I SAW THE ANGEL IN MARBLE
AND I CHIPPED UNTIL I SET HIM FREE.

Michelangelo had said it. Was that the key here as well—to chip away at her defenses, at that wall of ice she had encased herself in, until he set her free?

Nicholas jerked her against him and savagely covered her mouth with his, kissing her with shocking intensity.

"You want us both . . . you want neither of us . . . you don't know what the hell you want. But by God, I can help you make up your mind."

The more she resisted, the more intensely he kissed her.

"I want you, you beautiful little witch! So much I'd do almost anything to have you. You remember that the next time that fop kisses you. The ghost of his lovemaking has stood between us too long," he said, dropping to the floor and taking her with him. Trailing kisses across her throat, licking the hollow behind her ear, he whispered, "Now you can deal with another ghost as well."

Also by Elaine Coffman:

ESCAPE NOT, MY LOVE
IF MY LOVE COULD HOLD YOU
MY ENEMY, MY LOVE

ANGEL
IN
MARBLE

>-<

Elaine Coffman

A DELL BOOK

Published by
Dell Publishing
a division of
Bantam Doubleday Dell Publishing Group, Inc.
666 Fifth Avenue
New York, New York 10103

ISBN: 0-440-20530-1

Printed in the United States of America

Published simultaneously in Canada

March 1991

10 9 8 7 6 5 4 3 2 1

RAD

For my daughter, Ashley, and her classmates, the senior class at Madeira.

Thou art thy mother's glass, and she in thee
Calls back the lovely April of her prime.
—Shakespeare, *Sonnet III* (1609)

PROLOGUE

They used to tell how the Comanches were the fiercest Indians in the Southwest.

But they were no more than a falling star that blazed brightly for a time and then faded out of sight. For over a century the very name Comanche was synonymous with the word Indian. They were the lords of the southern plains, unsurpassed at stealth and plunder. Magnificent thieves and excellent horsemen, the mere mention of their name struck terror in the hearts of Spaniards, Mexicans, and the other Indians of the southern plains as well. Even their designation in sign language elicited fear: the index finger wiggled and drawn backward, signifying snake.

But with the settlement of a place called Texas, this conquering, warlike horde was faced with a new enemy, and one more formidable than any they had faced before: a group of warlike men called Texians.

In these single-minded, stubborn, purposeful men the Comanches met their match.

It was about this time, as the legend goes, that a band of hawk-faced Comanches with black braided hair and war feathers rode into history, their war cries penetrating and strangely prophetic.

It was the time of year when the crops were no more than green sprouts in the fields and new spring calves followed at their mama's flanks; a time when horse apples were green and hard and the sun had not yet reached its full intensity.

On such a day—a sunny May afternoon in 1836—a group of

Comanche horsemen under a flag of truce rode into Fort Parker, Texas. After learning that only five or six men protected the small stockade, they rode peacefully away. Moments later they returned, their high cheekbones and coppery skin smeared with paint, red ribbons tied in the tails of their ponies. Armed with lances and bows they swooped down on the small stockade, killing and plundering.

When it was all over they rode away, taking five captives: Mrs. Rachel Plummer, nine-year-old Cynthia Parker, six-year-old Margery Mackinnon, and two others.

Only that morning, Margaret Mackinnon and her six-year-old daughter Margery had gone to Parker's Fort to visit friends. Normally, the Comanches did not raid this far east, and the news that his only daughter had been taken captive was at first hard for John Mackinnon to believe. But a few days after the attack, John Mackinnon and five of his six sons saddled up before daylight, ready to find the band of Comanches that had taken Margery.

Before they left, John said to his son, Andrew, "Stay here and take care of your mother."

"But Pa, the Indians never come this far east, you said so yourself."

"That's what I thought before. I won't be fooled a second time. You heard what I said. You're the oldest. It's your place to watch over your mother. She barely missed being killed last time. I won't give those red bastards a second chance."

John Mackinnon and his five remaining sons turned their horses westward to begin their search. Two months of intense searching produced lead after lead, but in the end they all proved fruitless. Tired, discouraged, and wondering what he would tell his wife, John and his sons returned home. But instead of finding Margaret standing on the wide front porch drying her hands on her apron as he had found her countless times before, he found his home burned, with nothing but the chimney remaining, Margaret and Andrew missing.

The Mackinnon place lay in the smooth, rolling hills of Limestone County, along Tehuacana Creek, not far from

Groesbeck, where the treeless blackland prairie begins to give way to post oaks. On the far edge of their land the road to Waco ambled along, crooked as a dog's hind leg, weaving its way over the endless sea of grass. The creek itself was fringed with clumsy hackberry, their rough, warty bark overrun with mistletoe. But further over, not far from the house, stood as fine a grove of pecans a body could ever hope to see.

It was while riding past this pecan grove that one of the Mackinnon boys spotted two new graves. Riding closer, John, his voice cracking and raspy, read the names on the crude markers.

"Margaret Mackinnon, wife of John," he read. Then looking to the second marker, "Andrew Mackinnon, son of Margaret and John."

"I figured you'd want them laid to rest in this grove, seein' as how you and Margaret always talked of building a house here one day."

John wearily turned in the saddle and lifted red-rimmed eyes to see his closest neighbor, Jubal Sawyer, ride up, leading Andrew's strawberry roan. "My boy, Jonas, saw you coming up the road. Figured you'd like to have Andrew's roan back. He showed up at my place a couple of days after I buried Margaret and your boy. His mane was braided with Indian feathers, so I figured they planned on keeping him."

Jubal handed the lead rope to John. "I'm sorry as I know how to say, John. You know that." Jubal paused a moment. "Is there anything I can do?"

John shook his head. "No . . . but you have my thanks for seeing to Andrew and Margaret."

"You would've done the same for me and mine. My Mary said you and the boys were welcome to put up at our place for as long as you like."

For a long moment John sat there, astride his great gray horse, his mind on Margaret as she had been the day her father, a native Scot and a Presbyterian minister, had married them. In some ways it didn't seem so long ago, but as his weary eyes traveled along the line of horses beside him—five bays standing abreast—he saw what was left of his family. Five strapping sons.

His eyes roamed over these five boys that looked so apprehensive and full of fear—young birds on their first flight. His gaze settled on his second son, fourteen-year-old Nicholas—big enough to look like a man, but too young to prove it. Once again, John's mind traveled back, this time to his twenty-fifth year, when he and Margaret had migrated to Texas—Andrew barely walking; Nicholas born along the way. Backbreaking work and Scots determination had made them prosperous.

And for what?

John was never the same after the day he saw Margaret and Andrew's graves. Over the months that followed, he made repeated attempts to ransom and rescue Margery, following one false lead after the other. A year after Margery was taken captive, John struck out again, this time going alone, pausing a moment before he rode off, looking at his boys—his wild colts, so skittish and in need of a bridle. But they were good boys and hard working, and that was what he thought to himself that day, as he left his sons behind to rebuild what they could of a dream that had already crumbled.

He never returned.

It was a cloudy November morning when the sheriff rode out to the Mackinnon place on a broomtail bay with a Roman nose, riding into the yard like he was in a hurry, and scattering chickens in fifteen directions. Over by the woodpile, Nicholas and twelve-year-old Tavis heard the chickens squawking and clucking and stopped chopping, but the eight-year-old twins, Adrian and Alexander, were too busy throwing cockleburs at each other to hear much of anything. Down at the house, ten-year-old Ross was grumbling about having to work at all, using a bunch of broomweed to sweep the porch of the small house their father had constructed over the previous site.

"Morning, Sheriff." Nicholas buried the sharp blade of his axe deep in a stump. "What brings you out to this neck of the woods when it's looking like rain?" he asked, feeling that it was incumbent upon him to sound as much like his father as he could, since it didn't look like his father would ever give up looking for Margery.

"I thought it best if I rode out here with the news for you boys instead of sending someone else. Although God knows I hate like the dickens to be the one to tell you. We received word about your pa today. Comanches lifted his scalp a couple of weeks ago."

"You sure it was my pa?"

"Yes. The description I received fit John right down to the dimple in his chin."

"Maybe it was somebody else that looked a lot like him," Nick said.

"No, dern his ornery hide. It was John. A feller over near the mouth of the San Saba knew your pa and identified him. I told him not to go . . . tried to talk some sense into him . . . tried to tell him to stay put. But there was never any telling John Mackinnon anything."

Over the next few years, the Mackinnon boys tried to make a go of the family farm. It couldn't be done, of course. They had been taught to work, and work hard, at an early age, but alongside their father. They were still hard workers, but with the loss of both parents the Mackinnon boys lacked what some of the neighbors called direction. Something these same neighbors said they would acquire for themselves somewhere along the way.

In 1845, Nicholas, who was by then twenty-three, was the first to go seeking his own direction. He called it quits, giving in to the fascination he had always had for the sea. He had never seen the sea, of course, but that hadn't stopped him from daydreaming about it—and often enough to get his ears boxed on more than one occasion.

He made his mind up to go to Galveston and work long enough to earn passage to Nantucket. Once he arrived he planned to look up his uncle, Robert Graham. His mother had weaned him on stories about her brother, Robert, whom she described as "a rascal too ornery to do a hard day's work." It always intrigued Nicholas to learn how a man became a wealthy shipowner and merchant if he was too ornery to work, and he was determined to find out. When he left, Tavis went with him.

On February 19, 1846, Texas became a state. On April 24, the Mexican army, led by General Mariano Arista, crossed the Rio Grande into Texas and attacked American forces. The remaining Mackinnon brothers, Ross, Adrian, and Alexander, who didn't have a drop of mariner's blood in their collective bodies, joined the Texas Rangers and fought in the Mexican War. In 1848, the war ended with the signing of the Treaty of Guadalupe Hidalgo. Adrian and Alexander were lured west by the promise of gold. Ross Mackinnon returned to the Mackinnon homestead and remained there until a letter came from John Mackinnon's family in Scotland. Unable to contact any of his brothers, Ross Mackinnon answered the urgent summons and returned to the Mackinnon estates and their father's birthplace on the Isle of Skye.

The Mackinnon boys were no more than pollen when they were orphaned, and now, borne by the wind, they scattered. Although Margaret and John Mackinnon were gone, their legacy lived on.

Adrian and Alexander struck it rich in the goldfields of California, and were using their money to build a lumbering empire in the Pacific Northwest at about the same time Ross was doing his best to tame his unruly ways and adapt to the life of a titled Scottish gentleman. But it was Nicholas and Tavis that answered the call of their blood—a love of the sea inherited from the distaff side. Tavis, a natural-born businessman, took over the running of their uncle's shipping and whaling interests, while Nicholas became a shipbuilder and mariner whose enterprises took him all over the world.

One such journey was to a little town in Texas by the name of Indianola.

I saw the angel in the marble and I chiseled until I set him free.
—Michelangelo

➤ 1 ◄

INDIANOLA, TEXAS,
FEBRUARY 1849

Man wasn't meant to go to tea parties.

Nicholas Mackinnon was six feet, three inches tall. He weighed close to two hundred pounds. Balancing one of Miss Sukey Porter Merriweather's delicate china teacups on his knee wasn't exactly his idea of a good way to spend a cold winter afternoon.

"Well now, don't that beat all," Miss Merriweather was saying. "Come all the way to Texas to build a ship, you say?"

Nick nodded. He was afraid to do more, seeing as how he was feeling mighty awkward, all knees and elbows, as he tried to drink from a cup that couldn't hold more than a mouthful. Dern his hide if he couldn't spit and fill it up! He couldn't get his finger through the handle, yet holding something this delicate by the rim seemed mighty risky—and Miss Merriweather didn't look like she would take too kindly to having one of her teacups smashed by his big hands.

"Fancy! I've always wondered what it would be like to spend a few weeks on a sailing ship. Never rightly figured I would, though. There are just too many things that can go wrong with a boat, don't you think? I hear they're famous for springing leaks and such. And what would I do if it decided to spring while I was on it? The way I see it, the Good Lord put me on dry land for a reason. If he had wanted me in water he would have made me a fish."

Nick thought about that for a moment, remembering the size of the whales he'd seen and how graceful they were in the water. Maybe Miss Merriweather should've been a fish. On dry land, as she put it, she was clumsy and lumbering as an ox. But Nicholas didn't give two slaps for Miss Merriweather or her size, or even her precious teacups for that matter, but his mama had brought him up proper, and that meant being polite to his elders. On top of that, he doubted she would rent him the house if he broke anything. It was a bad habit with him, but once he got his mind set on something there was no turning back. "Stubborn as Pa," Tavis was fond of saying.

Tavis was probably right. Nicholas wanted to rent that house she owned, and he would sit here sipping tea from these silly cups of hers until the cows came home, if that's what it took. She was telling him that she had had a "most proper young man" by earlier to inquire about the house, and that houses for rent in Indianola were "as scarce as hen's teeth." Nick knew that well enough without her going on and on about it, and as for that proper young man, he could wait until hell froze over, but he wasn't getting Miss Merriweather's house.

Miss Merriweather sniffed, to express her distaste for Nick's obvious lack of attention, and spoke in an overly loud tone, "*If you don't mind my prying, Mr. Mackinnon, why do you need a house in Indianola for just six months to a year?*"

Nick looked at Miss Merriweather, her tightly laced bulk mounted upon a tiny rosewood chair as dainty and light as the one he was uncomfortably perched upon. With a voice of authority, and the self-confidence of a hurricane, she had asked him a question. The bulge of eyes, protruding from a flat face that was worse than plain, told him she expected an immediate answer.

"It takes a long time to build a ship."

She sat a little straighter and forced the rigid lines of her mouth into a shape that was probably as close as she could come to a smile. "Oh . . . You build as well as sail, how lovely."

"Yes, sailing helps me design and build better ships. I guess you could say it's a policy of mine; I never release a vessel I've built until I've sailed her first—although I rarely take command of a ship."

"And where do you usually do your building? I ask because I know that although Indianola is the leading seaport here in Texas, it isn't exactly the shipbuilding mecca of the world."

"No, it's not. I have shipping interests with my brother and uncle in Nantucket. That's where most of our ships are built. But occasionally we get a request to build elsewhere, as was the case here." Nick was hoping this would suffice and they could get on to the business of renting him the house.

But rapt and radiant Miss Merriweather—who by this time had insisted upon Nick's calling her Miss Sukey, as most of the folks in Indianola did—was just in the first throes of gleaning information. The Ladies of Indianola's Quilting Society was meeting tomorrow and she was determined to have enough information about this handsome bachelor (she considered a man's marital status of prime importance) to hold the attention of the society's members indefinitely. "I daresay it's a real shame to hear you'll only be living in Indianola until the ship is built . . . six months to a year, did you say?"

"Exactly. It's hard to pinpoint just how long it will take. So much of it depends on the availability of workers, the timely arrival of supplies, and of course, the weather."

"Our winters are much milder down here than they are in Massachusetts, Mr. Mackinnon. I think you'll find the weather much to your liking."

"Yes, ma'am. I know that. I'm a Texas boy myself."

"Are you, now!" She scooted forward and the little chair creaked. Nick was praying it wouldn't collapse. He had no idea how one would go about getting a woman of such tremendous proportions on her feet. The teacup balanced on Nick's leg rattled. "What part of Texas do you hail from?"

"Limestone County."

"Whereabouts in Limestone County?"

"I'm from a little place east of Waco, on Tehuacana Creek called Council Springs."

"How on earth did you get to a place like Nantucket from Texas?"

"I went by ship."

That wasn't what she wanted to know, of course. She didn't care how he traveled as much as what prompted him to do so. There was no mistaking Nick's irritation with the way things were going—all these questions and such—but poor Miss Sukey, not being overblessed with perception, did not detect this. She only perceived that Nick had misunderstood her question, quite accidentally, dear man. She decided not to embarrass him by pointing his misconception out. Ordinarily she wouldn't have been so tactful, but he was here to rent her house, and it had stood vacant long enough.

"You mentioned you had a brother in Nantucket. Did he go there when you did?"

"Yes, ma'am."

"I'm sure the two of you leaving at the same time like that must've upset your parents—"

"My parents are dead. Comanches," he added, knowing as well as he knew his own name what her next question would have been.

Her hand came up to her throat. "Oh, how dreadful. There's hardly been a family that hasn't been touched by misfortune, in one way or the other, at the hands of those red devils."

"I would be inclined to agree with you on that."

"And now you're back in Texas. Strange how things work out sometimes. You just never know what's going to jump up when you least expect it."

Miss Merriweather rambled on like an old country road, twisting and winding around, going nowhere. Any other time Nick would've made his excuses and hightailed it out of there, but she had the only house for rent in Indianola. It wasn't that he begrudged her owning the only rentable house in town, but he'd have to seek lodgings in a boardinghouse if she decided against renting to him. Boardinghouses were almost always run by widow-women or spinsters. He wanted nothing to do with either. He'd had enough widows and spinsters try to squeeze him into a marrying suit. It wasn't for him.

He liked women.

But he liked his freedom more.

It was trying, being a bachelor with so many marriage-hungry women about. But there hadn't been a woman in all his twenty-seven years who could hold his interest for more than forty-eight hours. He seriously doubted that the woman who could existed.

Two cups of tea and an hour later, Miss Sukey Porter Merriweather declared Nick the proud possessor of the house she had to rent.

"I'm mighty obliged, ma'am."

Before she had time to arm herself for another round, Nick grabbed his hat and coat and made his way to the door. But Miss Merriweather had encountered woman-shy men before. She collared him before he got the door open. "There's one more thing I forgot to mention. I don't allow no wild carrying-on, no loud parties, no . . ." She had been about to say no women visitors, but a man that looked like he did wasn't about to swear allegiance to a request like that. Still, she had her principles to uphold, so she said, "I'm sure a nice, upright man like yourself would never consider having an unchaperoned woman in his home."

In answer, he tipped his hat and flashed her a smile, and slipped through the door.

The goose was following Tibbie Buchanan down the road as she headed toward town. It wasn't a friendly follow either. Every time Tibbie walked a little faster, the goose did too. Coming down the road like a parade in a hurry, they were getting a few strange stares from those they passed on the road, and why not? It wasn't every day you saw a woman chased into town by an old gray goose and a trail of floating feathers.

The goose was still mad at Tibbie for picking up one of her goslings. Tibbie had long ago turned the downy little creature back to its mama, but apparently Mama wasn't appeased. Her long neck stretched out, her wings flapping to beat sixty, the goose was honking angrily as she closed the distance between them. For those who have never encountered the likes of a goose hot on their trail, there is nothing quite like it. A goose, when she is mad, is a formidable foe indeed. For this reason, Tibbie, seeing the goose was gaining on her, started running, thankful that the weathered gray buildings of Indianola weren't too far away. Once in town, she was certain she could lose this pesky goose.

But a mad mama goose is hard to shake, and this mama goose was mad. Hearing the hissing honk behind her and feeling the draft stirred up by the angrily flapping wings, Tibbie ducked down a narrow alleyway that ran between two buildings. When she reached the end, the obstinate goose trumpeted her fury and spread her ruffled wings in threat. This drove Tibbie across the wooden sidewalk, where she leaped over the wagon-tongue protruding between two parked wagons piled high with barrels and crates. She stepped into the street.

After leaving Miss Merriweather's with a smile on his face, Nick flipped the shiny key in his hand a couple of times before dropping it into his pocket. He looked at the sun. Only a couple of hours of daylight left. He removed his pocket watch and flipped open the lid. Seeing he had been right about the time, he closed it with a snap and went immediately to the livery to buy himself a horse.

The leggy chestnut must have been as anxious as Nick to get out-of-doors, for he took off down the street at such a fast clip Nick had a fight on his hands just trying to hold him to a nervous trot. The chestnut danced sideways, tossing his head, fighting to get the bit between his teeth so he could bolt down the street, and Nick, his muscles unaccustomed to being on land after months at sea, had his hands full.

He had no more than seen the woman, bundled in thick layers of somber brown clothing and a green cape, when he yanked back on the reins so hard the chestnut's neck arched as he pulled him aside. But she had already stepped between the

two wagons directly in front of him. He felt the slight thump
of impact just as the chestnut reared, the pawing forelegs frantically raking the air so close to the woman's head the curls
around her face fluttered.

The breath slammed from her body as the horse's massive
shoulder knocked her backward, Tibbie came close to losing
her balance. Then she looked up and saw the size of the horse,
and froze. Nick, fighting the animal for control, shouted, "Get
back, damn you!"

She leaped back just as the chestnut reared again, clamping
her hands over her mouth, a look of horror in her wide eyes as
she watched the chestnut rear again, then whirl, the man's leg
slamming with a sickening crack against one of the wagons.
Then, as quickly as it had happened, it was over. His horse
under control, Nicholas stared hotly at the woman, fully expecting her to come screaming and shouting the moment she
recovered. She had dropped her basket, spilling the neatly
wrapped packages in the mud. He saw the way her eyes swept
over him, lingering on the gold watch chain; the shiny new
boots. As plainly as she was dressed, she would probably
snatch the opportunity to demand retribution—monetary, of
course. He had had that sort of thing happen to him before—
more than once.

Nicholas saw the determination in her eyes and the stubborn
thrust of her pointed chin, saw, too, the look of deliberate
distaste the poor always had for the well groomed and more
fortunate. The clanking sound of a cheap piano reached his
ears, and his eyes were drawn to the saloon behind her. Had
she come from there? Was she a housekeeper, or a woman
whose profession charity forbade him to mention out loud?
His inclination was to guess the latter. Why? He had no answer for that.

His hands were trembling, and his heart still pounded furi-
ously from the thought that for all practical purposes it should
be her lying in the street splattered with mud instead of her
packages. The same charity that forbade him to mention her
possible profession did not forbid him to lose his temper at the

hostile way she looked at him. "Look your fill, damn you, and satisfy your curiosity."

He saw her eyes glance furtively around at the gathering throng of people, seeing, too, the shadow of panic that was born not of the danger she had passed so close to but of the fear of humiliation. He watched the woman turn and pick up the basket she had dropped, going down on her knees in the mud to gather her packages. Without looking at him again, she turned away.

What's this, he thought. *Whores are not humble.* He had obviously misjudged her. He watched her go, feeling a tightness in his chest. The easy flow of words normally so available to him deserted him. He nudged the chestnut to follow.

"You almost got us both killed. Don't you have anything to say?"

She turned and looked at him for a moment. "I—"

Whatever she was going to say was interrupted suddenly when a honking, flapping goose shot from between two buildings and headed straight for her.

Just about that time old Emery Enoch was coming down the sidewalk, swinging his one leg between two crutches. As the goose dashed in front of him, Emery lifted one of his crutches. "You *varmit,*" he muttered, and gave the goose a chop to the neck and sent it tumbling. "That ought to rattle your slats a bit," he said with a raspy chuckle, then settled himself on his crutches and shuffled on by.

Walking like she didn't know which way she wanted to go, the goose wandered around in a dazed state until Karl Heist, the postmaster, chased her off with a broom.

Nick missed that last episode because his eyes were on the woman. Even bundled as she was, he knew his first impression had been a mistaken one. This woman was as fine as a glass of French cognac. The icy wind blowing off the water had pulled at the thick woolen muffler she had over her hair and wound over the lower half of her face. Another frozen blast had loosened it enough for him to get a quick look at her before she hastily covered herself once more. Somehow, he had a feeling her haste had been more to hide herself from him than to protect herself. It didn't really matter though, because in spite of her diligence, he had seen enough to interest him.

Her hair was a dark, tobacco blond, the color of old Spanish doubloons, while her skin looked like it had been bathed in honey, and he was willing to bet it tasted just as sweet. When she glanced at him, the sunlight struck eyes that were as clear and golden as a string of polished amber beads that had once belonged to his mother. He had never seen a blonde with eyes that color. Blondes were blue or green-eyed.

"You travel in dangerous company," he said, indicating the retreating goose.

She said nothing. Perhaps she was shy. Whatever the cause of her silence, he was determined to talk to her. She didn't look ready for a smile yet, so he kept his humor to himself. "A friend of yours?"

There were times to retreat, times to attack, times to remain silent, and times to placate. She had tried retreat and silence. Attack was out. So that left placate. Perhaps then the brute would be satisfied and be on his way. She glanced around. The crowd had lost interest and was diminishing. "Yes . . . I mean Aunt Rhody is our goose," she said, her voice coming soft and muffled through the layers of wool. "It was my fault. I disturbed one of her goslings. She was just being a good mother."

"Then you—"

He doesn't look too humored yet. Try apology. Try anything. Just get rid of him. Quick! "I was in a hurry. I should have been watching where I was going. I'm sorry if I inconvenienced you." *There! That should satisfy even a pushy ogre like him.*

His deep blue eyes studied her thoughtfully for a moment, then with a nod in her direction he made what could only be construed as a mocking bow. "It was entirely my fault, I'm sure."

If he saw the way her eyes were suddenly charged with anger, he did not acknowledge it. The harsh, clipped tones of his words had expressed the most terse civility, but there remained little doubt that he had effectively chastised her, and in so doing had lumped her into the same category with the very young, senile, or mentally incompetent, while at the same time overriding her own apology. Anger boiled within her. Five years ago she would have tossed a clod or two at his arrogant head, or given his horse a start by slapping her basket against his rump. But those options were closed to her. Things were different. Now she had to watch herself.

She noticed Miss Merriweather peering through the dotted Swiss curtains in the window of Milly's Marvelous Millinery, keeping her customary sharp eye on everything that went on, from hat purchases to bank robberies and everything in between. There were few people in Indianola who could intrude with such fervor into the things that went on around them, and still find time to attend to their own rat killing; but Miss Sukey Porter Merriweather could do a bang-up job at both. It could be said that Miss Sukey ran Indianola. And in the midst of all this running she frequently drove people from town—she had, thus far, driven thirteen people away from Indianola.

Five years ago Tibbie had come uncomfortably close to being number nine. She had no intention of being number fourteen.

When she did not respond, Nicholas did. "Don't stand there like a frozen lump, lass. You put a powerful tear in my britches; you didn't kill me." But the woman before him looked anything but relieved—or amused—at his attempt at humor. That didn't deter him. "So, you can see for yourself that everything is under control and I'm hale and hearty, and assuming you didn't harbor some dark wish to throw yourself beneath the pounding hooves of a horse, nothing has gone amiss. But I would advise you to pay a little more attention to what you're about. An ounce of prevention is well worth the effort."

He nodded his head in her direction, wondering if he had eased her feelings any after he had embarrassed her in a moment of flaring Scots temper. But the woman gave no indication of what she was feeling. She simply turned around and disappeared between the same two wagons she had stepped from only moments before. For some strange reason, Nicholas felt a tugging sense of disappointment that he hadn't seen all of her face or heard her voice without the hampering layers of wool.

He started back up the street, tying the chestnut to a sturdy post. A moment later he stepped into Twitwiler's General Store to purchase a few things he would be needing at the house he had just rented. While he waited for the proprietor to gather the items on his list, Nick warmed himself by the fire.

The door opened, sending a chilling blast of cold air into the store, the bell overhead clanging loudly when the door slammed. Nick turned, recognizing the woman immediately. For a moment he stood watching her remove her thick gray mittens, thinking she didn't look any friendlier than she had a few minutes back when he'd almost run her down. He was about to turn back to the fire when she began to unwind the long woolen muffler from around her face and head, dislodging the tightly coiled bun at her nape and spilling the most unbelievable length of rich, honeyed hair down her back. His eyes went to her face. The woman was undoubtedly a beauty. A thousand descriptive words jammed his brain: Incredible. Exquisite. Unbelievable. Absolute perfection. None of them fit. Not one descriptive word that came to mind seemed adequate, let alone descriptive of what he was looking at. The woman's eyes connected with his, ever so briefly, before she hastily looked away. Nick felt the breath drawn from his body. Before he could draw in another one to replace it, the woman had twisted the shimmering length of hair into a tight coil and rewound it into a bun, thanking two young boys who retrieved her hairpins from the floor and handed them to her. She jabbed the pins home and turned away.

He watched her move about the store, graceful and quick as a hummingbird, never lighting in one place long enough for him to get a really good look at her. It took him a moment to realize that this woman had to be accustomed to being looked at constantly, yet she seemed immune to it.

Only once did she come near him, to pause in front of an oak barrel and lift the lid. The scent of vanilla and roses lingered long after she had passed. He watched as she withdrew three scoops full of sugar before reaching for the lid.

"Allow me, ma'am." Nick bent over and retrieved the lid, his face just inches from hers as they both came to an upright position.

The scoop fell from her hands, striking the floor with a clatter. She took a step back, then gained control, giving him a look a few degrees colder than the wind that howled around the small store. "Do you live around here?" he asked, watching her bite her lip as if he had just put an extremely difficult question to her. He laughed. "A simple yes or no will suffice."

"Please don't force me to embarrass you by calling Mr. Ridley to throw you out," she said.

"I've been thrown out of places before . . . a lot worse than this," he said. "Enough times that I'm afraid I'm beyond embarrassing. But you might consider that in all likelihood it would be yourself that would be embarrassed." A brief smile touched his mouth, then Nick turned to replace the lid. When he turned back, the woman had slipped away, quiet as a whisper, without his ever knowing she had moved. He watched her rewind her muffler around her face. She pulled the gray mittens from the deep pockets of her dark green cape and put them on, before taking the string-tied bundle and dropping it into her basket.

"Thank you, Mr. Ridley. You'll put this on our account?"

"Done before you asked. I'm not forgetting how sick my little Priscilla was and how many trips Dr. Buchanan made to our place in the dead of night, refusing to charge me any extra for the trouble. And those medicines you mixed up for her—"

"I'm glad they helped," she said, turning away. "Tell Priscilla that for me, will you?"

"Sure will. You take care going home now, you hear? Ol'

Ambrose was in, a little while ago . . . said there were a lot of icy spots on the road."

The woman nodded. The bell tinkled when she opened the door, then clanged loudly as she slammed it behind her.

Nick felt the cold blast of air and rubbed his hands over the stove. "Who is she?"

Mr. Ridley looked at Nick, then toward the door. "Who? The one that just left, or the one standing over the yard goods?"

"The green wool cape."

"No point in telling you who she is. Wouldn't do you an ounce of good. Waste of time is what it would be."

"I'll be the judge of that. Who is she?"

"I'm telling you, mister. It won't do you any good to know who she is. That gal is off limits."

"She's married?"

"No, but she might as well be."

"What does that mean?"

"It means you'd be beating your gums together. You could chase her from hell to Jericho and still have about as much luck as a cross-eyed owl walking a straight line. You're not the first young buck to inquire about her, you know."

"Are you going to tell me who she is, or not?"

"Or not," the man said and turned away.

Nick felt irritation toward the scrawny-necked clerk. He watched as the bespectacled man went back to wiping the counter, obviously absorbed in the meticulous care he took to arrange the horehound sticks in a candy jar. Nick had never punched a man with glasses before. He toyed with the idea for a minute or two, then decided the man didn't look much more substantial than one of Miss Merriweather's teacups.

The wind lashed angrily at him as he left the store, but Nick hardly noticed. His Scots dander was up again, and that produced enough heat to warm half of Indianola. Even the chestnut seemed to sense his foul mood, for he didn't try any of his previous shenanigans as they rode down the road toward the tiny gray house that faced the harbor.

Once he was inside the house he started a fire and made himself a stout drink of hot rum and spices. Standing in front of the window nearest the fire, he pulled the curtain back while he stared outside and drank his rum. By the time he had finished half of it, Nick felt his body relax. His eyes moved over the cold, gray depths of seawater, watching the wind tip each wave it created with fine white foam. The water looked about as hospitable as the woman. Yet he couldn't shake the way those eyes of hers had looked at him. She had eyes like a cat; aloof and mysterious. Would she purr as well?

The woman was obviously not interested, but that had never stopped Nicholas Mackinnon before. In fact, if the truth were known, it only served to intrigue him more.

"By God," he said, bringing the mug to his lips and taking a healthy swallow, "I'll stay here long enough to build fifty ships if that's what it takes. But mark my words and mark them well. Your days are numbered, my fair-haired lass. And when I set my mind to something, I always get what I want." He dropped the curtain in place and finished the last of the rum.

"Always."

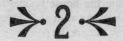

2

"I must tell you what Granny found inside that chicken's gizzard when she cut it open this morning."

Effie Buchanan finished cutting the slice of apple pie and looked at her husband, just as the piece of chicken fell from his fingers and landed in his mashed potatoes.

"Good God, Effie! Can't you see I'm eating?" Dr. Coll Buchanan scowled at his wife, who gave him a blank look as she put the slice of pie on a platter and carried it to the table, placing it next to his plate.

His eyes peered through thick, bushy brows to look at Effie. "Why are you standing there looking like a piece of paper with nothing written on it?" he asked.

Effie looked at him in a somewhat puzzled way, for in truth, she was perplexed. "I think you're working too much," she said. "Your color isn't good."

"The devil with my color!" Coll said. "And while we're at it, would it be asking too much to let me do the doctoring around here?"

"But—"

"Mrs. Buchanan, do you have a medical degree?"

"You know I don't."

"Good! One doctor in the family is enough."

Satisfied that what he had just quelled would stay quelled, Coll picked up his chicken and was about to take a bite when he remembered what had wreaked all this havoc in the first place. "What in the name of all that's holy did your mother find in that blasted chicken's gizzard?" he asked, waving the chicken leg in Effie's direction to emphasize each word. "And why did you wait until I ate three pieces before you mentioned it?"

"I could tell the Mississippi to stop flowing easier than I could have pulled you off that chicken, Coll Buchanan. Cramming it in with both fists, you were."

"Licking them too," said Granny Grace, who sat by the stove in her rocking chair, cutting out scraps of silk and taffeta to be pieced together for the top of a Texas Star quilt she was starting—she cut scraps for her Texas Star quilt when she wasn't bent over the Postage Stamp quilt she had stretched over the quilting frame in the spare bedroom. A bunch of clutter is what Coll called it. But then, what did a man ever know about the work of a woman?

Granny Grace Stewart was Effie Buchanan's eighty-year-old mother. Her mind was as sharp as a tack, but she was a little absentminded and forgetful at times.

"Granny, what did you find in the chicken?" Coll asked.

"Innards," said Granny.

The back door opened and Tibbie came into the kitchen, dropping her basket on the table and removing her mittens and muffler as she hurried to the stove. "Brrrr. It's freezing out there," she said, holding her hands out to warm them. She smiled at Granny rocking in the corner by the stove, recognizing the fabric of her old yellow taffeta dress. She thought the blue satin looked a lot like the lining of an old cape that had belonged to her mother. When no one spoke, she turned around and looked first at her father, who was looking strangely at his piece of chicken, then at her mother. "What's the matter? Doesn't he like the way that chicken is fried?"

Granny stopped rocking. "Who died?"

"No one died, Granny," said Tibbie.

"I wish people around here would consider that just because I'm old doesn't mean I don't like to know what's going on. Nobody ever tells me nothing. The only way I ever know what's going on in the world is what I overhear—"

"And that's always wrong," Coll said sourly.

"Gracious me," said Tibbie. "What's the matter with Papa? He looks as friendly as a boa constrictor."

"You ever see a boa constrictor?" asked Coll.

"No, but I saw a picture once." Coll went back to looking friendly. Tibbie looked at her mother and raised her brows in question.

"Your father and I were having a little discussion about nothing," Effie said.

"*That,*" Coll said, "is the kind of logic that put Christians in with the lions."

"I better go get my new black dress," said Granny, struggling to stand.

"The one you have on looks fine. Why do you want to put on your new black one?" asked Effie.

"For the funeral," Granny said, coming to her feet. "Coll said the Christians were standing in lines."

"Sit down, Granny," said Effie. "There is no funeral," she said loudly, for it was commonly understood around the Buchanans' that besides being absentminded and forgetful at times, Granny Grace was also hard of hearing.

Granny sighed and dropped back into the chair, mumbling something to herself about being the last person in line.

Tibbie, who was accustomed to these kinds of goings-on around the Buchanan household, took no notice. "Did Mama tell you what she found in the chicken's gizzard this morning . . . or rather what Granny found?"

Coll groaned and rested his forehead in his upturned palm. One of his cardinal irritants was the aggravating habit his wife and daughter had of asking questions when a simple statement was in order. "Women," he said, "I've never understood them. I probably won't ever understand them. Physics I understand. Medicine I understand. The laws of nature I understand. I even have a fair understanding of politics and religion. But my wife and daughter? When it comes to understanding, they are like strangers to me."

When he finished, Effie looked at him and said, "Coll—"

"Who is Coll?" asked Granny.

"He's the one eating the chicken," said Tibbie with a stifled laugh.

"Did you tell him I found a ring in the chicken?" asked Granny.

"A ring?" Coll said.

"Not exactly," Effie said, then she looked at Coll. "Actually, it was a ruby, but I recognized it immediately. Remember the ruby that Rosemairi lost a month ago?"

"Why didn't you tell me that to begin with, instead of making me think the worst? What if I had been eating poisoned chicken? Would you have waited that long to tell me?"

"I would never be that lucky," Effie said, then seeing Coll's increased exasperation, added, "You didn't give me any time to say anything. You were too busy blustering."

"Effie, you are cursed with a chronic desire to irritate me. Would that God had made you more prone to silence . . . or mute."

"Keep talking like that, Coll Buchanan, and I'll put opium drops in your coffee. See if I don't."

"If this nonsense continues, I'll be tempted to drink it."

"It wouldn't be the first time," Effie said.

It took a minute for that to soak in. "What do you mean, it wouldn't be the first time? Do you mean to tell me you've put opium drops in my food before?"

"Not in your food . . . your coffee."

"In my coffee then. Well? Have you?"

"I just said I had, Coll. On a few occasions and only in your coffee."

"May I ask why you find it necessary to drug your husband? Are you trying to kill me?"

"Don't be ridiculous."

"Putting opium drops in my food isn't ridiculous?"

"Of course not. I never put enough in to harm you," she said.

"That's reassuring," he said. "Just how many times would you say you've done this?"

"Not many. Only when you're acting like an old goat with one butt left."

While Coll was mulling that one over, Tibbie asked, "It seems awfully quiet around here. Where is everyone?"

Effie answered. "Beth is upstairs. Mairi is over at the Mabry's helping out with the cooking. Mrs. Mabry had her baby today."

"Another girl, I'll wager," Tibbie said.

"That makes six so far," said Effie. She poured tea into a cup and offered it to Tibbie. "Why don't you come with me to the town meeting tonight? There's going to be a little social after the meeting."

Tibbie took the tea and sipped it thoughtfully. "You know I don't care for things like that. Why don't you ask Mairi?"

"Because I'm asking you, that's why. If I wanted to ask your sister I would have asked her. What's wrong with you getting out once in a while? You're only twenty-one years old, Tib. Why must you live like an old woman?"

"Mama, we've had this discussion before. I still feel the same way I did then. Nothing has changed. I'll socialize when I'm ready to and not a minute before." Tibbie cut herself a thick slice of bread and buttered it.

"It just seems like such a shame to me. Mrs. Tripplet said her son George would give a month's wages to have one dance with you."

"George Tripplet is a fool," Coll said.

"Why? Because he's sweet on Tibbie?"

"He was a fool long before that. Got it from his mother."

"Just because you and Maude don't get along, that's no reason to talk about her."

"I get along with her as well as anyone. That woman wouldn't like God," said Coll.

"Speaking of God," Tibbie said, "I saw the Reverend Woolridge today. He said Mrs. Woolridge is having trouble with her throat again."

"I guess I'd better drop by and check on her after I eat," Coll said.

"I told the reverend to make her tea from angelica roots. Why don't you wait until tomorrow? She might be feeling better by then," Tibbie said.

"She should eat some of the root too," Coll said. "That would ease the soreness."

"I told him that as well," Tibbie said.

Coll pushed his plate away and stood up. "It's a shame you weren't a boy. You'd have made a fine doctor."

"I'm a doctor now," Tibbie said. "You said I know everything you know."

"And you do. You're my right arm. I couldn't get all my doctoring done if I didn't have you here to help me."

"You'd get it done."

"I'm not so sure. Here I am now, eating an hour after everyone else has finished dinner—and that's with you helping me. Without you here I probably wouldn't get to eat at all."

"And I'd miss all these interesting discussions we have," said Effie.

"Woman, if you had a neck, I'd wring it."

That brought a laugh from Tibbie. "Now you've done it," she said.

"You want a neck to wring? Here!" Effie picked up the raw chicken neck and tossed it to Coll, who, without thinking, caught it.

While Coll disposed of the chicken's neck and wiped his hands, Tibbie said, "I think I'll go over to the Mabry's and see how Mrs. Mabry is doing."

"Why don't you take Granny upstairs first," Effie said. "She's sound asleep."

Tibbie went to her grandmother and removed the sewing from her lap. "Granny?" She shook her shoulder lightly. "Granny, let me help you upstairs."

"Is it time to get ready for the funeral?" asked Granny, coming to her feet with Tibbie's help.

"In a little while," Tibbie said, leading Granny Grace from the room.

Once she had helped Granny to her room, Tibbie went into

her father's office and opened his black bag, taking out a few things she might need and placing them in her basket. She paused at the door to pull on her mittens. That's when she heard her mother's laughter, then a muffled voice.

"Coll Buchanan! What's gotten into you, you old fool!"

"Must be buck fever."

"It's not spring yet. And you're too old to get buck fever anyway."

"You're never too old. Now, stop talking and come here."

"Coll . . . not in the kitchen."

"What's wrong with the kitchen? It's nice and warm in here. Cozy as a—"

"Coll Buchanan! Mind what you say! Someone will hear you."

"Effie, will you shut up?"

"But one of the girls might—"

"It's damn hard to kiss a yapping woman."

"I'm not yapping now, Coll."

Tibbie clapped her mittened hands over her mouth to stifle the laughter and hurried out the door, closing it gently behind her.

Outside, the wind was still blowing, but the rain Tibbie had expected earlier in the afternoon didn't appear to be any threat now. It was terribly cold, and she pulled her muffler higher over her nose so only her eyes were showing, and then she set out. She didn't have too far to go; the big rambling house where the Buchanans lived was just up the road a few miles from town. Hugging her basket to her side, she hurried down the dirt road, telling herself it would be warmer as soon as she reached the buildings that lay on the outskirts of town.

The four-mile walk to town was a nice walk in the summertime, with honeysuckle and dewberry vines trailing along the fencerows, and an occasional tree some thoughtful soul had planted providing a nice spot of shade—knowing the exact location of these spots of shade was of premier importance when one was going barefoot.

Yes, everything was lovely along this road in the summertime. Why, even the road was pretty then, with wildflowers blooming in profusion along the strip that ran down the middle of the road, between the wagon ruts. In the summer the air was warm and sweet with a tang of salt from the gulf's steady breath, and the mellow hum of orchard bees could be heard until you got close enough to the ocean, when the waves drowned them out. But today the air was thin and cold, the gulf's breath slapping her like a sneeze. In weather like this, Tibbie was taking no note of her surroundings, thinking it was a good thing most folks stayed indoors. That way she could bundle herself up and bow her head, following the ruts in the road without bothering to look up.

Summertime was different. In the summer you had to pay attention to your surroundings, taking note of who was coming and going, making it a special point to nod and smile at each passerby—for it was somewhat of an unspoken rule here in Indianola that you had to smile or at least nod at all and sundry that you met, friend or not. Nod and smile. Tibbie always did both, for insurance. Usually she dreaded meeting people on the road, for they usually wanted to stop and chat, and Tibbie had precious little time for that.

There were times she was glad her father had built their house on the outskirts of town, but at other times, like tonight, she wished they were closer. She pulled her basket close against her body and ducked her head, hoping to keep her muffler in place. The wind was blowing against her back, buffeting her along as if she weighed no more than a lost hat. Fighting to hold her skirts down and keep her basket in her hand, she reached the boarded sidewalks by the livery, then hurried along with a faster gait. Passing the post office and saloon, she stepped down to cross the narrow alleyway that ran between the newspaper office and mercantile.

"Well, well, well. If it isn't Little Red Riding Hood with her basket of goodies."

Tibbie's head snapped around so fast she threw a crick in it. For a moment she couldn't see anything, as her eyes searched the deep shadows and faint pools of light coming from dimly

lit windows. She could see a few barrels stacked near the building, but nothing that looked like a man. Suddenly, a dark form
stepped out of the shadows, moving to stand in front of where
she stood. Unable to move, her breaths came in short, frightened gasps.

"It's a little late to be going to grandmother's house, isn't it?
Aren't you afraid of the big bad wolf?"

The voice was so near, she could feel the warmth of his
breath brush against her cheek. He was a giant of a man,
whomever he was, for she had to tilt her head back to see him.

The moment she did, she recognized him: The man in the
street. The same man who had cornered her in the store. Two
meetings in one day were too many. Three times went beyond
coincidence.

Without saying a word, she lifted her skirts in one hand and
stepped around him. "Wait a minute," he said, his hand closing around her upper arm.

"Take your hands off me, or I'll scream."

He laughed. "Scream away, then. But I doubt you'll be
heard over that out-of-tune piano and those warbly notes of
that fairest of all damsels, Poker Alice." He turned her toward
the light, to see her face better, wondering if she would be as
lovely as he had imagined her to be.

His hand came up slowly to unwind the muffler around her
face. When he had finished, he dropped his hands and stepped
back.

And when he did, the air seemed to rush from his lungs.
The girl was a beauty all right. More than he had first thought.
This was the kind of face that brought men to their knees and
toppled empires; the kind of face a man could not forget; the
kind that made a man just a little crazy.

Her beauty and his fierce attraction to her brought the reminder of just how long it had been since he'd had a woman.
He curved a forefinger beneath her chin and lifted her face.
Never could he remember making love to a woman as exquisite as this one. Bringing his other hand up, he pushed the rest
of the muffler from her head. She had cameo coloring, and

amber eyes that a man could lose himself in. They were watching him now, wide and incredibly pure, yet unfathomable. Her cheekbones were high; her nose perfect and straight; her mouth not red, but a dusky rose that reminded him of nudity and made him wonder if her breasts would be tipped with that color as well. It also reminded him that he was getting mighty uncomfortable in a certain spot he couldn't acknowledge right now.

In the deep shadows and filtered light her hair was the rich color of honey-butter. The moisture from the gulf was working its magic on the tightly twisted bun, loosening some of the shorter, finer filaments and coaxing them to curl in an angelic fashion around her face. His fingers itched to loosen the bun, to see just how her hair would feel in his hands. But the girl looked frightened enough to bolt, and finding out her name was more important . . . at least for now.

"I don't know who you are, but you obviously have mistaken me for someone else," she said. "I'm not *that* kind of woman."

His teeth flashed incredibly white in the dim light. The smile was both amused and taunting. "And what kind of woman are you?"

"I don't have the time or patience to stand here freezing to death while you amuse yourself. Indianola is full of willing women. I suggest you find one and leave me alone."

"I'm not interested in the willing women of Indianola. I'm only interested in you, willing or not."

"I'm not willing and I most certainly am not available. Now, release my arm."

"You're not very friendly either."

She jerked her arm, but he held it tightly, increasing the pressure when she resisted.

"Don't be in such a hurry. You can't rush a fairy tale, you know."

"If I remember right, the wolf let Little Red Riding Hood go."

"Only after he knew where she was going."

"Where I go is none of your business."

"Then tell me who you are."

"I'm Little Red Riding Hood, remember?"

"Give me your name."

"Give me yours."

"Nicholas Mackinnon, at your service, and soon to be, I hope, in your debt."

"Where you will be, Mr. Mackinnon, is in jail . . . after I give your name to the sheriff. You are detaining me against my will, sir. I neither solicited, nor desired, your attentions. If you don't release my arm right now, I will be forced to file a complaint. There are laws to protect women from the likes of you."

He threw back his head with a shout of laughter and Tibbie had her first good look—her first really thorough look at him. This was a man who definitely did not have to resort to accosting females in dark alleyways. Whatever his shortcomings were, none of them were in the area of looks. Not with a face like his—that wide, curving mouth with its teasing uplift at the corners, that arrogant, masculine jaw, the Roman nose that would have looked ridiculous on any other man, but with his looks and stature, was perfect. And so was his hair, a dark brown that picked out and held the softly diffused points of light. She didn't know what made her guess at the color of his eyes—blue. And that irked her. She didn't even care if he had eyes, much less what color they were.

In spite of her conjecture about his eye color, the most disturbing thing about him was the cleft in his chin. Like a woman's dimple, but on his chin. She had never seen such before, and she was sure it was just the strangeness of seeing one for the first time that made her want to touch it.

But Tibbie was neither as susceptible or impressionable as she had been at sixteen. She wasn't the same naive little girl to be won over by a man's charm and good looks. She had seen his kind before. Many times. And she had been approached before. Many times. They were all the same, talked the same, and whether or not they said the same words, they were after the same thing. She felt her anger and irritation increase. True, this man was like all the others and after one thing, but this man fathered a string of chain reactions within her that no man had—at least not for five years.

Why him?

Why would this man disturb her when so many others had failed?

A couple of drunks staggered out the doors of the saloon, and it was all the break she needed. The moment he glanced toward the saloon, Tibbie jerked and then twisted her arm, catching him off guard. Once she was free, she hitched up her skirts and ran, not even feeling the freezing bite of wind until she got to the street where the church and parsonage were located.

The first thing Tibbie noticed the next morning was that the wind had stopped blowing. It was cold as a block of ice in her bedroom, and that prompted her to dress quickly and take the back stairs two at a time. She stopped by the kitchen, and finding it empty, she poured herself a cup of tea and carried it with her to her father's office. Coll would already be seeing patients, she knew that, even though the rest of the family was still asleep. Tempting though it was to stay in bed, she knew her father would be needing her. There was a lot of croup and whooping cough going around this time of year, and only yesterday they had received word that a dozen or more cases of diphtheria, or "putrid sore throat" as it was commonly called, had been reported in San Antonio.

Her father was looking down little Herbie Gillingwater's throat when she came in. Seeing the somber expression on his face, Tibbie dispensed with the usual light banter she exchanged with her father. "Morning, Papa," she said, then nodding at the woman beside him, added, "Mrs. Gillingwater." She moved to the cabinet and took out a clean apron, tying it around her waist as she heard her father say, "diphtheria."

Tibbie had never seen a case of diphtheria before, but by four o'clock that afternoon she had seen the yellowish-gray patches on the throat or tonsils of five patients. And the most disheartening part of it was that they were all children; for diphtheria, as her father said, usually struck children over six months of age.

Tibbie wiped the perspiration from her forehead, knowing she reeked of powdered brimstone, which she had boiled in limewater and dropped into the nostrils of the sick children, using a goose quill. By the time the last patient had been tended to, she was too tired to eat, wanting only a bath and a bed.

While she scrubbed the brimstone from her body and hair, Nick Mackinnon was sulking over a whiskey at the Tarnished Angel Saloon. What a day! What a town full of closemouthed, unfriendly people. He had asked a dozen residents of the fair city of Indianola about the honey-haired woman—people who were friendly enough until he described her. Once he did, they turned a deaf ear on him.

Thorn Newberry told him to mind his own business. Mrs. Weatherby told him he was "barking up the wrong tree." Miss Merrilee Jackson said, "Go do your snooping someplace else." And the good reverend had said, "Get thee behind me, Satan!" Nick had actually turned around and looked behind him to see who the good reverend was talking to. Only when he saw there wasn't anyone else around did he realize who those caustic words were directed to. The barber took a hunk out of his ear with the scissors when he inquired about the woman. The blacksmith threatened to apply the hot horseshoe he was holding to Nick's backside. Even the whore in the Tarnished Angel reacted in a hostile manner by pouring the glass of whiskey he had just bought her in his lap and telling him to take his business elsewhere and leave the decent women of Indianola alone.

Over and over it happened, the same sort of rebuffs every time he inquired about the angel with the spun honey hair. The shoeshine boy left one boot unshined; the woman in the restaurant yanked his plate of eggs and ham right out from under his nose while he was still eating; the sheriff advised him to take his lustful yearnings to New Orleans. By the time he reached the newspaper office, the proprietor must have heard he was coming, for he was watching his approach through the glass-paned door. The moment Nick put his hand on the door to open it, the man threw the bolt, turned the CLOSED sign around, and pulled down the shade.

Nick finished his drink, his mind still on the girl. She might have slipped her mooring and eluded him the night before, but there would be other times. He would find out who this mysterious lass was. And then he would find out just why it was that everyone in Indianola was so protective and closemouthed about her. What power did she hold over everyone here? Finding the answer to that was close to engaging as much of his thought processes as finding out who she was.

The next morning Nick was down at the timber-strewn shipyard where they would begin construction on the ship he had come to Indianola to build. The man who wanted the ship was an eccentric if he'd ever seen one—Josiah P. Bitterworth, a man who was on a personal campaign to provide the state of Texas with only "Texas built" ships. When Nick tried to explain to him that the ship could be built much faster in their shipyards in Nantucket, the man had simply replied, *"This* ship must be built in Texas." Nick had learned a long time ago that the less you knew about a man's affairs, the better off you were. The man's money was good. He was asking nothing of him that was illegal. It was enough.

His hull designs were rolled into tight cylinders and tucked under his arm as he walked along the street. His first stop was by his office, which overlooked the shipyard. His longtime friend, Porter Masterson, was bowed over his desk. He looked up as Nick walked in.

"Nick, good morning! I was just going over these instructions you left yesterday. I've had the model carried up to the mold loft. The men are there now, tracing the contours on the floor."

"Are the battens ready?"

"Since day before yesterday. They were pinned to the floor yesterday. If all goes well, we should be cutting the templates by next week."

"Then let's go have a look at her."

Nick was frustrated. Not that anything was going wrong with the chalk lines that were being marked on the floor. His frustration came because he couldn't concentrate. More than once Porter had asked him a question, only to find Nick wasn't listening. He found his mind wasn't on shipbuilding at all, but rather on a certain honey-haired lass that he couldn't seem to push aside long enough to get some work done. If this kept up, the ship would never be built.

It was half-past four when they quit, but the February day was already tapering off as if anticipating the darkness that would soon follow. Nick stood outside the office and talked to Porter for a few minutes. Then turning the collar of his overcoat up over his ears, he headed toward town.

He wanted a drink.

He needed a whiskey.

The road was already freezing in places, and the land around him seemed stern and gaunt and somber. His thoughts, as they had been doing all week, turned to the woman.

Over on the other side of town, Dr. Coll Buchanan's thoughts were doing the same.

Tibbie was sitting on his bed talking to her mother when Coll went upstairs. He stood in the doorway for a moment, watching the two of them. They made quite a picture in the mellow light of the lamp, Effie showing the dark coloring of her Russian grandmother, her dark hair barely streaked with silver, and Tibbie, all sun-kissed and golden like his own Scottish parents, her eyes alight with yellow points of light as she spoke with animated gestures. His daughter's eyes had always fascinated him, primarily because he had never seen such a color: light brown, sprinkled with yellow, the color of a pair of old amber earrings his mother had once owned. In fact, the way she was laughing as her mother brushed her long hair reminded him of his mother. And he remembered how his father always brushed his mother's hair. He looked at his daughter. *Such a waste . . . such a pitiful waste . . .* She ought to have a sweetheart to do that for her, he thought.

3

"I don't know why you always want to cut across the pasture like this instead of taking the road like normal people do. You know how our crossing his fields irritates the blue blazes out of old Mr. Harkington. Besides, Papa will skin you alive if he finds out."

The slim girl with serious brown eyes paused, looking down the road her sister had just described as a "dull, monotonous road." Finding it neither dull or monotonous, Mairi said simply, "I just don't understand you."

And well Tibbie could understand that. She didn't understand herself either, or the spirit that left her in a state of hypnosis half the time. She certainly could not understand how it was that she seemed to hear melodies that no one else heard, or why it was, exactly, that her mind had a magic door that opened into a sunny garden of imaginings and dreams. Her papa said she had a mad boarder in her attic; her mother called it fancy; Granny likened it to seeing with the mind. Mairi said she was just plain crazy.

And perhaps she was.

She looked beyond the fence, gazing out across the pasture, where the most golden of hazes scarfed the gentle, rolling hills, the dry grasses whispering to the wind as it passed. She marveled that in one short month she could stand in this selfsame spot and see everywhere the dancing brilliance of the bluest of bluebonnets, the dazzling orange of flameflower, the shocking contrast of fire wheel's red and yellow, and the deep gold of

Maximilian sunflower. This called to her like no flat, brown
stretch of road ever could.

It also made Mr. Harkington's size and bluster diminish and
fade from a position foremost in her mind.

Mr. Harkington's farm adjoined the Buchanan place on the
east side, and in order to take full advantage of the shortcut
home, a short slice of his property had to be crossed. Mr.
Harkington had been here almost as long as Indianola, and it
was rumored that his father had been one of the alligators that
inhabited the marshy inlets of coastal areas, and that his
mother was a crab. As Tibbie had grown older she had seen
some justification for these rumors, since Mr. Harkington did
inherit a few of the obvious characteristics of these two, being
snappish and crabby.

Granny said he was an old crank and was crazier than a
loon. Tibbie wasn't sure just how crazy loons were, but as for
the cranky part. . . . Well, perhaps that was what made him
post a sign on the road that led to his house that read: NO
FOOLS, FEMALES, OR FREELOADERS ALLOWED.

"What would possess a man to put out a sign as absurd as
that?" Effie said as they passed the sign one morning on their
way to church. "Fools, females, and freeloaders indeed. Why,
there's absolutely no connection whatsoever."

Coll, who had learned a long time ago how to keep peace in
the family, simply raised a questioning brow and clucked the
mare into a faster pace, which made Effie give her immediate
attention to keeping her bonnet on her head.

Mr. Harkington was a little strange, Tibbie had to admit.
No one had ever seen the inside of his house, partly because he
never invited anyone in. Tibbie suspected the primary reason,
however, was the old Henry rifle he greeted them with. And in
spite of being a bit odd himself, he had the strangest assort-
ment of animals in the state of Texas. Anyone who saw his old
buckboard parked in town knew to stay clean away, for his
horse, a swaybacked red roan named Sourpuss (because she
was a female) was a biter. And what a record Sourpuss had.

Drat Wilson, the town drunk, got his right ear bitten clean

off, and once she took a swipe at the sheriff's cigar, taking a good-sized chunk of his lip with it. That's why folks called him Harry, which was short for Harelip. Mr. Harkington also had an old bluetick hound called Cooter, that "ran the legs off chickens," as Effie said; but fortunately for Cooter he only chased and never had been known to harm one—other than leaving them winded and walking around the barnyard with their wings outspread to cool off.

But it was his old red bull, Hammer, that put the fear of God into Tibbie's heart. She suspected Mr. Harkington called him Hammer because he had hammered a few people into the ground. More than once she had come close to being hammered herself, feeling Hammer's hot breath blowing down her neck as he came out of nowhere to give chase. And if that wasn't enough, she still had a scar on her shoulder where he'd gotten close enough to do more than breathe, and for that reason Coll had forbidden her ever to take the shortcut again.

And she hadn't.

For at least six months.

But Tibbie had a way of letting the good in things outweigh the bad, and in this case, the shortcut across Mr. Harkington's strip of pasture far outweighed the monotony of a country road or a nasty old red bull. And it seemed to be weighing that way today. Mairi shook her head as she watched her sister climb through the fence and strike off across the pasture like someone had set her heels afire, the basket looped over her arm swaying to and fro.

Tibbie had a way of walking that was rapid and resolute, as though she always knew exactly where she was going and what she would do when she got there. And that didn't make much sense to Mairi, who was content to amble along, drifting from one side of the road to the other, stopping to pass the time of day with every person that passed.

"Tibbie!" she called. "Tibbie Anne Buchanan, I know you hear me!"

But if Tibbie heard, she didn't let on. "Fine!" Mairi shouted. "Have it your way. Fill your skirts with burrs and your shoes with mud and see if I care. I'm taking the road." She started up the road in a huff, walking five feet or so, then pausing to look over her shoulder to see if Tibbie had thought better of it and come to her senses. But all she saw of her sister was the last bounce of her golden braid as it disappeared over the hill.

"Stubborn! Stubborn! Stubborn!" Mairi said, giving her foot a stomp. "I swear, if that woman had been born a chicken she'd lay square eggs." In spite of her insistence that her way was not only the best and most logical but the one any normal person would choose, in the end she looked in every direction, and not seeing Hammer anywhere, climbed through the fence and broke into a run to catch up with her sister.

Breathless and red of face, she caught up to Tibbie a few minutes later, still grumbling, one hand slapped down over her hat, the other working the stitch in her side while giving Tibbie her list of grievances one more time. "Just look at our skirts! We're ruining them in this wet grass. And look at my shoes. They're covered with mud."

"You can clean them when you get home," said Tibbie. "After you pull the burrs from your skirts."

"I've never understood why you put yourself to all this extra work and danger, just to take a shortcut," Mairi said, still loping a little in order to keep time with Tibbie's determined strides.

"It's not for the shortcut. I just like walking in the pasture. Taking the road can be awfully boring."

"And this is not?" wailed Mairi, looking around her and seeing not one thing of interest. Noticing Tibbie was putting too much distance between them, she hiked up her skirts and started after her.

"Are we in a hurry, Tib? Have you seen Hammer?"

"Not that I recollect."

"Then why must you walk so fast?"

"Stock-still would be fast to you."

To anyone passing by, the girls would have never been taken for sisters. Tibbie, showing the Scottish ancestry of their father, was blond and of small stature, while Mairi had the darker coloring and taller height that came from their mother's side of the family. In fact, the only similarity between the two sisters at all was the brown eyes, but even they were different, Mairi's being a dark, rich brown, while Tibbie's were much lighter. Mairi always teased Tibbie, saying hers were "the color of pulled taffy."

Tibbie, never one to be outdone, would retort by telling Mairi, hers were "the color of unsulfured molasses."

Mairi had never been able to see the difference between unsulfured molasses and the other kind, but Tibbie assured her there was, and she said it with such firm conviction that Mairi was inclined to believe she was right.

In front of them the pasture sloped gently, a gray-green field of last summer's dry grasses, damp from the cloudburst that left the grasses wet and lying on their side. Tibbie inhaled deeply, exclaiming, "Can't you smell it, Mairi? How delicious and fresh everything seems? I love it after a rain."

Mairi sniffed the air. "It smells like wet grass and cow patties to me."

Tibbie was about to give her a lecture on seeing everything in tones of brown, when at that precise moment she caught a flash of movement out of the corner of her eye. And it was red.

"Hammer has seen us!" she shouted to Mairi, giving her a shove. "Run!"

They broke into a dead run. When they reached the fence, Tibbie tossed her basket over, and she and Mairi dove through the slats in the nick of time. For a moment, Tibbie thought Hammer was going to come through the fence after them, but he just stood there, snorting and tossing his head at them. Winded and too terrified to move, they stood stock-still, wheezing and gasping for breath. "Uh-oh!" Mairi said between breaths. "Here comes trouble."

And trouble it was, for here came Mr. Harkington, looking madder than a disturbed hornet, hurrying like someone had soaked his drawers in turpentine and struck a match. By the time he reached them, his bald head was fire red, his face splotchy and mottled with purple rage. "I've told you more

than once to keep off my property! And what do I find? You!"
he said, stabbing a long, bony finger at her with such force,
Tibbie took a step back.

"We didn't harm anything."

"Don't back talk me, Missy! You've left muddy tracks
across my field and upset my bull, that's trouble enough."

"Your bull is always upset, Mr. Harkington, and well you
know it. As for tracking up your field, you and that bull of
yours have done far more damage than either my sister or
me."

"I've warned you enough, Miss Uppity. I'm off to see your
pa about this . . . the sheriff, too, if need be."

"The sheriff won't give much *lip* to anything you say, sir."
Tibbie replied, too angry to heed the warning in Mairi's horrified gasp. Mr. Harkington's face was solid purple now.

"You're a fine one to go digging up the past, you cotton-
headed little strumpet!"

At that precise moment, something besides Mr. Harkington's bull was red.

"I'd rather be cotton-headed than thick-skulled . . . and at
least I don't have to grow my hair out a foot long to cover my
bald spot. As for the other, you—"

Mairi's arm shot out, locking around Tibbie's arm. "Tibbie
. . . please . . ."

Tibbie took advantage of Mr. Harkington's being so sensitive about his hairless style, using the time he choked on his
anger to gain some control over her own raging temper.

"I would like to say I feel sorry for you, Mr. Harkington,
because you're the most miserable person I've ever known, but
I only find myself feeling sorry for those who have no control
over their adversity, while you take delight in manufacturing
yours. You just keep living out here with your crabby old disposition and your nasty-tempered animals and see where it
gets you. One of these days you're going to need some of these
people you've treated so shabbily, and what will you do then?
What if the next hurricane blows your house and all your
buildings down like it did the Ramsays's last time? Think you

can rebuild all that with the help of your dog and chickens and mean-tempered goat? What will you do if the next epidemic of yellow fever or smallpox strikes you? Send your horse after my pa? And what will happen when you die, Mr. Harkington, as you surely will. Do you think this fancy red bull of yours will lay you out and see to your burial? Or will he go right on chomping grass while the buzzards polish you off?"

"You cross my property again and I'll get my Henry after you," he said, sounding vaguely subdued. He turned and slapped his bull up beside the head. "Go on . . . get out of here!" He stomped off in an angry huff, muttering about how he should have shot her with his Henry a long time ago.

Tibbie and Mairi exchanged relieved glances. "He's gonna do it, too," Mairi said. "Mark my words if he doesn't. One of these days you're going to provoke him and he's going to shoot you with that old Henry of his."

"The firing pin of that old thing is so rusted over it wouldn't fire a candle wick."

"He can always use it for a club."

The two girls turned away and struck out across their own pasture this time.

"This is the last time I'm doing this," Mairi was saying.

"You always say that."

"But I mean it this time. I absolutely refuse to ever"—she looked heavenward—"God strike me deaf and dumb if I ever put as much as my little finger through old Mr. Harkington's fence again."

"Come on."

Mairi struck out after her sister, calling to her after a minute or two when she noticed they weren't going straight home. "Have you lost your sense of direction? Our house is over there," she said, pointing for emphasis.

"We've got an errand to do first."

Mairi picked up her pace, drawing even with Tibbie. When they neared another fence line, Mairi balked. "Are you out of your mind? That's *his* land," she said, pointing again.

"I know that."

"I won't set foot through that fence."

"You afraid of a few hogs?"

"I'm afraid of anything that belongs to Mr. Harkington." Mairi eyed the thirty or so hogs through the fence. Then she turned to watch her sister pulling jimsonweed.

"What are you going to do with that?"

Tibbie carried an armful to the fence and tossed it over. The pigs gathered around, snorting and squealing as they polished it off.

"My God! Jimsonweed will kill those hogs."

"I didn't give them that much. They'll just get a bellyache."

"Oh, Lord, we'd better get out of here."

This time Tibbie agreed and they retraced their steps, soon passing the place where they had encountered Mr. Harkington. Suddenly Tibbie looked down the fence row and saw their jersey cow with her head poking through the boards in the fence, trying to reach the grass on the other side.

"Oh no, not again!" said Tibbie. "Drat her stubborn hide!"

Mairi stopped and looked at her sister. Before she could ask what was wrong, Tibbie turned toward her. "Take this basket on up to the house with you. Tell Mama I'll be there as soon as I can." Tibbie handed a basket full of dried fruit to her sister.

"What's in it?"

"Just tell Mama Mrs. Pinckney sent the basket for all Papa and I did for Horace when he broke his leg. She's to keep the basket and the cloth as well."

Mairi took the basket, giving her sister a bewildered look. "But where are you going, Tib?"

Tibbie looked across the field. "Down the fence row. Bertha has her head caught between the boards again."

Mairi looked in the direction Tibbie had looked just moments before. "Stupid cow! You should just leave her that way. Maybe she'd think twice about poking her head through like that if you did."

Tibbie took the long braid lying across her breast and tossed it over her shoulder. "She's too good a milk cow to leave with her head caught between the boards. She'll stop giving milk if she gets too upset. I'll have to help her . . . unless you'd rather do it."

Mairi pushed the basket further up her arm. "You were always better with animals than I was."

Turning away, Mairi pulled her shawl tighter around her shoulders. "Don't dawdle none now, you hear? You know how Mama likes us to be on time."

"She's used to Papa and I coming in late," said Tibbie.

"She's not used to it," said Mairi. "She just tolerates it." Mairi started off across the pasture. "I know one thing," she said over her shoulder. "I'll never marry a doctor."

"There are worse jobs, and it keeps beans on the table. Besides, it makes Papa happy."

"It makes *you* and Papa happy."

The cold snap was apparently over, for today had been unusually warm for a day in February. Feeling as frisky as Bertha must have felt when she poked her head through the fence rails, Tibbie watched her sister disappear over a low rise, then tilted her head back and let the full force of the bright sun flood her face, before she drew her fringed shawl more tightly around her shoulders and spun around two or three times. Her encounter with Mr. Harkington forgotten, she was laughing at the wonderful feelings she was experiencing. Another month and signs of spring would be everywhere.

Spring.

Her favorite time of year, when the whole earth seemed to throb with the energy of nature. Spring. Before the heat and insects drove her inside. She whirled around again, spinning faster and faster until she was so dizzy she collapsed in a puff of skirt and petticoats on the soft, dry coastal grasses. Plucking a blade, she was about to put it in her mouth when the silhouette of a figure on horseback coming up the road came into her line of vision. The figure was a man, she could tell that much, but it was too far away to see the face. But whomever he was, he had pulled up his horse, obviously watching her. She tossed the stem of grass and gathered her skirts as she came to her feet. Hadn't anyone ever taught him it was impolite to stare?

She turned her back to him, standing on a grassy knoll covered with coastal bluestem and salt grass, a knoll that had been a sand dune years ago when a hurricane had driven the gulf inland to cover the land. But now the wind was calm and the bay shimmered in the sunlight, sparkling like broken glass. Across the grassy slopes and over a brackish pond lay Matagorda Bay and beyond that the Gulf of Mexico, while further inland lay the mud flats, marshes, and scrub that were scattered between shallow bays and inlets.

She loved to come here, often bringing a blanket and lying in the grass for long periods of time, looking out across the bay, wondering what the world was like out there beyond the barrier islands. Her papa had told her of so many places, but Tibbie could only imagine what they would be like, for she had never been further east than New Orleans, north than San Antonio, or west than Corpus Christi.

Then she remembered poor Bertha with her head stuck in the fence, and started off, glancing over her shoulder as she did. The figure on horseback was gone.

Her mind on other things now, she headed toward a motte of live oak trees, wind-bent and deformed by the wind and salt spray. Her coming disturbed a tiny marsh wren who flew into the twisted trees not far from where Bertha stood patiently waiting.

Sweet Bertha, she thought, *with her wet nose and her trusting brown eyes, always getting into trouble.* This wasn't the first time this had happened. Bertha was never content with what she had. If she was in the pasture she wanted the grass on the other side of the fence. If she was in the barn, she wanted to be in the pen. If she was in the pen, she stood gazing wistfully at the lush grasses growing in the pasture just beyond. And when it came to milking it wasn't any different. If Tibbie wasn't punctual about milking her, Bertha would "raise hell and put a chunk under it," as her papa said. But when she was being milked, you had to watch her carefully, or she'd kick over the milk bucket. Bertha just didn't ever seem to be completely happy—just like some people she knew.

Following the fencerow, Tibbie walked parallel to the road. When she reached the end of the fence line where it made a sharp turn, she cut diagonally across, skirting a stagnant pond. A few yards away, another fence cut the pasture in two. It would have to be crossed in order to reach Bertha.

Hearing a loud booming sound behind her, Tibbie turned to see a couple of prairie chickens going through their mating ceremony, just as they did every February. It was something to see, too. She crept closer. The cock and hen were so intent on their ritual that she was able to get quite close. Finding the spectacle very humorous, she clapped her hands over her mouth so she wouldn't be tempted to laugh—which was hard to resist. Seeing the male inflate the large orange air sacs on each side of his neck and then strut in front of the hen, bobbing his head up and down to gain her attention was a spectacle to behold. The entire time he was going through his comical routine, he made that loud booming noise.

By this time Bertha was growing impatient and gave her head a shake. Hearing Bertha's bell, Tibbie turned away from the prairie chickens and hurried toward her, breaking into a run. She stopped running when she neared Bertha, not wanting to startle her. A few yards away, she hitched up her skirts and went through the fence so she would be on the same side as Bertha's head.

"Drat," she said, as she was yanked back, a sharp pain jabbing into her scalp. She tugged at her hair, but it was caught fast. "Drat and double drat." Feeling along the rail she found her hair held fast by a rusty old nail.

Caught in the fence, just like Bertha.

Tibbie managed to climb through the fence so her feet were both on the same side, but in order to keep from pulling her hair out by the roots, she had to hold her head down, which wasn't too bad except for one glaring fact: When one's head is down, one's posterior is up.

Which is exactly where it was when Nicholas Mackinnon walked up behind her and said, "Is that an invitation, sweetheart?"

Tibbie jumped a country mile, smacking her head against the rail. She jerked back, getting a good idea of what it would feel like to be scalped. When she yanked her head back to ease the tension on her hair, she struck the back of her head on the fence rail with a loud crack.

"There's just no end to the excitement in your life, is there?"

Something about that voice was vaguely familiar, and she lifted her head to one side, hoping to get a glimpse of the ill-mannered clod doing all the clever talking. Seeing her predicament, Nick moved next to her and dropped low, sitting on his haunches, his face just inches from hers. She recognized him immediately. "What do you want?" she said coldly.

He sat looking at her, his features clear and disturbing at this close range. She had never considered herself timid or self-conscious, yet that was precisely how she felt now. Her breathing accelerated. Her throat grew dry. Her hands began to feel for the nail, pulling at it and tugging at her hair until she was breathless from the exertion. In spite of all her effort, the only thing she accomplished was pulling the braid loose, which sent the incredible length of her hair spilling downward to be caught by the breeze and ensnaring it worse than before. His eyes went to the tangled mass of hair, and then back to her face, as a slow-spreading grin crept across his handsome face.

"Looks like you're caught fast," he said. *At last, I've got you where I want you. You've no choice now, sweetheart. You'll have to talk to me.* His eyes went back to her shapely little rump up in the air—and close enough to pat. By God, he wanted to. *Lord! What an invitation!*

"Why don't you go back to whatever you were doing before you started pestering me? Can't you see I'm busy?"

He laughed at that. "Oh, I can see that you're busy all right. I can also see that you're going to be busy for the rest of the day. There's no way you're going to get your hair loose. You'll have to cut it."

"When I want your opinion, sir, I'll ask for it."

"You're lucky I'm such a patient man . . . content to wait right here until you ask me."

"Where you're concerned, I'm not lucky at all. You are a pest, sir. Worse than a horsefly." She tried to angle herself around to ease the cramp in her back. "For all I care, you can wait until you petrify. I want nothing to do with you. I thought I made that plain."

"Oh, you've made it plain enough. Too plain. A bit over-done, in fact. And that, sweet face, makes me wonder why." He lifted one hand to stroke the curve of her cheek with the backs of his fingers. "So soft on the outside to have such a hard heart."

Tibbie studied him, trepidation simmering in the back of her mind like a carefully watched pot. A long-unfelt tingling of excitement seemed to rob her of her steady breathing. The way he stood there with such powerful shoulders and long, muscular legs spread confidently wide—an unsettling thought that he was like a large, sharp-eyed predator swooping down upon trapped prey. A shiver that had nothing to do with the cold rippled across her as his hand left the curve of her cheek and drifted over her ear, dropping lower to follow the winding trail of a strand of honey-gold hair.

"Such beautiful hair . . . it's a pity to cut something so lovely."

She drew in her breath sharply as one fingertip lazily slipped beneath the curl, following it across the curve of her breast, the briefest whisper of his knuckles teasing her through the wool of her dress. She pulled back from him, wincing at the jab of pain that pierced her scalp. His hand continued its quest, following the curl until it went behind her to where it lay hopelessly ensnared in the fence. She tried moving back, away from him, but the fence rails behind her afforded her little space.

"Kindly remove yourself from my presence."

"Why? Do I bother you?"

"You, sir, are unwanted. And as for your assistance it is unsolicited and unnecessary."

"My goodness! What a pest I must be." He cocked his head to one side and studied her. "Is that all?"

"No. Your behavior is most inappropriate."

"It is? In what way?"

"You are taking liberties with my person."

He looked surprised at that. "I am?" Then an ear-splitting grin crossed his face. "What kind of liberties?"

"A gentleman does not put his hands on a lady."

"I see. Well, in that case, you just tell me how I'm going to get you untangled *without* touching you and I'll give it a go."

"*You* aren't going to do anything. I've told you . . . I don't need your help."

"You're a bit cocksure, aren't you? This dauntless attitude of yours may get you nothing more than a night spent here in this pasture. If I were you, I'd try being a little more demure."

"Demure women make me sick!"

He threw back his head and laughed. "A peahen with all the swaggering confidence of a peacock. Damn me for a fool if it doesn't go well with you. You're a contradiction, girl . . . the perfect picture of femininity, the ideal woman with a pretty, demure manner, but inwardly you're as dauntless as they come."

"Are you going to stand here all day boring me with your trite remarks?"

"Only if you continue to refuse my help."

She began to pull and tug at her hair in earnest now, wincing when she rammed a splinter into her knuckle, but still she did not stop—not until his hands came up to close over hers, stilling them. "You're only making things worse." He lifted her hand, pulling the splinter out. "I hate to see such beauty marred."

She jerked her hand back. "Then leave me be."

"Does it pain you to be civil? To my recollection I've done nothing to warrant this type of reaction from you. Whenever our paths have crossed my behavior has been, to my belief, at least civilized. I've tried friendly conversation, which you've spurned; an invitation or two, which you've turned down. I've spoken to you in passing, which you pretended not to hear. I've tipped my hat, which you've ignored. At least *I've* been honest about my attraction to you."

"Humph! Being stung by a bee can be called honest, but it hurts all the same."

"Even now," he went on, "I've offered you my help, which you promptly rejected. Tell me, what does it take to get close to you?"

"Did it ever occur to you that I might not want you to get close to me? That I just might prefer to be left alone? That being pursued by you or any man may not be to my liking?"

She tried to shift her position to ease the ache that was beginning to lodge in the small of her back and promptly bumped her head again. Her usually level-headed temper was beginning to be replaced by acute irritation. A woman should not have to put up with the likes of this. "When will you get the message? I do not wish to be friends or even acquaintances with you."

"What do you have against men?"

She rounded on him hotly. "I am not against all men, just certain ones . . . mainly lechers with less than honorable intentions. I've seen your kind before. They come into town all the time. Do you honestly think you're the first man to flash me a smile or sing my praises with a few flattering words? I'm made of sterner stuff than that. I don't topple into a man's hands, or his bed, simply because he takes notice of me. You may have a silver tongue and the devil's own blue eyes, but inside you have the blackest of hearts and the most wicked intentions."

Nick smiled, feeling the flood of elation. She had more spirit than a racehorse and enough tenacity to erode solid rock, not to mention a tongue that would cure leather. She was as stubborn as they came, and without a doubt the most opinionated woman he'd ever come across. He was on the verge of doing as she asked and leaving her be, but suddenly he remembered something she had said, something he was sure she hadn't meant to let slip.

The devil's own blue eyes.

With those words she had sealed her fate. She wasn't as

immune to him as she let on. It was all the encouragement he needed.

This woman, he realized, was different. She wouldn't give a man the time of day if she didn't trust him. "If I give you my word that I only want to talk with you—"

"Your word is worth about as much to me as a sack of beach sand."

"I might remind you that you're in no position to quibble. I haven't done anything to hurt you, but sweetheart, I damn well could have."

For a moment the two of them eyed each other. He was right, and she knew it.

"I'll make a deal with you," he said.

"No deals," she flung back at him.

"You win." He sighed and rose to his feet.

She angled her fanny around, pointing it in the opposite direction so she could see what he was doing. The man was too good-looking by half, and there had been a time in her past when she would have given a brute like him notice. But she was wiser now.

She knew there was more to being a man than having eyes as blue as the clear skies overhead, or a body that moved like water flowing over rocks. He was a handsome devil, all right. Not in the Greek god manner, but in a more rugged, raw-boned way that made you terribly aware—not of his charm, for in truth, she didn't know if he possessed any or not. No, his handsome appeal was in the way he seemed so terribly masculine, yet at the same time gentle. He had called her a contradiction. The same could be said of him. Masculine strength and a gentle nature rarely dwelt together. But gentle or not, this blue-eyed brute was all male.

Blast him! What is he doing?

He was leaving! She felt anger rise to the top of her head like a kettle full of steam. *How dare he leave me here like this. It might be hours before that rattle-headed sister of mine even remembers she has a sister, let alone think to come looking for me. And my back is breaking . . . my legs are cramped . . . my scalp is split . . . my head hurts . . .*

Supremely frustrated, she wound her hands around her hair and began pulling for all she was worth. By now, whatever hair that managed to escape being snared by splintered wood was blowing wild as a waterspout all around her. Because of its incredible length and the gulf breeze, it was caught in a dozen places. If she only had a pair of scissors.

She glanced back in the direction he had taken. He was some distance away now, walking toward his horse, his hands in his pockets, whistling a tune. The vile son of a salamander was leaving. *Well, let him go. I'll stay here till I rot before I'll ask for his help.*

On the verge of tears, she closed her eyes, resting her forehead on her arms. She crossed them over the rail. Feeling a little more in control, she peeked in his direction, thinking, brute or not, he wouldn't go off and leave her here like this. All hope of seeing him walking back toward her was shattered when she watched him mount his horse.

She would have preferred to be boiled in oil than to call after him. Trying to ingratiate herself with anyone was not of her ilk, and admitting that she was wrong was harder for her to swallow than castor oil. But her back was breaking and he might be the only help she would receive. One more quick glance and she saw him turn his horse away. She would worry later about the damage to her wounded pride.

"Wait!" she called after him. And if that wasn't humiliating enough, she had to add, "You can't leave me here like this!" He pulled up, turning in the saddle to look at her as if he were expecting her to say more. She bit her tongue. She'd said far too much already.

Fool! She couldn't believe she would give in so easily. *You sniveling ninny! You crybaby! You dope! Calling a man like him to help you. Serves you right!* If it were possible, she would have kicked herself. But then she saw him shrug and turn around, giving the chestnut the go-ahead. "Wait!" she cried out with panicked overtones. "Please!"

She could almost hear him sigh with exasperation as she watched him turn his horse and ride toward her. But she wasn't too concerned with what he was feeling right now. She was too anxious about her own conflicting emotions: elation that she would soon be out of this predicament; humiliation that he had won this first round. Her only consolation was in knowing there would probably be other opportunities to get the best of him. Yet, eyeing him at close range, she decided he didn't look like a man anyone got the best of very often. Nor did he look like a quitter. She had the feeling that by calling him back she had just scooped out another shovel of dirt from her own grave.

"You called?"

It didn't help her humor any to have him rub it in. She felt the urge to tell that blue-eyed devil grinning down at her to take his good-humored smile and get lost.

Nicholas sat upon his horse, watching her, fighting the urge to laugh at the battle pride and desperation waged upon her lovely face. As much as he hated being so ornery, he wasn't about to make this easy for her. Letting a woman like her gain the upper hand, well, there would be hell to pay. When she didn't answer, he shrugged and turned his horse away.

The high, stiff collar on her dress was choking her, her scalp was sore and stinging, her hands were full of splinters, her feet were going to sleep, her neck felt like it had calcified in this uncomfortable position, and now, her back was paralyzed. There are some things that overrule pigheaded pride, she told herself. "Yes!" she screamed. "Yes, I called, and you damn well know it."

He was fighting laughter that did not want to be contained. *Dear Lord, don't let me laugh. She's got more pride than a peacock. . . . One laugh, Mackinnon, and it will set you back weeks. You'd best remember that.*

The desire to laugh subsided somewhat. He had no hankering to lose any ground with this lass. He rode back to her and dismounted. All she could see of him, through the tangle of hair that covered her face, was a long pair of well-muscled legs

—a pair of legs that were too long and too well-muscled for a woman who was trying to forget men.

But it was of no use. The feelings she thought she had repressed, the desires and longings of a woman for a man were alive deep within her breast, beating just as strong and urgent and discomforting as they had done five years ago, in spite of the strict discipline she had forced upon herself. For the last five years she had struggled to prove to herself that she didn't need a man in her life—didn't need or want one.

But she had been wrong.

Why did God find it necessary to throw another temptation, like a stumbling stone, in her path, just when she'd overcome the last one. And why did temptation have to look so downright tempting? She earnestly wished she'd left Bertha to choke. But even as she thought it, she knew she couldn't blame it on poor, sweet Bertha.

The problem wasn't Bertha.

The problem was herself.

"You've decided to let me help you, I take it?"

She twisted around to get a better eyeful of him. He was here and willing to help, but his look had a bit of a taunt to it, and she had never been any good with dares, always giving in to them. But her predicament prohibited her from saving any face whatsoever. She couldn't even raise her chin, and with all this hair in her face, even a haughty, disinterested look would go unseen. "If I remember right, you offered to help me. I have accepted your offer. I see no reason to dicker further."

"I'm at your service," he said, "after we have a little agreement."

"Agreement?" she repeated, irritated at the warbling sound of her voice. "What *kind* of agreement?"

"Since my word isn't worth a sack of beach sand, I'll settle for yours. I want you to give me your word."

"About what?"

"That you will give me two hours of your time each week."

"To do what?"

"Whatever I wish." Hearing her outraged gasp, he chuckled. "As long as it is within the bounds of normal behavior between a man and woman."

"That leaves you an opening big enough to drive a hay wagon through," she said quickly.

"Perhaps, but you're in no position to quibble. You can agree, or spend the night in the pasture. Which will it be?"

"For how many weeks?"

"For as long as I wish."

She could have a long gray beard by then, or she could make his time with her so miserable he'd be ready to call it off after one week.

She took a moment to ponder. She didn't have any leverage. She either accepted or she didn't. And that meant she either got to stand up straight before her back calcified, or she didn't. But it was so hard just to say the words.

"Do you agree to my terms?"

"I suppose," she whispered.

"Speak up, lass. I can't hear you."

"I suppose so!"

"That's not a very definite answer."

"It's all the answer you're going to get. Now, are you going to help me or not?"

"I might."

"You might? What kind of answer is that?"

"About like *I suppose so,* I would reckon."

"All right," she said wearily.

"All right what?"

"All right! I agree to your terms."

"Two hours of your time each week, for as long as I choose?"

She nodded weakly.

"I only accept written or verbal agreements. Bodily gestures are out."

She thought of one bodily gesture she would like to give him. "Yes."

"Good," he said. "I don't think you'll be sorry."

"Humph! I'm already sorry."

He laughed, then stepped behind her, the hardness of his thighs pressing against her buttocks. "Do you have to stand there?" she asked.

"Where else would I stand, besides on the ground?"

"You know what I mean."

"No, I don't have to stand here . . . unless you want your hair freed."

She grimaced when he pressed closer, but she didn't say anything. He worked behind her for some time and she was beginning to wonder if he was making any headway at all when he said, "I'm going to have to cut some of your hair."

"You can shave my head for all I care. Just get me loose."

"A woman's hair is her crowning glory. A good, church-going girl like you should know that."

"I'm not interested in a woman's crowning glory."

"The way I see it, you're not interested in much of anything. You're not interested in making new friends. You're not interested in men. You're not even interested in just a little pleasant conversation. Now, you tell me, girl, just what are you interested in?"

"I'm interested in getting free of this blasted fence and putting as much distance between myself and you as I possibly can. Aren't you finished yet? My back feels like a bent nail."

"Almost finished," he said, then fished around in his pocket until he found his knife. She shuddered when she heard the sawing sound of his knife against her hair and felt the telltale tug, imagining what she would look like when he was done.

"There," he said, giving her a wink. "Stand up, lady bright. You're free at last."

Slowly, her hand pressing the small of her back, Tibbie rose to her feet, feeling the pull of hair he still held in his hands. "What are you going to do now?"

He grinned in a way that reminded her of a fox at a rabbit hole. "What would you like for me to do?"

"Disappear."

"Be nice, or we'll be here all night."

"For starters you can let go of my hair," she said, giving it a yank. But he held her fast. Then, without saying a word, his eyes never leaving her face, he used her hair to draw her closer, winding the golden strands around his hand, again and again. She was already close enough to feel the heated current of his breath caressing her cheek like a warm palm, when it struck her that she should have protested. For some reason she had been too stunned to realize what he was about, and now, when she tried to protest, the words caught in her throat.

"Would you like me to help?"

"What could I possibly need your help for now?"

"I'm only guessing, but I would think the reason you're out here might have something to do with that cow with her head caught in the fence over there."

"Bertha!" she said, her eyes following the fence line down to where Bertha stood patiently switching her tail, her head in the fence. She knew her face must be flaming, judging from the surge of heat she was feeling. How could she have forgotten about poor Bertha like that? "I can manage, thank you."

"Then I'll claim one of my hours now." Her eyes went wide when he lifted her hair to his mouth and kissed it. "It's a crime to cut hair as beautiful as yours," he said, releasing it to fall against her shoulder. "But at least I have a token to keep." She looked down and saw a healthy length of her hair in his hand. Automatically, her hand went to her head.

"Don't worry," he said, rolling the hair into a curl and tucking it into his shirt pocket, "you still have plenty left, more than most women could ever hope to have."

He reached into his pants pocket and extracted a pocket watch, flipping the gold lid open and checking the time. "One hour," he said, then snapped the lid closed, dropping the watch back into his watch pocket. He took her arm at the elbow and guided her along the fencerows until they reached Bertha, who lowed softly and looked at them with soft, liquid brown eyes.

When Tibbie reached for her, his hand came out to grasp her arm, not hard, but firm enough to stop her. "Let me," he said, taking Bertha by the horns and twisting her head to the side, forcing one horn back under the rail. He did the same with the other horn and Bertha was free. Giving her head a good shake, Bertha turned and trotted across the pasture toward the barn, her milk bag swinging to and fro, the bell at her neck clanging as she went.

A sudden gust of wind swept across the field, rippling the dry grasses and rattling seed pods. Tibbie pulled her shawl tighter around her, turning her face toward the wind so her hair would stay out of her face. *Now what?*

"Are you cold?"

The look on his face was neither flirtatious nor taunting, but simply an honest question deserving an honest answer. "No," she said, "not really. The temperature seems to be dropping and the wind is picking up."

"We're in for some cold, windy weather," he said, looking at the horizon. "Good chance of rain, too, I suspect." He took her arm again, and she decided to see this thing through. She had given her word and that was justification enough. But if she were entirely honest, she would have to admit the man had a certain manner about him that was easy to be around.

He was older than her by several years, but not too old. And she had already discovered he was a wee bit of a tease. But there was an element of sincerity and honesty about him that she didn't often see in a man. She didn't think this man would whisper sweet promises in a woman's ear with no intention of keeping them. She had a feeling this man would make no promises, and if he ever did, that he would keep them. But what did that matter to her? She knew the pitfalls that awaited a woman foolish enough to believe the beguiling words and charming smile of a man.

He walked with her in the direction Bertha had taken, making a few comments and watching her step along the deep-rutted cow trail, the hem of her skirt skimming the tops of dry grasses with a dry, swishing sound. Over and over he tried various subjects, hoping to hit upon some topic she would discuss freely with him. He was about to give up when he asked her if she knew Miss Sukey Porter Merriweather.

"Of course I know her. Everyone in Indianola knows her. How do you know her?"

"I've taken a house she had to let."

"Oh . . . not the one on Grapevine Street?"

"One twenty-nine Grapevine, to be exact. Why did you say it like there was something wrong with the house?"

"I didn't, did I?"

"You did. Now tell me why."

"It's just that there was a man murdered there last year."

"Miss Merriweather didn't have anything to do with it, did she?"

Tibbie burst out laughing at that one. "Have you seen Miss Merriweather?"

"Every overplumped inch of her."

"Exactly. Can you imagine Miss Merriweather wielding an ax?"

Nick cringed. "Is that how the fellow died? Hacked to death?"

"Papa said the first blow killed him. So the other thirty or so didn't matter much after that."

"Thirty? Saint Sebastian! Are you sure that old Merriweather cow didn't have something to do with it?"

"She was never a suspect. Of course they never had a suspect . . . never had any idea who could have done it or why. I personally don't think she had anything to do with it. Miss Merriweather is a little odd, I'll grant you, but she comes by it honestly. The Merriweathers have always been odd, but harmless. She's the most agreeable of the lot, if you can imagine." Tibbie paused a moment in thought. "She's not such a bad sort, really. She just takes a little getting used to. And you can get used to anything, even being hanged, as the Irishman said."

"Which Irishman was that?"

"It's just something my granny says."

"If your granny is anything like mine was, I bet she says a lot of things," he said.

"Oh, she does, she does."

Nick watched her, surprised to find her in a state of quiet humor, her bright eyes alive with life, a reflective smile hidden behind her hands. He couldn't help smiling at her. And then she did the most amazing thing. She broke into laughter, racing down the trail ahead of him, the trilling sound of her merriment trailing over her shoulder and wrapping him in warmth. It was the absolute last thing he would have ever expected to see her do. If this was the sort of response he got from her just mentioning her grandmother, he couldn't wait to meet the woman.

He slowed down a bit and watched her pull ahead of him, just so he could watch her follow the cow trail in her somber clothes while managing to look like she'd stepped out of a shaft of sunlight. He had a feeling she rarely forgot herself like this—and what a sight she was, her hair billowing out behind her, a sudden flash of a well-turned ankle, a glimpse of frothy white lace. At the top of the rise she turned and looked back at him, her face flushed and rosy from her exertion, the residue of laughter lingering in her lovely eyes and upon her lips. How unbelievable she was, how enchanting she looked this way, all flushed and warm and limp and laughing. He thought it odd that he found such contentment just in watching her. It was something he'd been doing a lot of lately—partly because she was the loveliest thing he'd ever seen, and partly because she was the hardest damn female to talk to he'd ever encountered. Him. Nicholas Mackinnon. A man who had, up to now, had any woman he'd ever wanted and quite a few he didn't.

But this one. Here was one female that wanted no part of him, and damn him for a fool if he didn't believe she meant it!

When they drew even with the orchard, he changed their direction. She stopped and looked at him. "This path only goes into the orchard," she said.

"And I've a hankering to see an orchard," he said, taking her by the elbow and starting up again.

"There's nothing in there this time of year."

"We're on my time," he said, "so humor me." They entered the orchard through the gate—a creaky old iron one that sagged on one side, leaving the earth beneath scraped bare and smooth. Keeping his hand at her elbow, he guided her through the bare trees until they came upon a three-sided shed that had a few crates stacked along one wall and a pile of sawdust in one corner that was used for mulch.

Her heart gave a sudden lurch, then throbbed in panic when he removed his jacket and spread it on the sawdust. He turned and took her by the shoulders, pushing her gently down to his jacket. She was wondering if she was close enough to the house to be heard if she found it necessary to scream, but another look at his face showed her a man who had probably done this a thousand times with as many women, but also a man who only took what was offered. She judged that he wouldn't use force—of course, he probably never had to before. But there was a small glimmer in his eye that said he wasn't above using a little persuasion. She had handled his kind before, true, but there was an element of newness to this one.

He stood over her for a while and she kept her eyes on her hands, which lay still and folded upon her lap. Her senses were acute now, her body sensitive to the slightest increase in warmth when he shifted his weight and drew nearer. Then he dropped down beside her, the sound of his breath coming strong and in complete harmony with the rustle of dry grasses. A breeze whispered through the bare fruit trees, and somewhere in the distance a dog barked. She jumped at the piercing cry of a killdeer hurrying down the orchard path. The wind carried his scent and she drew her shawl together and tied the ends in a knot across her breast.

He had watched her tie her shawl and then stare off into the distance. "Are you afraid?" he asked.

"Of what?"

"Me. Are you afraid to be here with me?"

She wanted to tell him no, but she didn't want to offer him any encouragement. She had no place for such as he in her life. But she didn't say so. He would realize all that soon enough. "Do I act as if I am?"

"You act as if you are ill at ease. It could be fear. Or shyness. Or even—"

"Or even the fact that I'm here when I don't wish to be."

"You've nothing to fear from me. If you aren't afraid of Beulah, you shouldn't be afraid of me."

She laughed and he thought he had never heard a more musical sound. "The cow's name is Bertha."

He watched, fascinated, as something as simple and basic as laughter transformed her entire face. He had always seen her as beautiful, but now she was radiant, illuminated from within. He felt a stabbing twist of envy for her family, friends, anyone who had seen her like this. Open. Free. At ease. "You're lovely when you laugh."

She stopped.

"I didn't tell you that to make you stop."

"I don't know why you told me that at all."

"Why shouldn't I? Aren't you used to men paying you compliments?"

"I'm not used to men at all, save my father and brothers."

"Oh, dear! Brothers, you say?"

She glanced up and saw the mock horror light up his face like an invitation. "Several brothers," she said. "Frightening. And mean. Tougher than whitleather."

He laughed. "And at least half a dozen of them. Right?"

"Half that."

"I suppose they're older than you . . . and bigger."

"Much older and much, much bigger."

"How big?"

"Huge," she said, indicating this with outspread arms.

"I'm terrified," he said.

She laughed. "You're full of prunes."

He grinned. "You see? There's nothing to fear around me."

She tossed a small clod of dirt at him. "Go do your apple-polishing someplace else . . . on some poor, unsuspecting girl. I'm immune."

He grinned, looking around him. "So, I'm apple-polishing,

am I? I would guess you know a lot about that, seeing how many apple trees there are here."

She glanced around her, taking in each beloved tree, hearing the rustle of dry leaves, the creak of bare branches calling her back in time.

"You like this place, don't you? It's someplace special to you."

The sound of his voice startled her and she turned to look at him. He indicated the outlying terrain with a nod of his head. "You came here often as a child, I think. I imagine it holds a lot of memories for you." He leaned back, bracing his back against the shed. "I had a place like this when I was a boy. Even now, I can close my eyes and remember it just as it was —the pecan grove, the sound of the creek running over rocks, the shouts of my brothers giving chase." He opened his eyes, looking at her. "You have those kinds of thoughts, too, when you come here, don't you?"

She nodded, drawing her legs up and locking her arms around them, dropping her chin to rest upon the flat support of her knees. He was right. She remembered coming here as a child, watching her father plant his fruit trees and skipping over the plowed ground, sweating and panting while she hunted for worms. She could almost see it now as it was then, the branches of the older trees sagging under the weight of heavy fruit, the sweet smell of freshly turned earth and cut grasses, the lazy droning of orchard bees, her own shrill laughter mingling with Mairi's and that of their three brothers, Barra, Calum, and Robbie as they gave chase.

Everything had been so green back then.

But the orchard wasn't green now. Now the gray-brown branches looked as thin and inhospitable as the yellow grasses lying flattened and dry. There were no fruit-weighted branches now, nor the shrill sound of children's laughter. Now there was only the discarded and abandoned residue from last summer and the disturbing presence and distracting nearness of this man.

As if sensing that the magic of the moment had vanished, he said, "Tell me about yourself."

She shrugged. "There's nothing to tell."

"Your name would do for a start." *But I'd rather hear why you wear those drab clothes, why you hide yourself away, why a woman that looks as good as you doesn't have a husband and a clapboard full of kids, or at least a steady beau.*

"You haven't told me yours."

"Quick," he said. "You're very quick."

"You're pretty quick yourself."

Ah, sweetheart, that's where you're wrong. I'm a man with a slow hand. "I told you my name the other day."

"If you did, I don't remember it."

"Ouch! I made a real impression, didn't I?"

Nick looked down at her. He had removed his hat and his golden brown hair was rumpled; he looked as though he wasn't ruffled in the least that she had forgotten his name. "Nicholas Mackinnon."

For a short while she lost her train of thought, becoming absorbed in the smooth yet forceful way his hands moved over his extended thigh, rubbing and pressing, as if he were trying to alleviate some kind of pain. It was then that she felt his eyes upon her and when she realized she had been staring she said quickly, "Do you always go by so formal a name as Nicholas?"

"I've been called a lot of things much less formal, believe me." She smiled in spite of her efforts not to, but he was disappointed in that. He had hoped to hear her laugh again. "I'm usually called Nick by my friends. I can't repeat what my brothers call me. My sister called me Nicky. My mother called me Cole."

"Called? You mean you were Nicky to them when you were a child, but now you're too grown up for that?"

A shadow passed over his face, faint, and was quickly brought under control, but Tibbie was a woman who caught such things. "No. What I mean is they used to call me that, but they don't anymore. They're both dead."

"Oh, I'm terribly sorry. I didn't mean to bring up painful memories."

"It's all right. It happened a long, long time ago. I was fourteen."

"Did you lose them both at the same time?"

"Close, but not at the same time. I'm sure you've heard of the Comanche raid on Fort Parker . . ."

"Everyone has heard the story of Cynthia Ann Parker. She was taken along with several other people."

"Five, to be exact. One of them was my six-year-old sister, Margery."

"You never found her?"

"No. My father and four of my brothers and I set out immediately to search for her. My older brother, Andrew, was left behind with my mother. When we returned without a trace of Margery, we found our homestead burned, my mother and brother dead. My father never recovered. He said life wasn't worth living without Margaret."

"Your mother's name?"

"Yes. After her death, my father was obsessed with finding Margery, leaving the five of us to rebuild the place as best we could. About a year after my mother and brother were killed, we received word that John Mackinnon had been killed and scalped by Comanches."

His words seemed to have a deeper meaning for her, as if by telling her these things, he was showing her the world was full of pain, that there were others besides herself that had suffered and risen above it. Somehow that gave him another dimension, one she had failed to see. Humanness. She had not thought of him as human—a person with mother, father, or family; someone who loved and cared and knew what it felt like to laugh and cry—to feel ten feet tall when everything was going his way and to find the strength to pick up and go on when it was not.

He tossed a pebble at a small mouse sitting on a clod of dirt. The mouse squeaked and ran. Tibbie was wishing he'd toss a pebble or two at her so she could do the same. But all he seemed in the mood to toss were questions. And he looked primed and ready to throw another one. "Here I've told you my life story," he said in the softest tones, "and I don't even know your name."

There was something about the softness of his voice, the pensive, almost melancholy feel of the moment that drew her to him. For the briefest instant the scars of her past fell away and he was nothing more than a lonely man who offered her friendship.

"Tibbie . . . Tibbie Buchanan."

⇥ 4 ⇤

"How did you injure your leg?"

"Comanche lance." He said that without thinking. A moment later his head whipped around to stare at her. "How did you know my leg had been injured?"

"By the way you've been rubbing it."

"You know a lot about things like that."

"My father is a doctor."

"My father could speak Gaelic, but that doesn't mean I can."

"I'm what you might call my father's assistant. He's taught me practically everything he knows."

She didn't venture another word. Beside her, Nicholas Mackinnon was equally silent, his brows drawn together in deep thought. What was he thinking about so seriously? Was it something to do with her? She thought perhaps that might be the case, since his glance would slide over her frequently. Although he was quite still as he sat beside her, she could feel the restlessness in him as if it reached out to touch her, and in a way it did, making her restless as well.

Now she began to wonder just why he was going to such lengths to be around her. She wished she had some way of knowing what he was thinking, but his thoughts were impossible to read. He narrowed his eyes and tilted his head to one side, as though he were appraising her. A man such as he could have any woman he wanted, so why did he bother with her? She could have nothing to do with this man. She had tried to make that plain enough—on numerous occasions. If only things were different, then she might. . . . She dismissed the thought, replacing it with one of speculation. How much, she wondered, did he know about her? That thought led to another. How much did she know about him?

Not much.

She stole a look at him and studied his face from the side. What few things she knew about him were of a very general nature. Snatches overheard when she was in town, or bits and pieces of conversation she picked up when helping her father in the clinic. But even these weren't things of a concrete nature, but more the self-absorbed fancywork of feminine minds, like Drucilla Fielding's description of him in overly flamboyant tones, or Tansy Peabody's bursts of enthusiastic praise for the romantic way he held the door open for her when she went to Appleton's Apothecary last week.

Tansy had stared at her like a dunce when Tibbie said, "Well, what did you expect him to do, Tansy? Hit you in the face with it?"

She had let her mind wander and now he was staring at her, a half-grin upon his face. She decided then and there that she did not like this man. Even if things were different and she were free to be courted like other girls her age, she would not be interested in him. *He'll probably grow fat in his old age. Fat and bald.* But fat and bald seemed quite harmless, and there was nothing harmless about this man. He was male and on the prowl. He was someone she should stay away from. Someone she should fear.

"I think your hour is up, and I've stayed way too long. Bertha is probably having a fit to be milked and Precious is probably driving my mother crazy."

"Precious? Who is that?"

She froze, a near-panicked look coming over her face. She didn't want to reveal any more about herself to this man. She had revealed way too much already. She inhaled deeply and dropped her gaze to the toes of her shoes, dust covered and peeking from beneath her dull brown skirt. Dull and brown. A mirror of her life. How she longed for something different.

Dear God! How she longed to have a splash of color in her life. If only for one day.

One day. It was only one tiny, insignificant slice from a year. She wouldn't even be particular about what day it was, or what month either, for that matter. One day. Just one whole day to laugh and dance and forget. One day to remember what life was like for her before.

But this wasn't before. This was after. Now. The present. There would be no going back. Not for her. Not ever. For her there was no way to return to the past, no hope for the future, for indeed she had no future, at least no more than she had right now. She was like that dull, brown road that stretched on and on without one bend or curve to break the monotony.

"Just why are you pestering me?"

"I wasn't aware that I was. I simply wanted to talk."

"I have two subjects I will talk about, Mr. Mackinnon: Weather and medicine. Take your pick."

"Everything else is taboo?"

"Everything."

"You still don't trust me, do you?"

"I don't even know you. How could you possibly expect me to trust you?"

"You don't have to know me to trust me."

"I don't trust anyone except my family."

"And why is that?"

"My granny always said, 'Anything that can lick can bite.' "

He smiled. "My grandpa always said, 'A woman that resists is a woman won, and her passion is equal to the fervor of her resistance.' "

The sudden turn of the conversation disappointed her. She wouldn't have admitted it, but it was a break from the ordinary to talk to him. But now he had guided the conversation toward an area that was taboo. "Your grandpa never knew me."

"What are you afraid of?"

"I never said I was."

"But you're uncomfortable around me."

"I'm not uncomfortable, I just don't associate with anyone but my family or my closest friends. You are neither."

"I could be your friend, if you'd let me."

"Friendship, for us, is out of the question."

"Why is that?"

"For one thing, we have nothing in common."

He grinned. "I bet it wouldn't take long for us to find something. I'd sure like to try."

"Oh, I've no doubt about that, no doubt you're experienced at that sort of thing."

"And you're experienced at diverting every attempt. I'd say we're about even."

"An experienced man when he's not bent upon seduction and an inexperienced woman when she is—still they are not even."

"Which are you? Inexperienced? Or bent upon seduction?"

He watched the play of emotion across her lovely face, still dazzled by her fresh brand of beauty, her lack of beguilement, the complete absence of flirtatious behavior, her naturalness, her almost believable disinterest in the opposite sex. She was like a beautiful woman who had had her mirror broken before she had a chance to look in it. She was pinkly scrubbed and squeaky clean, her hair shiny and, after the run-in with the fence, neatly rebraided. No scent adorned her, save that of soap and the warm kitchen scent of yeast and vanilla. She was a woman of no frills or decorations or gee-gaws. No bows graced her dress. Not one embellishment could he see on her person, yet she was the most electrifying creature he had ever laid eyes upon. He guessed it was because she was natural. The way a mountain is natural. Or a waterfall. Or a rain-dappled flower.

She wasn't certain what brought her mind back to shrewd consciousness. Perhaps it was the discomfort she felt whenever she was around him. Or perhaps it was the fear of what might happen if she stayed. She began gathering her skirt in one hand, which made him think she was about to rise. He studied the faded skirt gathered in her hand, picking out the faint tracery of a line where the previous hem had been. It was paradoxical—her preference for plain and somber clothing when the rest of her family dressed as their means and position in the community dictated. He reached across and picked up her hand, ignoring the way she flinched and tried to pull it back. As if it were nothing out of the ordinary for him to be holding her hand, he turned it palm up in his own, tracing the obvious indicators of hard work with his finger. "Such a tiny little hand to be so calloused. Don't you have help with your work?"

She jerked her hand back, hiding it in the folds of her skirt. "Of course we have help. There are just some things I prefer to do myself. The good Lord gave me two strong arms and a good back, Mr. Mackinnon. I see no reason why I shouldn't use them."

"They could be put to other uses," he said softly, noticing she had a way of acting like he wasn't anywhere around. He marveled at her hostility and the reason behind it. She was uncomfortable and secretive as hell around him and anxious to be on her way. He wondered at her secrets, and their cause. She didn't have the look of a woman with a past, or was she all pure innocence in need of a mast? Either way, she was entitled to keep her secrets, just as he kept a few of his own. He might insist on knowing what hers were, but he was determined to know her better. "There are a lot of other things a woman as beautiful as you could be doing. Your beauty could serve you well."

"When I'm sewing up lacerated flesh or slopping hogs, beauty doesn't serve me too well. I would rather God had seen fit to give me a little more height or a few extra pounds in its stead."

He came to his feet, pulling her up to stand before him. When she kept her eyes affixed to the fourth button on his shirt, he lifted her thick braid in his hand, judging its weight. "I think your size is perfect, at least considering the parts of you I can see."

She was unaccustomed to a man touching her. To have a

man like him do so was unsettling. She looked at the dark
hand that held her plait, noticing the perfect white cuff of his
fine cotton shirt. His clothes were expensive and well kept. The
boots alone she guessed cost well over twenty dollars. He was a
man with money—so let him use some of it to hire himself a
woman, and leave her alone. She felt frustrated and distraught.
She realized what he had said . . . *considering the parts of
you I can see.*

She placed both hands against his chest and pushed him
away, then she took a step backward. It was either bravery or
stupidity that made her meet his eyes as she said, "You've seen
all you're going to see of me, sir. I consider my debt to you
paid. There might be some women in town that might have
their heads turned by your kind, but I'm not one of them.
Fortunately, I recognize a crock of slop when I see it."

He grinned at her, trying to decide if he had just been called
a crock of slop or likened to one. He had seen her and her
sister come into town, watching them pause in front of the
mercantile, Tibbie looking like a drab little peafowl in her
brown skirt and gray-fringed shawl standing next to her sister
in her sassy dress of grass-green. He watched them go their
separate ways, her sister flitting about town like a paisley but-
terfly, chatting with this one and that, laughing and flirting
with every young man that stopped to talk, while Tibbie went
about her errands with a businesslike air. After an hour or so,
they had met in front of the mercantile and started walking
from town. Intrigued, he had followed.

He had to admit he was amused with her and her proper-
ness. She acted far, far older than she looked. Dressed that
way too. He bet underneath all that loose fitting, lackluster
clothing, she was as fine as a two-dollar cigar—slim and
shapely in all the right places and stuffed with prime tobacco.
He couldn't help admiring her spark of principle and assurance. A woman as unconcerned about her appearance as she
was had to feel pretty strong about herself. She was like an old
woman trapped in a young woman's body. He wished to God
he knew how to set her free from her little-old-lady ways.

He tried to imagine what she would look like all gussied up. Put her in amber silk, put her hair up under a fashionable hat —or better yet, leave it down. Put jewels at her ears, a ruby at her throat and she would shine like one. He almost laughed, imagining her reaction if she knew what he was thinking, and wondered if she did when she gathered her skirts in one hand and swept around him, coming at him with a doubled fist when he reached to detain her by the arm.

He grabbed the fist easily in one hand. "You sure don't like to be touched. Why?"

For some time she simply stared at him in insolent silence. At last, realizing he was determined to stand there looking at her as long as she was standing there looking at him, she said, "I just don't like it. Isn't that enough? Does there have to be a reason for everything?"

Nicholas had been staring at her in much the same fashion that she stared at him. But that is where the similarity ended. Despite his casual stance, his lackadaisical manner, he had been studying her closely, noticing the sudden paleness, the immediate stiffening of her body, the signs that told him he had touched upon something this yellow-haired lass was mighty sensitive about. For a moment he backtracked, mentally reviewing everything that had gone on between them, examining, weighing, comparing. Was it possible that she had been badly handled by some man in her past? If so, what? Rape? A father that beat her? A brother that made her life miserable? His impression, his gut feeling was that it was none of these. He'd bet his sleekest ship on that. His feeling now was that her apparent dislike of men wasn't born of fear, but of an absolute ill will. Someone had pierced her very soul and substance. She hadn't just been hurt. She had been wounded. Deeply. And she carried the burden of it still.

He studied her perfect profile as she turned her head and gazed out across the orchard, her long, dark lashes drifting down upon a pale, translucent cheek. Lord! She was a lovely thing. Lovely and calling out to him as mournful as a dove. What was the secret that burdened one so young and so lovely? And why did the desire to answer that question lure him so? She touched him, this taffy-eyed lass did; touched him in a way no woman had since his mother. Around her, his customary lighthearted flirting was absorbed into a deeper, stronger current, like sea spray when it falls back into the sea.

"There are reasons for everything, whether we want to admit them or not. Take you, for instance. There's a reason why you avoid men; a reason why you try to make yourself as unattractive to them as possible; a reason why you appear to be years older than you really are."

Stricken, she felt panic churn in her stomach, her nerves bunched together in wary knots of apprehension. Like a lighthouse beacon, her mind flashed her a warning. *Caution. . . . Caution. . . . Caution.* This man played a more dangerous game than the others. His interest in her and her past went deeper than just simple attraction. He was smart, determined. And he used gentleness and understanding like a weapon, slicing and revealing, layer by layer. He asked her to trust him, but that would be handing him another weapon. This wasn't just another man to be avoided. This man was as dangerous to the smooth sailing of her life as a coral reef, lying submerged and deadly in what seemed such calm waters.

"I can't stay here any longer," she said, fighting the panic swelling in the back of her throat. "I've stayed way too long as it is."

"There's a reason for running away from things, as well as a reason for choosing to stand and fight. What are you running from, Tibbie? Why are you so distrustful?"

"I don't distrust you. I'm just needed at home," she managed in a raspy, choked whisper.

"I was talking about you—your own distrust of yourself." His hand came up, cupping her chin and lifting her face up until she had no choice but to look at him. There it was again, that overpowering gentleness in his eyes, in the soft touch of his flesh against hers. She almost swayed against him, stopping herself only when he said, "Are you really needed at home, or is that an excuse to run away?"

"I'm . . ." She was about to say she was really needed at home, but the look in those deep blue eyes of his, that conquering understanding—and that gentleness again. She couldn't lie to him, and it terrified her because she didn't know why. Her voice was shaky and unsure. "You're a threat to me. I fear for my survival around you. Not all predators have fangs and sharp talons. You make me . . ." Her voice broke and she drew her head back and turned away. She couldn't go on talking to him like this. All she wanted was to be away from here in the shortest amount of time. She wanted what she had before he came riding that chestnut beast of his, thundering into her life: peace, order, tranquility—and if she were honest—loneliness.

"You make me feel a bit confused too." She looked so close to tears that he reached out to her, his strong hand going around her arm with a touch that was as gentle as the words he had just spoken.

"Please," she said shakily. "Please let me go. I don't want to touch you and I don't want you touching me."

"It's too late for that, I'm afraid. You've already touched me, lass. More than you know." He stroked the softness of her arm with the pad of his thumb. "Is that so bad? My touching you?"

When she didn't answer, he stepped around her, bringing himself around to face her, his hand still gentle upon her arm. She kept her eyes upon the dusty tips of his boots while feeling the stirring of her hair each time he breathed. "I've got all day," he said. "And I'm a very patient man."

She knew he spoke the truth. The desire to put distance between them as quickly as possible forced her to lift her head and look at him, unable to hide the quickly gathering moisture that collected in her eyes.

Seeing the shimmer of what would soon be tears was his undoing. "Damn, but you're a beauty. I'd give a year's income to kiss that trembling mouth of yours right this minute. But I have the feeling that would send you bolting like a startled doe."

His words brought a curious flutter to her stomach. What would it be like to kiss him? Would his kiss come with all the gentle persuasion of his softly spoken words? Suddenly, she gained control of her thoughts. Well she could imagine the kinds of things that would follow a kiss like the kind he would probably give her. Just the suggestion of it was enough to send her bolting. She jerked her arm from his grasp and turned away.

"Tibbie," he called, and she stopped. She didn't turn around, but she did say, "What?"

"Running away won't keep you from wondering what it would have been like. Curiosity is harder to beat back than a prairie fire."

"I'm not running and I'm not curious."

He laughed. "Yes, you are. I'll lay you odds that you'll feel the soft persuasion of curiosity when you're lying in bed tonight thinking about it."

"Humph! I've more important things to think about than the likes of you."

"And what might that be? What do you think about at night, Tibbie? What thoughts occupy your mind at night when it's dark and no one knows what you are thinking?"

"I mostly think about the lengths I can go to to avoid the likes of you. You're worse than a wart on the sitting-down place."

He laughed again. "As long as it was on your sitting-down place, I wouldn't mind a bit!"

She shouted her outrage and stomped off. Her sudden movement startled the horse grazing nearby and he jerked his head up. Nick shook his head. She was a sassy little thing. In spite of his desire to paddle her shapely little backside until it was as red as a pokeberry, he couldn't hold back the laughter when she waved her hands at his horse and said:

"Get out of my way, you lumbering lump of leather." When the horse didn't move, she kicked a clod and went around him, saying, *"You're* as obnoxious as *he* is."

He gathered the reins in his hand and watched her head

down the cow trail. In all his twenty-seven years he'd never heard anyone refer to a horse as a lumbering lump of leather.

"If you don't hear different, I'll meet you here a week from today," he called after her. "Same time. Same place. I'll be waiting, so don't be late."

"I won't be late," she called back over her shoulder, "because I have no intention of coming at all. You can wait until you petrify and grass grows between your toes."

She said some other things, too, but Nick couldn't make them out. He pushed his hat back on his head and watched her until she disappeared from sight, a grin on his face and an extra lighthearted little beat in his pulse. She was something else, this little hot-tempered Scot.

When she reached home, she banged the back door a little harder than necessary, but her mother was placing fried chicken on a platter and didn't bother to look up.

Tibbie looked at her mother. Effie was a fairly tall, well-rounded woman, "more curves than angles," according to Coll. Her hair was still dark as Mairi's, but it was showing a few streaks of silver. It was pulled back into a fashionable coil and held with two ivory combs, but by this time of day there were always a lot of loose tendrils floating about her head. Her eyes were brown, her disposition pleasant, and her wit almost as dry as Granny Grace's—of course, no one had wit as dry as Granny Grace. And no one was as absentminded, or as hard of hearing. Without missing a beat with the chicken she was piling onto the platter, she asked, "You get Bertha milked yet?"

"Not yet. I was just coming in for the pail."

"Who's in jail?" asked Granny, who was in her customary place this time of afternoon, her rocking chair by the fire, rocking like she was trying to make up for lost time, a basket of darning on the floor beside her.

"No one is in jail, Granny," said Tibbie.

"Well, why not? Why'd we build that new jailhouse if we aren't going to put somebody in it? Should've used that money to put a steeple on the Methodist church, or build a clock tower in the center of town." Granny went on mumbling to herself, picking up a vinegar bottle and pulling a sock over it and pulling it tight so she could better see the hole she was about to mend.

Effie stopped piling chicken on the platter and looked at Tibbie. Tibbie looked back at her mother and shrugged. Effie looked a lot like Granny, except, of course, Granny Grace's hair was snow-white. Like Effie, she always wore it up, but instead of a fashionable coil, it was twisted into a hard little knot and jabbed full of tortoise-shell hairpins. She couldn't hear a foghorn at three paces, according to Coll, but her eyesight was remarkable. If she didn't hear it, she could see it, and her imagination was second only to Tibbie's. For that reason, there wasn't much that went on that Granny Grace missed. She was a woman of vast experience and a generous conscience who taught her granddaughters to live life to the fullest, which caused a lot of headaches for Effie and Coll.

"You got some young feller after you? Is that why you came charging through that door looking like it was raining soup and you had a fork?"

Tibbie assumed that meant she looked a little put out, but according to her book, questions like that didn't deserve answers. But that didn't bother Granny Grace none. "You need to find you some nice young man and settle down before you get too old."

"I've got other things on my mind right now besides more tribulation," said Tibbie.

"Fornication!" shouted Granny. "If that's what you've got on your mind, you've got it worse than I thought."

That was another comment that didn't deserve an answer. And the same as before, that fact didn't bother Granny Grace one wit. She gave Tibbie a chastening look. "It's a good thing the Lord Almighty didn't have you in mind when he conjured up a helpmate for Adam, or mankind would've never gotten off to a start."

"You're right," said Tibbie. "It's a good thing God didn't pick me. If I had been Eve, I would have said 'Pick someone else.' "

Effie laughed. "That would have been a little hard for Adam, since Eve was the only woman around."

Tibbie shrugged and picked up the milk pail and stared at her grandmother, whose hairpins poked from her off-sided topknot like points of light radiating from some distant star. A pair of small wire glasses had fallen halfway down her nose, and a pair of diamond and sapphire earrings shimmered in her ears—earrings that had been given to Granny's grandmother when she married the brother of the Russian czar. A magnificent cameo brooch was pinned at the throat of her black silk dress.

Granny Grace always wore black.

Not because she was still mourning her late husband, who had been dead for some forty years, because she wasn't. And not because she had purchased sixty bolts of the finest Chinese silks—all black—when she turned fifty, which she had. No, it was simply because Granny loved black. It was her favorite color. "When I was young, girls weren't allowed to wear black. And when I was old enough to wear black, I was told it was appropriate only for mourning and for old people. Well, by all that's holy I'm old folk now, and in the prime of senility, so there's not a dad-blasted reason why I can't wear black . . . and black is all I'm going to wear. And I don't give a bug's ear if anyone likes it or not."

By this time Effie had finished piling the chicken on the platter and turned to look at Tibbie. "You look plumb tuckered out. Let me feel your face."

Tibbie looked reluctant.

"Tibbie Anne, come over here and put down that pail."

"Who fell down a well? Whose well was it? Did they drown?"

"Granny, get your mending finished," Effie said. "No one fell in a well."

"Well, if they did, I'd be the last person to know about it. No one around here ever tells me anything. How's a body to know what's going on if no one will tell them a blasted thing?"

"If they told you, you'd get it all wrong," Effie shouted.

"Now, get those socks finished before Coll comes after them. He'll be ready to go to the Skinnermeyers' place in a little while and he wants to take those socks with him. Poor old Mrs. Skinnermeyer has a house full of young'uns and Mr. Skinnermeyer's laid up and no money coming in. They need those socks and here you are dawdling!"

Granny got back to her darning, still mumbling to herself. Effie crossed the room to where Tibbie stood. "I still think you look flushed. You runnin' a fever?" Her hand came up to check the temperature of Tibbie's face in four or five places. "You don't feel too hot."

"I'm alright, Mama."

"Then what's wrong?"

"Nothing."

"Something is going on here, Miss Secretive, and I intend to find out just what it is. I've been your mother for twenty-one years. I know you like the back of my hand. Now, tell me what brought all that color to your face."

Tibbie knew there was no fooling Euphemia Stewart Buchanan, for there wasn't a woman alive that had more insight and perception, or a better dose of feminine intuition than Effie did. So Tibbie placed the pail on the table and told her mother about Nicholas Mackinnon.

And just as Tibbie expected she would, Effie encouraged her to see more of him. That was the problem. She'd seen far too much of him already. It was time to get out of the kitchen and do a little thinking for herself. She picked up the pail.

"You mind what I said, Tibbie Buchanan."

"I will, Mama. I'll give it some very serious thought. I promise."

"When the devil's boots begin to squeak!" said a high, fluttery voice coming from the rocking chair by the fire.

"There are times," said Tibbie, "when I could swear Granny's hearing is better than her eyesight."

"I shouldn't wonder," said Effie, giving her mother a pondering look. But Granny had gone back to her darning. "Children are a lot like old people in that regard. They hear only what they want to." Effie pulled the shawl up around Tibbie's shoulders and turned her toward the door. "Off with you now. It's almost dark."

It was dark by the time Tibbie finished milking and returned to the house, just in time for supper. But Tibbie didn't get to eat that night, for just about the time Coll returned from the Skinnermeyers' and sat down to supper, someone was banging on the front door.

"It's a wonder I'm not skinny enough to wash in a gun barrel," Coll said, tossing down his napkin and rising from the table.

"Maybe it isn't for you this time," Effie said.

"Oh, it's for me, all right. I never sat down to a plate of fried chicken in my life that some emergency or the other didn't come up and call me away." Coll had reached the door by the time Mairi had come in the back door saying she had seen the Carpenter boy ride into the front yard. "Looks like Papa is gonna miss his supper again tonight."

Five minutes later, Coll came back into the kitchen. "Tibbie, get my medical bag while I bring the buggy around. Be sure to replace the things I used at the Skinnermeyers'."

"I've already done that, Papa."

"Good girl," said Coll, and then he disappeared through the doorway.

"You'd think a body would be used to this by now," Effie said as she plopped a few pieces of chicken into a napkin and tied the ends together. "But I'm not. I can tell you one thing, though. If there is such a thing as reincarnation, I won't marry a doctor in my next life."

"Where'd you get flowers this time of year?" Granny Grace asked.

"Flowers?" Effie said. "Granny, what are you mumbling about?"

"You said the doctor gave you carnations. I want to know where he got them. This is February. Where did he find carnations in February?"

Effie shook her head and said to Tibbie, "See that your father eats something before he gets there. I've packed chicken and biscuits and a canteen of milk."

"I will."

"Sometimes," Effie said, handing the napkin to Tibbie, "I wonder why I bother to get out of bed in the morning."

"Because you can't resist the temptation to see what the day has in store for you," Tibbie said and laughed, giving her mother a peck on the cheek as she picked up the bag she had brought from Coll's office.

"Nothing but trials and tribulations is what awaits me, I know that much."

"Now, Mama, don't complain about your destiny, because it won't change a thing. You know what Papa says: 'He that is born to be hanged will never drown.' "

"I thought you said no one was in jail? Now see what you've made me miss!"

"What have you missed, Granny?" asked Tibbie.

"The hanging. They've already hanged the man they put in jail and now Coll is going to take him down."

"Papa and I are going to the Carpenters'. Mrs. Carpenter is going to have her baby and Papa is almost positive it will be twins. We've got to hurry. Willie Carpenter said his mama was in constant pain."

"Bah!" said Granny. "She doesn't need a doctor. Give her a handful of Rush's Thunderbolts. That'll fix her."

"Rush's Thunderbolts are for constipation."

"Well? Isn't that what Willie said she had? Constipation?"

Tibbie shook her head. "Willie said she was in constant pain, Granny. Constant pain."

"I'm going to bed," said Effie.

"I'm going to the Carpenters," said Tibbie.

The birth of the Carpenter twins took most of the night, and by the time Tibbie crawled out of bed the next morning at half past six, she had had two hours sleep. After all that had happened the day before and being up half the night, it wasn't looking like it was going to be one of her better days. By the time she fixed herself a cup of coffee and a bowl of oatmeal and put the brown sugar in the coffee instead of the oatmeal as she had intended, her usually sweet mood was sour at best.

It was in this sour disposition that Coll sent Tibbie into town to see if the medical supplies he'd ordered out of New Orleans had arrived by the packet that had come in the day before.

"You better get Hiram to hitch up the team and take the wagon," Coll said. "There will be too many crates to load in the buggy. And while you're in town, stop by the smithy's and tell Clovis Rafferty to have a look-see at that axle. Something doesn't sound right."

Coll was right about one thing. Tibbie thought as she sat on the hard wood of the wagon seat and looked down at the broad backs of Nip and Tuck, the geldings Hiram had hitched to the wagon. The axle, or something in that vicinity, was making a strange sound. Halfway to town she decided she would stop by the smithy and let Clovis look at the wagon before she went to the freight office. About a mile from town she amended her previous decision to *if I ever reach town,* for it was here that the axle gave a mighty groan and the wagon collapsed in the middle of the road. That in itself was bad enough, but coming down the road toward her was Rafe Tucker and the Buckner boys. And there wasn't a meaner, more worthless collection of misfits in the state of Texas than Rafe Tucker and the Buckner boys.

"Well, if it isn't Miss High 'n' Mighty herself, perched like a little yellow bird on her wagon seat, just waiting for some fair-haired knight to come along and rescue her," Clive Buckner said.

To which Rafe replied, "She's already had her fair-haired knight, wouldn't you say?"

"Leave me be, Rafe."

"Why are you acting so uppity with me, when everyone in town knows what kind of woman you are?"

"Whatever *kind* I am, I'm not your kind, so go on about

your rat killing and let me alone. I've got pressing business in town."

Rafe dismounted and walked around the wagon. "Looks like you got a busted axle, angel face. You ain't going to town or anywhere else in this wagon. Why don't you let me take you wherever it is you need to go?"

"No, thank you. I can manage."

"How you plan to manage with a busted axle?"

"I can walk, Rafe. I have two good, strong legs."

"I can think of a better use for two good, strong legs than walking. Wrap them around my waist and I'll take you all the way to New Orleans."

"And how would you know? Your mind is better suited to putting frogs in lunch pails or dipping pigtails in the inkwell," Tibbie said, picking up the whip. "I wouldn't go to a hog killing with the likes of you. Now, you get on away from here, or I'll put my mark on you in a place you'll see everytime you look in a mirror. You wouldn't want that pretty face of yours all marked up, now, would you?"

"No need to get all riled up, Miss Tibbie. I'm just trying to help you out a little."

"Thank you, but I don't need any help."

"Come on, Tib. Why walk, when I've got a good, strong horse that can easily carry us both?"

"I'd rather walk."

"You ain't got no call to be so uppity, Tibbie Buchanan. Any woman that can be had by one man can be had by any."

"I wouldn't walk across the street with you, Rafe, if you were the last man alive."

Rafe's words had been slow and smooth, but Tibbie wasn't distracted or lulled into a false sense of security. She saw how he was inching his way toward her all the while he was talking. He was up to something. She snaked the whip out and brought it around to her side in readiness. But before she could get it into position, Rafe sprang, grabbing the whip and wrapping it around his hands, giving it a yank, knocking Tibbie to her knees. She climbed from the wagon, ready to run up the road screaming for help when Rafe and the boys cut her off. Backed up against the wagon now, she was breathing hard, Rafe's eyes upon that part of her that heaved the most.

"Unhitch that team," Rafe said to Wiley Buckner.

Wiley unhitched them.

"Now turn them loose."

"Why?" Tibbie shouted. "Why turn them loose? It'll take us a week to track them down."

Rafe ignored her, giving Wiley a look. A moment later Nip and Tuck began to head into town at a steady pace, the tracings and reins dragging along behind them and stirring up a cloudlet of dust. Her eyes on Rafe now, Tibbie watched him coil the whip. "I never showed you how good I was with a whip, did I?"

Tibbie swallowed hard, pressing herself against the wagon, her eyes still on Rafe, who was still talking. "Take her arms," he said. Will and Wiley wrestled with her for a minute, Will howling and holding his privates after Tibbie rammed him with her knee. Will backhanded her one, looking immediately apologetic, and Tibbie felt the blood trickle down her chin.

"I'm sorry, Tibbie. Honest I am. I didn't think. But you shouldn't ought to have hit me like that."

"Get that fool out of the way," Rafe said.

Dexter Buckner moved in to take Will's place. Wiley on one side and Dexter on the other, they soon had her backed against the wagon once more, her arms pulled out as far as they would go on each side.

"Now I'm going to show you fellers how to go about undressing an unwilling woman." With that, he let fly with the whip and it lashed across the distance with a crack, licking at the bodice of Tibbie's dress like a burning tongue of fire, snapping her button off. Over and over again.

Crack . . . Crack . . . Crack . . .

One by one, her buttons fell away. Then her bonnet was yanked from her head and her hair spilled down from its tightly wound coil. Rafe drew back the whip for another go when a shot rang out.

The whip flew from his hand.

All eyes hastily looked in the direction the shot had come from, to see Nicholas Mackinnon mounted on his prancing chestnut, a pistol in his hand. "You've got until I spell chicken to vacate the area. After that I start shooting, and I won't be too careful where I aim."

"We got no quarrel with you, mister."

"But I've got one with you. Now, move!"

"Listen—"

"C!"

"This is none of your affair—"

"H!"

"You're meddling in something you'll regret—"

"I!" Nick cocked the pistol.

Rafe swallowed loudly and looked nervously around him. The Buckner boys had all mounted up.

"C!" Nick raised the pistol higher.

The Buckner boys hightailed it.

"K!" This time Nick took careful aim.

Rafe Tucker lit out after the Buckner boys.

Nick waited until they were out of sight, then nudged the gelding forward. "Whoa, Horse."

"Why don't you give him a name, instead of calling him horse?" Tibbie said, yanking her bodice together.

"I did name him."

"What?"

"Horse."

"Figures."

"Funny, that's what I was fixing to say about you. It seems to me you have a talent for getting yourself in one pickle after another."

"It's *my* pickle, and I'll eat it as I please, so why don't you mosey back to where you just came from and leave me alone?"

"Careful that you don't bite off your nose—"

She was looking downright huffy now. "I wish to heaven someone would bite yours off! Then you couldn't go around sticking it into other people's business."

Tibbie clutched the bodice of her dress together. His first reaction to her dressing-down was to make some comment about her appearance and embarrass the bloomers off her, just to irritate her. But the moment he looked at her, he was distracted, and not by her gaping bodice either—which was something of an oddity for him. What distracted him was the way she looked, standing there with her dress torn, her hair wild, her eyes flashing fire, when any other woman would have been reduced to tears over what had just happened. It was an oddity to find a woman such as this, especially one so young who exhibited the traits of a much older woman. A woman did not dress a man down, no matter what. But he had noticed that happened much more frequently here in Texas than it did elsewhere. In Nantucket, it was almost unheard of.

"If I appear to be pushing my way into your private affairs, I must apologize. I merely thought you needed help. Would you like a ride into town?"

"Thank you, no," she said harshly. "I can manage."

"And how do you plan to do that?"

"I'll go into town as planned and find the team, then I'll stop by the smithy and tell Rufus to send someone out to see to the wagon. He'll have a wagon I can borrow to pick up the medical supplies."

His eyes went over her slowly, from top to bottom. "The team is already at the smithy's. They came running through town like their tails were on fire. After we caught them and had them settled down a bit, Rufus told me who they belonged to. I figured I'd ride out this way and check things out. It's a good thing I did."

"Yes . . . well, thank you again." She wiped the blood from her mouth.

He watched her turn toward town. "I don't think that would be a good idea."

"What?"

"Going into town looking like you do. You let any male with even the most diluted red blood see you looking like that and you'll have a war on your hands."

Tibbie looked down. Although she was clutching her bodice together, it was impossible to cover everything, giving him a clear view of what lay beneath her clutched fingers.

"You can't go into town like that."

"No . . ."

"And it would be my guess that you can't go home looking that way either."

She frowned. He was right again. If she went home looking like this, her father would find out what had happened and he'd ride out to the Buckners' and then the Tuckers' to settle matters. The last man that had tried to settle something with the Buckner boys was six feet under. She didn't want that for her papa. He'd been through enough on her account.

Nick watched her piquant face, or at least he tried to, but it was damn hard because his eyes kept going back to the bodice of her dress. Although she was clasping it together with one hand, he still remembered what beautiful breasts lay beneath the thin chemise she wore. The girl was a beauty. Enough to make a man's pump stay primed for a solid week just thinking about her. And he knew all about that, firsthand, for he had done precious little, other than think about her, since the day he'd almost run her down in the street.

Swinging down from the saddle, Nick opened his saddlebags and took out a small leather kit. He closed his saddlebags and turned back to her, stopping closer than she deemed necessary.

Tibbie stared at him in surprise. She saw the look of longing in his eyes mingled with resignation. She closed her eyes. For the briefest moment she let her imagination do what she could not. She imagined the pressure of his lips upon hers, warm and firm, then his tongue in her mouth, touching, seeking, asking. Her heart raced, pumping an oversupply of blood into her body with its ebullient pulse. She was dizzy, elated; she found it hard to breathe. Gasping, she looked up to meet Nick's gaze and saw reflected there the understanding of what she was about. Reality covered her like a chilling rain. "What in the devil do you think you're doing?"

He didn't answer, but simply turned and began walking

around her, searching the ground, kicking clods of dirt and crushed shell this way and that, dropping down to a crouch now and then to pick something up.

"What are you doing down there?"

"Looking for your buttons."

"Why? Do you collect buttons?"

"Only yours," he said with a laugh. "In truth, I'm looking for them so I can sew them back on, then no one will be the wiser."

But she would. She knew just where his hands would be if he sewed a button to her bodice, and she had a quick mental flash of that. "No, thank you. I'll sew them on myself."

"You'll have to take your dress off to do that."

He knew an awful lot about feminine things, but as her eyes traveled slowly over him, she could plainly see why that was the case. But that was neither here nor there. She didn't give two bits for anything he did when he wasn't around her, which was where she wanted him. But he was right about one thing. She would have to take her dress off to sew on the buttons. She was caught in a dilemma. He would either touch her sewing on the buttons or get his eyes full watching her do the job.

"You can't go to town looking like that, and you certainly can't go home. I've just offered my help in sewing your buttons back on, unless you have a better idea."

She didn't, of course, and that's what irked her. "I'll think of something."

"Don't be such a little fool," he said, picking up the last button and moving toward her. "Stubbornness to that magnitude borders on stupidity." She backed up until she thumped against the wagon and could go no further. Then she looked away in confusion. She did not understand the things that were happening here, or in her life for that matter. How could she explain her inclination to touch his face to see if it was, in reality, as smooth as it looked, or to take his hand and lead him away from this place and show him all her childhood hiding places? She must be daft, thinking thoughts like this. She had to be.

"That's about it, I reckon," he said, when he heard her head knock against the wagon.

"I beg your pardon?"

"I could almost believe you move faster going backward than going forward. Practice often?"

"Only when I'm being accosted."

"What you're being, my pigheaded little friend, is helped." He opened the small kit and took out a needle and thread. She watched, fascinated, as he threaded the needle. He was no stranger to the task.

Curiosity overrode caution. "Where did you learn how to sew?"

"I own sailing ships, Miss Buchanan. And sailing ships have a lot of canvas."

She would have thought the owner of ships, or even a man as polished and well cuffed as he, would be above menial tasks, and certainly above sewing. "Here," she said, reaching for the needle and button. "Let me do it."

With a sigh he handed her the needle.

She hadn't expected him to give in quite this easily, and for a moment she simply stared at the needle in her hand. Then seeing the odd way he was looking at her, as if he thought he were dealing with a first-class dope, she jabbed the needle into her bodice and immediately pulled it right out the other side.

"I think you're supposed to put a knot in the end first."

"Oh . . ." Her face heated and she knotted the thread, swearing she would sooner stick a thousand needles in her eye as look at him.

On her second try, she jabbed herself in the thumb. The third attempt ended when she dropped the button. On the fourth try she got a crick in her neck. The fifth try, well, actually, the fifth try never got very far, for it was about that time that he swore softly and took the needle from her hand.

He paused to grin at her. "I know a stitch in time saves nine, but at this pace we'll be here all night. Sooner or later you're going to have to face the truth of it and let me help you, galling as it must be."

Blast his ornery, cantankerous hide! People who were always right irritated the stuffings out of her. *Galled* her, as he'd said.

"Well, what's it to be, Miss Obstinate? You gonna strip and sew . . . or go marching home with answers to a lot of questions?"

When she didn't say anything, he said, "I suppose as a last resort you could—just this once, understand—swallow your pride and let me see to the task."

"You will understand, of course, that I am permitting this slight indiscretion *only* because I have no other choice?"

"Of course," he said, grinning widely.

By the time he had the words out, she was already twisting her hair up, and finding no pins to secure it, she looked thoughtful for a moment, until she noticed he was watching her. "I'll remind you to give faithful attention to what you're about."

To her consternation, he smiled slowly. "Oh, I intend to do just that," he said. "I'd be a pure and utter fool not to."

She plopped the bonnet on her head, stuffing her hair inside, and yanked the ribbons together, tying them in a lopsided bow. Somehow, she had the feeling that what she thought she had said and what he thought she had said were two different things, but before she could figure it out, he said, "Come here and let me sew your dress."

She gasped and turned her head away.

"Are you embarrassed?" he asked softly.

"No," she blurted out. She was mortified. "I was just stretching the crick out of my neck."

"Tell me about those men." He studied the arch of her brow, felt the tension in her body. "They obviously know you—"

"They know me, and *I* know them . . . good-for-nothing troublemakers with more money than common sense and too much free time."

"Still, they didn't look like the sort you would . . . socialize with."

"They aren't, and I don't *socialize* with anyone, I'll have you

know. There are times that things happen in people's lives,
things that make lowlifes like Rafe and the Buckner boys think
they have a right to meddle."

"And that has happened to you . . . something that makes
them think they have a right to mistreat you?" He paused, his
eyes coming up to hers. Then his hand came up, his thumb
coming to the corner of her mouth.

She flinched.

"You still don't like me, do you?"

"It's nothing personal, you understand. I simply know your
kind."

"You can't know the wine by looking at the barrel."

" 'An ape's an ape, a varlet's a varlet, though they be clad in
silk or scarlet.' "

He laughed and reached for her. She flinched and drew
back.

"Don't panic. I'm not going to hurt you. Mistreating and
abusing women, that isn't my way. Your mouth is still bleeding
a little," he said, touching the corner of her mouth with his
thumb.

"It's all right. I'll clean it with camphor when I get home."

"No need to leave it this way, drawing unnecessary attention to yourself," he said, then brought his handkerchief up to
clean the blood away.

She turned her head, looking off across the flat, rolling land.
He took advantage of that to study the almost winsome pastel
of her peach-tinted complexion. "Do you always wear this
bonnet?"

"When I'm outside."

"Why do you find it necessary to hide behind it?"

"I wasn't aware I was hiding. A bonnet is for protection,
Mr. Mackinnon. From the sun."

"That's what hiding is . . . protection."

"I'm talking about protection from the elements, sir—wind,
rain, sleet and sun, to be exact."

"Oh, I see."

"No, I don't think you do, but it doesn't matter."

"And these somber colors you wear? Are they for protection as well? From the *elements,* I mean?"

His nearness was disturbing her again, the warm current of his breath bringing back memories that were best left forgotten. She didn't want to remember the feel of a man's arms around her, the exhilaration that comes from two sets of lips when they touch. Her eyes went to his face, too handsome by a country mile, as she tried to decide if he was being deliberately suggestive, or just innocently attempting conversation. One look at that face, however, said he was anything but innocent. This man looked good enough to know a great deal about sin. Curiosity was swelling within her like a water-soaked sponge —something she neither wanted, nor welcomed, but she possessed, nevertheless, the ability to push it aside. His suggestive frankness made her wonder if he had heard about her, if he knew, but his behavior was still gentleman enough to make her think he had not. A borderline gentleman is what she dubbed him. "Do you find something wrong with my clothes?"

"Frankly, yes. They're too old and matronly for you. The colors belong at a funeral. I see nothing of you represented here. Are you forced to wear them? Is it your father?"

"My parents don't use force, Mr. Mackinnon. I dress as I see fit."

"It can't be money, because I know your father is the only doctor for miles and I've seen the house you live in. So what is it then? What makes a peach-tinted flamingo dress like a little brown wren."

"Perhaps I don't like the attention I get as a flamingo."

"And it's safer being a little brown wren?"

"Exactly."

"Hmmm. That's understandable enough. Problem is, I keep seeing the flamingo behind the poor little wren feathers and I'm itching to set her free."

"You mean to force yourself upon—"

"No. No. No." He started laughing, still holding her with his eyes, fighting the urge to take her in his arms and pull her tension-filled body against his and kiss her until she went as soft as pudding. Lord, to have a woman like her again, after all the seaport wenches he'd bedded. His tightly held desire for her strained against him, and he wondered if he possessed the restraint necessary to hold off until he won her trust and confidence, which would eventually lead, he hoped . . . to where? The impact of that thought hit him suddenly. When had he started thinking of her in terms more serious than a warm body in a cold bed? And when had his intentions turned so honorable? He wasn't, at this point in time, sure exactly what his intentions toward her were, but he knew for certain he would never be satisfied with just one night.

He looked at her, losing his train of thought at the sight of her. Her hair had slipped out from beneath her bonnet. She made a sound of displeasure and yanked the bonnet off, releasing her hair and giving her head a shake in a perfectly innocent gesture that was seductive as hell. She raked her fingers through her hair several times and then began plaiting it into one long, honey-gold braid. She glanced up just then, seeing him standing perfectly still, his eyes on her, watching her every move. Something about the look on his face, the expression in his eyes, made her drop the braid. The spell was broken, but the repercussion of it was not. The thoughts it evoked lingered like a warm, intimate look. It occurred to her suddenly that this man was alarmingly alive, something that made her limbs go weak and her heart hammer painfully in her chest. His look and her reaction to it seemed to penetrate the rules of social etiquette. She opened her mouth to speak, frantically thinking for something to say, anything to detract from the moment. But nothing came from her throat except the release of a long-held breath.

"Tibbie," he said, feeling mounting desire and exasperation, "if you don't want to be kissed senseless this very minute, I suggest you get away from me the quickest way possible."

She couldn't have been more stunned if he'd slapped her, and that kept her standing there. In this dazed state her wits gathered about her slowly, but not so slowly that they prevented the realization of one thing: He was on the verge of kissing her, and he didn't look like he was in any mood to be talked out of it.

The moment she made a move to go, he took her arm, holding her in place. Watching the stunned expression on her face had a sobering effect upon him. He had a feeling he was going to be honorable and leave her unkissed, and that made him speak in irritated tones. "Don't be such a henwit! You can't go anywhere looking like that. Here! This will only take a minute." His hands came out, warm and steady, to hold the edge of her bodice, one hand slipping beneath, his knuckles brushing against the soft curves of her breasts as they rose above her chemise.

His touch was shocking, not because she detested it, but because it made her remember things better left forgotten. She felt the flood of shameful memory rise to her face. Would it always be like this? Would there never be any peace for her? She turned her face away, feeling the fight drain away from her. Sometimes it was so hard being a woman.

Nick finished sewing and looked up, seeing the fight go out of her, and that surprised him. *Poor little mite, you need a nudge or two.* He leaned forward, biting the thread close to the button. And that put his face against the sweetest mound of soft feminine flesh he'd ever come up against. It was pure instinct more than raw, naked lust that prompted him to press his mouth against that sweet flesh with a kiss.

And when he did, the fight that had slowly drained out of her a moment ago came rushing in.

Nicholas Mackinnon got his kiss.

But he also got his ears boxed for the effort.

And he swore on the spot that they would be ringing for days.

It might be said that Tibbie Buchanan could be pushed down, but it was a known fact she wouldn't stay there long. While his ears were still ringing from the boxing they had just received, Tibbie wound up and let fly with another one.

His ears ringing quite smartly now, Nick couldn't help laughing when Tibbie shoved him away and marched with determination to his chestnut and mounted. She headed toward town without giving him so much as a second glance. He was still laughing when it occurred to him that he would have to walk. The laughter died away.

"Damnation!" he said, catching a glimpse of a cottontail staring at him from a cluster of grass. "What are you looking at? You're afoot the same as I."

The cottontail hopped away.

He didn't feel much like laughing after that. In fact, all the way back to town he thought about all the things he was going to do to that honey-haired little witch when he caught up with her next.

Delicious things.

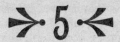

5

"Tibbie?" A knock rattled her door. "Tibbie, are you in there?"

Tibbie closed her eyes, her brooding silence interrupted. "I'm here."

The door opened and Mairi stepped inside, her dark hair plaited and swinging like a thick rope over one shoulder. "Mama said you didn't come to supper." She looked Tibbie over from head to foot. "Are you unwell? Want me to get Papa?"

"No. I'm fine. Really." Tibbie looked away from her sister, her gaze drawn to the window once more.

"You're not sick. You're upset about something. What's wrong?"

"Nothing. I'm just tired. Papa and I both are. There's a lot of sickness going around. We've been staying up late and—"

"Hogwash and slops! I'm your sister, remember? Older than you, if not wiser. I know you, Tib. I changed your nappies when you were a baby and taught you your first word. I made the Buster boys stop teasing you in the third grade and got a bloody nose breaking up a fight between you and Audrey Schneider in the eighth."

Tibbie turned toward her sister and half smiled. "It was Audrey's fault, as I remember. She's the one who bloodied your nose."

In spite of Tibbie's attempt at levity, Mairi saw the pain in her sister's eyes, pain that had been there too long, pain that never completely went away. She crossed the room and put her arms around Tibbie. "When are you going to stop using Papa's medicine as something to hide behind?"

"I don't."

"You do, Tib. You know you do. What are you afraid of? Don't you see your fear of losing something, your hiding behind your devotion to medicine is hurting you? You've lost your direction in life. You don't take the initiative anymore, you don't risk being hurt. You let the world go on around you and *you* react to *it*. You didn't used to be like that."

"I don't need your preaching, Rosemairi Buchanan. I've had enough of that to last a lifetime. Just leave me alone. I'll be alright in a little while."

"Not this time. This time you're going to listen."

"Go on. I don't feel up to one of your inspirational talks. I get enough of those at church."

"I know what you want. You want to be left alone to wallow in all those things you do to protect yourself from life. When you first started helping Papa in the clinic, I thought it was a grand idea. It gave you something to do, some way to achieve, something to be recognized and praised for. But you've let your devotion to medicine become your prison. It's time you stepped outside of the secure little world you've built for yourself. It's time you lived."

"Why? So I can be hurt again? So I can go back through all that pain again? People don't forgive and forget, Mairi. They don't want me to forget. They want me to remember. They want me to pay."

"And you do, don't you? You remember every single day. You're the one who won't let yourself forget, Tibbie. And sadder still, you're the one who can't forgive."

"That's not true!"

"Yes, it is. You can't forgive yourself, and so you keep believing you deserve to be punished. And that's what you do. You punish yourself. Over and over. You don't live. You exist. And that's sad, far sadder than what happened to you."

"Leave me alone . . . please."

"Why? So you can throw yourself over your bed and cry? So

you can feel sorry for yourself? Poor Tibbie Buchanan with all her misfortune and that horrid shrew of a sister! Stop and think, Tib. It would be easy for me to leave. Easy to walk away. I don't like making you cry, but someone needs to shake you up a little."

"Mama and Papa don't—"

"Mama and Papa are too close to the problem. They can't see the forest for the trees. Mama wants you here, her little girl, just like it was before. And Papa dotes on your devotion to medicine—he always wanted one of the boys to follow in his steps. You know how it hurt him when Barra and Calum went to sea and Robbie went to law school. You're sacrificing your life, Tibbie. For a cause that is not your own."

"I'm not. I love healing. I'm a natural with it. You've said so yourself."

"Yes, I have. And you are. But you can't make it your whole life, your whole existence. Papa loves medicine, but he took time out of it to have a wife and family." Mairi sighed. "I'm not trying to hurt you, Tibbie. You've had enough pain, I know that much." She turned Tibbie toward the mirror, her hands on her upper arms, giving her a shake. "Just look in the mirror, Tib. What do you see?"

Tibbie studied herself. "That's a ridiculous question. I see me, of course."

Mairi shook her again. "No, you don't. You don't see Tibbie. Tibbie hasn't been here since Eric abandoned you. What you see is a woman growing old before her time, unripened fruit shriveling on the vine. Don't do that to yourself. What happened to your sense of adventure?"

Tibbie shrugged, looking across her laid-out nightgown, past her turned-down bed to the window beyond. The sun was settling like a big red ball in the dust. Mairi went on talking, although she suspected her sister wasn't hearing anything she said. It was always a source of irritation to her, how her sister could always mentally disappear whenever she wished. A sudden fierce anger swept over her. Her wrath was born over the habit Tibbie had developed of doing this whenever things got uncomfortable for her. Her face flushed with annoyance, Mairi slammed her hand down on the tabletop. "If you keep this up you're going to make yourself sick. Sick with loneliness and bitterness and regret."

Tibbie jumped, startled by the sudden bang of Mairi's hand on the table. This time she didn't drift off into another world, but when Mairi said, "You should at least try to make an effort to think about what I'm saying, instead of rejecting it flat-out," Tibbie let out a pained cry and clamped her hands over her ears. "I won't listen to another word."

Mairi pulled her hands down. "Yes, you will, because you know, Tibbie. Deep in your heart you know I'm right. You aren't happy, are you? You haven't been happy since he deserted you."

"And what if I haven't? I loved him, damn you!"

"I know you did, but he was never right for you. I pray one day you will find that out. But that's not why you're unhappy. You're unhappy because you're dead inside. I know my sister, my real sister. She's full of life and laughter and living. She was never afraid of anything before."

"I'm not afraid of anything now."

"Aren't you?" Mairi gripped Tibbie's arms more firmly, almost shoving her nose in the mirror. "Then take another look, Tib. Take a good, long look. Do you see a happy, carefree, fun-loving young woman? Do you?"

Two tears rolled down Tibbie's cheeks.

"Do you?" She shook her again. "For once, be honest with yourself. Do you?"

"No!" Tibbie said, crying in earnest now. "No! No! No!"

"You're twenty-one years old, for God's sake! And look at you! You can't keep running away from your fear. And you can't hide from it forever, either. It's always going to be there, waiting for you." She shook her head. "I don't know why you punish yourself so. You look and act and dress fifty. And whose fault is it? Is it Mama's or Papa's?"

"No."

"Is it mine?"

"No."

"Then whose fault is it? Tell me! Who? Who decreed that you had to live like this? Who is the most relentless in punishing you?"

"Me," Tibbie cried, stabbing herself in the chest with an accusing finger. "Me! Me! Me!"

And she was right.

Sitting on her bed, Tibbie buried her face in her hands and cried. Her arms around Tibbie, Mairi cried too. "I won't let you do this to yourself anymore. I want my sister back. My real sister. I'm sick of this self-sacrificing imposter."

Tibbie was sick of her, too, but Tibbie doubted she could ever rid herself of the imposter. It grieved her to know Mairi was right about so many things, grieved her to know she could not change. She didn't know how. Her life as it was had become too comfortable. She would never have admitted it to anyone, but deep within her, Tibbie was afraid. Afraid to be herself again. Afraid to trust. Afraid to care, to love. Afraid to let her guard down. Because she had done all that once. Done it all and been hurt. Better to be safe than sorry.

Mairi sighed. "Oh, Tibbie! I'm not trying to make life miserable for you."

"I know that."

"And I'm not trying to ruin your day."

"I know that too," Tibbie said.

Mairi sighed and stood. "I'll tell Mama you were asleep."

"Thanks, Mairi."

Mairi kissed her sister and quietly left the room.

After that day Tibbie tried to avoid Nick completely. But that wasn't always possible.

Whenever their paths crossed by accident, he would tip his hat politely and say, "Good morning, Miss Buchanan," or "Good afternoon, Miss Buchanan," and she would reply coldly without giving him so much as a look. But she gave him plenty of thought. And that irritated the daylights out of her. She didn't want to think about him, didn't want to feel her heart flutter like a silly schoolgirl's every time she saw him.

What right did he have to come into her life looking better than a body had a right to look, worming his way into her life and into her thoughts? And what right did he have making her think about pretty dresses again, or hair ribbons and rosewater? Why did she find herself humming like a fool when she set the table in the evening, getting all kinds of strange stares from her family because of it?

He had noticed her the moment he first came into Indianola and had kept after her until she had begun to notice him, had even looked forward to seeing him. And she didn't want to. _That_ irked her more than she could say. She needed him to stay away from her, because, God help her, she felt so weak where he was concerned. The pressure from it all was making her a stranger to herself, made her think the strangest thoughts. Why, just last Sunday she was angry enough to want to bring a hymnal down on top of his thick-skulled head simply because he had the gall to come to _her_ church and distract her thoughts. She couldn't even pray anymore, without thoughts of him creeping in.

The only thing she could do to save herself from ruination was to dodge him every chance she got. She painstakingly avoided each and every place he was known to haunt, even when she knew there would be a crowd of people present, thus increasing the chance that she might not really see him at all. Once in a while she would catch a glimpse of him walking down the street with his friend, Porter, or coming out of a shop in town, and she would find herself wishing that blasted ship he was building would burn to the ground and perhaps then he would go away and leave her mind in peace.

And sometimes she found herself wondering what it would feel like to have him court her like a real beau. Oh, to act young and carefree again, to dance, to . . . _Get out of my mind, Nicholas Mackinnon. Get out and stay out. And get out of my life as well. I don't want to lay eyes on you again._

And she didn't for almost two solid weeks. Of course, all of this frustrated the dickens out of Nick. He was accustomed to dealing with women, but he felt like a trembling beginner when it came to Tibbie. Funny how ironic life was. He knew he could have had the pick of any of the young women in town, but none of them interested him. He knew one local gal that interested him, but she wanted nothing to do with him.

He reared back in his chair and crossed his legs, resting them on his desk, careful not to put them on the ship plans he had scattered about. He lit a cigar and clamped it between his teeth, then folded his hands behind his head. He had absolutely never in his entire life seen a woman as hard to get to know. He went back over the time they had spent together in the orchard. Had he been wrong to decide the conversation they had had—the almost friendly way she had talked with him—had been a sign that she was warming up to him?

Apparently he had been.

After his last meeting with Tibbie things weren't going so well—at least not for him, considering how many times he'd tried to cross paths with her and how many times she'd managed to put him properly in his place or avoid him altogether. The girl was harder to pin down than a politician. He never saw more of her than glimpses and snatches. And he was so irritated at her he could have throttled her if he had.

Primarily, his anger concerned the fact that she had blatantly reneged on her word. That day in the pasture when he freed her cow, she had granted him a tiny part of her time each week. But twice now, she had failed to keep her appointment or her word. There were few things Nicholas Mackinnon hated worse than lying or deceit, for dishonesty in any form was something he could not tolerate.

Finally, after two weeks of not seeing her, his luck changed, and he came across her at a time when she was all alone. Feeling elated over his good fortune, he approached her and she brushed him aside like a pesky insect. He surmised his disappointment lay in the fact that she obviously did not share his desire that they see more of each other. Her curt dismissal had irked him and he had let it show in the frown on his face and the sudden stiffness of his body. He cursed himself for not having concealed his displeasure.

She was consistent. He would have to grant her that much, for each time he had seen her he had come away feeling about as welcome as a bastard son at a family reunion. She simply wasn't interested in him and she had made that plain enough. In fact, during his last attempt at conversation, she had said as much. "What will it take, Mr. Mackinnon, to get the message through your thick skull? I am neither intrigued nor charmed by your flattery, attentions, or pleasing countenance. You and your dogged persistence are something I find irritating. I am not interested in you in the least, sir. You would be wise to admit as much and move on to more receptive arms."

But Nick wasn't about to let a trivial thing like rejection deter him—not when there was something in the way she spoke that lacked conviction, something in the way she looked at him that didn't agree with her harshly spoken words. For some reason he felt she was making a point to show him she was self-reliant and quite content without any attention from him, but he couldn't shake the feeling that she was vulnerable, and that for all her seeming strident behavior there were times when he sensed a sadness in her that attracted him powerfully.

She was the loveliest thing he had ever seen and he was drawn to her strongly, but the realization that she had a life separate and apart from him, that she had secrets he knew nothing about, intrigued him. There was something about all this that made him feel a certain power, a power he wanted to use to break down her defenses and enter her unapproachable sadness.

He didn't know exactly what made his mystery lady, his lady of the dark colors, behave so. But he would. With or without her cooperation.

He had jumped higher hurdles before—many times. He wasn't about to give up on this one simply because it was proving to be such a challenge. He knew persistence ran in his blood. He had determined blood, just like his father and his brothers. If the Mackinnon men were known for anything, they were known for tenacity, and Nick Mackinnon wasn't about to let a tiny slip of a girl—even if she did have a Scots temper—get the best of him.

One afternoon, Nick was sitting on an overturned nail barrel in front of the mercantile. It was Saturday and Indianola was as busy as a beehive in the spring. *Every farmer and business-man within fifty miles of this place must be in town today,* he thought. *I've seen half the residents of the county parade down the street since I sat down here.* But he hadn't caught a glimpse of the one resident he was looking for. He hadn't seen hide or hair of Tibbie Buchanan.

Rube Weatherspoon, who ran the freight office, was sitting in a canebacked chair next to the nail keg, with the chair reared back to rest on its back legs, the back resting against the building. Rube was peeling an apple, and the peeling became one long corkscrew, which touched the sidewalk's wooden planks. Nick had just given Rube an order for the canvas he would be needing for sails.

Rube finished peeling the apple and tossed the peeling into the street, where it was soon attacked by five or six chickens. Rube cut a segment from the apple, then speared it on the knife point and offered it to Nick.

"No, thanks."

"You sure?" asked Rube. "Came in this morning off Strik-er's ship. Don't get apples around here this time of year, you know."

"I know," said Nick. "Maybe some other time."

Rube swung the chair forward and stood up. "Don't wait too long. They won't last long. Going faster than hotcakes, these apples are." Rube paused and looked down at Nick. "You ain't done much since I sat down here. Boat building must be slow work."

Nick nodded, then watched Rube cross the street, tossing the apple core to the chickens. Rube was right. He hadn't gotten much done. He tried to get his mind back on the sketch of deck beams he had lying in his lap, trying to decide if he was going to keep the standard inch-and-a-quarter measurement on the treenails. But it was of no use. He couldn't get his mind on deck beams or treenails. All he could think of was one honey-haired lass with eyes as warm and brown as molasses cookies. He would have never thought it possible that any woman could have him tied in such knots.

He knew it was commonplace for small annoyances to crop up now and then during the courting process, just as a great river will form sandbars that slow down its speed, but he had never as yet heard a reasonable explanation as to just why it was the female's habit to act so disinterested, when the male was doing his all-out best to be noticed. In fact, he had already decided that it wasn't even a habit. Feigning disinterest was a basic component of a woman's behavior, something deeply rooted within her instinct to attract and entice the male. And it was causing him all sorts of trouble. But sometimes Tibbie didn't feign disinterest. She slapped him in the face with it.

Here he was, trying to act the male rampant around this gentle female creature, being totally ignored and constantly avoided, in spite of his efforts. It was puzzling and frustrating as hell—a woman's ability to attract and hold a man's interest while appearing as remote and indifferent as all get-out.

It had occurred to him that one fast and efficient way of dealing with this would be to turn his interest elsewhere. But whatever divine power arranged things of this sort wouldn't hear of it. The girl had gotten to him and gotten to him bad. She might as well have been the only woman in the world, in fact. That's just how bad it was.

He thought it sad, but ironic, that the infamous avoider of love and matrimony, previously attracted to no woman for any length of time—no matter how willing—would find himself so enamored by one who wouldn't spit on him if he were on fire.

Over the past two weeks she had slammed a barn door in his face and damn near broken his nose. She had shoved him away from her with such force that he lost his balance and stumbled backward, knocking the physically substantial Mrs. Witherspoon into the muddy street. Another time she had dumped a pail of water over his head ("to cool your ardor," as she had said). Not to mention that she had promised to meet him on three separate occasions—one of which she sent as her replacement what had to be the ugliest woman in the state of Texas.

The second time she sent him a note of apology with a basket of cookies, pepper cookies that set fire to his mouth and scorched his throat. The third time she was surrounded by a score of townsfolk and gave him a look that made him feel as welcome as death when she asked, "Did you want something, Mr. Mackinnon?"

Hell yes, he wanted something! He wanted her to give him some small token of recognition. He wanted her to look at him with something other than boredom or loathing. He wanted to see her laugh at something he said. He wanted to see her eyes light up when he walked into the room. He wanted to see her flirt with him, if only just a little. He wanted to see what she would look like dressed like other women, in something beside dull, depressing, somber colors. He wanted to see what she would look like dressed in nothing.

He wanted her. Period.

But it didn't look like he was going to get what he wanted, or anything close to it. He'd been sitting on this nail barrel until he had callouses on his rump, and for what? He hadn't caught so much as a glimpse of her. He looked down at the drawings in his lap and shook his head. "You poor, stupid fool," he said like a curse.

He was behind on his work.

He couldn't concentrate.

He couldn't go on like this.

Something had to give.

He was afraid it would be his sanity.

"Okay," he said, looking heavenward. "If you have anything up your sleeve, now's the time to use it, because I'm fresh out of patience, as well as ideas."

Half expecting an answer, Nick was put out when he saw only a whirlwind move slowly up the street, stirring up bits of chaff and paper, then moving on, leaving them to fall where they might. "All right!" he said. "I'm finished, washed out, fed up, calling it quits." He came to his feet. "Find someone else to toy with. No woman is worth this much grief. I've got a ship to build." He was rolling his sketches up, tucking them under his arm, when he noticed Rube standing in the doorway of the mercantile, a knowing grin on his face.

"Having a little heart-to-heart with the almighty?"

"Something like that."

"Bet you've got a woman on your mind."

"Yes, and there are better places to have them."

Nick was about to step off the sidewalk into the street when he saw *her* coming into town, sitting in the buggy beside her father. They passed in front of the mercantile, and although Tibbie didn't give any sign that she had seen him, Nick didn't take his eyes off her.

"Beats me," Rube said, "why you're standing around getting older. God's handed you the milk. Whadda ya want now? A pail?"

Dr. Buchanan pulled up in front of the smithy's. Nick figured Tibbie and her father had come after their wagon. Watching her father drop her off, Nick stopped rubbing the crease in the crown of his hat and placed it on his head.

He headed in Tibbie's direction.

Rube scratched his chin. "Some people want their good fortune buttered," he said, then stepped inside the mercantile.

By then, Nick was almost in front of the smithy's. "How about going to the Independence Day dance with me next Saturday?" he said.

Tibbie's heart lurched. How well she knew that voice, but she refused to turn around. The good Lord knew she had stepped into enough of his well-laid traps to be more than justified in avoiding him at all costs. The man had to be twins. There was no way on earth one man could turn up in as many places as he did.

"I don't think she heard you," said Fisher Huffington, the smithy's helper.

Nick looked at the young man working the bellows. "You think not?" asked Nick.

"Appears that way," replied Fisher, his tone as brawny as his build.

"Well, I can fix that straightaway."

Hearing no sound, curiosity overcame her, and Tibbie turned around. Nicholas Mackinnon was down on one knee before her, his hat in his hand and held over his breast. "Fair Mistress Buchanan, will you do me the honor of going to the Texas Independence Day dance with me?"

"Get up," she whispered, glancing quickly around. Then louder, "Get up, will you? Are you insane?"

He grinned. "Probably."

She looked around her again, her discomfort evident. She didn't know if she should ignore him or bolt. Either way would draw attention to her. "Will you get up?" she whispered a little louder. "Did you hear me?" Then, not bothering to whisper, she shouted, "Get up, you half-wit! People are staring at us! Have you no shame?"

"No . . . nary an ounce. How about you?"

"Ohhhhhh!" she said, stamping her foot. "Will you get up? You're making a spectacle of yourself!"

"Answer me and I will."

"No," she whispered, looking all around her. "Some things don't deserve answers." She turned away.

Nick was having second thoughts, wondering if humor was the right approach. Instead of seeing her laugh (he would have settled for a faint smile) he found he was staring at the backside of a young woman who responded to his teasing humor with a cold, hard stare and a turned back that left him feeling like the village idiot. He looked up and saw Fisher was watching him. "Looks like I'm not making much headway."

"Appears that way," said Fisher. "I'd say you weren't making any headway at all."

Nick scowled. He was beginning to see why Fisher was a smithy's helper instead of a smithy. "Well, I guess I need to use more flamboyance," said Nick.

"Or brains," said Fisher.

His eyes went back to Tibbie. She had turned around and

was looking at him with her lips in a sour pucker. If her idea
was to indicate in the most abstract manner that she was the
helpless victim of his aggressive attention, and that his attentions were not only unwelcome but annoying, she was doing a
damn good job. Nick looked at Tibbie. He looked at the
smithy. He looked at his helper.

All of them were looking back at him like he had been
smartly put in his place. Any other time, any other woman, he
would have called it quits. But his Scots blood was singing the
old Mackinnon battle cry and from somewhere in his mind
came the reminder that there was more than one way to skin a
mule. He looked at her again. The sour expression, the hostile
look, the rosy flush of embarrassment, they all made him think
the girl didn't laugh enough.

*Okay, Mackinnon. You've already made a fool of yourself.
How much sillier can you look?*

And he decided to find out.

If Tibbie Buchanan thought he looked like the village idiot
now, she hadn't seen anything yet. "Come to the dance with
me," said Nick. He put his hat on his head and stood up. Then
he said it again, louder. "Come to the dance with me."

By this time Tibbie could see a crowd of people were gathering, quite a few of them drifting toward the smithy's.

"Come to the dance with me, Tibbie," he said in louder
tones. "I've got my little Scots heart set on taking you." By
this time he was literally shouting.

"Go with him, Tibbie," shouted Laura Shrewbush. "You'll
break his little Scots heart!"

There were a few scattered laughs, a snicker or two, and a
cheer from a group of schoolboys.

"Mr. Mackinnon, you don't know what you're doing. Just
leave me be! Please!"

"Do you want to be the only person in the whole town of
Indianola that is sitting at home next Saturday?" he shouted.
He was walking toward the horse trough now, and when he
reached it, he jumped up, putting one foot on each side, arms
outflung. "I want you to go to the dance with me. I won't go if

I can't take you. I'll get a haircut. I'll buy a new suit. I'll bring you a box of candy. I'll take dancing lessons and give you my word I won't step on your foot."

More laughter erupted. This was drawing a bigger crowd than a hanging or a parade.

I'll probably get my face slapped, but it would be worth it, he thought. Then he went on, "The only way you're going to get me down from here, the only way you can make me shut up and stop embarrassing you, the only way you can convince me to leave you alone, the only way you can get me to stop making a spectacle of myself is to agree to go with me."

From the spectators came a roar of agreement, a lot of cheers and a few catcalls and whistles. "Do you hear that?" he asked. "The good people of Indianola think you should go. I think you should go. You're the only person here, Tibbie, that doesn't think you should go." He thrust both hands into the air in supplication. "Tell me you'll go to the dance with me and you'll never have to hear me ask you again. Say yes, and you won't have to be embarrassed anymore. Give me your word and I'll stop making a fool of myself over the horse trough." He paused and looked directly at her. "Say yes, or we'll both be here all day."

"Yes!" she shouted at the top of her voice.

Nick let out a war whoop and sailed his hat into the air. And then he did something she had never seen anyone do, and certainly not a nattily dressed man like Nicholas Mackinnon. With outflung arms and a smile of rapture on his face, he leaned back, farther and farther, until he fell in.

He made a huge splash and the startled horses nickered in terror and broke their ties, bucking and snorting. This upset a team parked in front of the mercantile and they started running, the load of chicken crates stacked in the back of the wagon spilling out with a loud clatter. Chickens and children and feathers and bucking horses were everywhere.

"You won't be sorry," Nick shouted over the melee. Then he stood up, slapping his arms against his chest and saying, "Brrrrr!"

"Serves you right if you catch the croup," she said, thinking she had never in her life seen a grown man do such a thing.

Come to think of it, she had never seen a child do such a thing.

She decided she had never seen *anyone* do such a thing— including the half-wit that lived in the tar-paper shack on the outskirts of town. Before she could think anything else, Nick was arrested by Harelip Harry, and the sheriff escorted him to jail for disturbing the peace and causing a stampede.

She learned later that Harelip had added "destruction of property" to the growing list, because Heck Tucker's old blue mule got so riled up he ran through the door of Fletcher's Barber Shop. That was bad. But to make matters worse, Mr. Fletcher grabbed a cane and began beating Mr. Tucker's blue mule. When the mule decided to leave, he exited through Mr. Fletcher's brand-new glass window that had come all the way from Chicago. That was real bad.

Tibbie went straight home after that, and didn't leave her house until the next morning when Dr. Buchanan loaded his family into the carriage and drove them to church.

An old blue norther had hit Indianola during the night and it was colder than anyone could remember, so when Dr. Buchanan pulled the carriage up in front of the church house, Tibbie and her family departed in haste. Once in the vestibule, they removed their wraps, though Tibbie decided to leave her shawl on because her teeth were still chattering.

In spite of the downward turn of the weather, the good people of Indianola had turned out in record numbers. The Reverend Timothy Woolridge was making announcements from the pulpit while his wife, who was almost as large as the piano she was sitting in front of, fought off a spell of sleepiness. Making more racket than they should have been making in God's house, the Buchanans walked down the aisle to their pew and stopped.

Something was wrong.

The widow Hevers and her nine children were sitting in the pew the Buchanans had occupied since coming to Indianola twenty-five years ago. Looking at the row just ahead, where the widow Hevers always sat, they saw the problem. Old Mr. Dimmesdale sat with his daughter and her family on Mrs. Hevers's row. And ahead of them, the Gutcher family sat on the Dimmesdale row. And in front of the Gutchers, sitting on their row was the head of the Bank of Indianola, Hector Peabody and Mrs. Peabody and all the little Peabodys. And sitting in front of the Peabodys was none other than that disturber of the peace—the reason for all this disturbance in the first place—Nicholas Mackinnon. And since Mr. and Mrs. Peabody had so many little Peabodys that they needed an entire row, Nicholas was occupying the Peabodys' row all by himself.

By this time, the Reverend Woolridge realized he might as well stop making announcements. No one was listening anyway. They were all watching Dr. Buchanan move the widow Hevers and her nine children out of his pew. And the widow Hevers, in turn, slapped old Mr. Dimmesdale up beside the head with her Bible, moving him and his daughter, along with her entire family, out of her row; which, of course, made old Mr. Dimmesdale rout the Gutchers; who gave notice to the illustrious banker, Mr. Peabody, and Mrs. Peabody, and all the little Peabodys. All of this pew switching to get everyone situated in his correct pew meant quite a bit of moving and shuffling around, and that, of course, was all on the wooden church floors, which made it sound like a stampede had been sidetracked through the church.

"Dooooooctor Buchanan!" intoned the Reverend Woolridge. "Would you be so very merciful as to permit me to take the liberty of beseeching you to have the charity to bestow the favor upon me of giving me the blessed rapture of seeing you get your family squared away?"

"I'm sorry, Reverend, but I didn't catch that. Would you mind repeating it?"

"Do you suppose you could get your brood set to roost so we might get on with the Lord's work?" the good reverend fairly shouted.

"I am working on that, Reverend. I sure am working on that."

The Reverend Woolridge tapped his fingers on the pulpit as he waited, then seeing at last that Coll and his family was indeed settled, he said, "Dr. Buchanan, trying to get you and the Lord together is like forcing an owl upon day."

Of course, Nicholas Mackinnon, who started the whole disruption, slipped quietly to the back of the church, sitting next to Marvalene Bruce, who sighed so loud she blew three feathers off the widow Dudley's black hat.

After church, Tibbie and Beth were waiting for the rest of the family beside the wagon. Beth was busy making faces at Timmy Satterly through the large spokes of the wagon, and Tibbie was wishing everyone would hurry up when Nick walked up. Seeing Beth squatted down in front of the wagon wheel, making a terrible face, he chuckled and moved to the other side of the wagon. Dropping down beside the wheel opposite Beth, Nick made the ugliest face imaginable. Beth squealed with delight and stood up, clapping her hands. "Do it again! Do it again!"

Tibbie looked around to see what all the commotion was, just in time to see Nicholas Mackinnon screw his face up into what looked like a dehydrated plum.

"Having fun?" she asked.

Nick grinned and came to stand beside her. "I used to be pretty good at that," he said, wiping the dirt off his britches.

"You still are," she said with a laugh, still unable to believe she had seen him do what he did.

Beth ran up to Nick and grabbed his hand. "Come and show Timmy. Show him how to make a face like that."

"Not now," Tibbie said. "Beth, don't bother Mr. Mackinnon."

Nick smiled at Beth and gave her pigtail a yank. "You're no bother, are you, Beth?"

"Nope," Beth said, tugging on Nick's hand again. Nick went with her, and Tibbie followed him with her eyes. Never in all her born days had she seen a man so unruffled by what others thought. There he was, standing by the big oak making a complete fool of himself, showing five or six children how to stretch their faces hideously, not seeming to notice that half of Indianola was looking at him strangely.

A few minutes later Nick and Beth returned to the wagon. Just as he walked up the church bells began to chime and Beth said, "Listen!"

Nick looked down at Beth. "When I was a little boy, my mother used to tell me that every time church bells rang, an angel got his wings."

"Golly!" Beth said. "There must be a lot of angels!"

"There are," said Nick, "and a lot of them don't have their wings yet." His eyes were on Tibbie as he spoke. She put her nose in the air and Nick laughed.

"I'm going to tell Timmy," Beth said and tore around the wagon.

After she was gone, Nick said, "Well, I guess I'll be on my way. Good day to you, Miss Buchanan."

Tibbie nodded and said, "Good day," as Nick pushed away from the wagon where he had been leaning.

As he passed Tibbie, he tipped his hat, and leaning closer whispered, "It's a shame you aren't as carefree as your little sister. If you work on it real hard you might get *your* wings someday."

Tibbie stared, dumbfounded, as Nick mounted his chestnut and rode away. *Little sister?* Did he think Beth was her little sister? *Bah! Let him think what he will.* Tibbie climbed into the wagon and opened her parasol.

Two days later Nick and Porter Masterson were walking down the sidewalk at half past four. Having just called it a day at the shipyard, they were headed for the Wooden Nickel Saloon to talk business over a drink or two. It was a fine day for March and not too cold. The customary wind seemed content to do no more than stir up a flutter of dust and long-dead leaves now and then. Without a cloud in sight all day, the sun had ample time to warm things up a bit, and there were more folks than usual in town today.

When Porter and Nick reached the corner of Butternut and Pecan, they turned onto Pecan St. The Wooden Nickel was only a block away. And so was Tibbie Buchanan.

Seeing her walking toward them, Nick stopped listening to what Porter was saying. All he could think about was that beautiful creature coming toward him and how badly he wanted some time alone with her. It would be Saturday in a couple of days. Would she remember her promise to go to the Texas Independence Day dance, or was she planning another surprise for him?

Nick was so busy thinking about Tibbie that at first he didn't notice the little girl walking beside her. Once he noticed her, though, he recognized her: Beth, Tibbie's little sister. And once he noticed Beth, he couldn't stop looking at her, comparing her with her sister, whom she favored somewhat. Beth, like Tibbie, was blond, but where Tibbie's hair was honey-colored, Beth's was the color of flax, so pale it was almost white. As they drew closer he saw her eyes were different too; the color of blue-grass beads and just as bright. Beth was smartly dressed in a red velvet coat trimmed with white fur, sporting a matching white fur hat and muff. Tibbie, as usual, was dressed in drab colors—a deep burgundy skirt that looked like it couldn't decide if it wanted to be red or brown peeked beneath a black cape. A matching burgundy bonnet did nothing except hide her lovely hair and place her face in shadow. Nick felt the frustration of wanting to yank that bonnet off her head and drag her into the nearest dress shop and buy her the most daring of dresses, both in color and design.

Porter and Nick were just passing the mercantile when two women about Tibbie's age stepped out. For a moment Nick thought he saw a pained look come over Tibbie's face, but decided he was mistaken. Stepping aside to let the women pass, Nick watched Tibbie and Beth glide between the two women as gracefully as a clipper ship passing between two icebergs.

The two icebergs stopped and turned, watching Tibbie and

the child enter the mercantile. The bell over the door jingled, then grew silent.

Nick looked at Porter and Porter looked at Nick, then the two men headed up the street. As they passed the two icebergs, one of them said to the other, "Who does that hussy think she is? Parading her bastard around decent people like we ought to congratulate her."

"She has more gall than a government mule, if you ask me. Mamma said . . ."

But Nick didn't hear. All he could hear was the shattering echo of the word, *Bastard . . . Bastard . . . Bastard . . .*

No wonder Beth favored her.

Inside the mercantile, Tibbie gripped Beth's hand until she squealed, "You're squashing my hand!"

"I'm sorry, pumpkin." Thrusting her hand deep into her cape pocket, Tibbie pulled out a coin and handed it to Bethany. "Here. Go buy yourself a peppermint, like Grandpa said. Hurry now, we've got to be going."

Beth hurried to the counter, squeezing her money tightly in her fist, but Tibbie wasn't watching. Looking through the storefront she saw the Carter sisters pause in deep conversation, then she recognized the shocked look on Nicholas Mackinnon's face.

So now he knows. . . . Good, she told herself. *It's better this way. He would have known sooner or later. It's a good thing I didn't build up false hopes. I'm glad now that I stuck to my guns. He's a charmer, all right. But that sort of thing is closed to me. Forever. No man wants . . . a woman like me.*

Tibbie finished her errands so fast that Beth complained heavily. "Mama, why are we walking so fast? Why can't we go to Mrs. Hibbets and get the book she said we could borrow?" With a final effort, she asked, "Mama, are you mad at me?"

Tibbie pulled up short. Turning toward Beth, she placed her hands on each side of Beth's rosy cheeks. "No, my angel. I'm not angry with you. I'm angry with myself."

"Oh," said Beth, tucking her hand in her mother's once more. "Why?"

"You wouldn't understand now. I'll tell you when you're older."

"When I'm fifty, like you?"

"I'm not that old yet," Tibbie said sourly. *But Lord! Do I ever feel it! Fifty and more!*

They walked in silence the rest of the way home, Beth apparently satisfied and her attention given to the peppermint stick. Tibbie, feeling anything but satisfied, didn't feel much like talking.

Cycles. Life always went in cycles.

First came a comfortable lull when talk died down and life seemed to go on as if nothing had ever gone wrong in her life. These were the times when Tibbie could almost forget; the times when she could act the carefree, happy girl of twenty-one.

Almost.

But it was always there, a dark stain on her consciousness, an obscure cloud that relentlessly blocked the sunlight from her life, a cold, bitter chill that no amount of warmth could penetrate.

One afternoon she walked down the road that led to town and stood on a gently sloping rise, seeing in the distance the shipyards where Nicholas Mackinnon worked. The sails were gray and bleak beneath overcast skies and were shrouded in cold, creeping fog. Occasionally, a patch of it would thin out or threaten to lift and she would catch a glimpse or two of town, every so often making out a dark, blurred shape to be a coach or wagon going up the road toward Indianola. Between those two, the shipyard and town, stood the small cottage where Nick lived, but she never got a glimpse of that. And it was just as well.

That night she sat, propped up in her bed, writing, as she often did, in her log. Tonight she wrote that life was one long, linked chain and there was no way to see all the way to the end of it, no way to handle anything more than one link at a time. She could not choose her destiny. But even as she thought it, she knew the way she handled it was of her own choosing.

"Please," she said, dropping her head to her chest. "I don't know what to do. Help me. Help me to live again. Show me what to do, who to trust. Give me some indication, some way to know. I'm so tired of my life the way it is, but I'm afraid to do anything about it. Help me. Show me the way. Give me a sign."

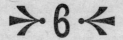

6

Was it the Reverend Woolridge or Cervantes who said, "Man appoints, God disappoints"?

As she thought upon it, Tibbie decided those words sounded more like Cervantes than anything the good reverend would say. And she was right.

"I ask for a sign, and what do I get? A revelation that God has a sense of humor." She was thinking that, when it came to prayer, one could do with more good fortune and less wit.

The first thing Tibbie had done that morning was to remember her earnest prayer the night before. A moment later she shot out of bed and hurried to her bedroom window. She looked outside. She saw the sun.

Sunshine! That could be a good sign.

But then the sun went behind a cloud.

She saw Beth playing with her pig, Precious.

Laughter! That's a good sign.

But then Beth tripped and fell, and ran into the house crying.

She opened the window. It was as balmy a day as she'd ever seen in springtime—much too nice for the first of March.

The day held promise. And that could be a good sign.

Then she saw Nicholas Mackinnon coming up the road toward her house.

That was not a good sign.

She looked heavenward with a questioning eye. *You wouldn't. . . . Would you?* The sun came out from behind the cloud.

Tibbie buried her face in her hands. "Not that sign," she whispered. "Anything but that."

But when she looked back, Nicholas Mackinnon was still there, coming toward her house, grinning like a pure fool, the sun at his back.

It was hard to ignore God when he whacked you between the eyes.

With a dejected sigh, Tibbie hurried away from the window, pulling her gown over her head and tossing it on her unmade bed. If she hurried, she could be gone before *he* got here. She put on her dress and ran a comb through her hair, plaiting her hair as she left the room and hurried down the stairs, taking them two at a time.

She should have known better.

Trying to sneak out of the house undetected. Her. Tibbie Buchanan. The same Tibbie Buchanan who never got away with anything.

And whose fault was it that she got caught? This time the honor went to Precious. Who'd had the brilliant idea to name that blasted pig of Beth's, Precious? He was anything but, if you asked her. For it was Precious who gave her away. And not in a way she would have called subtle.

There is something nerve-wracking about the squeal of a pig; something nerve-wracking and quite noticeable. A pig's squeal, for those who have never had the pleasure, is not something to be ignored. A real attention getter, it is. As it was when Precious spied Tibbie's rapid descent down the back staircase and gave chase, his horny little trotters clipping smartly over the wooden floors, while a squeal that would have put a banshee to shame pierced the otherwise quiet, peaceful morning.

"What in the name of heaven is that pig doing in the house?" Coll roared as he came out of the kitchen, looking dark as a thundercloud.

"He comes into the house all the time," Effie said calmly, following Coll out of the kitchen, drying her hands on her apron as she went.

"Not when I'm here, he doesn't!"

"He does, you just don't notice him unless he makes a ruckus," Effie said.

"Don't notice him! How could anyone not notice a two-hundred-pound pig in his house?"

"I'll never understand that one either," said Effie. "I think you noticed him this morning because he was squealing at Tibbie."

Coll looked at Tibbie. "Why was he throwing such a ruckus over you?"

"I don't know," replied Tibbie.

"I do," said Beth. "Mama was sneaking down the back stairs and Precious saw her leave. He doesn't like to be left alone."

"How do you know she was sneaking?" asked Effie.

"'Cause she came down the stairs real fast and on her tip-pie-toes . . . and she had her shoes in her hand."

Coll still had his eye on Tibbie. "Why were you sneaking down the stairs?"

"I think I might have something to do with that," a deep, rumbling voice behind them said.

They all turned in unison toward the doorway, seeing Granny Grace leading Nicholas Mackinnon into the foyer. "See," she said, pointing toward Tibbie, "I told you she was here."

The Buchanans looked at Nicholas Mackinnon, wearing a buff-colored pair of buckskin pants—way too tight, in Tibbie's estimation—and a dark-blue coat. His hat was held loosely in one hand. He was quite a contrast to Granny Grace, standing to his left, her hand on the door. Granny apparently was having a slow start this morning, for she was still wearing her dressing gown and a nightcap that rested like an afterthought on her frizzled white hair.

What is he doing here? Surely he wouldn't come after what he had heard said about her in town, after seeing her with Beth. She looked at her grandmother. The white knot that had been on top of her head yesterday was dangling over one ear.

Tibbie leaned against the wall and folded her arms. "Granny," she said in an irritated voice, "why did you open the door like that, without giving anyone any notice?"

Granny didn't beat about the bush fishing for an answer, but said straightaway, "Because he knocked."

Tibbie gritted her teeth, and Nick almost choked. He was finding it hard to contain the laugh that crowded in the back of his throat. He looked at Granny standing there, not much bigger than his thumb, looking frazzled and gray and sharper than a tack. He thought suddenly how he would have loved knowing Granny when she was a young woman. He looked at the old woman facing her family in a showdown. And damn if he didn't think she'd get the best of them.

"Heavens above, you should know better than to ask Granny a sensible question," Coll said.

"Coll, don't say things like that in front of company. You'll embarrass Granny," Effie said.

If Coll was taken aback, he didn't show it. "Embarrass her? How? How can you embarrass someone who takes communion, drains the chalice—in front of the whole congregation, mind you—then hands it back saying, 'That was so good, I think I'll have another'?"

"She just forgot where she was, Coll. Just you wait. Your time is coming."

"Please do me a favor when it does," he said. "Lock me up! Shoot me! But don't turn me lose on decent society when my wits have wilted."

Nicholas looked around him. Never in all his years had he encountered such a family. He looked at Dr. Coll Buchanan, a large, robust man with a bald head ringed in silver, and a look of supreme irritation on his face that didn't harmonize with the warm expression in his eyes. From there, Nick's eyes moved over to Effie Buchanan, who looked too youthful to have a daughter as old as Tibbie—her figure was still girlishly slim, her dark hair showed only a few streaks of silver. And of course, Tibbie looked beautifully serious and somber in her dull, matronly clothes.

But it was Granny who stole his heart. When he looked at her, he didn't see an aging old woman who had outlived her usefulness. Cloaked in yards and yards of black dressing gown, her nightcap cocked to one side, her gray hair poking every which way, he saw ever-wise Merlin, performing magic.

Granny, seeing four pairs of eyes upon her, said, "What is everyone looking at me for? Did I do something wrong?"

A resounding, "Yes!" broke the silence.

"You shouldn't answer the door dressed like that," said Coll.

"You should check with me before you tell someone I'm in," said Tibbie.

"It would be better if you let the housekeeper answer the door, Mama," said Effie. "It's her job."

"Who's the housekeeper?"

"My Lord!" groaned Coll. "She's the woman that's been bringing you your breakfast for the past three years!"

"Well, I never knew Gladys was the housekeeper. Nobody ever tells me anything," said Granny. "All I ever hear is complaints."

"You don't hear anything!" Coll said. "You're as deaf as a stone."

"Humph!" said Granny, casting a quizzical eye about the room. "I'm going back to bed," she said, heading for the stairs. She paused at the first step and turned, her eyes narrowed in on Nick. "If I were you, I'd pay my respects somewhere else. This bunch looks as happy as a pig in a poke." She started up the stairs again, mumbling to herself. "Nobody ever tells me anything. It beats me how they expect a body to know anything, when no one wants to tell me. All they ever tell me is what I shouldn't do, or what I should do, or what I did wrong." She waved her hand as if dismissing the whole thing. "Children," she said like a curse. "Bah!" Her voice got higher. " 'Blessed is he that has a quiver full,' " she quoted, then shook her head. "Grace," she said, nodding to herself, "You should have stayed a virgin."

The sudden sound of Nick's laughter echoed throughout the house.

"I've got work to do," said Coll. "If I'm going to listen to complaints, I might as well get paid for it. My office is full of complaints. Those I can do something about."

"Oh, dear," said Effie, her hand coming up to touch the lace at her throat, "I think I smell my muffins burning . . ." She whirled around and disappeared through the kitchen door. That left Tibbie looking uncomfortable, standing a few feet away from Nick, frantically trying to think of a good line to exit with, and failing miserably.

"Looks like you're stuck with me," Nick said.

Tibbie sucked in her breath and clenched her fists. "Why not? Granny gets her nap. Papa gets his patients. Mama gets her burned muffins. But lucky me, I get *you*!" She gave him an icy stare and said under her breath, "I'd rather have burned muffins."

It was a beastly warm day and her father was fractious, her mother's muffins burned, Granny was in one of her absent-minded moods and now this devil appeared on her doorstep. "Is there someplace we can talk?" he asked.

She turned away with quick impatience and led him into the parlor. "We can talk in here," she said coolly, while moving to the large front window and drawing back the drapes, "although I have nothing to say to you."

Without a second thought, Nicholas said in a voice that was very controlled and very rigid, "But I have something to say to you, *little mother.*"

So he knows. She knew he did, of course, since she'd seen him in town, but there was something final and frightening about standing here alone with him and knowing it.

His words came like sharp daggers piercing her flesh. *Little mother . . . little mother . . . little mother . . .* Over and over the sound of his voice echoed in her brain, searing and choking her with its putrid smoke. Tibbie gripped the draperies as a frigid tremor swept over her. Immediately, her entire body went stiff and cold. She stood perfectly still. Her hands clutched the draperies, as if their coarsely woven length alone supported her. She closed her eyes and concentrated on her thoughts.

The great clock in the hall ticked on, as if nothing out of the ordinary had happened. In the kitchen, her mother's voice could be heard scolding herself over the burned muffins, while upstairs, Granny's rocker creaked out a rhythm passing over a squeaky plank in the floor. Outside, the smithy's hammer told her a horse was being shod, and Beth's pig, Precious, let out a sharp squeal. Around her the familiar sounds of home and family went on as before, reminding her that everything about her had survived the anguish of recently spoken words. She alone felt their destruction. The musty aroma of dust and age clinging to the draperies rose like a sickening vapor to surround her.

From somewhere beyond her a faint hollow echo of a voice from the past reached out to touch her. It was her mother speaking, that horrible night she told her parents of Eric's abandonment and her pregnancy. "It might be best if you went to stay with relatives, pass yourself off as a widow. God knows I hate to see you leave, but people can be so cruel. I can't bear to see you taunted and beaten down, Tibbie. As long as you remain in Indianola, there will never be another life for you. People won't forget. The past will always come back to haunt you. You must do something to protect yourself—you and the child."

But she had stayed. She had faced her accusers, absorbed their scorn, lived with their rejection. It had been Granny who had encouraged her to work in her father's clinic, Granny who taught her that misfortune can destroy or strengthen and the choice was hers alone. "Seeing the suffering and pain in others helps us forget our own," Granny told her. "People won't forget, but they will forgive." And she had been right.

From that day on Tibbie made a vow to herself, a vow so intensely pledged she had never wavered from it, not once. *No man will ever do this to me again.* She would never allow herself to be infatuated with a man again. She would never fall for smoothly spoken promises, or put faith in a few stolen kisses. She would never allow a man to get close enough to her to stay her from her purpose, to weaken her resolve, to make her forget. She would remember with every breath she drew. She would show them, show them all—those who criticized and blamed her, those who called her names and pulled their skirts aside when she passed, as if by touching her, her taint would be passed on to them. It had not taken her long to learn the best way to avoid persecution was to make herself as inconspicuous as possible, to be quiet and reserved, to lead a life that no one could fault. She kept to herself, avoided men altogether, spoke politely, even when snubbed, and when she had to go to town she went about her errands with well-bred dignity.

Even now, Tibbie remembered with absolute clarity the way things had been; the betrayal, the blame, the rejection, the suffering, and after a while, the long, difficult climb back to respectability. She had been through all that once and survived. Her head came up, her back straightened. She had endured looks and slurs and accusations before, had endured and become stronger.

The tension in her body flowed outward as she opened her eyes and turned to face Nicholas Mackinnon, fixing him with a fiercely determined stare.

Nick's eyes swept over Tibbie, so beautiful, so bold and self-assured. No matter how colorless and ugly her dress was, it could not hide her willowy figure, her unadorned beauty, her graceful way of moving. Framed in a backdrop of sunlight, her lustrous hair was warm and alive and golden, swept up and coiled, revealing a slender, white neck. She was the picture of grace and poise and confidence. But in her eyes, her lovely golden eyes, he saw apprehension. But the thing that almost sent him to his knees was recognizing the lingering residue of pain.

His face thoughtful, Nick stared at her. He quickly determined that she had imagined him shocked and, more than likely, disgusted by her past. It wouldn't take a flickering of a second to set her straight on that account, but there was something else that bothered him. There was no sign of discomfort on her face. Her expression was controlled, reserved and aloof. But pain runs deeper than facial expression. He remembered his mother had once told him, "Lips are the instrument of deceit, but the eyes never lie."

He focused on her eyes. He cursed himself for his choice of words, confronting her with his discovery by calling her little mother.

His discovery about her child had added a new dimension to her, like a pencil sketch that comes to life when touched with color. His sudden insight was so profound it was close to overwhelming. So many things were explained, so much brought to light. She was a mother, and not only that, but the mother of a child born out of wedlock. What she had been through—experiences he knew nothing about—would have changed her. Suddenly her aloofness, her hostility, her refusal to have anything to do with him were explained. *Once burned, twice shy.*

It hit him so hard, the breath rushed from his body. Tibbie had been transformed from a laughing, loving young girl to a cautious, self-protective woman. God! How he wished he could have known her before. His fists clenched with fury. He could kill with his bare hands the bastard that did this to her.

Nick sighed, feeling a sudden transformation within himself. Earlier, when he had found out about her child, his desire for her had given way to anger. Now anger had become sensitivity and perception. Answers to a few questions would bring what he desired most: understanding. "Would you tell me about it?"

"No," she said quite adamantly, "I won't."

She had seen, some time ago, the softening in his features, but she would put no trust in that. And now even the gentle tones of his voice didn't put her at ease. She had fallen for soft looks and kind words before. Looking at him, Tibbie had the feeling he was dead-set upon talking—and well she knew that he had no shame, falling in the horse trough like he did, drawing all sorts of attention to her, making her the topic of discussion around Indianola for days—something she had lived a quiet, discreet life for the past five years in order to avoid.

A few minutes passed and Nick said nothing. "I haven't much time, Mr. Mackinnon. There's a lot of croup going around. I'm needed in the clinic. If there's something you have to say, please say it, so I can be on about my business, although I'll warn you now, I've heard it all before."

"I'm sure you have, but I haven't."

"There are plenty of people in Indianola who would be more than happy to fill you in on *any* details you are missing."

"I'm not interested in hearing it from anyone but you."

She was more of a mystery to him now than ever. But he decided then and there, no matter what it took, if he had to bar the door against her entire family and threaten her with starvation, he would have her story and have it now.

She sighed and walked away from the window, her skirts swishing as she passed him. She walked as far as the horsehair sofa, then turned, her hands clasped in front of her. "I don't understand you. You said you came here to build a ship. Why don't you go build it and leave me alone? I've made it clear enough, I think. I don't want your companionship, your attention, your friendship, or anything else. Why do you persist?"

"Because you have something I want. Because I don't think you're as immune to me as you'd like me to think. Because I came here to get some answers and I'm not leaving until I get them." He moved to the door and threw the lock. "And *you,* sweet Tibbie, aren't leaving until you give them to me."

She watched him lean confidently against the door, crossing his arms over his chest, and she felt irritation explode in scarlet upon her cheeks. "How dare you lock me in here with you like this!"

"I dare," he said with a smile as confident as his stature.

Tibbie Anne, this may take some doing. This man is harder to get rid of than a gopher. Why is he so persistent? How much longer can I put up a fight against odds like this? Her eyes roved over his face and long, lean body. *Dear Lord, what odds!* The room was getting smaller by the minute. She was so sensitively aware of his closeness, of the fact that he had locked the two of them in this room. And there he stood, her tormentor, leaning against the door, dripping charm and good looks and masculinity like a melting candle. He was better looking, and taller, and broader, and more determined than all the others that had tried and failed. There was an understated strength about him, an implied male dominance, an earthy sensuality that frightened her out of her wits. She may have borne a child, but she was inexperienced against a man with his powerful ammunition. Her mouth felt dry. Her heart quickened, beating hard and fast, like it wanted to remind her of its presence. She felt closed in, trapped, cut off from her defenses. A strange, tingling sensation swept over her, penetrating into the very center of her being. Panic swept over her.

Perhaps that is what prompted her to pick up her mother's best pewter candlestick and hold it like a club. "I'm warning you now, you'd better unlock that door and do it right now."

"And if I don't?"

She waved the candlestick. "I'm going to let you have it."

"That," he said with a knee-weakening smile, "is what I have been waiting for."

Her pulse raced. Her irritation mounted. "You don't think I'll throw this, do you?"

"Oh, I've no doubts about that. I've always suspected there was a little red in your hair. Point is, it won't do you any good to throw it. You'll miss me, and put a dent in your mother's lovely wallpaper, and more than likely break her prized candlestick. And then, when it's too late and the damage has been done, you'll realize it wasn't me you punished at all, but your mother." He pushed away from the door. "Now, why don't you put that down before you do something you regret."

He took a step toward her and she drew her arm back in readiness. But the look of indecision was still upon her adorable face. He sighed and shook his head. "You're a stubborn lass, for sure." Then he grinned. "Of course, I'd really prefer you to throw it. Then, when you see the damage you've done to your mother's wallpaper and candlestick, you'll be full of remorse. Chances are you'd be so overcome you'll start crying, and me, being the soft-hearted lad that I am—well, I've never been a man who could stand to see a lass cry. I'd have no choice but to take you in my arms and give you comfort." He lowered his voice a note or two and added in husky tones, "In the only way I know how."

She had a pretty good inkling as to what way that was. Her eyes grew wide with supposition. Down went her confidence. Down went her arm. Down went her mother's candlestick to rest on the table. About the only thing that didn't go down was Tibbie's frustration. That, if anything, was on the rise.

He had to hand it to her. She put up a good fight. He wanted to shout with the pleasure he found in her. He didn't know where her grit came from, but it was limitless and her resistance boundless. She was feisty and full of spirit and he bet next Sunday's dinner that she'd be wilder than hell in bed. He realized what he had thought to be a drab little peahen was really a fighter, a real little gamehen, and a tough one at that. Not many women could have gone through what she did with the cards stacked against her as they had to have been and come out on top. He admired the hell out of her, for he knew what effort and endurance it must have required of one so young, to overcome the odds she had overcome to win a place of respectability within the community. So many feelings were emerging, he was feeling a bit of her confusion. His desire for this woman was so intense he was losing sleep over it, yet he was afraid to express himself for fear of surrendering his chance with her, slim as it was. He was at a quandry as to how to proceed. *Fool,* he thought, feeling the frustration of not knowing whether to go forward or back up.

She was about to come back with another cold remark, but she saw the change that had come over him. Before her stood a different man. He still wore the same too-tight britches and blue coat, and he still possessed that handsome face and the devil's own blue eyes, but there was something in his bearing, in his manner, in the tone of his voice, and in those eyes!

Well she knew, she could withstand insults, accusations, or

even anger, but she feared the softer things—his patience, his understanding, his conquering gentleness, for they would be her undoing. Here was a man that wielded gentleness like a two-sided sword. Even now she felt him hacking away at her resolve, even when he stood there in complete silence.

They had crossed over an invisible line into territory that was foreign to her. No man had been able to push her this far before. The realization of it held her frozen in place, even after he crossed the room to stand before her. She knew that look of confidence, knew it would soon be followed by a look of possession, for she had seen it often enough in Eric's eyes.

And she knew what it meant. A strange warmth spread throughout her belly like fullness. A shudder rippled through her. As if he sensed what she was experiencing, he slowly lifted his hand and trailed his fingers down the length of her arm, from her shoulder to her fingertips, then he took her hand and lifted it to his mouth and kissed it. He broke the kiss, but he did not release her hand.

Tibbie swallowed, waiting to see what his next move would be.

"It's a different game we play from here on out. You know that, don't you?"

She nodded, pulling her hand back and feeling the shiver ripple across her once more when he cupped her chin in his warm palm and tilted her head up so she was looking at him. "This time we're playing for keeps."

For the life of her, Tibbie couldn't think of a thing to say, but she bristled at the thought of going down in defeat when she had overcome so much.

He smiled in confidence at the thought of holding her in his arms at last.

She stiffened, scraping together the last bit of resolve she could muster. She couldn't give in so easily a second time. Hadn't she learned anything before?

And so it began, Tibbie's most dogged determination to resist Nicholas Mackinnon, and for Nick, the most relentless pursuit of a woman he had ever embarked upon. The groundwork had been laid, and without speaking a word they both knew only one of them would win.

Thankfully, a child's bubbling laughter and the shrill, piercing squeal of a pig broke the silence. Tibbie looked toward the window and saw a flash of Beth's red coat as she dashed by the window, Precious running and squealing as he gave chase.

"Your daughter," he said.

"Yes."

"And your . . . husband?"

She turned on him like a spitting cat, and Nick instantly regretted his use of "husband" instead of asking about the child's father.

"I have no *husband,* as you well know. Beth is a bastard, for want of a better term. Please don't think your attempt to be snide and insulting will have any effect upon me. I've been through that many times before. After a while you become calloused and numb. There is just so much pain that can be inflicted. After that, it becomes painless."

"I didn't mean—"

"I know what you meant," she said, doing her best to control the quiver in her voice. "You're all alike. Hypocrites, all of you."

"I think you misunderstood—"

"Ohhh no! That's *one* thing I don't do. Not about that. It's been five years now—almost six. If there's anything I know, it's how the job is done. Don't think you're the first to try being subtle. As for flagrant name calling, it has fallen a thousand times on these deaf ears." She took a deep breath, composing herself. "There is nothing you can tell me at this point that I haven't heard before, no name you can call me I haven't been called a million times."

Her pain from the past reached out and touched him. *God, what she must have endured.* "I didn't come here to tell you anything," he said. "Quite the contrary, in fact. I came because I wanted you to tell me a few things."

"Like what, sir?" she said with a snarl. "What is it that you want to hear? The details, Mr. Mackinnon? All the nasty, sordid little details, like everyone else?"

"Details perhaps, but not sordid—"

"Don't lie, please! I'm no fool. I know why you're here. It's obvious. You want to be satisfied, don't you? You look at me and there is still some doubt. I don't exactly *look* like a strumpet, do I? And I don't dress like a *whore*. I don't work down at The Glass Slipper, and I've never been seen with paint on my face. That puzzles you, doesn't it? Here I am, surrounded by a loving family. I go to church. I have some semblance of respect in the community. Nothing seems to fit. Isn't that what you've been telling yourself?" She paused for a breath, seeing the look of denial. "Please, don't bother to deny it. I know what you've been thinking. 'Surely, there must be some mistake. Perhaps she was married or engaged and the young man died tragically. Or perhaps she was a victim of cruel, misunderstanding parents, who forbade her to marry the man she loved.' Well, I can tell you it was none of these things. What happened was, I fell in love. *That* was my crime. I fell in love with a man, and I believed his lies. And when it was all over, when he had gotten what he wanted, he left. Nothing tragic *or* glorious there. I made a mistake. I sinned in the eyes of God and the church. I was condemned by the community. I bore a child out of wedlock. And oh, how I suffered for it." She paused, drawing herself up in readiness for what was to follow. "Now, you go ahead ask me the details you came here for."

"Are you still in love with him?"

She hadn't expected that, and it showed on her face. She let out a ragged sigh and turned away from him, giving him a view of her profile. For a moment she considered not telling him anything more, but he would hound her and stay after her until they were both exhausted from the effort. Perhaps if she gave him the answers he wanted he would go away and leave her in peace.

She brought her hands together, prayerlike, and placed them against her mouth, her thumbs hooked beneath her chin, then said honestly, "I don't know. Sometimes I hate him so much I think I could load a gun and blow his brains out if I ever laid eyes upon him again. At other times I find myself wondering what it would have been like if things had turned out differently, if he had loved me in return. And there are times that I wonder what I would do if he came back."

The thought pierced him and he waited a moment for his voice to steady. "And if he did? What would you do?"

She dropped her hands to her side, then lifted them in a questioning gesture. "I don't know." She turned to face him. "I honestly don't know. I have no answer for that, though God knows I've thought about it often enough. I loved him once. His leaving almost killed me. I bore his child. That formed an unbreakable link between us that can't be denied. I bore his child. I suffered for it. Does one wipe the other out? I don't know."

He was looking at her as if he were in a trance. And in a way he felt like he was. She still loved this man, that much was obvious, and the thought of that made Nick want to place his hands on each side of her head and squeeze until the memory of him was pressed out of her head. Her loving him in the past he could understand. Her bearing another man's child, he could live with. But the thought of her loving another man now, he could not take.

He felt a sinking in the pit of his stomach. He had just been dealt a blow he was not prepared for. But he had her talking and he couldn't let his own trampled feelings interfere. He had to get the subject off that bastard who kept her heart closed to him.

With a ragged breath he said, "Tell me what it was like for you."

"Why?"

"Because it concerns me. Because I want to know. Because I'm cursed with curiosity. Because I know what you went through, but I want to feel it, too, and the only way I can do that is through your eyes. Goddammit! Whatever the reason, Tibbie, humor me."

There was such desperation in his voice that she never considered not telling him what he wanted to know. "What was it like? You mean when he left? When I discovered I was going to have his child? Or after Beth was born?"

"Did you know you carried Beth when he left?"

"Yes."

"Did he know?"

She laughed harshly. "Of course. That probably helped him decide it was time to go. Wouldn't you?"

"No, but that's not the topic of discussion right now. You never tried to contact him afterward, to tell him of the birth of his child?"

"No. Why should I? He wanted no part of me. His only interest in his child was making sure he was gone long before it was born. Why would he want to know anything about us after that?"

"And now? Where are you now?"

"How do you mean?"

"As far as making a life for yourself and Beth."

"As you can see, I've done that already."

"I mean apart from your family here."

"You mean live alone?"

"That, or marriage," he said softly.

She looked stunned. "Marriage? Me?" Her voice cracked and she laughed to cover it. "Oh, I think not. Don't you know what the men around town think? They may not say it to my face, because they know my father is the only doctor in town. And many of them are beholden to me for the lives I've helped save. But the thought is there. There will always be men who think, Once a whore, always a whore."

He winced at the word. "I don't think—"

"Then perhaps you should. I'm sure once you do, you'll come to your senses and get the hell out of here. That's what they all do once they find out, and they always do, you know."

"I'm sure there are plenty of men who would be willing to overlook the fact that you have a child. You're a beautiful woman, unusually so. That alone will get a lot of things overlooked. I would think you would've been asked out countless times by now."

"Oh, yes, I certainly have. And it doesn't take long to find out why."

"I think you may be jumping to conclusions. I don't think people around here hold you in such low regard. In fact, they're quite protective of you. It sure took me a hell of a long time to find out anything about you. As best as I could discover, the people around here have a great deal of respect for you and your devotion to healing."

"Yes, but unfortunately *those* aren't the people who seek my company. As for my medical knowledge, it's respected because like my father, I possess a much needed skill. My 'good' reputation is based on that, yet it's a flimsy sort of security at best."

Desperate to have this discussion over and see this nosy Scot on his way, she said, "Now, has that satisfied your curiosity, or whatever it was that brought you over here today?"

"I had a few questions I wanted answered, but that isn't what brought me here today."

"And what did?"

"You."

"Me?"

"Come now, don't tell me that surprises you. A woman as beautiful as you?"

She wanted no compliments from him, for in truth she didn't know how to handle them.

He saw her discomfort and added, "But to be perfectly honest, it was to get one more glimpse of that lovely dress you're wearing."

"Thank you very much."

"I suppose it fits you in a way."

Her brows lifted in question.

"A drab, colorless dress for a drab, colorless life."

Color flooded her cheeks and in her eyes he saw a spark of indignation. "I see."

"No," he said, "I don't think you do."

Nick studied the pure features of that exquisite face. Flaw-

less was all he could think of to describe it. Besides beautiful,
of course. She had perfect features, the kind a master would
define in the rarest of marble. And in a way, even her coloring
lent itself to that concept, with her cool blond tones and taffy-
colored eyes. An angel in marble; cold, hard, and set in stone.
Was there no way to set her free?

Is that what Michelangelo meant when he said, "I saw the
angel in marble and I chipped until I set him free"? Was that
the key here as well . . . to chip away at her defenses, at that
wall of ice she had encased herself in, until he set her free? He
reminded himself that he had a ship to build for an eccentric
man with more money than patience. And he had a time
schedule to meet. There was no allocation for time spent on a
woman. But as he watched her, he knew his mission would be
shot to hell unless he found some way to thaw her a little. She
was an enigma to him and he didn't understand why. All he
knew was that he wanted her. He thought about that for a
moment. Want, a word that had so many different meanings
for him. He had always wanted her, but over the course of
time that want had developed so many different definitions. In
the beginning, his want had been based on pure physical attraction. She was a beautiful woman, whom he desired. He
was a man who enjoyed lovemaking. But later, after he had
observed her, he was intrigued to the point that he wanted
something more than just a night in bed with her. He began to
discover that he actually wanted to know more about her, this
lady of mystery. And then, after his encountering her in the
pasture that day, after spending time with her in the orchard
he found he actually enjoyed her company and wanted more of
it. And now?

He pondered that for a moment. His sexual desire for her
was still there, running wild in the forefront, but now it had
dimension. There were so many qualities about her that attracted his affection. He felt a tenderness for her that he had
never felt for a woman before. It occurred to him that his
desire now included a warm, fond attachment. He liked her,
admired her, enjoyed her presence, and took immense pleasure

in watching her, in learning more about her. In spite of her rejection, he felt like a rose in sunshine when he was with her. Was that love? Then it came to him. It wasn't so much what he wanted or felt when he was with her, but more of what he felt when he wasn't. And that, he had a feeling, was love.

He realized he had let his thoughts wander, and when he looked at her, he saw the look of unease that made him think she was just a little apprehensive about what was going on inside his head. *Sweetheart, if you only knew* . . .

Problem was, Tibbie had a pretty good idea. But what really scared her was that she knew, deep down inside her, that she wanted the same thing. Words she longed to speak jammed in her throat. She couldn't speak. She couldn't think. She had difficulty breathing. A curling warm pressure of desire began low in her stomach. She felt dizzy and took a step backward, bracing herself against the wall beneath a copy of a picture Gainsborough had painted. Her head, coming to rest against the wall, tilted the picture, but she didn't notice.

She didn't notice that Nick stared at her strangely, or that he had closed the distance between them, until he said, "Why don't we stop all this nonsense and pretension and resistance and get down to some serious courting?"

Courting. Not lust. Not sexual desire. Not something vulgar or demeaning. Courting. Dear God above, how long had it been since someone suggested courting to her, or looked at her as this man did? A warm flush of comfort raced across her like a shiver. Courting. She relished the word. Was that his intention? When his head leaned forward and lowered, so much blood rushed into her head that she was dizzy, her hand coming out to grip his arm to steady herself. She closed her eyes, hoping the dizziness would pass. When his lips touched hers lightly, warmly, briefly, she felt no insult, no invitation, no shame, nothing, save pleasure.

The clock in the hallway chimed, pulling her back from a dream into reality. Wide-eyed, she looked at him, trying to steady herself and maintain some composure. "You shouldn't

have done that," she finally managed to say, not feeling she
had completely overcome her surprise and shock.

"I shouldn't have," he admitted, "but I'm glad I did."

"The clock . . ."

He tilted his head, a half-smile lingering but not really form-
ing.

"The clock," he repeated. "Is that what we're going to discuss next?"

A smile curled itself across her mouth. "No, I meant to say
the clock just struck."

He smiled. "They've been known to do that regularly, I'm
told."

Firm resolve replaced her smile. "It's one o'clock. I really
must go. There are so many sick people waiting to be seen. We
worked until eight o'clock last night and still had to turn people away."

He nodded, following her to the door. When she reached
out to take the handle, his hand came out to close over hers.
Unable to pull her hand back, her eyes flew to his in accusa-
tion. He saw the look, felt the trembling response of her hand,
but he did not release her. *Angel, you're lucky. . . . If I did
what I really want to do, I'd take you in my arms and kiss you
until that pretty little mouth of yours was as startled as your
eyes.*

"About the Independence Day dance," he said, hesitating to
see if she was going to interrupt.

"I can't go with you."

"You accepted my invitation in front of half the town.
You're going to look pretty miserable if you back out now."

"Better to look miserable than to be miserable. I thought
you would have changed your mind after—"

He looked angry enough to slap her. "Let's you and I get
something straight here. I don't care if you've bedded half the
state of Texas and have enough children to fill a twenty-room
house. I've invited you to the dance and you accepted. That's a
commitment I don't intend to let you break." He saw she was
about to say something else but he cut her off. "You need to

understand one very important fact here. I invited you because I saw a beautiful woman I felt attracted to, one I wanted to get to know a little better. I still feel that way. The things we've discussed here today don't change anything, they just make it a little more complicated, that's all."

"Complicated?"

"For you," he said. "Not me." He saw she was confused. "I'm not a callous, unfeeling brute, Tibbie, in spite of what you think. I know the kinds of things you must have suffered, the snubs and rebuffs, the cruel comments, the lewd suggestions, and I know it won't be easy for you to be seen with a man in public, if this is the first time since—"

"It's the first time."

"Then I understand your apprehension. I don't want to add to what you have already endured. I simply want to squire the best-looking woman in six counties to a dance and spend a few hours forgetting a little of my own bruised past. I want to dance until we're both exhausted and you have a few holes in your slippers. I want to spin you around the room until all those gawking bystanders are nothing but a blur in your memory. And I'm going to do my damndest to see you laugh. And when it's all over, I'm going to walk you to my buggy and drive you home in the moonlight, praying until then that the weather is cold enough to make you sit just a little closer to me than you ordinarily might."

"*If* I go with you, Mr. Mackinnon, you must understand one thing. There will be no . . . well, what I mean is, I don't intend to let you . . . I have no desire to . . ."

His arms came around her so fast, she didn't have time to realize what was happening. He spun her around the room a time or two before dropping her to her feet. "You may not have any desire to right now, Tibbie my lass, but I intend to do everything in my power to see that you do by the time I bring you home."

"There will be no display of affection," she said succinctly.

"Public or otherwise?" he asked with a teasing grin.

"Anywise," she said, without cracking a smile.

"Then that will be solely up to you to put a stop to it."

"I have what it takes to do that, Mr. Mackinnon. I surely do."

"Do you, lass?" He lifted a hand and stroked the back of his knuckles across her cheek. "I wonder."

"Don't take that as a challenge," she said. "You'd be wasting your time."

"Perhaps. But you haven't seen me turn on that old irresistible Mackinnon charm," he said, giving her a kiss on the forehead that was no more than a peck. He whisked his hat off the chair, where he had tossed it when he entered, and a moment later he was gone.

Tibbie closed the door behind him, her arms braced behind her as she rested against it and closed her eyes, feeling strangely disturbed. *That old irresistible Mackinnon charm* . . .

The reverberating sound of those words broke her heart. He seemed so different from the others. If only she could believe him, believe that his intentions were born of attraction and a desire to spend some time with her, to dance, to laugh, to understand and know her.

If only.

There were too many if only's in her life now. If only she hadn't succumbed to Eric's captivating words and Nordic looks. If only she hadn't believed he loved her, that he wanted marriage. If only she hadn't become pregnant. If only she had decided to leave Indianola, to present herself elsewhere as a grieving widow. If only this charming Scot with the teasing blue eyes hadn't tried to run her down in the street that day. If only he had left her alone and let things be. If only he wasn't so blasted attractive. If only he didn't remind her of how much she denied herself. If only he didn't stir these feelings within her. *That old irresistible Mackinnon charm* . . .

If he only knew . . .

She found him so utterly charming already. Oh, he was irresistible, all right, and the blue-eyed brute knew it. And just how did one go about resisting someone irresistible, pray tell?

Tibbie Anne, you're in a peck of trouble, she told herself. *If you had a goose, it would be cooked.*

The hall clock struck the quarter hour. Her father would be knee-deep in patients by now and wondering what in the name of heaven was detaining her. But Nicholas Mackinnon had stirred up too many remembrances for her to pull away. An eerie sensation passed over her, not unlike a shudder, and she could feel herself going back in time, back six years. She could see herself now, hurrying up the boarded walks of town toward the docks, carrying her father's medical bag, her new lilac taffeta petticoat rustling with each step she took.

They reached the ship that had summoned her father, a Norwegian ship, the *Nordic Star.* Pausing to confirm that he was in the right place, her father had taken his bag, instructing Tibbie to wait for him where she was, since he had no idea what he might find once he was on board. What Coll had found was eight crewmen down with fever and one wealthy young passenger who happened to be the grandson of the owner of the *Nordic Star.*

The young man was deathly ill, and after much persuasion by the ship's captain, Coll agreed to have him removed from the ship and taken to his clinic. And that was the first time Tibbie had seen Eric Neilson. Over the ensuing weeks, Tibbie had nursed Eric, bathing him in apple-cider vinegar, spooning a mixture of juice and honey into his mouth at fifteen-minute intervals. And as the handsome young giant regained his strength, he turned his attention on sixteen-year-old Tibbie.

Looking back, Tibbie could see how Eric, at twenty-seven years of age, had had plenty of time to learn a great deal about women. She knew now the things that had seemed so unimportant to her then, things that would cause the older, wiser Tibbie Buchanan to steer away. But at sixteen, she didn't know to hold at bay any handsome scoundrel who was the spoiled baby of a doting father and mother, a man who had been born with a silver *and* gold spoon in his mouth, a man with such handsomeness that to look at him overly long had the same effect as staring at the sun.

Anything Eric had ever wanted had been his. Any trouble he had ever gotten into, his father had smoothed over with money. Because things came so easily to him, Eric had no regard for their value. Things or people. They were there for one thing and one thing only. To be used. And when they had served their purpose, they were expendable. Tibbie had learned the hard way that she was no exception.

But Lord, it had been beautiful for a time. She had felt his powerful lure the first time she had laid eyes upon him. He was blond and beautiful, and full of life and love and laughter; and he had made her feel ten feet tall when he looked at her, and like a princess when he touched her lips with his. He had been the first to kiss her, the first to touch her in a place no man had a right to know. But she had loved him then. And what terrified her was the fear that after all this time, she loved him still.

He was so difficult to forget. Even now she could recall that night, the first time he had come to her room in the hush of night and aroused her sleeping body; the first time he had made love to her.

She had dreamed of Eric that night, as she always did, but that time it had been different. She felt her body open like a flower petal, like the tide flowing out to sea—a rich languor blended with lethargy and inertia, then building and building, becoming so intense she felt her body stiffen in a spasm that was so real it woke her in the middle of her dream. For a moment she drifted, light as a leaf swirling in a torrent left by spring rain. Her limbs were heavy, her breathing deep, her mind awake and yet feeling as if it were not.

And then it came again, the warm lazy feeling, the heaviness in her legs. "That's it, my little passion flower, open your legs."

Her eyes flew open. This was no dream. She was no longer asleep, yet the room was still dark. Instant awareness told her she was still in her bed, and it also told her she wasn't alone.

"Eric!" she gasped, drawing her legs together.

But Eric pinned her before she could succeed, placing himself over her and between her legs. Panic flooded her. "No, Eric! Please!"

"You liked it well enough a minute ago."

"What are you doing?"

"Wait," he said softly, his hand coming up to tease the coral-tipped softness of her young breasts, and she flinched. "Tight and smooth," he said. "You've never been touched by a man before, have you, Tibbie, my love?"

"Not like this," she said, with a quiver to her voice.

"But you like it."

"No, I don't, Eric. I'm afraid."

"Shhh, love. It's the unknown you're afraid of. Once it's familiar you'll wonder why you denied yourself for so long . . . you'll see." His hand came down between them, touching her in the place that had throbbed so in her dream.

"Eric, no!"

"I thought you said you loved me."

"I do."

"Then let me."

"I can't. It's wrong."

He moved his fingers and she gasped. "Does it feel wrong, Tib?"

"I don't know. It feels . . . strange."

"I love you, Tibbie. And when a man loves a woman, he wants to make love to her, wants to touch her like this. It isn't strange. It isn't wrong. It's natural for this to happen between a man and a woman."

"When they're married."

"Is that what you want, Tib? Marriage?"

"They go together, don't they? Love and marriage? Making love and marriage?"

"Is that what the problem is? You want to, but only if there's marriage?"

"It's what I've been taught, Eric."

"If marriage is what you want, Tibbie, my love, marriage is what you'll get. Now, tell me you love me."

"I love y—"

Before she could finish the word, Eric drove into her swiftly.

But in the end, marriage wasn't what she got. What she got was being awakened out of her sleep a few nights a week over the next month. But two weeks after Coll pronounced Eric well, he was gone, leaving nothing behind but a note of apology and a tiny rose carved from a piece of coral that hung from a golden chain.

No, marriage isn't what she got.

What she got was pregnant.

When she told her father, it was the first time she had ever seen him cry. No, she hadn't gotten marriage. She didn't get a husband. But she did get a child. And she got something else as well. She had gotten wiser.

That old irresistible Mackinnon charm. As far as charm went, Nicholas Mackinnon certainly had it, but in a much more subtle way than Eric. Nicholas was the kind of man who slowly wore down a woman's defenses, a grain at a time, like erosion. But Eric swept in like a tidal wave, wreaking havoc wherever he went. While Nick was certainly handsome and possessed eye appeal, it wasn't the knock-you-on-your-bustle kind that was so outstanding in Eric. Eric was a diamond— hard, flashy, brilliant—a real attention getter, but without much purpose, other than ornamentation. Nick was like gold —shiny, but not dazzling—pliable and multidimensional.

Comparing Eric and Nicholas wasn't her real point of concern, for Eric was gone, nothing more than a part of her past. Her real concern now had nothing to do with Eric. Her concern was Nicholas Mackinnon. She stared at a fixed point across the room, not really seeing anything, save the turmoil going on in her mind. Perhaps it would be best if she were to leave for a while; take Bethany and go to visit relatives back East. But she knew she could never do that. This was her home. She had too much invested here to quit now. And there was her work and her dedication to it, which was as great as her need to thwart the advances of one Nicholas Mackinnon.

She reminded herself to be cautious. Remember what you went through before: the humiliation, the pain, the feeling that life just wasn't worth living. And now . . . even now, remember how you still ache for Eric as much as you hate him.

Oh, Eric. Why? Why did you do it? Why did you deceive me? Why did you lie? You were so very convincing at what you said, so very good at what you did. I was so sure; so sure you loved me, that you meant what you said. But you meant none of it. Is that what it is to be a man?

→ 7 ←

"Wars and Conquests" would have been the title for the month, if Tibbie had been prone to giving titles to the months, like Granny Grace was.

According to Granny, March was named in honor of Mars, the god of war. And before the month was out, Tibbie saw a great deal of wisdom in that. It was, she supposed, only natural to dedicate an entire month to the deity of war, since wars and conquests played such a big part in the lives of the early Romans. Not much different from today, as far as she could tell.

Wars and conquests.

Conquests and wars.

Would this month never end?

As always, March was a blustery month, a rude and boisterous month, yet it brought to life hope for what lay ahead: spring.

One unusually calm, sunny afternoon Tibbie packed a basket with cider and cookies, a book and a blanket. Basket in one hand, she took Beth by the other hand and headed for the beach, Precious following close behind. Beth, who seemed at age five to be in a constant state of excitement and questions, didn't hold her mother's hand for long. Soon she was running ahead, picking a flower or two, and running back to ask its name. "Bluebonnet," Tibbie said, pointing to the lovely periwinkle-blue flower.

"And this one?" Beth asked, holding up a white flower.

"Angel's-trumpet."

Beth turned the flower in her hand, studying it. "What's a trumpet?"

"It's a shiny horn that you blow into and it makes music."

"Like Grandpa's fiddle?"

"They both make music, but Grandpa uses a bow to play the fiddle. Have you ever seen him blow it?"

Beth giggled. "Maybe he will if I ask him to."

Tibbie fluffed the curls on Beth's head, then chucked her under the chin. "My sweet angel, if *anyone* could get Grandpa to blow on his fiddle, it would be you."

Beth looked at the flower again. "Do angels really blow on this?" She brought the flower up to her mouth and blew. The flower fluttered out of her hand and Beth looked questioningly up at her mother. "It didn't make any noise."

Tibbie gave Beth's cheek a soft caress, then bent down to pick another white flower. "Angel's don't really blow this flower, people just named it that because its shape reminded them of a trumpet." She turned the flower to its side. "See?"

"Why didn't they just call it trumpet flower?"

"I'm not sure, but I'd be willing to bet it was because it's such a pretty flower, all slim and white, just like an angel's long white robe."

Beth took the flower from her mother's hand and eyed it with newfound reverence, then she placed it in her pocket. "I'm going to give this one to Granny to press in my book."

The next moment Beth was running over a sandy slope, shouting for her mother to hurry up. Tibbie hurried, and soon she was sitting on the blanket, the sound and smell of the sea filling her with renewed vigor.

She was reading Granny's *Book of Months* to Bethany. She would pause occasionally and frown, or lay the book facedown upon her lap and gaze across the water. There were just too many parallels between the month of March and her life. Take, for instance, the fact that the birthstone for March is the bloodstone.

Enough said.

Or take, for another instance, the old belief that the bloodstone could stop bleeding, heal inflammatory illness, and stop anger and discord—she could use a little of these powers. It was also claimed that this same stone could make water boil, and could bring its wearer popularity, courage, and wisdom. Wisdom? She could use a little of this as well.

"The March flower is the jonquil or daffodil," Tibbie read. "Daffo-down dill has come to town/in a yellow petticoat and a green gown," Beth chimed musically. She stood on the end of the blanket opposite her mother and bent over at the waist to peer between her legs at her mother. "You look funny, Mama! You're upside down!"

Tibbie laughed and got to her feet. She turned away from Beth and hitched up her skirts, bending over as Beth had done and peeked between her legs. "You look funny too! You're upside down!"

Beth collapsed in a fit of giggles and Tibbie followed her down, tickling her on the way. Beth gave her mother a wet kiss and said, "I like you that way. I like you upside down."

"Why not," Tibbie said, giving Beth one last tickle as she reached for the book. Then she added, "It's a parallel to my life," in tones low enough for Beth not to hear.

"What?"

Tibbie shook her head, forgetting what ears children had. "Nothing."

"Why are you always saying 'nothing,' when you really did say something? I *saw* your lips move, Mama. I did. Are you listening?"

Tibbie laughed outright at this. She never tired of listening to Beth's musical chatter, her grown-up thoughts. "Of course I'm listening." Then Tibbie hugged Beth close and kissed her hard, stopping her laughter and looking suddenly as if tears had come into her eyes. She kissed the top of Beth's head, and looking heavenward, whispered a soft "Thank you."

From out of nowhere, a seagull shrieked and coasted low over their blanket, scoring a direct hit with a dropping that landed on the corner of the blanket with a *splat!*

Beth said, "Ugh!" and scooted closer to her mother.

Tibbie looked heavenward once again. *You will note,* she thought solemnly, *that I am not asking for signs anymore, but if that was an indication of my blessings to come, would you please bless someone else for a while?*

Her attention was distracted by Beth, who, after covering the gull's *blessing* with sand, began searching around the blanket, looking in her pockets and in the basket.

"What are you looking for?"

"My flower. I put it in my pocket, but it's not there."

"You probably lost it when you ran. We'll pick you another one on the way back."

"Maybe I'll find that one, then I won't have to pick another one."

"Perhaps, but lost things have a way of staying lost." Tibbie began reading once again, pausing occasionally to look at Beth, who seemed as lost as her flower, a queer little look of thoughtfulness on her small face.

After some time, Beth said, "Mama, where do lost things go?"

"What do you mean?"

"You know, things we had but don't have anymore, like Grandpa's knife and Grandma's pillbox, and the stick of sealing wax Aunt Mairi was looking for. I lost my best blue ribbon, and you can't find your silver thimble. With so many things being lost they must take up a lot of room, so why can't we find them? Where do they all go?"

"They're in a lot of different places, but mostly they're just lost . . . misplaced."

"Oh," said Beth. "When red dog died, did he get misplaced?"

"No, he was buried, remember? We put him in a box and then in the ground. We know where he is, so he isn't lost."

"But my flower is lost, because I don't know where it is. So, where did it go, Mama? It has to be someplace!"

Tibbie pondered that for a minute. She wished Granny were here. Granny always had a wonderful explanation for everything. Reminded of that, she felt a little guilty for the multitude of questions similar to Beth's that she had asked Granny when she was Beth's age. Did Granny have as much trouble with answers as she was having now?

"Mama? Are you listening?"

"Yes, sugar plum, I am. I'm thinking. Lost things don't *go* anywhere. They stay right where they landed when you lost them." She looked at Beth to see if that answer was going to satisfy her or not. Judging from Beth's expression, Tibbie guessed it was "or not." She shook her head and smiled. *I might as well jump into this with both feet.* "What are you thinking about now?"

"Grandpa. He said good people go to heaven when they die and lost souls go . . . down there!" Her eyes got very round and she pointed in the proper direction. "He said Mr. Pomfreet's son got lost at sea, and poor ol' Mrs. Adderley lost her hope . . ."

"Lost all hope."

"Lost all hope," Beth repeated. "Did her lost hope stay where she lost it?"

"No. Objects, like your flower or my thimble, stay right where they were dropped, but hope isn't something you lose like a flower. Losing hope means you give up, you quit. Mrs. Adderly didn't really *lose* something, she was just very, very tired."

"Then she should have taken a nap."

Tibbie laughed. "She does that in church."

Tibbie's eyes rested on the small pig tracks in the sand. "Where's Precious?" she asked. "I don't see him anywhere."

"Oh, dear," said Beth, "I hope *he* isn't lost."

"No such luck," said Tibbie.

"Oh, there he is, under the blanket. I forgot, I covered him up."

"Why? It isn't cold."

"He'll get sunburned." Beth eyed the pig. "But I don't think he likes it much."

A minute later, Tibbie decided Beth was right, for Precious wiggled out from under the blanket and began rooting around in the sand, grunting. Then he turned the picnic basket over and ate three cookies before Tibbie and Beth could set things right. "We need to put him on a rope," said Tibbie. "He's getting too hard to handle."

"He won't like it," said Beth.

"He doesn't have a say," said Tibbie. She stood, extending her hand to Beth. "Come on, let's go for a walk down the beach. Maybe we can make Precious tired enough that he'll want to sleep when we come back."

They walked down the beach a half mile or so, Beth and the pig running ahead, Beth looking for shells, Precious squealing and running after Beth. Watching them, Tibbie wondered if Precious enjoyed anything as much as eating and squealing.

When she caught up to them, Beth looked at Tibbie and said, "Can we go back now? I'm getting hungry. Can we have our treat now? Are you hungry, Mama?"

"Starved."

"I'll race you," Beth shouted as she took off running.

"You little rat!" Tibbie shouted after her as she took up the challenge. When Precious saw Beth running off, he took off behind her with a terrified squeal, running in front of Tibbie and squealing like a stuck hog when Tibbie came tumbling down upon him.

"Shut up, you stupid swine," she said, rising up on her elbows and releasing Precious from the twisted maze of legs and petticoats. For a moment, Precious stood looking at her, tilting the flat pink disc he called a nose back and forth. "Go on!" Tibbie shouted. "Get out of here, you porky porcine . . . get away from me." She clapped her hands together. "Shoo!"

But Precious simply stared at her, his tail held aloft. "All right!" Tibbie said, relenting. She gathered her skirts into one arm, mumbling, "That blasted pig will be the death of me." She took off, knowing that Precious would squeal at the thought of being left alone, and would soon be working those horny little trotters of his double-time.

And she was right. Hearing the pig behind her and knowing he was gaining on her, Tibbie looked down the beach, catching sight of Beth far ahead of her, just rounding the curve. Tibbie hiked her skirts higher and cut a diagonal slice across the beach, cutting through the shallow water. Precious loved water, but he was a little unsure of an ocean full of it. He kept running up to the edge of the water, then retreating. After a few times he began to squeal, seeing Tibbie splashing through the surf, gaining on Beth and putting way too much distance between her and himself.

"Just you wait until I catch you!" Tibbie shouted to Beth with an exuberant laugh as more warm gulf water splashed over her, spraying her face. Beth turned, and seeing her mother fairly soaked to the skin and splashing in the surf like a frolicsome puppy, she immediately did a right turn and came running and splashing toward her.

"You can't catch me! You can't catch me!" she shouted, as Tibbie made a dive for her and came up clutching a length of ugly brown seaweed.

"You're in for it now," Tibbie squealed with a laugh, spitting salty water from her mouth. Beth let out a squeal that rivaled Precious, then she took off toward the shore, stumbling over her sodden skirts just as she cleared the water. Tibbie caught up to her at that moment and they both tumbled into the sand. Their joined laughter, laced with squeals from Precious, was loud enough that they didn't notice the low, swelling rumble of masculine laughter that rolled across the dunes behind them.

Knowing that he might reveal his hiding place, Nick lifted his head higher, looking over the sand-swept log as Tibbie and Beth played. Never had he seen such a sight. He felt an intense aching at being so artistically inept, for truly this was the sort of thing that inspired painters and poets, or a musician would set to song, while all he could do was bumble around in the sand like a tumblebug.

He was learning and observing things about Tibbie Buchanan faster than he could catalogue them. He had longed so to see her smile, never imagining what it would do to him to see her like this, laughing freely and rolling in the sand, her skirts up to her hips, the absolutely most divine-looking legs he had ever hoped to encounter thrashing the air. And when she came up to rest on her knees and he saw the way her water-logged dress clung to her body, he was mighty uncomfortable lying in the sand like this. Hell! He was hard again.

Sometime later, Tibbie and Beth were finishing their snack. Precious, having polished off the leftovers, was snoring from his corner of the blanket. Nick was debating whether or not he would interrupt this scene when Tibbie's sister appeared down the beach, walking toward them.

"Hullo!" she called. "Tibbie, hullo!"

"Mairi," Tibbie shouted back and waved. "Come join us!"

Mairi came to the edge of the blanket and stopped. "I can't. Mama sent me to find you. Mrs. Rafferty is coming to give Beth her piano lesson. Did you forget?"

Tibbie clamped her hands over her mouth. "Oh, saints preserve us! I did forget. What time is it?" she asked, fumbling around in the basket, looking for her timepiece. "Half past four! My goodness! We've been here since one!"

"I know. Mama was afraid you two had drowned. 'Course, Granny said that wasn't likely, since you promised to stay on the beach and out of the water." Mairi eyed Tibbie's wet dress, the tangled hair. "Looks like Granny was wrong." She laughed. "You'd better let Beth come on back with me, while you try to get yourself in some kind of order. You look like you've been sorting briars."

"What is that supposed to mean?"

"It means you're a mess and you know what Mama will say."

Tibbie had a pretty fair idea, and that was enough to make her agree with Mairi. "Okay, you take Beth on up to the house. I'll be along shortly."

"Take all the time you need," Mairi said with a teasing grin, her eyes traveling slowly over her sister. "You're gonna need it." With that, she grabbed Beth's arm and took off, dodging the fistful of sand Tibbie flung at her. "You never could hit the broad side of a barn, Tib," she said, laughing.

"Well, you're certainly as broad as one, so you should know," Tibbie called after her.

For some time, Tibbie sat there, digging her toes into the warm sand, staring out across the water. With a drowsy sigh, she stretched out across the blanket. "I'll close my eyes for just five minutes," she said, feeling warm and full and terribly sleepy.

Half an hour later Nick was standing over her, fighting the impulse that was almost stronger than he; an impulse to drag her into his arms and hold her against him, kissing away all signs of protest. He looked at her tranquil face. Dear God! To sleep like that, to sleep that peacefully once again. A swelling tenderness flared briefly, extinguished before he could give in to the feeling. To continue this dogged pursuit wasn't, in all likelihood, in her best interest. But there were some things a man had to do. And seeing this through to the end was one of them.

For what seemed ages Nicholas had watched her, allowing her carefree frolicking to heighten his passion for her, knowing it would only make it more difficult on him when the time came to turn away. *Get out of here, old man. Now! Quickly! Before you do something you'll both regret.*

But Nicholas Mackinnon had always been a stubborn man. His eyes traveled over her. He had seen sleeping women before. Many times. And mostly without a stitch on. But never had he watched a woman sleep like this. Sweet. Peaceful. Content. And so damn beautiful, he ached.

He closed his eyes, hoping to diminish or at least ease the painful swelling in his groin. But it was no use. Every detail was etched on the back of his lids, every wonderful, feminine curve, every mole, each indecently long lash that framed those amber eyes. Observing her as much as he had over the past weeks, Nick had learned that everything this girl did, she did with passion, including sleeping.

Would that extend to lovemaking as well?

He listened to the soft, gentle lapping of the waves washing over warm sand. In the distance a gull cried out. The sun was warm upon his face, the wind gentle at his back. It was quiet here. Peaceful. Like an uninhabited island. He let his thoughts run amok, imagining himself marooned with her on an island, having her all to himself for months and months, no longer having to steal snatches of time, or spend hours trying to catch a glimpse of her. More elusive than a mud minnow, she was. Always darting in and out of his line of vision with the same frequency she flitted in and out of his mind. With a sigh, he opened his eyes.

She was looking at him as though she were having some difficulty focusing.

"Well," he said, "what have we here? A piece of driftwood? A beached mermaid? A tangle of shapely seaweed? Tell me, just how did you manage to escape Poseidon, little beauty?"

"Luck," she said, so softly that only the slow outrush of breath confirmed she had spoken at all, then she closed her eyes. She opened them quickly, as if she had just, at that moment, realized he was there and she had talked to him.

"What do you want?"

What did he want? He dropped down to his knees beside her and she responded by hastily coming to a sitting position and giving her attention to loading the picnic basket. What did he want? Desire surged through him. She had released more of her inhibitions, had given more of herself to her frolic in the surf than any woman had ever given him in bed.

"What are you doing here?" she asked, using more volume, showing more irritation this time.

"You might say I've come to collect my hour of your time. You've been mighty frugal with honoring your word."

"Something tells me you've had your hour and then some. How long have you been watching?"

He grinned. "Long enough to know you're half water sprite."

He saw the smooth, peaceful look of tranquility ease from her face, replaced by the one he was so familiar with: hard, wary, controlled.

Involuntarily, his hand came out and slipped around her

neck, his fingers lacing through the hair at her nape, his thumb stroking the hollow in her throat, as if this one, insignificant action would still the fear that he sensed so strongly he could almost smell it. "You've nothing to fear from me," he said as he leaned toward her.

She had the sweetest mouth—succulent, warm, soft—sweet as tree-ripened fruit. Nuzzling her with his nose, he learned her fragrance—woman, sunshine, and salty air. He felt his knees tremble, recognized the quiver trapped along the length of his arm. How long had it been since he felt this schoolboy awkwardness? Is that what her innocence did to him?

And she was innocent, in spite of her bastard child.

At first she didn't seem to react to him at all, kissing him like the piece of driftwood he had accused her of being. Then the faintest flutter of warm, fragrant breath brushed against his cheek and he turned his head to draw it in, to mingle with his own breath. There was something potent about her brand of freshness, something that stayed with him as a reminder of who she was and what he was about, like a new pair of shoes that pinched his toes. His hands came up under her arms to lock across her back as he lifted her up, and drew her against him.

From the moment she had opened her eyes and realized he was no dream, no vision from her healthy imagination, Tibbie felt separated from herself. And for the last few minutes, she had been desperately trying to find her other half; that curious, expressive side of her nature that was too inquisitive, too prone to snap judgments, too quick to submit. Finding him here had surprised her. And so had his kiss. And the way he had kissed her was startling. The way it made her feel was terrifying. All she could do was repeat to herself, *Tibbie, haven't you learned anything? Are you still on that same road to destruction you walked down with Eric? Have you no inkling of what this man is about, what he wants?*

Nicholas felt her resistance and increased the pressure, twisting his hands more tightly in her hair until she almost cried out from pain. "Stop! You're hurting me!" But he only kissed her harder, an agonized groan coming from deep in his throat. "Please!" she said in a breathless whisper. "What do you want from me?"

"I want you," he said. "I want you to kiss me like you mean it."

She took a swing at him and he chuckled. "I ask you to kiss me, little hothead. In case you don't know, that isn't an insult!"

"It is as far as I'm concerned!"

"Good Lord! How would you react if I said I wanted to bed you?"

He didn't have to wait long for the answer to that one, for she boxed his ears good and proper this time. "You pervert! You . . . you . . . You scaly-tongued lizard!"

His ears were still ringing, both from the boxing and the dressing down, but that only served to push his rampant male drive higher—and it was high enough as it was. His brief surge of anger at having his ears boxed dissolved quickly, and his only form of punishment was to pull his arms around her more tightly, pressing her hard against him with insistent pressure and washing away her feelings of caution and restraint. He kissed her hard, not coaxing her lips apart, but demanding, plunging his tongue into her mouth.

Tibbie was restless and uneasy. She had called herself experienced and knowledgeable about men—after all, did she not bear a child? But now her confidence was severely undermined. As Nick kissed her, his control slipping away as his passion mounted, Tibbie was acutely conscious of her pitifully poor knowledge about the opposite sex.

Her mind, she knew, was rational and functioning, but his kisses left her reeling, and feeling as if someone were forcing brandy down her throat. She knew what he was about. She knew what she should do about it. But somewhere between knowing and performing, the urge was lost. Almost eagerly Tibbie leaned against him, thinking of how good it felt to be held like this, if only for a moment, not realizing the devastating effect her young body had on a man like Nick. He groaned in a way she could only describe as frantic, his arms crushing her against him, his mouth invading and demanding and filling her with thoughts she had no business thinking.

But it had been so long since she had felt the closeness of a man, the soft pressure of a determined mouth against hers. Her sensible half reminded her about guilt and shame.

Deeds and consequences. Sorrow and pain. Punishment and suffering. She couldn't go through all of that again.

He kissed her again and she broke away. "If it's a response you're looking for, you're wasting your time. Your kisses move me about as much as eating raw liver."

"If I ever thought you had actually stooped to eat raw liver, I might be concerned. As it stands, you're doing nothing more than muddying up the water with all this thrashing about. Now, why don't you behave yourself and kiss me back. It's what you want to do, and you know it!"

She pushed against him, breaking his hold on her. When his hand came out, she slapped it away. "Keep your hands to yourself. I don't like to be mauled."

A hard freeze seemed to catch and hold his features in a stony expression she could only call anger. "You don't like anything that requires freedom or feeling," he said.

"I have my reasons."

His features thawed. "Yes," he said, softly stroking her cheek, "you do." He smiled awkwardly, and her heart, traitor that it was, swelled at the sight of it. He was getting through to her, cracking her thin ice shell, penetrating her frozen defenses. She felt herself weakening, forgetting, for a moment, her reasons to be bitter and withdrawn. But only until he said:

"But those aren't reasons enough to deny yourself, to spend the rest of your days on earth in eternal punishment. You've set yourself up as judge and jury. You have no right to condemn the good people of Indianola for their judgmental attitudes, their lack of understanding, their readiness to cast stones. You're your own worst enemy, Tibbie. You punish yourself far more than all these other things put together. It's time you stopped."

"Why? So I can be your victim?"

"My victim? Now, that's a rather morbid way of looking at it, don't you think?"

"Not when you know what I know."

He laughed. "Tibbie, my girl, I have a feeling you don't know anything more than the basic rudiments."

"I know enough," she said crossly.

He laughed at that. "Perhaps you do, but then, when has bare necessity ever been enough? You don't strike me as a woman to be long satisfied with the mediocre or average. You're the kind to go whole hog, an all or nothing sort of girl."

"You don't make sense!" she said, still sounding cross.

"Sweet, sweet little innocent," he said softly, touching his fingers to her lips.

"I'm no innocent," she said. "Anything but. You know that as well as I!"

"Do I?"

"You've seen the proof of my foolishness."

"Is that what it was? Foolishness?"

"I can call it no other name . . . save stupidity."

He caught her chin in his tapered fingers, his eyes boring into hers like piercing flames of light. Leaning toward her a fraction more, his words were concise and sharply flung, like a knife. "Why call it anything at all, save your past, for that is what it is. Your past. Something that is done with, over. Something that can't reach out and hurt you, unless you allow it."

"Shut up!" she screamed, clamping her hands over her ears. "I don't have to listen to this."

"Then you're a fool."

She glared at him in a way that was both intense and bitter. "Perhaps I am, Mr. Know-It-All, but then, that is my affair, is it not?"

"And the child? Beth? What about her?"

"Leave her out of this."

"Why? She's been left out of enough."

"In what way?"

"In denying yourself, you deny the child as well."

"I've denied her nothing. I devote myself to her."

"Yes, you do. But there are things that are impossible for you to give her."

"Then she doesn't need them."

"Every child has a right to, and needs, a father."

"She has a father!"

"Not one she knows. Not one to give her the love and security that is different from a mother's, love and security that only a father can give."

"She has my father."

"Who is too tired, too old, and too overworked to give her the attention and companionship needs. You'll end up passing this abhorrence you have for men on to your daughter. She will grow up fearing and disliking men. Is that what you want? To grow old watching her deny herself like you did, to watch her shrivel on the vine? Your daughter may not be as fortunate as you, she may never know what it's like to be a mother, and she'll have you to thank for it. When she's a grown woman, hardened and soured on life, do you think she'll look back and thank you?"

"She's no fool, Mr. Mackinnon. Beth is a smart child. She'll understand when she's old enough."

"If you believe that, then you really are an innocent."

"I told you not to call me that. Your persistence is nothing but mockery! I am no innocent! Far from it!"

His sudden laughter startled her. "You've had a man awaken your passions, sweet Tibbie, but nothing more. No man has touched your heart."

"And no man will!"

His eyes held hers. "Are you so sure of that?"

"Certain as well as positive."

"I think not. I think that's why you're afraid of me."

"I'm not afraid of you."

"Then come here," he said.

"No," she said, scooting back across the blanket.

He lifted one brow. "Then you are afraid of me, just as I thought."

"I'm not afraid. I don't like you, but I'm not afraid of you."

"Then come here."

She looked around her, like she was hoping to find help. He almost pitied her then, but he knew she had had enough of pity. She needed something stronger than pity. Something much stronger. Nicholas knew what she needed. He just wasn't sure how to go about giving it to her.

"One of these days you're going to wake up to your feelings."

"I doubt it. I haven't any . . . at least none where you're concerned."

He had the gall to laugh. "Oh, you'll come around soon enough. I'm a patient man . . . very patient."

I'd give five years' income to be on that island I've dreamed about with you. His eyes went over her thoroughly. *Make that ten . . .*

"You can wait until you get bunions on your"—her cheeks colored—"You can wait till doomsday, for all I care. I won't ever submit to you. I won't ever let you inside my heart. Never! Ever!"

His smile curled around her like a warm hand. "Many a drop is spilt 'twixt the cup and the lip, sweet face. You'd do well to remember that next time."

"There won't be a next time," she snapped, but Nicholas Mackinnon simply smiled as he came to his feet. He reached out and took her chin in his hand, staring down into her upturned face. "Many a drop," he said tapping her nose as a reminder, and then he turned away.

She watched him walk down the beach, then disappear over the rippled rise of dunes, the waves closing in swiftly to erase his footprints, as if he had never come. But the footprints he had left upon her heart. . . . What of those?

8

Besides Nicholas Mackinnon, church was the second-highest source of disquietude in Tibbie Buchanan's life.

"To commit a lustful act is a sin, but I tell you now that even to think lustful thoughts is a sin."

The Reverend Woolridge always made Tibbie a little uneasy whenever he decided to preach on moral issues. And today was no exception. Truthfully speaking, she had been thinking lustful thoughts. She had been thinking about Nicholas Mackinnon. That man was about as lustful as they came. Of course, it really wasn't Nick's fault that she was feeling a little guilty, no more than it was the reverend's fault that she was thinking about lustful things.

She might have been spared those feelings today had Granny not called her attention to what the reverend was saying. For it wasn't until Granny Grace placed her hand over her ample bosom, and said, "At my age, lustful thoughts is about all I have left," that Tibbie was aware she had mentally strayed from the sermon to become lost in her own thoughts.

She looked around her, noticing that everyone sat calm as a clock listening to the Reverend Woolridge talk, and this made her think she was the only person in the whole congregation that must be thinking lustful thoughts—and more than likely the only one who needed to be listening to the sermon.

When the reverend said, "I want to see every head bowed and every eye closed as we bow in prayer," Tibbie followed suit, claiming the reverend's words as her own, until he said,

"Cleanse this wretched vessel, Oh Lord! Give me chastity. Give me abstinence and self-restraint—"

"Don't pray for that!" Granny Grace whispered, her hand closing over Tibbie's and giving it a squeeze. "You'll have plenty of time for that later, when you're my age."

Tibbie opened one eye and looked at the dear and beloved woman sitting on her right; a woman possessed of the uncanny ability of knowing just what she was thinking. Once when she had asked Granny why this was, Granny had said quite simply, "Why? Because you're just like me! That's why!"

On Tibbie's left, Beth was squirming and Tibbie gave her a stern look, but that only caused Beth to look the other way. Beth was having "one of those days," the kind mothers abhor. A few seconds later Tibbie had to remind her, "Don't rustle your petticoats."

"Why? Because Jesus doesn't like me to?"

"No, because the Reverend Woolridge doesn't."

A few minutes later, Tibbie whispered to her again. "Close your eyes when we pray."

"Why? Because the Reverend Woolridge wants me to?"

"No, because I want you to be respectful."

A few minutes later that was followed by, "Don't turn around and stare at the people behind you."

"Why? Because you don't like it?"

"No. Because the people don't like it."

A short time later Tibbie was about to tell Beth not to sit up on her knees when Coll leaned across Beth and said to Tibbie, "We're about to receive Communion. Tell your grandmother not to drain the cup."

Tibbie passed the reminder on to Granny, who simply snorted and mumbled something under her breath. Tibbie then turned her attention back to the sermon, until Beth began yanking on her sleeve. Giving Beth a reproving look, Tibbie tried to focus her attention once more, only to have Beth tug harder. "What?" Tibbie whispered.

"What is everlasting life?"

"It's when you live forever."

"Like cats?"

"Cats don't live forever."

"Grandma said cats have nine lives."

"Yes, and after the ninth one, they die."

"Oh," Beth said, frowning. "Will I have everlasting life?"

Tibbie patted Beth's hand. "I'm sure you will. Now, be quiet."

Beth was quiet for a minute or so, then tugging on Tibbie's sleeve once more, she said, "When will I get it?"

"What?"

"Everlasting life."

"When you die."

"How can I have everlasting life if I'm dead?"

Tibbie Buchanan folded her hands in her lap and thought about that. After a moment or two, she leaned toward Beth and whispered, "Ask your grandpa."

On her way out of church, when she was just leaving the pew, Tibbie glanced up and caught sight of Nicholas Mackinnon. He was leaving the pew just behind them, stepping into the aisle just as Tibbie did. He turned those disturbing eyes of his upon her. "If your father doesn't know, tell Beth I'll be happy to explain everlasting life to her," he said, his eyes going over her with methodical scrutiny and an all-too-brazen boldness.

Her temper flared, but she remained in control. Some comments didn't deserve answers. She was no longer smiling, and if he couldn't see her putdown in that, he should have seen it in the stony countenance, the haughtily lifted head, the quelling look in her eyes.

All around them feet were shuffling; behind her someone coughed, reminding them it was time to move out. Tibbie looked around quickly for Beth, spotting her several pews ahead, walking out with her grandfather. Without looking at Nick again, she yanked her skirts aside and swept by him. *How dare he embarrass me like this, and in church!*

Nick leaned against the pew for a moment, dipping his head at an overstuffed matron and her homely daughter, who melted into smiles. But Nick's eyes were already locked upon another. He was watching that golden-haired temptress with the most superb figure—slender where it should be, swelling where it counted most—as she hurried away from him, the drab tones of her gray dress doing nothing to hide what Tibbie so obviously desired to hide. In retreat, she had the most regal yet supple form he had ever laid eyes upon.

His eyes caught on the tiny pearl buttons that ran from her curl-fringed nape to the small but deliciously draped and rippling train that billowed behind her.

How long would it take me to undo all of those adorable little buttons?

Too damn long, he told himself, for Nick was feeling more and more impatient as the days went by.

"That was quite a sermon, Reverend," said Granny Grace.

Taking Granny Grace's hand, the Reverend Woolridge said, "Why, thank you, Granny Stewart, I'm glad you liked it."

"I didn't say I liked it," said Granny.

Dropping Granny's hand, the Reverend Woolridge said, "Oh . . . yes . . . well, I do think the subject matter was appropriate . . . with spring just around the corner." He took Coll's hand and ignored Granny.

Tibbie looked at her father as Coll said, "You seemed to have everyone's attention with that sermon today, Reverend."

"Yes, I think I did," replied the Reverend Woolridge, giving Coll's hand a pumping shake. "I had them glued to their seats."

"How wise you were to do that," said Granny.

Standing by the carriage, Tibbie had her eyes on Beth, who was looking at Dorothea Winterbury's kittens. She thought how sly Dorothea's mother had been in bringing the box of kittens to church to give away. What mother could resist?

Beth fussed over the box for a long while, and then smiling, reached into the box and drew out a small, furry ball, which she promptly held aloft—in her mother's direction, of course—and said, "Can I?"

"No!" said Tibbie. "A thousand times no."

"But I want a kitten!"

"Fine," said Tibbie. "You get rid of Precious and you can have a kitten."

Apparently Beth knew when she was bested, or so thought Nick as he approached, for Beth put the kitten back into the box. A moment later she scampered over to stand beside Mairi, who let her hold her parasol. Nick looked at Tibbie, standing beside the carriage, her attention given to a pair of gloves she was pulling on. He felt a slow yearning to pull those gloves off and kiss each one of those delicate, but long, fingers of hers—after he gave her a piece of his mind for sending him that note and backing out of her promise to go to the Independence Day dance with him. He didn't believe that story about her sudden illness for a minute. She looked like the picture of health to him.

"Tibbie," came Nick's voice in soft tones behind her. She smoothed her hand over the last glove and looked up, catching the full effect of sunlight on those mastering blue eyes. For a moment she felt stunned, compelled to stand there and hear him out as best she could in spite of the drumming of her heartbeat in her ears, the spinning in her head.

"I must admit," she replied, amazed at the steadiness of her voice, "that church is the last place I ever expected to see you. Your regularity astounds me."

"Even us heathens have a moment of respite now and then. Do you find church a soothing balm for your conscience, Miss Tibbie?"

"A most effective one," she agreed.

"It makes life a little easier to take," he said like a suggestion.

"Almost filled with hope," she answered.

"And makes the sin-filled past fade into oblivion."

"I don't know about that," she said slowly, "perhaps you could enlighten me."

He laughed. "Ahhh, always the wasp with her stinger out. I had hoped that the good parson's sermon would soften you—"

"So I might repeat my sins of the past? If that's why you are here—"

"No," he said softly. "I never meant to imply that. Forgive me if it sounded so to you. It's not my way."

She knew how his way was: Kill them with kindness. She turned away from him. "I have a grand headache in the making, Mr. Mackinnon. If you don't mind—"

"Perhaps my presence will take your mind off it."

She whirled around, facing him once more. "Why are you here? It's obvious to everyone . . . the way you've practically flaunted yourself at church."

"I wanted to see you . . . hoped to catch you with a free moment."

"Why?"

"I want to talk to you."

"I can't imagine why. You know more about me than I do. We no longer have anything to talk about. And it is obvious to me that we have exhausted even those topics you manage to dredge up. Please go away."

"I believe you owe me some explanation."

"About what?"

"About the Independence Day dance."

"I sent you a note, didn't you get it?"

"Oh, yes, every lying word. You weren't any more sick than I am, were you?"

She looked at him for a moment, and he thought she was going to lie to him again. "No," she said calmly, "I wasn't."

"Then why did you lie?"

"I was trying to spare your feelings."

"You could have spared me a lot more by going with me. Why didn't you?"

"Primarily, because I'm not ready to face all the tongues that would surely wag if I were to go to a dance with you or any other man. Surely you can understand that."

"I can," he said. "But you could have told me."

"I'm telling you now." She whirled around and walked quickly away. He followed in a slow rambling way that wasn't

obvious. Passing a few feet from where she stood beside her
father, he heard her say, "I need some time alone, Papa. I'm
going to walk home."

"Walk? Are you sure? It's—"

"I'm sure. Tell Mama I'll be there in time to eat."

"And Beth?"

"She's with Mairi. I've already spoken to them."

"Enjoy your walk," he said, and she turned away.

Nick untied his chestnut, taking his time leading him along
the path that cut through the cemetery. When he came out on
the other side, he caught sight of Tibbie, her golden head reflecting light like a beacon in the distance. She was quite a way
ahead of him, and judging from her direction, walking toward
the beach. He mounted and headed the chestnut slowly in the
same direction.

He dismounted when he caught up to her, sure she had
heard him and a little irked that she chose not to acknowledge
his presence. He said thickly, "How long must we continue at
this cat and mouse game until you start being honest with
yourself?"

He observed the sudden tension in her stiffly held shoulders
and when she turned on him, saw the widening of her eyes in
surprise. Her coloring was so vivid to him now, in the full
impact of the sun's brightness. He saw the flaring nostrils and
the way her eyes picked and held all the gold that was in the
sunlight. Her mouth was set, and berry blushed, and very, very
kissable.

"Please, it would be best if I wasn't seen talking to you. It
can only cause problems for me. It would be best if you . . ."
She was distraught, her golden eyes looking at him with the
panic of a trapped animal, and he understood how she felt, for
he knew that if he did the decent thing, he would leave her
alone.

The sun blinded him, engulfing him in a molten, white ball.
The ocean roared so in his ears that he wondered if a gale had
come, unannounced and sudden. He was still looking at her,
but found his thoughts confused, his words jumbled. The roar

began to diminish. His eyes regained their focus. The sun faded in importance.

"It's a little late for that and you know it," he whispered.

She studied him calmly, but he knew she had sensed something was about to happen. She took a step backward. He took one forward. The sun was glaring again, growing warmer. She backed away further, looking at him in a concerned way. He continued to advance. She turned away quickly and ran until she could go no farther, her way blocked by a small stream—a result of the recent rains—cutting a path across the beach on its way to the sea. She stopped abruptly, looking frantically in one direction and then the other, seeing her route of escape cut off. She whirled and faced him, looking as magnificent and battle ready as her ancestors must have at the battle of Culloden. He was close enough now to hear her breathing, quick and uneven. He could almost smell her fear.

The color was gone from her cheeks. Distress ate at her until her stomach lurched. How long would he pursue her? As long as it took. He wasn't a man to give up. Nicholas Mackinnon was becoming a part of her life. And deep within her she knew she wanted it.

"No," she said with a shaky voice, "Dear God, no! Why can't you leave me alone?"

"You know why, Tibbie. And you don't want me to leave you alone."

She brought her arm up before her, as a knight would raise a shield. She looked to her left, and then to her right. She was trembling now and he could see the nervous quiver that claimed her lips. It was more to still her trembling than to nourish his crushing desire that he reached for her. But once he touched her, once she was in his arms, all resolve, all that he could call self-restraint was lost. He caught her arm, bringing his other hand out to capture the other one as it came up in self-defense. What he had seen was now supported by what he could feel; her flesh beneath his fingers was seized by quick, strong tremors.

The sun disappeared, passing into insignificance behind a

thick, gray cloud. The water took on a dull, brown cast, the wind seemed to carry more of a chill. A light sprinkling of rain misted the earth around them, but neither of them moved.

This time she did not shy from him, or attempt to pull away. He stepped nearer, bringing his body full against hers. She turned her head to one side, this small effort seemingly costing her much. He caught her chin and turned her face back to him, seeing the fine droplets that collected on her lashes, seeing the way their breaths joined, rising between them as one.

Now he was conscious of her, the way her heart thundered against his chest, the pulsing of her blood beneath his hands, the soft flutter of her breath coming soft against his face. That which he had thought velvet was, as he now learned, no more than cheap, coarse cotton, having a velvety sheen in the places it had worn thin. He knew she could afford more. It angered him to see her like this, to know why she did this to herself. His fingers dug deeper into her arms. "Why are you doing this to me?" she whispered.

"I wish to God I knew," he said softly, nuzzling her ear with his nose. He heard her indrawn breath just as she pulled away, looking at him with eyes that were passion-bright and confused. Something twisted inside his chest, a gentle emotion that urged him to let her go. And he wanted to, but this need to be with her was stronger, more potent than anything he had heretofore experienced. It was odd, but he sensed it was really the same for her too, because he saw the flicker of resistance shine brightly then fade before his very eyes. At that moment she released a strangled little cry, covering her face with her hands, and he knew she was like a small skiff lost at sea, wind-tossed and going in circles, and the reality of it touched him with a new, more violent force. He drew her closer still. She understood fully that he intended to kiss her. He came closer, surprising her when he said in an almost savage, pain-filled voice, "Get away from me, Tibbie. Go! Now!"

The savagery alone would have sent her running. Or even the scraping sound of pain in his voice. But the look of gentleness in his eyes—that quiet weight bore down heavily upon her and she was unable to move. "I can't," she whispered.

His arms came swiftly around her and he buried his face against the fragrant slope of her neck and shoulder, pulling her against the blistering heat of his body. Placing soft kisses along her neck from her shoulder to her ear, he let his hands coax the stiffness from her body before coming up to plunge into the wild, thick honey of her hair, releasing it from its knot so it was whipped over her face and his by the wind. His fingers dug deeper and he heard her moan. With a fierce, twisting groan that ripped his insides, he pulled her face toward him, covering her mouth with his own.

"Tibbie," he whispered, breaking the kiss and feeling the softness of her breasts against him and knowing her heart must be beating as frantically as his. "I'm like a wild man when you're in my arms."

She pulled away and turned to look off in the distance. "When I was little I had a rowboat, and I was caught in a storm and it capsized just as my father's boat reached me. The water closed over my head and I couldn't see anything and I knew I was going to die. At that moment, I felt like I was in a strange new place, suspended and floating somewhere between life and death, yet strangely I wasn't afraid. That's when my father found me and I felt his arms come around me as he pulled me to the surface. That's the way I feel when I'm around you, like I'm going to die, but I'm not afraid." She turned back to look at him. "And I don't know what I'm going to do about that," she whispered. Then she looked at him, as if she were just waking from a dream, then she turned, running and falling, crossing the shallow stream, falling and getting up, falling again.

Seeing her fall, he started toward her, but she was up again, the water-logged weight of her skirts pulling her back down. Her face was wet, but she didn't know if it was from tears or rain. She didn't care. Like Eve, she felt suddenly naked, for Nick had managed with those kisses to open her eyes to too many things she had fought so hard to cover up. To feel a man's arms about her; to know the softness of his mouth after so much time. Whatever she had felt before for Eric, it was so much stronger this time.

A need too long denied is what she chose to call it, telling herself there wasn't anything special about this man. Nothing special at all. But even as she thought those things, she knew she had to get away from him. Quickly. To flee was the only resource she had.

He reached her and pulled her to her feet, holding her dripping body against him. He would have kissed her again, for indeed he wanted to, but something in her eyes held him. "Damn you," she said. "Damn you to hell for what you've done!"

"Give in," he said. "Let me love you the way you were meant to be loved."

"I can't," she said, feeling the urge to cry more strongly now, and knowing a more urgent need to get away.

"I'll never leave you alone," he said, his voice breaking. "I'll follow you to your grave if I have to. You know that. What I feel . . . you can't deny it. . . . You feel it as well."

"I don't know what I feel! I should hate you . . . indeed, I *want* to."

"But you can't, Tib. Love is a stronger emotion than hate."

"I don't love you," she said.

"You do," he said confidently. "You just don't know it yet."

He pulled her against him, feeling her body in more detail now through the wet clothes. He lowered his head, putting his hand at the nape of her neck to draw her toward him.

"No!" she said, gasping for breath. Then with a small cry she shoved him away, turning from him at the same time and running up the beach.

He watched her, feeling suddenly deprived and cold. The rain was coming down harder now, in liquid sheets and carrying a chill. He sat in the middle of the stream, on his rump, where he had landed when she shoved him, his boots filling with sand and water, his best hat lying upside down next to him, filling with water . . . and his horse? He looked around him seeing nothing but flatness, all brown and gray. The chestnut could be halfway to hell by now.

He felt a sudden cramp in his fingers and he lifted his hand, staring stupidly as the sand and water fell away. With a blank expression he opened his hand, feeling dullwitted and slow to comprehend. Lying in his palm was a gray button, a few tangled strands of Tibbie's hair wound tightly around its base. He sat there, the rain falling all about him, and stared for a long, long time at that button in his hand—until the rain stopped and the sun was dropping low in the western sky.

→ 9 ←

The first day of April is a good day for fools, as any fool knows.

"Answer a fool according to his folly, is what the Good Book says," Miss Merriweather had said only that morning when she had dropped by Nick's house on her way to town.

Later that morning, when Nick had hurried Porter along, citing how late they were on the shipbuilding project, Porter had lamely said, "Fools rush in where angels fear to tread."

And so it was on this fine April day that Nick, standing on the scaffolding in the shipyard, kept finding his mind wandering from what Porter was saying to thoughts about Tibbie. And that made his concentration slip, which as it turned out, wasn't the only thing that slipped that day. As the sign over the doorway said: IT IS THE FATE OF THE COCONUT HUSK TO FLOAT, OF THE STONE TO SINK.

Unfortunately for Nick in this particular case, he had more in common with the stone than the coconut husk. He didn't sink exactly, but he did fall—some twenty feet off the scaffolding when it gave way. As he lay on the ground waiting for Doc Buchanan to arrive, he suddenly remembered hearing, in spite of the pain he was in, what Porter had said mere seconds before he fell. *Don't step on those boards near the edge, they haven't been nailed down yet.*

To keep his mind off how much he was hurting, Nick went back to thinking about Tibbie. But before long, he decided that dreaming about being marooned on a deserted island with a beautiful woman is as good a way as any to drive a man quietly and safely insane. It also makes him jumpy as hell, cross as an old, wounded bear, and unfit company even for himself. Feeling the ache in his groin, he told himself, *It isn't a good idea, old man, to dream of cream when you live on skim milk.*

Over the past two weeks, Nick had doubled his efforts to get Tibbie Buchanan alone, which wasn't something he had to push himself to do, since he couldn't stop thinking about their meeting on the beach that Sunday. Yet he knew, even as he pursued her so relentlessly, he was taking much needed time away from his shipbuilding. Already he had received a letter from the owner, asking when he could expect completion. And what had he done? Tried to hurry things along, that's what he had done. And in the process, he'd been careless. Something he would've fired any other man for.

By now the pain was getting the upper hand, shoving Nick's thoughts aside. He lay in agony for what seemed to be an eternity before blessedly losing consciousness. When he opened his eyes next, he was in Dr. Buchanan's clinic. He hurt like hell, and could only guess he must've passed out from pain. He watched Coll Buchanan. It was easy to see that he and Tibbie were related, for all the old sawbones did was poke and prod, screwing his mouth this way and that, while shaking his head in an ominous fashion.

Then Coll reached for a bottle and said, "I'll give you a little of this and you'll sleep like a baby."

Nick, who didn't like the way Dr. Buchanan kept poking at his right leg, feared the worst. "I don't want to be put to sleep. I want to be good and awake when you start getting ideas about cutting any of my limbs off."

"I don't practice deceptive medicine. I don't have time for it. I'm too busy delivering babies to babies that haven't been paid for yet, and hauling cords of wood, chickens, pigs, cabbages, potatoes, and goats to the bank for deposit, since that's my most customary form of payment."

"I'll pay you in cold, hard cash if I leave here with everything I came in with. But I don't want to be knocked out."

"Suit yourself," Coll said, "but from what all I can see,

you're busted up pretty good. Some of this is going to hurt like hell." He gave Nick's leg a hard yank, and Nick let loose with a curse.

"You could give me some warning."

"I just told you it would hurt like hell. You look more dead than alive."

"Then why don't you cover me with lilies and be done with it?"

Coll looked at him over glasses that had slipped down his nose and gave his leg another tug. "It's more fun this way."

"Sonofabitch!" Nick shouted. "That hurts like hell! What are you trying to do? Unscrew my legs?"

"He can't be as bad off as he looks," Coll said, turning to Porter. "A nasty temper is a good indication."

"His temper is always nasty," Porter said. "So where does that leave us?"

"I won't be flat on my back forever," Nick said, his words sounding like a low growl. "You'd best be watching your tongue, Porter." He finished with a painful grimace.

"I will," Porter said. He turned to Coll. "You think he'll be all right?"

Coll looked at the bruised and battered body lying in front of him, lingering for a moment on the white sliver of bone that had punctured his leg. "He's leaking blood like a sieve, and he's broken his wrist, both legs, and has more cuts than I can count, and he'll be black as sin over half of his body tomorrow, but he'll make it." Coll looked at Nick and shook his head. "Hear you fell off the scaffolding. That's coming down the hard way, if you ask me."

"I didn't ask you," said Nick.

"Yep," said Coll. "A real nasty disposition. He'll make it just fine." Nick grimaced and closed his eyes.

A minute or two after Porter left, Tibbie walked into the room. "Granny said you were looking for me. I was in the—" She froze when her eyes went to Nick. "Oh, my God! What happened?" Her eyes flew to Mairi, hoping to find the answer, but there was no hint of emotion on Mairi's white face. When she saw her father shake his head, Tibbie whispered to Mairi, "Is he dead?"

"Miraculously, no," Coll answered.

"He looks dead to me," Mairi said.

"He probably wishes he was," Coll said.

"What happened?" asked Tibbie.

"He took quite a nasty fall," said Coll.

Tibbie came to Nick's side; her only awareness was of him. She knew she was moving and that each step was followed by another and that those were tears she felt so warm against her eyelids. She stopped when she reached the bed and stared unblinkingly down at his perspiring face. His mouth was opened slightly, and he appeared to be wrestling for each breath. The sudden memory of the times she had been with this man left her with a terrible fear of what might happen. Mairi saw Tibbie's face grow paler, saw the way she gripped the side of the bed, and she came to stand between Tibbie and Coll, her face as pale as Tibbie's as she surveyed the damage.

Tibbie flinched like she'd been struck when Mairi said, "He banged himself up pretty good, didn't he? You say he fell?" Her eyes went over Nick once more.

In a voice that didn't sound like her own, Tibbie whispered, "It must have been a terribly long way."

"It was far enough to do the job right. Looks pretty bad, doesn't he?"

The control in Tibbie's mind snapped, exploding and flooding her with panic. Her voice quiet, tentative, she said, "Is he going to . . ." She paused, suddenly aware that Nick's eyes were open. She was aware of his scrutiny and the effect it had upon the color of her cheeks. Their eyes met and she felt a stab of desire so strong she was afraid she might groan.

Nick licked his dry lips. Tibbie. Lovely, uninterested Tibbie, looking so distraught and concerned. *Time,* he thought, *I need more time with her.* He didn't need to be disabled like this, to have a halt put on the progress he was making with her. He couldn't move a muscle in his entire body. How could he court her, woo her? How could he hold her and show her his passion? How could he make her understand the way he felt? And why would she want to listen to a beat-up cripple?

"He's got a difficult time ahead of him," Coll was saying, "but he'll pull through."

Nick saw Tibbie was close to tears. "Fortune favors fools," he whispered, his voice dry and cracking.

"From a foolish judge, a quick sentence," came Coll's chastening reply.

If he hadn't tried to be funny at a time like this she could have stayed in the room, but Nick's attempt at humor and knowing the pain he must be in—it was too much. Unable to stop herself or the sudden flow of tears, she clamped her hands over her mouth and rushed from the room.

"Blast and double blast! What's gotten into her?" Coll turned to Mairi. "Go see what ails your sister."

"Who? Me?"

Coll was losing his patience and snapped, "Yes, unless you see anyone else in the room."

"Humph!" snorted Mairi, sounding just like Granny Grace. "Why am I always the one that's so handy? I don't know why I have to go tell her to come back if she doesn't want to. I'll probably get my head snapped off."

"Forewarned is forearmed," Coll said and gave Nick's arm a tug. That drew a yelp of pain from Nick. "Sorry," Coll said, "but I've got to straighten these limbs before I can bind them." He glanced toward the door. "Where is that blasted daughter of mine? Underfoot all the time, and then when I need her she's as scarce as oranges in December."

A few minutes later Mairi came back. "Tibbie can't help you in the clinic today. At least not with that patient," she said, pointing to Nick.

Coll looked down at Nick. "And why not? What's she got against this man?"

"Honestly, Papa! Do you have to ask me that?"

"I suppose so, if I'm going to find out what's going on here. Tibbie has never acted like that before."

"Papa, she's afraid to come in here, afraid she'll make a fool of herself."

"She's a little late to be worrying about that. Now, I'm tired of beating around the bush. I need help and she's the only one that can give it to me. She can act like a woman later. Tell Tibbie I need her, NOW!"

Leaving the room like a shot, Mairi almost levelled Granny Grace, who stood in the doorway. Granny looked at Mairi and cackled, "Heh! Heh! Heh! It takes a clever woman to get the best of a fool!"

Mairi wasn't about to put a dog in that fight, so she ignored Granny Grace and took the stairs two at a time, calling Tibbie's name. "Tib, your goose is cooked," she said, rushing into Tibbie's room. "Papa is hopping mad and he wants you in the clinic right away."

Meanwhile, Granny Grace poked her head into the clinic. When she saw something of interest going on inside, she hobbled over to the table where Coll was working on Nick. "What happened to him?" she asked.

"He fell."

"Fell, you say?"

Coll nodded.

"Fell," she repeated. "Off what?"

Coll opened his mouth to say scaffolding, but he caught himself just in time. "Off his horse." It was a lie, of course, but as far as Granny was concerned, it was as good an explanation as any. He had work to do, and he wasn't up to giving Granny an explanation of the basic rudiments of shipbuilding. The way she messed up words she'd have a real heyday with a word like scaffolding.

"He's mighty pale," Granny said. "Pale as a gutted fish."

That brought a dry heave from Nick.

"Granny, what in the devil are you doing in here?" Coll asked.

"Well, this is my nap time and I was on my way to fetch my lap robe and take my nap."

"Since when did you start keeping your lap robe in my clinic?"

Granny didn't answer, of course, her mind having left all that talk about lap robes miles behind. She looked at Nick again. "Looks like he's been dead for quite a spell." She sniffed the air, testing the validity of her words. "You shouldn't leave bodies lying about for long. Not with the weather warming up as it is. He'll be smelling like a gut wagon in a day or so."

Nick heaved again.

"Why haven't you buried him?" Granny was asking. "Can't you find his next of kin?"

"The man isn't dead, Granny. He will probably live to be as old as you, if you'll let me get him patched up and quit interrupting my work. Now, you go on, you hear? Go find your lap robe."

If Granny heard that, she didn't let on. She looked Nick over good and proper this time. "Hmmmm. If he isn't dead, he must stay in out of the sun a lot. He's too pale. I bet he's an undertaker."

She gave Nick one last look. Then she looked at Coll, and finding him busy, she gave Nick a poke. Nick didn't budge. "You better check him again. It looks to me like you've sure-enough got yourself a dead one this time," she said.

Nick opened one eye. "Then I'd like to throttle the man that said pain doesn't hurt the dead, because I'm hurting like hell."

"That should be reassurance that you're still alive," Coll said. "Count your blessings."

Granny gave him another poke. "What's his name?"

"Nicholas Mackinnon," Coll said.

"Oh," said Granny. "Mac Nichelson . . . Hmmmm . . . I don't remember hearing anyone make any mention of Mac Nichelson having any kin—" She looked at Coll. "Who is Mac Nichelson?"

By this time Coll was ready to throw his hands up. "For the love of God! I don't know any Mac Nichelson," he said in exasperated tones.

"Then how do you know this fella is his kin?"

Coll was busy cutting the legs off Nick's trousers, so he simply shrugged, not bothering to answer—which was all right, because he didn't have an answer anyway.

That didn't bother Granny. She was used to being ignored, so she went on like normal. "You say you don't know any Mac Nichelson. Well, that makes two of us. Mac Nichelson . . ." She pondered, then shook her head, her frizzled gray curls going every which way beneath her lace morning cap. "Nope! I know I'd remember that name if I'd heard it before—"

"Good God!" Exclaimed Coll. At that moment, Nick was praying that he would mercifully lose consciousness. "Good God!" Coll said again.

Granny still wasn't discouraged—mostly because she'd been around long enough to know that whenever he was perturbed, saying *Good God!* was about as perturbed as Coll Buchanan would get. And although he would occasionally go so far as to say, *Good God Almighty!*, she wasn't intimidated by that one either. So she went on. "Well, if he's Mac Nichelson's kin, he can't be from around these parts, since we've decided we don't know any Mac Nichelson. He must've been passing through."

"Mackinnon . . . The name is Mackinnon," Nick whispered in a raw, pain-filled voice. "Nicholas Mackinnon."

Granny patted his hand. "Now, don't you worry none, Mr. Nichelson. Coll here will fix you up good and proper and then we'll find your kin." She squinted her dark eyes until they were tiny little beads. "You don't look too good," she said.

The door opened and Tibbie entered the room. "Come in, come in!" Granny said with a motion of her hand. She saw Tibbie pause, her eyes going over to Coll's patient and giving him a rather skeptical look.

"He just looks like he's dead," Granny said in her customary booming voice, "but he ain't. He's kin to Mac Nichelson and he's an undertaker. He was just passing through."

"Good God!" said Coll, wiping his hands and turning toward Tibbie.

Granny didn't pay him any more mind than she had the first time, but she did lower her voice a decibel or two to say in a loud whisper, "He was conveying one of the recently departed to the grave when he fell off his hearse." Her voice boomed again. "That's why he isn't feeling so good."

For a moment Tibbie simply stared at her grandmother. Then her eyes went to her father, who if he had been a storm cloud, looked dark enough to hail. She turned to Nick, who looked, as Granny said, like he wasn't "feeling so good."

Nick moaned and said in a hoarse whisper, "This place is a lunatic farm. Don't you have something strong you can give me?"

"I thought you said you didn't want to be put out," Coll said.

"I changed my mind. I didn't know what the alternative was when I said that," rasped Nick.

Coll nodded at Nick, then looked up. "Tibbie, get me the tincture of opium, and then *get Granny out of here!*"

Tibbie went to the medicine closet and opened the door. "What was she doing in here in the first place?"

"Looking for her lap robe."

She handed him the bottle. "In here?"

After giving Nick the drops, Coll measured a splint against Nick's leg. "Knowing your grandmother as well as you do, you still have to ask me a question like that?"

"Never mind," said Tibbie. "Come on, Granny. I saw your lap robe in the morning room."

"Don't be mourning him," Granny said. "I told you he ain't dead yet. He just looks that way."

Watching her grandmother open the door to the medicine closet, Tibbie said, "That's the medicine closet, Granny. The door is over there."

"I don't know how anyone expects me to find my way around this place, always moving the doors around and never telling me. No one ever tells me anything. I don't know how they expect me to know what's going on . . ."

She went on mumbling as Tibbie led her out.

Tibbie hurried back to her father's side and soon the call to heal, to give comfort, to perform the tasks she had done so many times before helped her lose herself in her work, forgetting for a time just whose battered body she was tending.

"He's got one nasty gash here on his thigh, where the bone protruded," Coll said, cutting away a little more of Nick's pant leg. "I've set the bone. You see to the cut. Get some yarrow roots and mash them."

"You want the pulp used as a dressing?"

"Yes. We'll let it sit there for a half hour or so, while we tend to his other wounds. That should give the root time to ease the pain so we can clean it out."

For over three hours they worked over Nick, and during this time he was mostly conscious, occasionally accepting small sips of opium to ease the pain. In between bouts of drug-induced sleep, Tibbie would catch his blue gaze resting on her face, his face pale and set, his lip beaded with perspiration. She looked at him, doing her best to keep her expression blank and her attitude professional, but she couldn't help giving him an encouraging smile, or taking a soft cloth dipped in cool water and placing it against his parched lips.

The fall had done enough damage on its own, but added to that were the cuts, gashes, and horrible bruises inflicted by the shower of lumber that fell upon him. According to Coll, Nick's friend Porter had explained the accident, saying Porter had escaped injury only because he was standing on a different section of scaffolding than the one that collapsed under Nick.

As Porter had told Coll, the only thing that saved Nick from being crushed was that the main support timber hit the ground on one end, the other end resting some five feet in the air, braced on a stack of lumber that formed a right-angled triangle. Fortunately for Nick, he had fallen in the center of the triangle, beneath the support timber, which protected him by blocking some of the heavier beams and holding them aloft and off his body. Not long after Nick had been removed, the main beam gave way. But looking at him and seeing the condition he was in, Tibbie had difficulty believing that Nick had been fortunate at all.

"There," Coll said, tying the last splint in place. "That will have to do until we take those stitches out, then I can fashion a splint that's a little stronger. By then, the swelling should be down and we'll know if there's going to be any infection."

"You think there's a good chance for that?"

"In his case, a damn good one. He sustained enough cuts, and landed in a busy section of well-traveled ground, where there was everything from horse-droppings to runoff from the city streets. Not the best exposure for open wounds." Coll removed his glasses and began cleaning them on his handkerchief. "You clean him up as best you can. Keeping his cuts and scratches clean is of primary importance here. See that you give proper attention to all the small ones we didn't suture. When you finish, get Mairi in here to help you change his bed."

"But—"

Coll looked at his watch. "Lord, where has the time flown? Looks like I'll be missing supper again tonight." He returned a few supplies to his bag. "I'll go ahead and start seeing patients. When you finish here, you can join me."

Tibbie wasn't sure how much longer she could hold up under the strain of seeing Nick like this. She needed to get out of this room, away from this place. She didn't want to see any more illness today, or any more injuries. The smell of blood and sweat still nauseated her; the vivid picture of Nick's torn and bleeding body still loomed like a nightmare in her mind. "Don't you think we've done enough here, that we need to see to the others? Don't you want me to come with you now?"

Coll looked at her for a moment like he was trying to decipher just what it was she was saying. "We never leave a job half done, Tib. You of all people should know that. Now, you see to this man's needs, then I'll put you to work."

Tibbie returned to his bedside and stood looking down at Nick, aware for the first time just how nearly naked he was. Every shred of clothing had been cut or torn away from his body, and only a small area below his midsection was covered with a bit of cotton sheeting. "Clean him up?"

Coll snapped his bag shut. "Isn't that what we usually do?"

"But he's nearly naked, Papa."

"Aha!" Coll looked at Nick, then looked at Tibbie, a glimmer of understanding lighting his eyes. "So! That's the way of it, huh?" He approached Nick's bedside and stood looking down at him. "Well, well, well. I wondered when it would happen, when some man would finally . . ." He paused, then said as he turned away, "I'll shake his hand later."

Tibbie stared after her father, thinking Coll made even less sense than she did, which wasn't saying much. With a sigh, she turned her attention back to Nick. Her only salvation here was the fact that he had been given enough doses of opium to sleep for quite a while. It was bad enough to be forced to bathe his half-naked body without his being conscious while she did it.

Not sparing a minute, she fetched a bowl of warm vinegar water and began to bathe him. Soon she had given her thorough attention to his face, arms, chest, hands, feet, and lower legs. Then she paused.

She looked at the section of sheeting.

She looked at his face.

She couldn't do it! She simply could not do it.

But then she remembered her father's admonitions. Tibbie was not a woman to do any job halfway. She was an all-or-nothing sort of woman, and that included just about everything. But looking at the well-developed male lying naked and prone before her, Tibbie fervently wished she had opted, in this particular case, for nothing.

She looked at his face again, and with a hard-set grimace of resolve, pushed the basin of vinegar water closer. Plunging her hand into the basin and fishing for the cloth, she raised it out of the water and, with her other hand, simultaneously lifted the sheeting.

The cloth fell into the basin with a loud *plop!*

Dear Mary, Jesus and Joseph! I can't wash there . . . that.
. . . But in spite of her reluctance she held her breath and lifted the sheet again, using only two fingers, as if by doing so she displayed a total lack of interest. For a moment she simply stared point-blank at that greatest of all mysteries.

Of course she had known a man, but Eric had always come to her room at night and made love to her in the dark. And of course she had seen male bodies before, but those had been the bodies of *other* men, *old* men, or babies. In spite of herself, Tibbie couldn't seem to drop the sheet, nor could she look away. She simply stared, spiraling shafts of fire shooting through her body at the sight of him. Asleep he might be. Unaware he might be. Injured he was. But there was nothing asleep or injured about what she was looking at. In fact, the longer she looked, the longer *it* became. And then slow recognition dawned.

Her eyes flew to his face and she saw, horror of horrors, that Nicholas Mackinnon, not unlike certain parts of his anatomy, was neither asleep nor unaware. She gave him a hot look. "You could have at least pretended to be asleep, you . . . you . . ."

"Perfectly normal man," he put in. "I'm sorry if that bothers you, Miss Prudie, but you'll have to tote that baggage by yourself."

"You're really enjoying this, aren't you?"

"What?"

"This opportunity to display such vulgar behavior."

Nick couldn't help feeling a stab of tenderness for his poor lass, her red face, the tears of humiliation and embarrassment lying in wait in her eyes, the overall expression of mortification. And for what? Because she'd given in to a normal curiosity? A perfectly rational fascination? A desire to see the unseen, to explore the unexplored? He remembered that this lass was no simpering, inexperienced virgin. This lass had borne a child. This lass should know what a man's body looked like and more. This lass should. But she didn't. That made Nick a little curious.

"I suggest, angel, that if you're sufficiently recovered, you refrain from doing what you're doing." When that didn't seem to soak in, he tried again. "Keep looking at me like that, and I'll display a little more vulgar behavior." When it still didn't register, he said blandly, "Sweetheart, any other time and place I'd give you free rein to look your fill, but I feel like shit, and it's colder than hell lying here with no clothes on. If I promise to give you another look when I'm up to snuff, do you think you could lower the sheet?"

With a horrified gasp, Tibbie dropped the sheet like it suddenly weighed a ton. She would have fled the room, but Nick, anticipating her move, latched onto her arm at the wrist. Tibbie collapsed in the chair next to him, her head resting facedown on the bed. For a moment he lay there, his hand still clamped tightly around her small wrist, and watched her, seeing the fine hairs of her head, the smooth braid, the edge of heated color about her ears, the heaving action of her back as she fought for breath.

"Tibbie, look at me."

She shook her head.

"Come on," he urged, giving her wrist a weak tug, "look at me."

"I can't."

"Yes, you can."

"No! I can't. Believe me! I can't ever look at you again."

He laughed.

"Are you through embarrassing me?"

"I don't want to embarrass you at all. Why should the sight of something as normal, functional, and in such common supply as a man's—" He started to call it by its proper name, penis, but thought the better of it. "Why would the sight of a man's manhood embarrass you?"

"If you have to ask that, you're loonier than I thought," she said through muffled layers of mattress and sheeting.

"Do you think I would be embarrassed at the sight of your nakedness?"

That brought her head up. "No! And we both know why!"

He refrained from smiling. "I'm afraid you've got me on that one," he said. "I haven't the faintest idea. Can you tell me?"

"Because you're a lecher and a pervert, that's why!"

"Because I'm a man?"

"Because you can't control that . . . that . . . that *thing*!"

He laughed, and just as he feared, it hurt like hell. It also sent Tibbie's head crashing back down to the bed. "I knew you'd laugh at me. I knew it."

"I see," he said finally. "Tibbie, tell me something. You say you're embarrassed. Why?"

"Good God!" she said, sounding just like Coll. "Good God!"

"If I had remained asleep, would you have been embarrassed?"

She didn't answer, so he prodded her a little, telling her that they would be there until Coll Buchanan came in and inquired about their unusual position, at which time he would be forced to tell Coll what had happened, word for word.

"You wouldn't dare!" she said, her head coming up off the bed again.

"Try me."

She tugged, trying to pull her hand back. Unable to do so, she looked away.

"Tibbie, answer me or we'll be here all night. Would you have been embarrassed if I had stayed asleep?"

She sighed. "I don't suppose so."

"Why not?"

She looked irritated now. "Because, you simpleton, if you were asleep you wouldn't have seen me, and if you didn't see me I wouldn't be embarrassed. You're only embarrassed when someone sees you."

He lost her about ten words back, but he didn't care. Just watching her was a delight. He looked at her thoughtfully and smiled. "Are you sure you're Bethany's mother?"

"What is that supposed to mean?"

"You don't seem very aware or experienced to be the mother of a child."

"I had a child, Mackinnon, I didn't conduct surveys."

He found her so utterly charming, it was hard to keep his mind on the fact that he was trying to put her at ease when what he really wanted to do was stir her up a little and heat her blood with passion.

"You assume a great deal, just like the good people of Indianola did. Don't confuse the facts. I made a mistake. I fell in love. My punishment was the ostracism I suffered; the wagging tongues, the jibes, the leering looks, the suggestive remarks, the embarrassment of being heavy with child and knowing the whole town knew I had no husband. My forgiveness was Bethany."

Nick was vaguely aware of what she was saying, but one remark stood more vividly in his mind. *I fell in love. . . . I fell in love. . . . I fell in love.* He didn't know just why it irked him so to hear her say that. It was the natural thing to expect that a woman like Tibbie wouldn't give herself to a man for any other reason. Still, it was a point of irritation, like a splinter in the thumb. His only consolation was knowing she had also said, *I made a mistake.*

He looked at her, seeing the beauty, the youth, the honesty, and then he was reminded of that day in her parlor, the revelation of how it had been for her. Small wonder that she shunned him and recoiled at his touch. She had been burned, badly. And that had taught her to stay away from the fire.

"Only people who have nothing to give hoard themselves, Tibbie. You were never meant to live that way. You have too much to give. The best way to free yourself is to talk about it."

"And what about you, Mackinnon? You're guilty of a little hoarding as well."

He looked surprised. "I am? About what?"

"Yourself. You pester me to tell you about myself, my past, even to the point of locking me in the parlor until I've told you my life story. But what about you? *You* never talk about your past."

Her words struck a chord of disharmony. He frowned. "I told you what happened to my family."

"Not really. You told me your parents were dead and your little sister was kidnapped by Indians."

"Which is true."

"Did you ever hear any more about your sister?"

"Nothing."

"And your brothers? How many do you have? Where are they now?"

His look was reflective. "Andrew, the oldest, was killed with my mother. I'm the next oldest. After me there's Tavis—he went to Nantucket with me. After Tavis, there's Ross, and—"

"Where is Ross now? Do you keep in touch with him?"

Nick grinned. "As much as I can, considering the distance between us. Ross is in Scotland, on the Isle of Skye. My parents were both Scots. Last year, we received word that a relative had died and I was the next in line for some fancy title. It didn't take me long to send word to find someone else. So they did. They wrote back and made the same offer to Ross. Damn me for a fool if he didn't take them up on it. Smart move on their part, I'd say." He shook his head. "His letters are a sight! I can't imagine my wild brother Ross playing the part of a titled gentleman, but he seems to have adapted quite well. He actually *likes* it!"

Tibbie laughed at the amazement on Nick's face. "And after Ross?"

"Twins. Adrian and Alexander, meaner than snakes, both of them!"

"Where are they now?"

"California. They joined the Texas Rangers for a while. After the war ended they heard someone yell 'Gold,' and that was it. They hightailed it for California and didn't let their shirttails hit their backs. If what they write can be believed, they're getting richer as we talk. 'Course, those two never could be stopped when they put their heads together."

"Don't you miss being with your family?"

"Lord, yes, but I've got my brother Tavis and my Uncle Robbie, so I'm not all alone."

"I would think I'd hate being away from my family."

"You feel that way now because you need them. They're a comfort and in a way a protection for you. One day you won't feel the need to stay tied to them." He saw her frown. "Cheer up, lass. Like I told you, you'll get your wings."

She ignored that last bit because she was still steamed up about what he said earlier. "I am *not* tied to them. I happen to love my family."

His gaze, still glazed with drugs and pain and not clearly focused, moved slowly over her, his hand releasing hers and lifting to stroke the curve of her face. "Poor little angel. Angel in marble. A wounded, distrustful lass reconciled to her fate, to look misfortune in the face and prove herself, with a noble heart, not to trust and not to mate." He drew the pad of his thumb across the fullness of her lower lip. "I find I like her better than the hard-hearted beauty . . . and strangely, desire her more."

➤ · 10 · ←

Tibbie armed herself with her best fulminating glare and entered the small room at the back of her father's clinic, where Nicholas Mackinnon had been moved after Coll had patched him up as best he could. But before the morning was over, she was feeling more like the frog that tried to look as big as the elephant and burst.

Some things just weren't meant to be.

She waited outside the door to his room and listened. It was getting harder and harder to face Mackinnon and act disinterested. Hearing no sounds coming through the door, she whispered a small prayer just in case: "Dear Lord, please let him be asleep." Thinking upon it further, she added: "And if you won't make him asleep, could you at least help me look fiercely strong, determined, and disinterested?"

With a deep breath of peaceful resolve, she opened the door.

She had spent the better part of the night lying in her bed awake and thinking about the things Nick had said to her. She was an organized, methodic person who liked order in her life. She was the kind of person who made a flower garden out of life and spent her time wandering along its rock-lined pathways, occasionally pulling a weed, or tossing out a stray rock —whatever was necessary to preserve order. Some things lent themselves to order. Some things did not. Nicholas Mackinnon was of the latter. Since he had come into her life, there had been nothing but disorder. He was a rock that needed to be tossed.

As she entered the room she was still praying Nick would be

asleep. Then she could put the breakfast tray on the table beside his bed and leave quietly. But his eyes were upon her the moment she opened the door. The moment she saw him looking at her, she felt neither fiercely strong, determined, nor disinterested. With a silent mumble to the Almighty, she thought, *Just what have you got against me?*

"How are you feeling?" she asked, more out of a loss for anything else to say, because she knew he probably felt like a bridge had collapsed on top of him.

He looked at her with a confused gleam of recollection, as if he were struggling to arrange his ideas, sorting fact from hallucination. He studied her for a moment, then said, "What?"

"I asked you how you were feeling."

"Like hell."

A battering like he took was bound to play a little havoc with one's disposition, so she bristled a little, but refrained from giving him a nasty reply as she moved to his bedside. Setting the tray on the table, she looked at him, seeing the pain and residue of opium in his dazed expression, the dark shadows they produced beneath his eyes. His usually healthy coloring was sallow, his features pinched and drawn.

He looked at the tray. "Take it away. I'm not hungry."

"You haven't eaten since yesterday morning. Papa wants you to get some food in your stomach."

"I said, take it away!"

"You need to eat whether you feel like it or not. All that opium on an empty stomach isn't good for you."

"Falling off that scaffolding wasn't exactly good for me either."

"That was an accident—"

"It was stupid!"

"Whatever," she said, feeling just a little put out, "but you really must eat."

He indicated both arms, which were heavily bandaged. "And how do you propose I do that? Grovel in the bowl like a pig?"

She hadn't meant to laugh, but at the mention of groveling

like a pig, she suddenly had a picture of Precious as he had been this morning, up to his ears in slops, his pink corkscrew tail waving at a frantic pace.

She stopped laughing when she saw the dark scowl across his face. Her gaze moved slowly over his face, where the skin stretched smooth and pale over high cheekbones, dropping to the white bandages bound tightly across his chest. He's too much man, she thought; he would demand so much from a woman that there would be nothing she could hold back.

She lifted his head with one hand and fluffed his pillow, then began straightening his sheeting. "Would you like me to open the window? How about a book to read?" She remembered his hands and added, "Would you like me to read to you?"

"What I'd like is for you to stop fussing over me and asking me all these stupid questions. I liked you better when you wouldn't talk!"

"You keep snarling like a starved wolf every time someone comes in here, and you're going to have a hard time finding anyone to help you when you need it." She picked up the napkin and opened it with a snap of her wrist, then tucked it under his chin.

With a low growl, Nicholas floundered around a bit with his bandaged hands before finally managing to move the napkin from where she had tucked it and tossing it toward the tray. "Next thing I know you'll be putting me in diapers. I don't like to be coddled!"

She was surprised at how easy it was for her to remain calm. Perhaps this was because he was in such a nasty mood that it was actually funny. "Some woman has spoiled you terribly, Mr. Mackinnon. And you are accustomed to having your own way."

"Something I've had precious little of since meeting you."

She took the cover off the bowl of oatmeal, catching his displeased look out of the corner of her eye. "If you'll behave yourself, I'll help you eat."

"Since you're being so accommodating, why don't you just eat it for me?"

"Oh, I couldn't eat another bite. We had a big breakfast this morning: eggs, ham, grits, fresh biscuits with lots of sweet butter—"

"Get that slop out of here," he said with a snarl.

But Tibbie had nursed surly, ill-tempered people before—most of them men. She knew there would be many more days like this before Nicholas Mackinnon would be back on his feet. *Men are the worst patients.* Perhaps his mood would be better tomorrow.

But by the following morning, Nick's mood, if anything, was worse. Balancing his breakfast tray in one hand, Tibbie pushed open the door to his room and stepped inside. Nick was propped up in bed looking burly, and cross as a treed coon, staring at the door, which meant that he was staring at her when she stepped inside. "Did you have a good night?" she asked cheerfully.

"Not particularly," he replied, not bothering to make any effort to sound pleasant, cordial, or for that matter, humane.

"Was there some problem?"

"As a matter of fact there was. I wasn't sleepy. Do you know what it's like to lie in bed for hours watching shadows move across the ceiling, wishing you could fall asleep?"

"You should have taken some of the sleeping draught my father mixed up for you," she said, crossing the room and placing the tray on the table beside him.

"I'm sick of medicine. I'm sick of being confined. I'm sick of lying in bed. And for that matter, I'm sick of this place. In plain English, I am bored out of my mind."

"Bored?"

"Bored," he said flatly. "That's B-O-R-E-D! I'm not allowed out of bed, and I don't have anything to do while I'm confined. The most exciting thing that's happened to me since I came here was having you wash between my toes day before yesterday."

She looked down, feeling her face grow warm. She had thought him asleep. "You remember that?"

"Oh, yes, but not too fondly. I've had more excitement shaving."

"Oh, I'm sure it isn't as bad as all that," she said, with a nervous little laugh. "Surely you've had other things to do."

"Oh, yes, I did forget a few things. Yesterday morning I watched a spider spin a web around a fly. And just before lunch I counted the knotholes on the door—there are fifty-seven, if you're interested. All in all, I can tell you just how many planks there are in this floor, how many cracks there are in the ceiling, how many times your father said, "Good God!" while examining patients yesterday. But the real highlight was when your grandmother came for a visit."

That surprised her. "Granny? Granny Grace came in here?"

"Oh, she came all right, every little gray hair."

"What did she want?"

"She said, 'Did you know Napoleon and Richard the Third were both born with one tooth?' "

Tibbie was laughing now.

"I don't remember saying anything funny."

"Well, did you?" she managed to ask between gasps for breath.

"Did I what?"

"Know about Napoleon and Richard the Third?"

"No," he said, trying not to laugh, "but I'll make sure I don't forget. Lord knows how many times I may be called upon to know that."

She looked down at his hands, remembering that Coll had removed the bulky bandage yesterday. The smaller one he was wearing now made it easier to use his hands. "Do you want me to help you eat?"

"No. I can manage."

"Well then, if there's nothing else . . . I've a number of chores waiting." She turned away.

"Tibbie . . ."

She paused halfway across the room. Then she turned toward him. "Yes?"

"There is something else . . ."

She prayed her face did not show the panic she was feeling. "Something else? You mean for me to do?"

"Yes."

"What?"

"Sit here awhile and talk to me."

"I really don't have time—"

"Then make time. I need some human conversation and a little companionship. I've been in this blasted bed for almost two weeks and I haven't had one decent conversation during all that time."

"Decent conversation? That's all you want?"

He nodded.

"What do you want to talk about?" she asked, moving slowly back to him. She sat down in the chair beside his bed.

"Anything. Tell me what you did yesterday."

She laughed. "Beth and I gave Precious a bath."

He smiled. "I would have liked to see that. I've heard a wet pig is hard to hold on to."

"You heard right. I'm glad the weather was warm. Before it was all over, Beth and I were both in and out of the tub with Precious. He gave us a thorough soaking." She paused a moment. "He always hates to be bathed. It makes him sulk for days."

"I've never heard of a moody pig."

"Oh, but it's true. Pigs sulk and they carry grudges too. He won't forgive us too easily for that bath. His feelings are hurt and his tail isn't curled over his back today. Mama said he's taken to his pallet on the back porch." Her face lit up and Nick looked rather skeptically at the mischief he could see there.

"I have a wonderful idea! We could bring him in here with you," she said. "That way, you could both sulk together."

"I wasn't aware I had been sulking."

"Oh, you have been! Believe me!"

"I think I'd rather count knotholes," he said sourly.

She came to her feet, a teasing smile on her face. "Mackinnon, you are spoiled! Terribly!" She moved to the door, then stood in the open doorway. "Spoiled," she said again. "Spoiled rotten!" She closed the door behind her.

That night Nick slept through the entire night without waking up once. He could feel the warmth of sunshine on his face when his mind first began to struggle with consciousness. *What is that noise?* He opened one eye, then the other. He didn't see anything. He closed his eyes. *There it is again,* he thought, opening his eyes and looking around the room. Still nothing. He closed his eyes again. As he had before, he heard the noise again. It sounded like someone was snoring. He opened his eyes again and listened. Someone was snoring. He eased himself close to the edge of the bed and looked down, finding what woke him up.

Beneath his bed, Precious was stretched out, sound asleep, snoring. Before Nick could sort through what he was seeing, he heard a muffled laugh. Looking up, he saw Tibbie and Beth peeking through the door. When they saw he was looking at them, they both broke into hysterical laughter. It was impossible not to join them.

A moment later, they entered the room, closing the door behind them. "We better get him out of here," Tibbie said. "If Grandpa finds out we've let Precious in his clinic, we'll be up the creek."

"Will Grandpa be angry?" asked Beth.

"Furious," said Tibbie. "Now, you go stand on the other side of the bed while I try to get hold of him before he wakes up. Otherwise, it'll be the devil to pay. You know how he likes to play chase. We could be in here all afternoon. Now, hurry."

Tibbie went down on her knees beside the bed, and seeing Beth was in place on the other side, she reached for Precious, intending to grab him by the collar. But just as she reached for him, Precious woke up with a grunt, squealing madly when Tibbie missed his collar and grabbed his ear. A split second later, he shot from under the bed like someone wanted him for bacon. "Oh, dear!" said Tibbie.

"Grandpa is gonna get us now!" said Beth.

A free-for-all is what happened next, with Beth and Tibbie

both trying to head Precious off, darting this way and that, while Precious, who was having great difficulty standing on the polished wood floors, was squealing for dear life.

"What in the name of all that's holy is going on in here?" Coll Buchanan said, opening the door and looking around the room. "Good God!" he said, then again, "Good God!" Seeing his daughter and granddaughter, he said, "What is the meaning of all this nonsense?" When neither of them spoke, he said, "Tibbie Anne, what is that *pig* doing in here?"

Tibbie was doing her best to look contrite, but it was hard. Inside she was feeling as happy as a singing teakettle. Just looking at the expressions on Nick and Coll's faces, she wanted to double over with laughter. Never had two men looked more bewildered, and less capable of understanding.

"Grandpa looks pretty mad," whispered Beth.

"And growing madder by the minute," Coll said. "Now, answer me! What is going on in here?"

"Oh, you wouldn't understand," said Tibbie.

"Try me," said Coll.

Tibbie sighed. "Well, you see—"

"No, I don't," said Coll. "And what's more, I don't think you do either. What in heaven's name possessed you to bring that pig in here?"

"We thought it might cheer Mr. Mackinnon up."

"Cheer him up? You thought that slobbering swine would do the trick?"

"Precious doesn't slobber!" Beth said. "Grandma said he was cleaner than a lot of people she knew."

Coll looked at Beth. "I'll speak to your grandmother about that." He looked at Tibbie. "Are you feeling all right?"

"Of course."

Coll was still looking at Tibbie. He looked at the pig. Then he looked at Nicholas, who was looking as bewildered as he. With an exasperated sigh, he said, "Get that pig out of here and see that he stays out, or I'll be carving ham Sunday week!" Instantly he looked at Beth, regretting his harsh words and expecting to see her burst into tears, but Beth knew Coll was more bluster than business, so instead of tears he got, "I'll get Precious out of here, Grandpa. Just like you said."

But Precious was of a different mind, for he had found a lovely patch of warm sunlight on the floor and had promptly plopped down. Lying on his stomach, his feet poking out before him, his head was positioned so the sun was full upon his face and his eyes were closed in a euphoric state of bliss. When Beth prodded him, he only grunted and opened his tiny little pig eyes for the briefest moment before closing them. She poked him again and he began to grunt in earnest. When she tugged on his ears, he came to his feet, squealing loudly, his horny little feet tapping out a message of extreme irritation before he stopped next to Nick's bed. Thrusting his head under the bed, he wiggled and grunted until he wedged himself underneath. Beth dropped down on all fours and began pleading and wheedling, but Precious did not budge.

Coll watched all of these goings-on quietly. Beth was getting more like her mother every day. He wished that wasn't so, but there was nothing he could do about it. Without another word, Coll shook his head and turned away. A moment later he closed the door behind him.

Coll took two steps away from the door and paused, his hand coming up to scratch his chin as he pondered a moment. He turned and looked at the door he had just closed, then shook his head. "Naah," he said quietly, then started off again. He took two more steps and paused once again, his hand coming back up to rub his chin. Once again he looked toward the door he had just closed, a puzzled look upon his face. He opened the door.

Beth was where he'd left her, down on the floor on all fours, still coaxing and pleading with that pesky pigheaded pig. Coll thought, *Any man who allowed a child to keep a Yorkshire hog for a pet ought to have his head examined.* Coll had gone along with it for a while, thinking if he didn't make too much fuss, Beth would soon lose interest in a pig and turn her devotion upon something more worthwhile. But that strategy hadn't worked, because in the devotion department, Beth never wavered.

But it really wasn't Beth or her pet pig that had Coll concerned. It was Tibbie. She was acting stranger than the weather. And he wasn't sure what to do about it. He went into the kitchen and mentioned it to Effie, but she was as perplexed as he. "I don't know, Coll. How about one of the remedies in Granny's almanac?"

"Lord, woman! I want to understand my daughter, not kill her. That blasted book ought to be burned. Have you read it?"

"No. What's wrong with it?"

"It's nothing but silly superstition, that's what. How would you like to have fried-onion juice poured in your ear to cure an earache?"

"Oh, how awful!"

"There's more. A dirty sock around the neck is called a sure bet for a sore throat, a stye will go away if you rub the tail of a black cat on it, and chicken pox can be cured if you let a rooster fly over your head."

"Be thankful Granny hasn't tried any of those yet."

"Give her time," Coll said, walking from the room. "Give her time."

He returned to Nick's room and paused inside the door, looking at his daughter. She and Nick were just as he'd left them moments before, only now a static charge hovered over the room that hadn't been there then. Even from this distance he could tell they were at loggerheads about something, for Tibbie was standing beside Nick's bed giving him what for, her hands slapped on her hips, her elbows poking out. Coll had seen this enough to know it was her perturbed stance. Tapping her foot would come next, indicating she had moved past perturbed into agitated, which judging from the look of things, was due to come along any minute now. Sure enough, he had barely finished the thought when that foot of hers started tapping. If the expression on her face indicated anything, Tibbie was mad enough to stomp something. Coll looked at Nick, who wasn't exactly passive about all of this. In fact, he was looking angrier by the minute. At first Coll was of a mind to dismiss the whole thing, knowing anyone with the kinds of injuries Nicholas Mackinnon had would be a trifle cross and justifiably so. The Lord only knew there was nothing a woman worshiped more than an argument. In fact, he was wondering if he should give Nick a little warning. As far as Coll knew, an argument never convinced a woman contrary to her inclinations.

The two of them were so engrossed in their discord, they took no notice of Beth still lying on the floor coaxing Precious, or Coll standing in the doorway, so he had an opportunity to monitor just what was happening here. That they were squared off like two cats trying to eat from the same dish didn't bother him. He had enough faith in Tibbie to know she could hold her own. She was, after all, Effie's daughter, wasn't she? In fact, by the time he turned away he was actually feeling just a little sorry for Nick. If Tibbie didn't get him, Beth and that pig of hers would. Coll quietly closed the door and turned his attention to the business of the day, whistling a tune now and then and making reference to the lovely weather.

"I think it's going to rain, Papa," Mairi said, giving him a strange look.

"Well, who's to say rain can't be lovely?" Coll said, and went right on whistling.

Mairi had seen her father act stranger, so she simply shrugged and went bouncing down the hall, opening the door her father had closed moments before.

Mairi looked at her sister, then at the pig under Nicholas Mackinnon's bed. She took in the situation, seeing Precious locked in rebellion, Beth pleading her head off, and Tibbie losing her patience and rounding the bed, grabbing Precious by the tail and dragging him, squealing and grunting, out the other side. Yet none of these things surprised her. If you've seen your sister pour a mug of pumpkin beer over the head of the town bully, what else can surprise you? Though she didn't understand any of what she was seeing, it just didn't surprise her. Still, the pig had been under the man's bed and there had to be a reason. She looked at Tibbie. "You didn't—"

"I did," said Tibbie, unable to recall the trinity of reasons she thought up for bringing the blasted pig into Nick's room. All she could remember was at some point she had thought it was a good idea. Looking slightly sheepish and wondering why she always seemed to be the victim of too much determination and not enough forethought, she wished she could be more like Mairi—mentally diffuse and hidden in a never-lifting fog.

Tibbie glanced around the room. Everyone was staring at her, everyone except Precious, that is. *Uh-Oh!* thought Tibbie. Seeing the way Precious was brooding over his recent indignity, she knew he was planning redress. A hog, for the uninformed, is always thinking up mischief and ways to repay any wrong done to him, for pigs are well known for bearing a grudge. There simply isn't anything worse than a grudge-bearing pig.

"Don't just stand there like a bump on a pickle," Tibbie said to Mairi. "Come and help us catch this unswayable swine!"

Mairi joined the chase and Nick had to admit that by the time the three of them had the pig cornered, his spirits were definitely lifted. He couldn't remember laughing so much. Only problem was, all that laughter made him ache all over. But that had been forgotten soon enough when Beth had come toward him dragging Precious behind her. "Isn't he the most *adorablest* pig you ever saw?"

Nick had agreed that Precious was indeed the most adorablest. Mairi picked Precious up and said, "Come on, Beth. Mr. Mackinnon needs to rest."

Beth climbed onto the chair beside Nick's bed and leaned over, planting a wet kiss on his cheek. "There!" she said with a satisfied sound. "That will make you ever so much better."

A moment later she was down and out the door with Mairi. Tibbie had never seen Beth take to anyone the way she took to Nick, and she wasn't one to go about passing out kisses—she was a lot like her mother in that regard. Surprise still on her face, she turned back to Nick. Their eyes met and held. For a suspended moment the two of them stared at each other, unable to look away. Tibbie felt her insides go soft and her body tremble—something that happened to her quite often, whenever Nick looked at her like this. Color rose to her face and her heart thudded in response. She couldn't look away from that face, those cobalt eyes so full of yearning—and she really didn't want to.

There was no use denying it. She was attracted to this man and he waylaid her emotions in a way that left her knees weak and her blood racing. Her long-passive feelings, barely awakened at age sixteen and snuffed like a candle, were emerging like tiny green buds and grew faster than weeds during a wet summer.

"Don't be afraid of me, Tibbie. I won't hurt you. Not ever."

Tibbie recoiled at those words, which hit her like an echo from the past. But then she looked at the man who spoke them this time, saw the gentleness in his eyes, the sincerity in his expression.

She sighed. "I'm not afraid of you, Nick," she said softly. "I'm afraid of Tibbie Buchanan. I'm afraid of who I am and what I want when I'm with you. I don't want to be hurt again. I don't want to make another mistake."

"I know, but it doesn't have to be that way."

"I understand that," she said in a strangled voice, "and that's the problem."

Before he could reply, she whirled and ran from the room. All that remained was the lingering scent of her, the sound of her hastily retreating steps echoing down the hall.

She didn't see Nick for three days. She couldn't. She felt so drawn to him, so vulnerable, that she had to put a little distance between them to give herself time to think things through. But it wasn't easy staying away from a man like Nick. *Out of sight, out of mind, my eye!* He was in her thoughts constantly.

Nick must have been in Beth's thoughts a lot, too, because she began visiting him regularly, bringing him pictures she had drawn, or a wilted flower or two, and one afternoon she brought him a gingerbread man she and Tibbie had made.

"Is your mother a good cook?"

"Yes, 'cept she burns things a lot. Granny Grace said that was 'cause she has her mind on other things, but Mama won't tell me what they are."

Nick smiled at her and started to take a bite.

"Eat the buttons first," she said. "They're raisins."

While Nick was eating the buttons, she said, "I don't eat the eyes *ever,* because they're licorice and I *hate* licorice."

"You do? Well, I'll eat the eyes. I like licorice."

"It makes your tongue black!"

Nick ate the eyes. "Here," Beth said, "you can have my eyes too." She pried the eyes off her gingerbread man and handed them to Nick, who promptly plopped them in his mouth. "Let me see your tongue," she said, standing up in the chair and leaning over him so she could examine his out-thrust tongue.

"Yep!" she said. "It's black all right. But don't worry. Mama said it will go away."

"So will you, Miss Priss," Mairi said as she came into the room. "It's time for your bath and your mother is looking for you."

Beth scampered from the room.

That night, after she had Beth bathed and in bed, Tibbie took a long, leisurely bath, reflecting and thinking about Nicholas. The man had entered her life, and from the looks of things intended to stay there. How did she feel about that? Confused. Terrified to let him into her life. Afraid if she didn't he might go away. By the time the water grew cold, the only thing she knew for certain was that her skin had never been so puckered. She stepped from the tub.

Once she was dried and dressed in her plain cotton gown, she crawled into bed, lay there for a moment and then crawled out. She tried the chair, and left it as well, moving to stand in front of the window. But that didn't hold her long either. For the next hour she did nothing but pace the room, going from the chair to the window to the bed and back again. Why was she so restless? *If you don't know the answer to that, you're dumber than I thought.* She wanted to be with Nick. *Should I go see him, talk to him?* Would she? *Would I what?* Talk. Maybe Mairi wasn't the only one in the family that was mentally diffuse and hidden in a never-lifting fog.

Her bedroom door opened and Effie stepped into the room. "Saints preserve us! You're as restless as a cat. I've never heard so much board creaking."

Tibbie had forgotten that her parents' room was directly below hers, and that naturally they would hear her moving about. "All that thumping and squeaking," Effie was saying, "it's enough to give a body indigestion." She gave Tibbie the once-over. "What ails you? Lately you're all nerves and twitches." She paused, coming over to Tibbie and lifting her eyelids, one at a time, not put off in the least by the fact that Tibbie was scowling fiercely. "You're looking a little pale around the gills. You feeling up to snuff?"

"I'm okay."

"I don't know," Effie said. "Even your father has noticed it, and that young man, Mackinnon—"

Tibbie's head snapped up. "Mackinnon?"

"He's been asking about you every time I take his tray in." Effie looked like she was seriously contemplating something. "He hasn't done anything to you, has he?"

"Done anything?" Her color darkened. "No, of course not."

"Then why don't you go pay him a visit?"

"Why should I?"

"Why shouldn't you?"

Tibbie shrugged. "Papa said he was over the worst of it. He'll be up and about in a few days."

"But until he is he is confined to bed, day and night. He's been asking for you."

Tibbie had a sudden memory of the last time she had seen him. Lord, the way he had looked at her. All she could think about doing was running to his room and lying her head on his shoulder so he could hold her. She sighed. *That* was reason enough to stay away from him.

It was three days later at breakfast that Coll said to Tibbie, "I notice you've been having Mairi or your mother take Mackinnon's meals into him. Is there some problem?"

"No," Tibbie said, "I've just been busy with a lot of other things."

"Well, your mother tells me Mairi is going to be busy for a few days. I guess that means you'll have to pick up the slack and start carrying those meals yourself."

Tibbie hesitated. "Can't someone else do it?"

"Who, for instance?"

Tibbie thought about Gladys, remembering she had gone to visit her sister, then she suggested Mairi, but Effie reminded her that Mairi was helping with the nine Dexter children, since Coll had just delivered Mrs. Dexter of number ten. Tibbie mentally ruled out Granny herself, for the last time she had given Granny something to do, suggesting she knit Mr. Mackinnon a pair of socks, she found Granny sitting next to Nick's bed, his leg pulled over the side while she tried to knit a pair of socks over his foot.

Her mind was still trying to dredge up someone to suggest when Coll said, "I've been called to Port Lavaca. Looks like the yellow fever that was reported in Galveston is moving this way. I don't know how long I'll be gone. You'll have to take over the clinic in my absence. And that includes Mackinnon."

Tibbie sprang to her feet, looking as surprised as old Harm Brewster had when he woke up in Mrs. Price's bed and saw Mr. Price standing over him with a rifle. "Yellow fever?"

"Yes. I don't know how long I'll be gone. You might as well start by taking Mackinnon's breakfast to him," Coll said. "And see that he eats it."

Walking slowly toward Nick's room, Tibbie was worried about her father. Yellow fever was a serious illness, and Coll was overworked and run-down. The trip alone would be hard on him. When she saw Nick's door down the hall, she suddenly wished she wasn't holding a tray in her hands, so she could wring them. She was worse than nervous. She wanted nothing more than to spend the afternoon with him, but she felt awkward as a schoolgirl. Talking to herself was, in her opinion, a poor second to hand-wringing.

Pausing briefly outside his door, Tibbie squared her shoulders and took a fortifying breath, then balanced the tray on her out-thrust hip and opened the door.

Nick heard the door creak and slowly opened one eye, to see an angel approaching. But he was furious with this particular angel for the cruel way she had avoided him over the past few days. He didn't trust himself to talk to her right now, because he was afraid he would say more than he should. He closed his eyes to a narrow slit, seeing her dimly.

Tibbie placed the tray on the table beside his bed, and looked at him. His chest was bare and beautiful, the bruises having faded to reveal smooth, tanned skin. The sheet was dangerously low, and she reached for it to pull it up and caught herself just in time. She sat down in the chair beside him, her eyes still on his face. Lord, he was a handsome devil. She wanted to wake him, but didn't want to be obvious. She scraped the chair. He didn't flinch. She cleared her throat, but he didn't bat an eye. She coughed and Nick slept on. She looked off, lost in thought, and he fought back a smile. Keeping his eyes closed, he waited to see what she would do next.

She looked back at him and sighed once again. "It's just as well," she whispered. "The way I'm feeling right now I don't think I could last one round with you."

Nick slept on, a warm, uplifting sensation spreading throughout his body.

"Why have you done this to me? Everything was going so well here until you came." She shook her head. "I can't," she said, coming to her feet. "I want to, but I can't." She jumped up and left the room in a hurry.

Nick opened one eye and slowly smiled. "Yes, you can," he whispered.

11

The following morning Tibbie said she wasn't feeling well and Effie insisted she stay in bed. After two days in bed, Mairi came into her room and said, "All right! This has gone on long enough."

Tibbie looked at her sister. "What has?"

"Tibbie Anne, you aren't any sicker than I am, and I feel fine. Now, I want to know what's going on, and I want to know right now, or I'm going to send for Papa."

About that time a deep rolling bellow, decidedly masculine, shook the very foundations of the house. "What is that dreadful noise?" Tibbie asked, sitting up in bed.

"You mean you're just now hearing it?"

"For the first time," Tibbie said. "What is it?"

"Mackinnon."

"Mackinnon? What's wrong with him?"

"He wants to see you and he's raising a fuss. That," she said as Nick bellowed again, "has been going on since eight o'clock this morning."

"Tell him to stop acting like a fool."

"You tell him. I've tried that and a dozen other things as well. You'd better go see him."

Tibbie dressed and made her way downstairs to the room Nick occupied. Carefully she opened the door and stepped inside, just as Nick let out another bellow.

"For the love of God!" she hissed. "Will you be quiet?"

"Come in here and sit down. I want some company."

"No!"

"Either you come in here and sit down or I'll start singing the 'Star-Spangled Banner'—every single verse of it."

"You wouldn't dare. Besides, I doubt you know more than five words."

He began bellowing again. After two verses she clamped her hands over her ears and came into the room, banging the door behind her. "What is your *least* favorite food, Mackinnon?"

"Liver," he said.

"If I hear one more note from you, if so much as a *tweet* comes from that throat of yours, I am personally going to see to it that you are given nothing to eat except *liver* for the rest of your stay."

As he watched her turn and leave the room, slamming the door behind her, he had a feeling he knew *whose* liver she would be serving.

Two days later Coll returned. Taking one look at her exhausted husband, Effie fed him strong chicken soup and put him straight to bed. The next morning he saw a few patients in the clinic, then stopped by Nick's room. Exactly three minutes later he came flying out of Nick's room and headed for his office, passing Mairi on the way.

"Find your sister and tell her I want to see her immediately. Liver!" he said. "For the love of God!"

Two minutes later Tibbie entered her father's office. "Close the door," he said, and she did.

Fifteen minutes after that, Tibbie left her father's office. When she walked out, she was looking as pale as a bedsheet, but by the time she marched to the kitchen her face was as red as roses. Once there, she went to a bowl sitting on the cabinet and picked up a quivering slice of reddish-brown liver and carried it to Nick's room. Without pausing a fraction of a second, she threw open the door and headed in, swinging that piece of liver as she went.

"Of all the despicable, conniving, low-down, underhanded, unscrupulous, callow, double-crossing tricks!" she said, slamming the door behind her.

If that weren't enough to throw Nick's slumbering consciousness into full alert, the loud *thwack!* of something cold and wet and horrible smelling slapping him in the face was.

Even with his eyes closed, he knew that smell. He felt his stomach heave in revolt. It heaved again as the smelly glob slid over to one side and nestled near his ear.

Before he could heave again or rid himself of the liver, she yanked it from his hand and hit him with it again.

"What in the hell has gotten into you?" he said, capturing the liver and flinging it across the room.

"Don't try to act innocent. It's impossible. *You,*" she said, poking him in the chest, "are lower than a snake's belly! How *dare* you!"

"How dare I what?"

She looked for something else to hit him with. "You told my father, you swine! You reprobate! You yellow-livered chicken! You . . . you . . . you sissy!"

"Sissy? Me?"

"I would've never believed a grown man would stoop so low. Do you know what you are, Mackinnon?"

Nick was mulling over the possibilities, wondering what profane name she would be forced to resort to.

"You," she said, poking him in the chest again, "are a tattletale!"

He lost it on that one, laughing so hard he was afraid his newly mended ribs had unmended themselves.

Tattletale? He studied the angry but still beautiful face, the eyes that were shooting daggers at him, unable to believe that he was lying so passive and so close to a woman that looked as fetching as she did while she was calling him, among other things, a tattletale.

Dear Lord! How long has it been since anyone called me a tattletale? Not since he was in knee britches.

The man in the bed raised his eyebrows and gave her a warm smile. Had she not been so angry, she might have been jolted to see the way the sun shafted off the warm brown tones of his hair—hair which half the women in Indianola would

217 *Angel in Marble*

give their eye teeth to have. His perfectly sculpted features were held in an expression of delighted amusement, and the deep blue of his eyes that swept over her were hot enough to scorch the drawers off an ice maiden. But Tibbie gave no notice to any of these things. She was feeling cold as charity. "Don't try to coddle me, you lily-livered coward."

His stomach heaved again at the mention of that word. "Tibbie Anne, could we talk about something besides liver? Are you upset about something?"

"Don't get formal with me, you sneak? You know very well I'm upset and, furthermore, you know why!"

"I do?" he asked, the perfect picture of innocence.

"You do. You told my father I refused to care for you and that I threatened to feed you nothing but liver!"

He was crass enough to look amazed. "Well," he finally said. "Didn't you?"

"I avoided you altogether. I didn't refuse to care for you."

"However you wish to phrase it, you didn't care for me and you did threaten me with liver." He wiped his face and said, "God, this stuff smells horrible!" Then he looked her straight in the eye and said, "I might add that that threat has now become a fact."

"*That* is not the point."

"What is the point, then?"

"The point is your tattling like some irksome schoolboy. What are you going to try next? Dipping my braids in ink? Frogs in my lunchpail?"

He grinned. "Do you have a lunchpail?"

"Don't try to avoid the issue, you shifty-eyed toad. You flapped your mouth and got me into a passel of trouble. Well, let me tell you something, once and for all. Don't you ever again mention so much as my name to my father," she said, sounding, if she had to say so herself, all persuasive and self-confident.

"I see. Well, then, I suppose I must apologize."

"I don't care whether you apologize or not. I don't give

that"—she snapped her fingers right under his nose—"for you or your apology."

"If I offended you, Miss Buchanan, if I caused you any discomfort, I am most contrite."

"You are lying through your teeth, you unprincipled informer. You are delighted to think you might have caused me a few problems. Why else would you do such a devious, manipulative thing like carrying tales to my father. Do you have any idea," she said in high pitched tones, "just how long it's been since I had my father threaten to paddle my backside?"

"He didn't!"

She opened her mouth to give him what for when her mind went blank. There he was, looking as calm as a dead mule, while she was wound up tighter than an eight-day clock. Why was it that every time she confronted him, she came away feeling she had done nothing more than run up and butt? Each and every encounter left her frustrated from wasted effort. He was as slick as a button and cagey as they come. A man like him, well, if you threw him in the river, he'd float upstream. There was just no getting around him. Truth to tell, a butting session with him just left her feeling all tuckered out. And there he sat, looking as frisky as a turkey in young corn, while she was feeling so low she could walk under a trundle bed with a silk hat on and have room to spare. Her father always said, "Tibbie Anne, everytime you have a fit you fall in it."

But she was ready to lick her flint and try again. "Don't think you're so clever. You aren't as dazzling as you think you are, you evasive troublemaker! What you did was cheap and childish."

"Don't blame me. You're the one that's responsible for my behaving like a schoolboy whenever I'm around you. You've built a wall around you that a mountain goat couldn't climb. And I'll wager it was intentional. You don't wait for a man to make a mistake or disappoint you, do you? You don't give him that chance. You'd rather convict him without a trial."

"That's not true."

"Oh, yes, it is. You perform a mental execution of any man

you meet within minutes, or I miss my guess. Why don't you put the sawmill where the timber is, Tib? You aren't riled at me because your father found out, you're mad over the result. You're being forced to spend some time with me and that makes you nervous as hell."

"Hah! You don't affect me in the least. I simply don't like you."

"But you want me." He could tell he'd hit the nail on the head that time, so he drove it home. "I'm a threat to you and that perfect little world you've created for yourself."

"Don't try to divert me. It's *your* faults and transgressions we're discussing here, not mine."

He gave her one of those slow-stretching smiles that unsettled her so. "Why, Miss Tibbie, do you have faults?" His brows dipped in the center. "And transgressions too? Surely not!"

She lifted her head to a loftier height, not looking at him as she spoke. "Ridicule me all you like. It helps me loathe you all the more."

For a man who had more cracks in his bones than a dropped cup, he moved surprisingly fast. One minute he was lying prone with a teasing smile on his face, the next moment he had her yanked across him so her feet were at least six inches off the floor. His arms might be bandaged, but there was more than enough strength in the arms pressing against her back to hold her in place. From the knees up, Tibbie's body was pressed against Nick's, close enough that she could feel his nakedness beneath the light sheeting. Her only salvation was seeing that the intimate contact of their bodies unsettled him as much as it did her.

She managed to get one hand braced against the bed and tried to push herself away, but Nick only held her tighter, moving one arm up to her shoulders, which put his lips against her neck.

Nick knew she was uneasy. He could see the new, rosier tint that darkened her skin. He felt the tension in the supple body that lay stiffly upon his own. "The woman you show to the world is such a strong one, I would have never suspected she had such a fragile core."

"Just because I didn't box your ears, doesn't mean I'm fragile. And just because I haven't boxed them yet, doesn't mean I'm not going to. I haven't forgotten your scheming ways or your conniving deeds. I was right to peg you as someone who couldn't be trusted."

"Don't go cynical on me."

"I've learned just how low you will stoop to get what you want, and if that's being cynical, so be it. I've been suspicious of you all along, but I'm even more leery of you now. You're as bothersome as a pesky fly and about as welcome. Now, let me up before someone comes in here and sees us."

"Why are you making such a big to-do over your father finding out you refused to feed me?"

"I'm not making a big to-do about his finding out, it's the *way* he found out. *You told him!* You wanted to get back at me, and you did."

He pulled her closer, his breath coming warm and strong against her neck. "I told your father, true. But you're wrong about my purpose in doing so. It wasn't to get back at you, Tib. It was simply to get you back."

She lifted her head as much as he would allow and looked at him. "You don't make any sense. You never had me. How can you get me back?"

He began nuzzling her neck again. "I hadn't seen you in days and it wasn't hard to figure out you were avoiding me intentionally. I knew you would probably go right on ignoring me unless I did something. I'm held together by bandages. I can't get out of bed. What other choice did I have? A man in love should be expected to do a few strange things. It may not have been a wise decision, Tib, but at the time it seemed my only choice."

Tibbie was no longer listening. *A man in love . . . A man in love . . . A man in love . . .* The thought distressed her. Surely he didn't mean it the way she thought. He hardly knew her, how could he be in love? She was still wearing a confused expression when his hand came up to cup her face.

"I love you, Tibbie. Surely you've suspected as much long before now."

Her hand came up to touch his forehead. "Are you running a fever?"

"Only when I think of you." He began to caress the sensitive skin of her throat with his mouth. His breath was warm and the brush of it across her flesh roused her with deep-penetrating sensations. His hand came up to stroke her hair with mesmerizing slowness, rubbing, stroking, pressing. He turned with her, rolling them both over so that they lay on their sides, facing each other in the bed. His hands were still on her back, one coming up to the base of her head, applying pressure and drawing her to him. Overcome with the numbness his declaration had produced, she watched with the sleepy dullness of sleep as his mouth descended toward hers.

"Ah, Tibbie . . . Tibbie . . . Tibbie . . . my blood runs thick and hot at the very thought of you."

Well she could understand those words, for her own blood was running a little thick and hot as well. That infusion of warmth was spreading more rapidly now, seeking its counterpart in the long, hard body that lay parallel and very, very close to her own. He was whispering words to her now, tender words, love words, words that spoke of his desire. Without realizing it she was returning his kiss, her body restless to get closer to him, her lungs struggling to deliver each rapidly exhaled breath. She was panting now, unaware that he had separated her bodice until he kissed the softly plumped flesh of her bare breasts. Everywhere he touched her, each place he kissed, burned intensely, a wake of fire that seemed never to cease.

She shouldn't be here with him like this—she knew that, but it had been so long since she had felt the warm, strong comfort of a man's arms about her. And this man's arms . . . her breath caught in her throat, blocking the panicked escape of air. She was unprepared for the firm softness of his lips, unprepared for the surge and depth of her desire for him, and that left her unprepared to resist. *No!* Her subconscious mind was screaming. *No, not again. Think, Tibbie. You have been here before. Remember. You have felt lips this soft and warm upon yours; listened to the same declarations of love. And after he left, you bore his child.*

"Don't fight me, Tibbie. Please."

Her eyes flew open and she saw Nick. Not Eric. Nick. Her face was burning with confusion, her head pounding with the memory of the moment before. She looked down, really seeing now her naked breasts, still damp and rosy from the scratch of his whiskers, the bathing of his tongue. Jerking her bodice together, she began to refasten her clothing. "I was right not to trust you," she said in a quavering voice.

He sighed, dropping his hands to rest beside him. "Maybe you were distrustful of the wrong person. You don't seem to have much more control than I do."

"No, I don't suppose I do. Now you know why I stayed away from you." Her eyes filled with tears. "I know now what will happen if I'm with you again. I won't let it happen again. You can rest assured of that much."

"You can try," he said softly. "But I don't think you'll have any more luck than you had today." He drew a finger down the side of her arm. She trembled and drew away, still occupied with putting the two halves of her bodice back together. "Why are you so determined to drive a wedge between us? I've told you of my feelings. Doesn't that put your mind at ease, even a little?"

"My mind hasn't been at ease since the day I met you."

"Then why won't you let yourself go, Tib? Release your feelings and let them flow free. That's all I'm asking. You don't have to love me back, at least not yet."

"I'm not the kind of person to take and give nothing back."

"I know," he said softly, taking her efficient little hand, so small and defenseless, in his, bringing it to his lips. "Ah, Tibbie, Tibbie. What am I to do? There hasn't been a single moment out of a day that you haven't been in my thoughts, weighing heavily upon my mind. So many nights I've lain here in this bed, knowing you were sleeping in your chaste bed somewhere in this very house. At times I wanted to go to you so badly I would have crawled to get there." He looked at her, afraid his words were frightening to her, but her expression was difficult to read. "I don't just want your body, Tib, if that's what you're thinking. I want *you,* all of you, your company, your laughter, your stubborn determination." He saw she was on the verge of tears. "Tibbie, I'm not Eric."

She tried to move off the bed, but Nick held her tightly. He dropped his head against her shoulder and sighed, laughing a dry laugh. "Maybe that's it. I'm not Eric, and that's the problem."

"No," she said, "it isn't. I've told you, the problem is me. That's what I've been trying to tell you, what I wanted you to understand. You've picked the wrong woman."

"You mean I should find someone else."

The thought twisted like a pain so severe she almost doubled over from the effect of it. He chuckled—a sad, hollow sound that made her shiver. "I'm afraid it's too late for that, my little love. This is one fish you've hooked that you can't throw back."

"Please, Nick. I'm so confused. I want. I don't want. I feel, but I don't want to feel. I want you to go away. I'm afraid you might." She was crying now. "I want to care again, but I'm so afraid I might."

He kissed her cheek. "I think," he said slowly, "that you're in love with a memory."

"It's more than that."

"I wonder." He paused, studying her face for a minute or two. "I'd be willing to bet that you'd feel quite differently if this man . . . if this man came back. I may be crazy, but I find myself almost wishing he would."

Tibbie turned a startled look upon him, catching his brooding blue eyes upon her. They seemed to burn through her skull, penetrating her mental defenses and leaving her weak and unable to shield her emotions. But in spite of their burning intensity, there was a bleakness, a barrenness she could only liken to pain. The strength of the sun penetrated the curtained window, bronzing the paleness of his face, catching like water droplets in his hair, in his wiry brows, and making more prominent the cleft in his chin, the squareness of his jaw. Between them rose a strange new tension and she had the sudden urge to turn and run.

A cold shiver caused her to tremble and she lowered her gaze, looking away. How would she feel if Eric came back? He wouldn't, of course, but *if* he did, how would it feel? For so long she had been convinced she was still in love with Eric. Only now, was she that sure?

Her eyes drifted over to Nick. *This man,* she thought. *This smiling, soft-spoken man brings to life so many feelings I thought I'd laid to rest forever.* How unfair it was that her woman's body would turn traitor and remember so much of what she strove to forget. Was it this man she wanted, or the memory of another? Was he only a spark to kindle to life the partially burned logs of her past, which had flamed so brightly for a time before burning down and growing cold?

Which man did she really long for in the sanctity of her moonlit room during those endless stretches of sleepless night? Was it Nick or Eric she desired when she hugged her pillow and sobbed out her plight? Which man could ease the tight ache between her legs that would sometimes awaken her deep in the mystery of night. It *was* Eric. Wasn't it? But if that were true, why did she find it impossible to impose Eric's fair features over those darker ones she saw in her mind: the clear, sharp features of Nicholas Mackinnon. Tears rose unbidden in her eyes, and she closed them against the emotion, hearing as she did his softly sworn curse.

"My poor little angel," he said softly. "My poor little angel in marble. So trapped. So cold. So beautiful." He lifted her cold fingers to his lips. "What would it take, I wonder? What would it take to set her free?"

"Please," she said, a strange tightness in her throat. "I'd rather you didn't talk like that."

"Would you? Then I'm sorry to go against you on that, for

it's been my desire to give you anything your heart desires. But there are too many things I've wanted to say to you, too many things I've dreamed of sharing." He paused as if he were deciding something, then with a sigh he continued. "One of those dreams became a reality today." She lifted her head and looked at him, wondering what he was getting at, trying to backtrack and imagine what dream he could have had. The answer shocked her.

"You have a beautiful body, Tibbie . . . and your breasts . . ." He caught her wrist in his bandaged hand. "Don't turn away from me. Closing your eyes and covering your ears won't stop what I have to say. I've dreamed of touching you like I did today, only more so . . . more touching . . . more places . . . more times. I've wondered what it would be like to see you enter my room, and to see your eyes light up when they met mine. Night after night I've thought about how it would be if you loved me, if you came to me of your own free will. I think about how I would watch you undress and take down your hair, see you lying naked and open, unashamed that the lamp still glowed beside the bed, aware of nothing but the feel of my hands on your body as I entered you."

The whole world seemed to disappear in silence, the normal sounds of the day seeming to vanish into thin air. So honest and open were the eyes upon hers that she could not look away. The silence stretched between them, circling and then gradually fading away.

"I know what you've been through, and the kinds of things you've had to endure. There are times I'd like to kill the sonofabitch that did that to you, and other times I feel a great heaving sadness that I have somehow been sentenced to suffer for another's crime. I can't change what happened to you, Tib. I can't make the memory of it go away. I can only promise to try."

12

Nick watched her eyes, those great luminous golden discs that told so much about her, things even she didn't know. Was that what drew him to her in the beginning, those huge amber eyes looking up at him as he fought to control his horse—eyes that drew his very soul from his body? The slightest shading of sadness had always been present, but today, this moment, he was seeing a new sadness, one he couldn't attribute to Eric. Funny, her face didn't look sad—only her eyes, as if they knew something she didn't.

The urge to pull her into his arms again was strong. He wanted to cover her face with kisses, as if by doing so he could drive the sadness from her eyes. But something held him back. Today he had given her enough to think about. Tomorrow would be time enough. He sighed, bringing his hand up to rub the deep furrow between his brows. This impetuous wooing was taking its toll on him. Like walking on eggs it was, where the slightest change in pressure would bring penalty or reward.

"Sometimes I wonder about you," she said, her eyes steady on him. "That look on your face doesn't go with the words coming from your mouth."

"And how does my face look?"

"Dark and brooding, like Lucifer."

"But Lucifer was the angel of light."

"Bah! Lights can be turned on and off. He was nothing more than a proud deceiver who wreaked havoc." She would have gone on, but a noisy blue jay settled itself on the windowsill, drawing her attention away.

"Tibbie . . ." He forgot what he was going to say, for when she turned her attention back to him she suddenly went deathly pale, her hand reaching out to touch the sheeting where it rested on his thigh.

"Blood," she said, as if she had never seen blood before. Then, as if the truth of it suddenly struck her, she said, "You're bleeding," her hand moving quickly away from the bright red stain that spread like red ink across the stark white sheeting.

He looked down, then back at her. "It's nothing," he said. "I don't feel a thing." Then with a bittersweet smile, he added, "After so many broken bones, what's a little thing like a bleeding heart?"

One brow lifted and a smile curled across her face. "It's a little low for that, don't you think?"

"All blood leads to the heart."

"Just as all roads lead to Rome?"

"Exactly."

She stood, that professional expression he had seen so many times settling across her lovely face. There would be no more wooing now. He felt tired, drained. He closed his eyes. She would take care of him now, his little lass would.

It wasn't Nick's heart that was bleeding, and Tibbie was more than thankful for that, since Coll had left again that morning, this time going to Victoria, where the town's only doctor had been kicked in the head by his horse. That left Tibbie to care for patients as best she could. And that included Nicholas Mackinnon.

Cutting away the binding across his thigh, Tibbie feared the worst. Well she could remember the day Nick had fallen, and never would she forget the sight of the small, white sliver of bone that protruded from his flesh when his pants were cut from his leg.

She wasn't aware that she had been holding her breath until she heard the relieved release of it after she examined the wound. "All that wiggling around you've been doing, yanking women into your lap like a pure-headed fool . . ." She looked up to see the amusement in Nick's eyes and looked quickly away. "The bone is still in place," she said. "You've torn the wound apart, but the bleeding is superficial." She examined the wound again. "I'll have to stitch it back, but only if you promise to behave yourself and keep your hands to yourself."

"No more angels in my bed?"

She ignored that and went on berating him for this morning's spurt of activity, but even as she chastised him, she accepted part of the blame. She had pushed against him, trying to get free. Although he never said anything, she knew the wound was probably reopened due to her reaction more than his movement. Still, he had no business grabbing her the way he had, holding her against her will like that. But as she went about readying things to stitch the wound closed, a small voice in the back of her mind said, *Yes, but wasn't it wonderful to be held like that, if only for a short time?*

She picked up the needle and thread, but her hands were trembling—she was afraid she might make this more painful than was necessary. She glanced quickly at his face and then looked away. If he noticed her trembling, his expression didn't let on. With a fortifying breath, she said, "This will hurt."

"A common occurrence when I'm around you," he said, offering her a teasing smile that accomplished what he obviously meant it to. She relaxed.

In no time, she had the wound closed and new binding wrapped around his thigh. The tincture of opium she had given him was taking effect now, judging from his slowly closing eyes. A few flutters of protest and the opium won out. Nick closed his eyes. Moments later his breathing was slow and even. For a moment she stood at his side, looking down at his peacefully sleeping face. Lucifer, she had called him, and even that he had taken in stride. She smiled and pulled the light blanket over him.

He loved her. Or so he had said. But Eric had said the same thing. There were men, she well knew, who shared words of love as frequently as they shared beds. She gathered the soiled bindings and carried them to the trash, returning to the bedside table to clear away the opium, thread, and scissors. She paused beside his bed. The sun was resting full upon his face and she moved to the window to close the outer drape over the curtains, blocking more light. But even in the dimness, she could make out his features so well.

Her hand came out to smooth the rebellious hair away from his forehead, much as she had done for Beth numerous times. *He was the darling child of some woman*, she thought, and immediately imagined him as such. Some woman had gone through the terrible pains of birth to deliver a beautiful child, just as she had endured with Beth. And he had grown, been spoiled, beloved—a beautiful little boy, both naughty and nice, the apple of his mother's eye. That woman was dead now, he had told her that much. She smoothed her hand across his brow once more. Had his own mother done the same?

With a groan of despair, she left quickly, not stopping until she reached her room. She stood before her dressing mirror for a long time, looking at her reflection, berating herself for her unsettling thoughts and telling herself she should do better. But no amount of reprimand could make thoughts of that morning vanish. How could she have allowed herself to do this again? After all she had been through, how could she care?

But she did. More than she was willing to admit, but deep within herself was a feeling, not a small voice but a feeling that a turning point had been reached. She stood staring at herself, thinking about her daughter and her life, and the man who had suddenly come into it.

She looked down, seeing nothing unusual—shoes peeking beneath her dress, the full skirts, the tiny waist. But as she looked, she saw her dress get tighter, her bosom severely flattened by the bodice, her stomach round and protruding below her waist. She glanced at her reflection in the mirror. This time she saw herself as she had been then, younger, rounder, and tired. Her hair had been neatly braided, the small nesting of curls at her nape damp from perspiration, for it had been in the heat of summer. Her eyes moved from her face to the large mound of her belly, where Bethany had been cradled. The image began to fade and now, transposed over it, she saw herself in the throes of labor, the bed about her soaked in blood and sweat, the concerned face of her father, the pain and then blessed unconsciousness. Like a sharp pain to the heart, the memory came forward—of how it had been afterward—the snubs from her friends, the scorn of neighbors, the whispers as she walked with her family down the aisle to their pew in church, and following that, the long period of isolation and seclusion.

Panic shot through her and she stared at her reflection until the image faded and the color drained from her face. She blinked, seeing herself not in the previously bloated form, but as she was now, slender, older, more composed. But in the background, coming toward her out of the darkness, was Nicholas Mackinnon, carrying a light.

"No," she whispered, the back of her hand coming up to cover her mouth. "Not again," she said through trembling lips. "Dear God . . . please . . . not again." The image of Nicholas in the mirror loomed larger as he approached. The closer he approached, the brighter the light he carried, the more rounded her body became. And still he came, until he was standing behind her, the light blinding her. She watched, her face ashen as his hand came up to rest upon her shoulder. Her eyes dropped lower, to her protruding stomach. She picked up the hairbrush on the dressing table beside her and hurled it toward the mirror.

The glass shattered and the sound of it brought her out of her stupor. The door behind her crashed open and she turned, seeing Mairi and her mother rush into the room. She opened her mouth to speak, but the room began to spin. She lost consciousness and fell to the floor, lying like a broken doll in a bed of shattered mirror, bright with the reflection of the sun.

She awoke in her bed, the draperies drawn, the softly muted voices of her mother and sister nearby. She lay there for a long time, fully awake, fully conscious. Her head hurt. Her body felt chilled. But those things were unimportant. Her head was clear now for the first time since Nicholas Mackinnon had come to upset the order and tranquility in her life.

One of the figures huddled in the shadows moved and started toward her. "She's awake," Mairi said, coming to her side and taking her cold hand. "How do you feel?" she asked. "You gave us a scare. What happened?"

"Not now, Mairi," Effie said, moving to Mairi's side and taking Tibbie's hand. "You run on now and help Granny with her mending. I'll see to Tibbie."

She heard the chair scrape as Effie pulled it beside the bed and sat down, still holding Tibbie's hand. For a long time she sat there, holding her hand while Tibbie stared at the ceiling. There was strength in that hand, strength to give comfort and courage, strength of understanding. Tibbie knew that. She could feel it as keenly as the warmth from that hand, which penetrated the cold of hers. "Oh, Mama," she said, turning on her side and giving way to the tears that had waited so long to come, and then, once they did, seemed to have no end.

Effie used her free hand to stroke Tibbie's head. "My poor little lamb," she said. "I would take this burden for you if I could. You're still so young to have suffered so much."

"I don't know what to do . . ."

"I know. For some of us answers come with so much difficulty, so much trial and tribulation. You've always been a good person, Tibbie. You have a good heart. I don't believe for one minute God has it in his plan that you should suffer like this for long."

"I think God has forgotten all about me."

"No," Effie said, "though the Lord knows, I sometimes think things would go much easier for you if he had." Effie patted her hand and stood, pulling the blanket over her. "Why don't you sleep for a little while. You've been burning the candle at both ends lately. I'll see that Beth gets to her piano lessons."

"But the clinic—"

"There's no one there but old Thaddeus Carlisle wanting

someone to give him a little attention and a shot of Kentucky bourbon. Mairi can handle that. Now, you rest for a while."

She nodded and closed her eyes. But Nicholas Mackinnon was there, even in her sleep, his blue eyes staring at her intently, his look frank and hungry, without apology or shyness.

She had no idea how long she slept, but when she awoke the light in the room had faded and someone had lighted a lamp beside her bed, its dull glow filling the room with shadows. Somewhere in the house a door opened then shut, voices spoke and then she heard the sound of Beth's laughter. Beth would be wondering about her. She left the bed and went to her dressing table, putting her hair in order and pinching a little color into her cheeks.

"You look much better," her mother said, when she entered the kitchen sometime later.

"She looks the same to me," Granny said, giving her the once over.

Tibbie looked at Granny, who was eating cornbread crumbled in a glass with milk poured over it. She stopped eating when she saw Tibbie watching her. "I heard Coll say Slap Johnson has been enjoying poor health and his sister Ruby is feeling a mite less than common. Must be something going around. You feeling sick?"

"No," Tibbie said, "just a little tired."

"I bet it was those rootybaggers you ate that made you sick. I used to love rootybaggers, but they're against me now. I get backed up everytime I eat them, then Coll has to give me some workin' medicine."

"I'm feeling fine, Granny. Really I am."

"You lay off them rootybaggers, you hear?"

"I hear," Tibbie said. She glanced around the room. "Where's Beth? I thought I heard her."

"You did. She and Mairi went to the barn to give Precious his weekly bath."

Tibbie sighed and picked up the copper kettle. "She'll be a mess when she comes back. I'll put some water on to heat for her. She'll be needing a bath as well."

"I'll do that," Effie said, taking the kettle. "Why don't you get something to eat."

"I'm not hungry," Tibbie said, turning away. "I'll be in the parlor if anyone needs me."

A few minutes later Tibbie was seated in front of the rosewood piano, her eyes closed as her hands moved, quick and graceful, over the keys. Everything that came to her today seemed to be long and mournful and melancholy. Once or twice she tried to play something light and gay, but the moment she stopped forcing herself, she would find she had slipped back to the melancholy tunes again.

It was half past eight when she stood, closing the piano and picking up the lamp. Beth was in the warm cozy kitchen taking off her clothes when Tibbie came in. "I hope Precious looks cleaner than you do," she said.

"Oh, Mama, you should see him. He looks ever so nice and he smells sweet too. And we even put a bow around his neck. He's quite the most precious pig I've ever seen."

"If he would only stay that way." Tibbie picked up a piece of cornbread, moving to the table and taking a seat. She began to eat it, watching Beth climb into the tub.

"It's time to wash her hair, too, don't you think?" Effie asked, rolling up her sleeves.

"Nooooo!" Beth said.

"It's time," Tibbie said, giving Beth a reproving look. Beth was going through all the motions of washing. She soaped the sponge and lathered her arms at least eight times. Once, she went as far as her shoulders. But she never went near her face or ears. She saw her mother looking at her and gave Tibbie a smile. There were times like this, when she would sit and observe Beth, that she was reminded so much of Eric. And that was to be expected, she supposed, for indeed, Beth did favor her father.

She had been thinking of Eric a lot lately, more than she ever had since he'd left. She wondered about that for a moment, then decided it was because of Nicholas, a man who aroused thoughts and desires in her she hadn't felt since Eric left. She tried to capture Eric's face in her mind, but she kept seeing Nick as he had been earlier. She couldn't begin to understand how she had allowed herself to be nearly seduced again. Yet what could she have done to change anything? She was no innocent, and for that fact alone she should have been on her guard. But there were times when everything seemed so set against her. First there was Nick, pressing his suit every time she turned around, stooping as low as necessary to see that she played into his hands. And then there was her father, always insisting that she do this or that for Nick, and going so far as to order her to feed and care for him while he was gone.

How she wished Nick would heal quickly and be on his way. Things were going fine until he stormed into her life. And now he had invaded the only place she had been able to find solace —the clinic. And since his coming here, she was finding it harder and harder to blame him for all the turmoil that had so recently come her way. Perhaps that was because she knew it wasn't really all his doing. Oh, it had been in the beginning, but now she had allowed herself to care for him, and that made her as responsible as he. When had it happened? When had she begun to care?

It wasn't a time she could pinpoint. It had been so gradual, the feeling had just slipped up behind her, quiet as a cat. Nick was such an easy man to please, good-natured, easygoing, and unpretentious as they came. A lot like her in so many ways. It was easy to see how she could like him, and she had from the very beginning, but now her feelings ran deeper than that. She cared about him. Deeply. But was that the same as love? She didn't understand how it could be the same. She loved Eric, yet in some way she had been falling in love with Nick for some time.

It was an hour later before Tibbie had Beth to bed and their bedtime story read. With nothing left to do except make herself ready for bed, she decided she had put off the inevitable long enough. There was no other way around it. She would have to see Nicholas now. Damn him for falling off that scaffolding. Damn her father for leaving and placing him under her care. And damn her for caring. This newly discovered feeling terrified her, for what was she to do with it? She couldn't tell Nick, not now, for she had no idea what his intentions were. He had said he loved her, but that could mean a lot of things. The next move would be his.

She dreaded seeing him, afraid he would see instantly what was going on inside her. Determined to reveal nothing, she would be even more cautious.

If Nick thought Tibbie had been difficult to sway to his purpose before, her behavior over the next two weeks could only be called impossible. Every day she would come into his room, glowing with health and loveliness that seemed to increase day by day. And each time she entered the room, Nick could feel his body leap in response. With a scowl and a temperament so foul he couldn't stand himself, Nick watched her moving about the room, chatting about the day's activities in the clinic or that blasted pig's latest antic or something funny Granny Grace had said: always pleasant, always cordial, always indifferent. It was this indifference that was slowly driving him mad.

"Good morning, Mr. Mackinnon," she would say—it was that Mr. Mackinnon bit that made him want to bite himself. She couldn't fool him. She was deliberately provoking him, thinking that if she kept him irritated enough he wouldn't have amorous thoughts on his mind. And to a certain extent, that was true. Night after night he lay here thinking about her and what he'd like to do to her, only to have her come flitting into his room the next morning, wearing that I-know-something-that-you-don't smile of hers, so smug and so damn desirable that he wanted to make love to her and choke her at the same time.

He had thought her so sweet and kindhearted, but now he decided he'd never encountered a more devious, spiteful, and downright mean woman in all his life. If he could only get out of this bed.

Cursing his stupidity for falling and his consequent stupidity for receiving not one but two broken legs, he longed for the day that he could get out of bed and walk. Feeling more out of sorts than he had heretofore, he almost snarled at her when the door opened and she came dancing into the room, smelling like sunshine, her cheeks flushed, her eyes sparkling to match the dazzling smile on her face, speaking to him like he was some barnyard pet or a total idiot.

"It's a lovely day outside, and you're going to miss it if we don't open these windows." With that, she gave the drapes a yank and sunlight came flooding into the room. "Why, Mr. Mackinnon, I declare that is the same displeased look I saw on your face last night. Aren't you tired of wearing it?"

"No. I like wearing it!" he snapped. He was tired alright, but not of that.

"Would you like me to shave you this morning?"

"No."

"How about a nice sponge bath?"

"No."

"Would you like me to move your bed closer to the window so you can see outside?"

"Not particularly."

She moved to the bed and yanked the pillow from beneath his head, not bothering to apologize when his head thumped against the headboard. Then she began plumping and fluffing the pillows. "I could change your bed linens today, if you'd like."

"Don't bother."

She glanced at his bedside table. "Have you finished reading the books I brought you?"

"I haven't looked at them."

"That's nice," she said, smoothing the sheet and drawing the blanket up.

With a growl, Nick grabbed her arm and yanked her forward. With a startled cry, she fell sprawled across him. Tibbie held her breath. Was he going to throttle her or seduce her? She gasped at the way he was looking at her, so hungry, so intent, a herd of goats could have been driven into the room and he wouldn't have taken notice. His hands digging into her arms, he said, "If I had just one good leg, you'd wish you'd conducted yourself a little differently over the past few days. I've never wanted to paddle a woman's fanny as much as I do yours."

She fought back a smile. "You wouldn't dare!"

"Only because I haven't the strength to wrestle you into position, but I won't be incapacitated forever. I owe you one, lass, and you can rest assured that I always pay my debts."

"You're a brute!"

"Probably."

"And crude as they come!"

"That too."

"Let me up, or I'll—"

"Shut up, Tibbie."

"Don't think you can—"

Nick didn't let her finish. "Let me point something out to you, sweetheart. *You* are lying on top of me in *my* bed. I am calling the shots now and you are in no position to argue."

"What are you going to do?"

"Something I should have done a long time ago. I'm going to kiss you and keep on kissing you every time you open that pretty little mouth of yours."

"You seem to forget that you are a guest here in my house and—"

"And you seem to forget what I just said." She was so stunned that all she could do when he pulled her closer was squeak. She told herself it was time to put up a little resistance, but to save her soul she couldn't manage even a pitifully weak protest. His hand came over her back and along her neck, his thumb pressing her head up, their eyes locking for only a moment before she felt his lips, hard, urgent, and hot, upon hers. Nicholas didn't care at this point if he frightened her with his passion or not. She had tempted and taunted him for weeks and he had finally called her bluff. If he had to scare the drawers off of her to get her attention, he wasn't above doing just that.

But one thing was harder than he imagined. Restraining himself was the most difficult thing he had ever done. He had thought and dreamed about her for so long that the moment her body had pressed its weight upon him, his body cried out for him to take her—here, and now.

He was concentrating so hard on his restraint, he wasn't completely conscious of what he was about. He wasn't aware that his hands had threaded into the silky skeins of her hair, sending hairpins clattering across the bed and floor, or that he had shifted her until she lay full upon him, his knee between her legs so that she was, in the plainest sense of the word, riding him.

But Tibbie was aware of it, and the pressure of him hard against her groin was making her mindless and forgetful. And to make matters worse, he was kissing her senseless, using everything he could throw at her to weaken her and leave her helpless and vulnerable to his will: his hands, mouth, tongue, softly whispered words, and artfully applied pressure. Oh, he was a devil all right, and he was tempting as well.

Never had she known that one person could possess such a strong sexual attraction, so strong that even knowing what she knew and knowing without a doubt what he was about, she was powerless to stop him. And stop him she should.

Was that his hand inside her drawers? Oh, God! "Nicholas—"

His breath coming hot and heavy against her ear, she heard him say, "I've wanted you like this for so long, and now that I have you here, I don't have a good leg to stand on." His frustration mounting, he added, "God! What a sense of timing."

She was feeling a lot of the same frustration and her restless body showed it.

"Easy," he said, his breath blowing warm and strong into her ear.

"What are you doing?"

"Just let me touch you. You'll see," he said.

He was right about that. She caught her breath, her head falling back as she moaned softly. He might have suffered several broken bones and lost the use of his legs, but there was absolutely nothing wrong with his hands, and he showed her just how true that was.

They were both so engrossed and breathing heavily that neither of them heard the door open. But they both heard Mairi's startled gasp. Simultaneously, Nick and Tibbie looked up, staring at the door, seeing Mairi's head poking through. "Mama wanted me to ask you if you wanted to walk down to the orchard with us. The weather is nice and she thought it would be good exercise"—Mairi paused, a wide grin coming across her face—"but it looks like you're getting plenty of that."

Before Tibbie could respond, Mairi was gone, the door closing softly behind her.

"Ohhhhh!" she groaned. "I'm ruined."

"I don't think it's as bad as all that."

"You don't know my sister," she said, rolling away from him. A moment later she slipped through the door.

Mairi was waiting for her at the end of the hallway. Before Tibbie could utter a sound, Mairi took her hand and pulled her along behind her. "We need to talk," Mairi said.

"Where are we going?"

"For a walk."

Once they were outside, Mairi said, "Okay. Start talking."

They walked halfway to town before Tibbie finished her long story, leaving nothing out. "Do you think I've gone mad?" she asked.

Mairi laughed. "If you have, I wish I could join you. You're in love, Tib. Enjoy it."

"How?"

Mairi gave her a disbelieving look. "You have a man that looks like Nicholas Mackinnon telling you he's in love with you, and you don't know how to enjoy it? Maybe you have gone mad."

"Somehow I knew you'd say that."

They climbed through the fence, Mairi spouting something about Mr. Harkington's mean bull, but Tibbie just kept walking. "Tibbie," she said, catching up to her, "I hope you aren't going to do something stupid like continuing this crusade of loyalty to Eric. Think back, Tib. Look what you've been through. Disappointment, rejection, suffering, more than most people endure in a lifetime. And you came through it, you survived. It wasn't easy, but you did it. And for what? To wither and die on the vine? You've got a chance for happiness. Take it in both hands and hold on to it tightly."

A weary, thinner Coll Buchanan returned the next morning, and after giving Nick a close examination, he removed the splint on his right leg and declared him well enough to take a few short trips with the aid of a crutch. "You'll be surprised at how weak you are and how quickly you'll get tired. Moving across the room to relieve yourself will leave you winded and gasping for breath. But it'll get better each time you get up."

After he finished with Nick, he did some paperwork in his office. When he didn't come for dinner, Tibbie went looking for him, finding him asleep at his desk. When she called him he did not stir, and when she touched his face she found it burning with fever. Tibbie feared the worst, thinking that Coll had come down with the dreaded yellow fever after having been exposed to the virus.

It wasn't yellow fever. Coll had awakened when she and Mairi and Effie put him to bed, putting their fears to rest. But he was still a sick man, running a high fever for two days before he broke out with chicken pox.

"Chicken pox!" Effie said. "After all the years he's been treating children with chicken pox and never caught it?"

"Well, he's got it now," Tibbie said, "and the worst case of it I've ever seen. And on top of that, Papa is the absolute *worst* patient I've ever seen."

Because of her father's illness, Tibbie had twice as much work to do, taking care of Coll and managing the clinic. It wasn't intentionally that she didn't see Nick, but that her time and talent was needed elsewhere. Mairi kept her up to date on his progress, which was fine. It was his disposition that was suffering. On the fourth day after Coll had taken sick, Mairi quit.

"What do you mean, you quit?" Tibbie asked.

"I mean I quit. That man is so irritable he can't stand himself! All he does is shout and throw things. Yesterday it was a bar of soap, today his drinking glass. He's been asking for you, and looks mad enough to kill me each time I open the door and he sees who it is. I'm telling you the truth, Tibbie, I think he might throttle me if I go in there one more time."

"All right," Tibbie said, "I'll see what I can do."

"Before supper," Mairi said, "because I'm not taking that tray in there to him. He can starve for all I care!"

Tibbie sighed. It had been raining cats and dogs all day, so thankfully the usual number of patients she had to see had been lower than usual and she had finished early. She had hoped to use the time to bathe and wash her hair. She looked at the clock and let out a sigh. She knew what awaited her when she opened the door to Nick's room.

It would have been a lie to say that Tibbie wasn't the least concerned about that. She knew the kind of man Nicholas Mackinnon was: proud, strong, sure of himself, and by now very, very angry.

She put it off as long as she could, until she had visions of Nicholas throwing a fit for attention and flinging his crutch across the room and banging his cup on the bedside table. The rain had blocked out so much of the sunlight, it was necessary for her to take a candle as she left her room. The hallway was long and dark, and the journey far too short. For some time she stood outside his door, debating just how she should go about this. She could try the light, frivolous approach, entering the room in a flutter of skirts and chirping in a high-pitched voice.

But Nick was a smart man. He wouldn't be fooled for an instant by any kind of frivolity—light or otherwise. Besides, she wasn't a frivolous woman, and chirping wasn't exactly her forte. Perhaps she should try being remorseful, slipping into the room as quiet and timid as a field mouse, playing upon his sympathy and throwing herself at the mercy of the court. But Nick was the kind of judge that would sentence her without a trial—fair or not. Of course, she always had the option of using the blustery approach, stomping in there mad as fire and giving him what for before he had a chance to give it to her.

But Nick would be angry enough on his own. Saints preserve her, if she should rile that Scots temper one degree more. In the end she decided she would just have to be honest. If he asked where she had been over the past few days, she would say truthfully, "I've been very busy." And that was that.

His room was looking its medicinal best when she opened the door and went in. Nick, however, was not.

She stood near the door with her candle in her hand, holding her breath and wondering if he would speak first or throw something. When nothing happened, she fortified herself with a deep breath and crept across the room. He was on his side, turned away from her, facing the wall. His breathing was steady and even, his body still, so she expelled a slow breath, thankful he was asleep.

Suddenly he flipped over, looking mad enough to kill. "Where in the hell have you been?"

The sudden movement startled her and she screamed, dropping the candle which immediately went out. She heard him curse and fumble with something. She heard a match strike, the flame bursting to life and making his features look even more threatening than before, as he leaned toward her, lighting the lamp beside the bed. When he finished, he leaned back and crossed his arms in front of him, looked hard at her and said, "Well?"

13

"Would you prefer the nasty truth or a bland lie?"

"I always prefer anything nasty," he said, impaling her with his glare. "Please. Enlighten me in your nastiest fashion."

"And the topic?"

"You know that as well as I."

"Humor me," she said, feeling almost giddy from the outrageous turn of events. There is a certain thrill that comes with danger, she thought, remembering Granny Grace had once told her that danger and delight grow on the same vine.

"I wonder why it is," he said slowly, "that audacity in a woman always augments courage, foolish as it may be."

"Foolish?"

"There should always be some shred of diplomacy in brashness, otherwise . . ." He lifted one dark brow in challenge. "When a mouse laughs at the cat, there should be a hole nearby."

"Who said I was laughing?"

"You've too much sass in you, lass. Someday some man is going to take it out."

"Really?" How calm the word sounded. How loud her knees were knocking. "I look forward to his trying."

He leaned back against the headboard, his hands folded together and resting beneath his chin. He studied her face, the energy in her bright eyes, remembering the breathy tones of her voice. "Have you issued me a challenge, then?"

"I thought I was responding to yours."

The blinding whiteness of his lazy smile did the strangest

things to Tibbie's heart rate. "It amazes me that I thought I could confront you and have you quaking in your boots." Then he surprised her by adding, "I should have remembered I have yet to come out of an altercation with you unscathed."

Tibbie was so stunned by this sudden turn of events she couldn't help smiling. "It would help, perhaps, if you remembered that if you play with cats, you must expect to be scratched."

"I'll keep that in mind," he said, "for next time." He looked at her, a ghost of a smile hovering at his mouth. "It would help, perhaps, if you would remember that Jupiter is slow to look in his notebook, but he always looks."

She groaned at the thought.

"I'd like to have a bath now, and after that my bedding changed."

So that was the way it was going to be. Jupiter might be slow, but apparently Nick wasn't. "Of course. I'll draw some water."

As she left the room, her fists clenched at her sides, he called after her, "I want the bath within the hour, Miss Buchanan, not sometime next week."

"Then get it yourself!"

"How is your father?" he asked, and Tibbie stopped dead in her tracks.

How dare he remind her of her father, and consequently of the fact that he wasn't above playing the traitor. *Let him tell Papa anything he wants. . . .* But as she thought that, she remembered the tiredness in her father's eyes, the way his poor body was covered with small blisters. The extra burden and worry about the yellow-fever epidemic had taken its toll on him. How could she even consider adding to that burden? Her father depended on her. She sighed. Nick would get his bath, but there was more than one way to skin a cat.

As she headed for the kitchen she wondered just how hot she could get the water without causing any permanent damage—none that her father could see, at any rate.

The water was blistering hot, or so Nick thought, and if that didn't leave his skin raw, the fiery, impassioned scrubbing that Tibbie gave him did. For a solid hour after his bath, his skin burned like fire and the discomfort of it brought a scowl to his brow. But then he began to think upon it, and remembering the bath, he couldn't help smiling.

She had entered the room carrying two large buckets of steaming water, Mairi coming right behind her, complaining as usual about having to carry a large basin, while Beth, who was always happy to be included, brought up the rear with a stack of towels and a flat cake of soap. For a moment Mairi stood beside the bed, watching her sister pour the water into the basin and make ready the soap and towels. But when Tibbie began removing the bandages that held the splint over his mending leg, she must have realized that there would soon be a half-naked man beneath her gaze. Mairi shot from the room, dragging Beth with her. If Tibbie noticed her haste in departing, she didn't let on.

Tibbie removed the splint, laying it aside. "You mustn't move, you understand. The splint must go back on as soon as I . . . you've . . . uh . . . washed."

With the bandages and splint off, Nick was feeling better than he had since his fall, and with his body feeling so good, his spirits lifted considerably. In fact, it could be said he was feeling downright frisky. Seeing Tibbie concentrating so earnestly on her work, he decided it was a downright shame for him to be the only one to enjoy this frisky mood of his. The Christian thing to do, of course, was to share it.

"Does your father smoke?"

"Goodness, no," she said, cutting another length of new bandage and placing it in the growing pile next to the splint.

"But he must have been given a cigar or two from time to time as payment or a token of appreciation?"

"Of course he has. He has a box full of them. Gives them to guests, since he doesn't indulge himself."

"I suppose he wouldn't mind if I smoked one, then?"

She stopped, her hands going to her hips. "Are you asking

me—in a roundabout way, of course—to go fetch you a cigar?"

"In a roundabout way, yes."

She started for the door, calling over her shoulder. "Don't
forget, you aren't supposed to move. You'll be sorry if you do."

"I wouldn't dream of it," he said. *Because I have too much
in store for you, sweetheart, and I wouldn't want to miss a single
minute of it.*

A few minutes later she returned and placed three cigars on
the table beside him. She picked up the bandaging. She measured the fabric and picked up the scissors.

"Have you any matches?"

"Aren't there any by your lamp?"

"Used the last one this morning."

"Why didn't you tell me when I went for the cigars?"

"I didn't think about it then." He smiled blandly. "Would
you mind checking to see if you have any?"

She sent him an irritated glance and put the bandaging and
scissors down, her hands going to her pockets. "I don't have
any matches," she said flatly, hoping that would shut him up.

She picked up the bandaging and was just reaching for the
scissors when he said, "Would you mind going to see if you
can find me some, then?"

Yes, you arrogant beast, I would mind! She glared at him.
"No, of course not."

She picked up the scissors and started to cut another strip,
but before she could, he said, *"Now, if you don't mind."*

She slammed the scissors down and left the room without a
word. Five minutes later she returned, tossing a box of
matches at him. They landed on the sheet, just where it covered a very vital part of him. "Contrary to what it may look
like," he said dryly, "that isn't a fuse."

Her face flooded with color. "You shouldn't be so vulgar."

"You shouldn't have such a good aim."

"I wasn't aim—" She caught herself just in time. Without
another word she finished cutting the stack of bandages, then

moved to his bedside, placing them on the table beside him. "Do you need anything else?"

"No."

When she started from the room, he called after her. "I'm sure you forgot, Miss Tibbie, but you'll have to do the honors. As much as I'd like to bathe myself, I'm not supposed to move, remember?"

"You've got one good arm now, and I think the other one is sufficiently mended for bathing."

"In your opinion, that may be true, but your father advised against it."

Leave my father out of this!

He could tell even from across the room that she gritted her teeth at him, yet she remained silent. He gave her his most innocent look as she returned to his bedside, taking up the bar of soap. Dipping it and the sponge in water, she washed one arm. As she did, he lit the cigar. When she finished his arm, she leaned over to get the other one. He exhaled a large puff of smoke.

When the smoke cleared and her coughing subsided, she said, "Do you think you could refrain from blowing smoke in my face?"

"Does my smoking bother you?"

"Everything about you bothers me, Mackinnon. Every single little thing you do."

That delighted him, of course, and he grinned.

If there's anything I want to do, sweetheart, it's bother you.

He took another puff from the cigar, exhaling the smoke, trying not to smile at the way she fanned the air around her. His little Scot had her dander up. He wondered just how much more of this she would take. He was a beast, he knew, but he had to find out. So he smiled and pointed at his leg. Her nostrils flared in revolt, but she didn't say a word. When she finished one leg, she moved to the other, and when it was done, she tossed the sponge back into the water.

It took the better part of the next hour to replace the splint and bandages. But once she was done, she breathed a sigh of relief, thinking she would soon be able to put some distance between them. All that cigar smoke had her turning green around the edges. How could he stand to smoke the ghastly things? She reached for the clean bed linens, intending to change his bed when he said, "I'd like my face washed, too, if you don't mind."

"Oh, for heaven's sake . . ." she said a little too loudly, exasperated beyond measure at the way things were going, but she picked up the sponge and gave his face a couple of swipes. Then she tossed the sponge back into the water, surprised that he didn't complain about it splashing on him. He retaliated by blowing another puff of smoke in her face.

I'd like to shove that cigar down his hateful throat and tell Papa he choked in his sleep.

"It behooves me to tell you this, Miss Tibbie, but that isn't all," Nick said with an air of authority.

It behooves? I'll just bet it does! It behooves . . . The preposterousness of it almost sent her into a gale of laughter.

"There is one other place . . ." he went on.

Tibbie had a pretty good idea just where that place was. "You can wash *that* place yourself. I wouldn't touch it with a ten-foot pole."

"That's encouraging," he said with a laugh, "because I prefer you to use your hand."

"And I prefer—"

Nicholas would go to his grave never knowing exactly what it was that Tibbie preferred, for at that moment he caught her by the arm and, as she had been twice before, Tibbie found herself in Nick's bed. "Shut up, Tibbie," he said. "You don't know what you prefer. You don't even know what you want. But I do."

"You don't know anything. You just like to provoke me." When he didn't say anything else, she said, "Nicholas Mackinnon, why are you behaving like this?"

"I like the way you say my name, Miss Tibbie. Indeed I do."

"Will you stop acting like a crazed fool, before someone comes in here?"

"No one will come in here. They all have a pretty good idea about us."

She was only play-acting when she opened her mouth to yell and said, "I can get someone in here." She said that, just to see what he would do. She found out all right.

Nick slapped his mouth over hers faster than a chicken on a June bug. His intent had been to shut her up. But when her arms went around his neck and her breasts flattened against his chest, he forgot everything. He kissed her like there was no tomorrow, and Tibbie was kissing him back like she had already lost today. He pulled her closer, lifting her and fitting her against him, feeling her arms tighten around his neck in response. He enjoyed kissing her so much and having her respond to it the way she was that he was content to kiss her for a long time. This was one sweet, long-awaited miracle he was going to enjoy.

At last, he pulled away from her, looking into her eyes with eyes so blue she could swim in them. While Tibbie lay speechless over what had just happened, Nick brought his mouth to hers once again, kissing her with an endless, demanding kiss that took her breath and left her limp and unable to think. Again and again his mouth moved over hers with a hunger she had never before known, yet at the same time a tenderness so gentle she wanted to cry. Somewhere, deep in the most private part of her, she sensed he was a lonely man who truly felt the desperation he spoke of. She was powerless to resist it, responding to that side of him more than any other. With a muted groan her lips molded to his and she melted against him. Feeling her response inflamed him, and with a groan of his own, the demanding pressure of the kiss deepened. Again and again he kissed her like this, putting every fiber of his being into it, showing her without words.

She had been kissed before, but never like this. And in spite of all her protestations, she really didn't want it to end. Judging from the way Nick was kissing her, he didn't either.

When he broke the kiss she looked up to see Nick watching her, and without really thinking about it, she raised her head and kissed him, full upon the mouth. Instantly, Nick's worried look vanished, and he laughed, a low, rolling rumble. "You outrageous little imp," he said, using his good arm to draw her closer to him. "Do you know I have spent many a night dreaming that you might someday kiss me like you did . . . voluntarily and of your own accord?"

"Have you, now?" she said, her eyes filled with teasing laughter. "If I had known that, I might have reconsidered."

"But it's too late for that now," he said, "for the moment is gone, but I have the memory."

Oh, Nicholas . . . you say such beautiful things.

"I wish," he said, pulling her closer, "that I could keep you here like this forever."

"We might get hungry," she said, "or you might decide you want another bath."

"I don't think I could stand another bath," he said. Then rolling up onto his elbow, he looked down into her face. "Do you have any idea what that did to me? To have you running your hands all over me?"

"I know what it did to me. Is it the same?"

"If it isn't, it should be," he said gruffly, and kissed her.

Breathless, she said, "I should be going."

"You," he said, biting her nose lightly, "should be doing a lot of things, but going isn't one of them."

"What kind of things, Nick?"

"Come closer and I'll show you."

"Why?" she asked in a trembling voice.

"Because you and I have a lot of unfinished business."

Tibbie pulled back and stared at him in a distrustful way, but at the same time her mind was racing with the possibilities. When she hesitated, he said, "I won't force anything on you. You should know that by now."

She leaned toward him, but his hand came up between them to rest upon her shoulder, detaining her. "Weigh carefully what I've just said, Tib," he warned, "because if you choose to find out what I'm talking about, you won't be able to blame me for the outcome."

It was difficult for her to change directions all of a sudden. All the time she had known him he had been doing one thing or the other to get her alone with him, to get her into his arms, to weaken her defenses. And he had finally accomplished all of that. She was here with him, alone and in his arms, and her defenses were as weak as a rained-on bee. And what was he doing about it? Nothing! No, worse than that—he was giving her fair warning. What was she supposed to do?

I'd know what I'd like to do.

Then do it!

I don't know if I can.

Why can't you?

Because he's making me do all the giving.

Believe me, he'll be giving plenty if you'll just cooperate.

Why can't he meet me halfway?

I don't know. Why don't you ask him?

"Can you meet me halfway?"

Nick's heart nearly leaped out of his chest, exploding with joy. Had he heard her right? He hadn't expected her even to consider what he'd said, let alone ask him to come halfway. *Meet her halfway?* Hell! He was itching to go the whole damn distance. But that wasn't his way, not with this lass. These first fledgling steps had to be taken alone. He had nurtured this love that he knew they felt for each other long enough. It was time to push her out of the nest.

He saw the small, anxious face watching him so earnestly, and his heart twisted with the fear that his next words would send her away. "No, Tibbie, not this time. This time, lass, you're going to have to come to me."

"But it's such a big step for me."

"I know. You've got so much holding you back: Eric; the past; feelings you're not yet sure of. There isn't much drawing you forward, except an honest invitation and my desire to see that you never regret accepting it. For too long the rule guiding your life has been denial. If you want that to change, if you want to come out into the sunlight, you're going to have to be the one to change all that. Stay where you are and deny yourself again, or come here and accept what I offer. I can't make it more simple than that."

The words were hardly out his mouth when Tibbie threw herself against him. He held her close to him for a minute, his hand stroking her hair, his heart listening to the sounds of her crying. "Go ahead and cry, sweetheart. That's the only way you're going to set the angel free."

Tibbie cried harder.

Nicholas wanted to lose himself in his passion for her, but he knew that that was the wrong thing to do. He had gained a lot of grass with this reluctant lass of his. He wanted no setbacks now. Tomorrow he wanted her to remember that she had trusted him—and that he had not violated that trust. It was one small stone laid in the foundation. Pray to God he had the patience and stamina to endure the torment of wanting and not having until the last stone was in place.

When someone knocked on the door, Tibbie jumped, pushing herself away from Nick, wiping her eyes and feeling the same frustration she heard in his softly sworn curse. There was never any privacy in this family, but perhaps it was just as well. She couldn't stay in Nick's arms crying for the rest of her life, no matter how wonderful it felt.

Smoothing her hair and hurrying to the door, she wondered who was on the other side. She opened the door to see Mairi, standing wide-eyed on the other side. She smiled at her sister, thankful that Mairi had the good sense to knock this time. "It's all right," she said softly. "You can come in. I've just finished with Mr. Mackinnon."

But Mr. Mackinnon isn't finished with you, sweetheart. . . .

"Mama wanted to know if you needed any help getting Mr. Mackinnon out of his bed so you can change the bed linens."

Turn that around and you'll have it right. Mr. Mackinnon needs help getting Miss Buchanan into his bed.

"Yes, I think I will. He's still a little unstable . . . with his crutches."

It took some doing, but the two of them managed to help Nick onto his feet, where he stood for a moment to regain his balance before bracing himself on his crutch and hobbling to the chair a few feet away. Tibbie took a hasty look at Mairi, to see if she was as disturbed by the sight of as fine a specimen of manhood as Nicholas, draped in a flimsy loincloth and nothing more. But if it disturbed Mairi at all, she was good at hiding it, and that made Tibbie wonder if she was the only one with thoughts like that on her mind.

Once the bed was made and Nick was back in it, Mairi gathered the dirty linens and left Tibbie to finish up. Replacing the light blanket over the sheet, Tibbie was tucking it under the mattress when Nick began teasing her again, making half-lunges toward her, telling her what he was going to do if he caught her. Tibbie was laughing at what he said, when Mairi returned.

"Cora Belle Hamilton and her cousin Ruthie are here," she said, coming into the room.

Tibbie turned to look at Mairi. "Cora Belle and Ruthie? Is one of them sick?"

"No," Mairi said. "They both look fit as a fiddle to me, all decked out like the Fourth of July. They told Mama they'd come to call on Mr. Mackinnon and bring him a little something they baked for him."

Both women turned to look at Nick, who smiled in a rather sheepish way and shrugged. "It's purely a social call," he said nonchalantly.

"Oh, I'm sure it is," said Tibbie. Then she turned to Mairi. "Well, don't stand there like a trapped fly. Show them in."

Mairi shot from the room and Tibbie moved to Nick's bed-side, giving the blanket a yank and tucking it snugly over him. "Ouch!" he said. "You don't have to take it out on me," he said, grinning. "I didn't invite them here."

"I'm not taking anything out on you. It's of no concern to me who comes to visit you."

"You look a little miffed to me," he said. "If I had known they were likely to come calling, I would have told you."

"I don't care if you have women hauled in by the wagon

load or smuggled in here in trunks." She gave the blanket one final yank and tucked it in.

"You've got this blasted blanket so tight I can't wiggle my toes."

It isn't your toes I'm concerned about. "Then the blanket should stay in place."

He grinned at her. "Why? Are you worried these lovely ladies might do a little peeking?"

"No, but you certainly aren't above doing a little showing!"

She picked up the tray with the supplies on it. "I'll be going now. Mairi will show your . . . visitors in."

"Tib," he called after her.

Halfway to the door she paused and turned. He told her, "You don't have a thing to be jealous about."

"Who's jealous?" she said, kicking a chair out of the way.

At the door, she was almost levelled by the stampede to get into the room and her tray and supplies went scattering. "There you are, Mr. Mackinnon," Cora Belle Hamilton said in tones that would make a parrot envious. "You do remember me, don't you? The Reverend Woolridge introduced us at church one Sunday. And this is my cousin, Ruthie Faye Brewster."

Tibbie turned to see the two of them sweep into the room like a blight.

"Charmed, ladies. I'm absolutely charmed that you would remember me, let alone go to all the trouble to pay me a visit." He looked at Tibbie, who had finished picking up her supplies and was making her way toward the door. *It won't work.* Grinning, he said, "You do know Miss Buchanan, don't you?"

Both women turned to look at Tibbie. "Why, yes, of course. You're looking well, Tibbie . . ." Cora Belle smirked and looked at her cousin and then at Nick. "And how is that darling daughter of yours?"

Tibbie's heart sank.

"You must mean Bethany," Nick put in, catching the pain in those translucent golden eyes. He wished these two plump cows were gone so he could take Tibbie in his arms and tell her he wouldn't trade her for five trainloads of women like these two. "I'm sure you find her as utterly adorable as I do," he said.

"Oh, yes . . . adorable. Utterly adorable." Cora Belle said with more passion in her voice than Tibbie had ever heard.

"Well, as I was saying, the Reverend Woolridge, who introduced us you remember, was telling me just last Sunday all about your unfortunate accident." Her eyes swept hungrily over Nick. "You poor, dear man. Does it hurt terribly?"

"Only when I breathe, but Miss Buchanan has been taking excellent care of me during her father's illness."

Two pair of eyes drifted toward Tibbie. "Yes . . . well, Tibbie is good at taking care of men. . . . When they're sick, of course."

"Of course," Nick agreed. "She is exceptionally good at it. So good, in fact, I'm sure half the women in Indianola envy her skills."

"Oh, absolutely!" Cora Belle said, looking crestfallen. "Isn't that so, Ruthie Faye?"

"Why, yes, it is. I am terribly jealous," she said, "just terribly jealous."

At that moment Granny Grace, who had been passing down the hall, took notice of Tibbie's pale face. She paused in the doorway, her eyes going from Tibbie to Nick to the two women dressed fancier than circus ponies. With a snort she hobbled into the room, her black silk bombazine dress rustling like she was walking on leaves, and everyone turned to look at her. "Hah! I thought I recognized your gig, Cora Belle. What brings you out to this neck of the woods? You on the scent of something?"

"We're paying a social call, Mrs. Stewart. After the Reverend Woolridge told us of Mr. Mackinnon's unfortunate circumstances, I had the brainstorm to bake him a lemon cake for his convalescence."

"A brainstorm? Cora Belle Hamilton, I've known you since you were knee-high to a grasshopper, and the closest you ever came to a brainstorm was a light drizzle."

"Heh! Heh! Heh!" Cora Belle tried to laugh, but it fell flat as her bustle.

Granny looked at Ruthie. "I see you brought reinforcements."

"Ruthie Faye has a little head cold. I thought we might have Dr. Buchanan look her over, but I understand he's feeling poorly."

"Yes, he is," Granny said, "but Ruthie might want to hang onto that cold of hers. I'm sure it must be nice to have something in her head."

"Well, I never!" Cora Belle said with a huff, her corset laces quivering unpredictably. "We'd best be on our way."

"Thank you, ladies, for coming," said Nick.

"I'll show you out," said Tibbie.

"Don't bother," said Cora Belle. "We know the way."

Tibbie watched the two women leave, then turned to her grandmother. "You shouldn't be so hard on them, Granny. They thought they were doing good."

"Those two do about as much good as a glass eye at a keyhole."

Nick broke into gales of laughter. "You aren't married, are you, Granny?"

"Nope, and I don't think there's a man alive that could put up with me."

"I'd marry you in a minute."

"Lordy! Lordy! I'm too old for you," she said, her dress rustling as she turned toward the door.

Nick called after her. "If you're an example of what it's like to be old, then I'm looking forward to old age."

"No, you aren't," said Granny. "Do you know what it's like to look at yourself in the mirror every morning and wonder where you've seen that face before?" And with that, she was gone.

And Tibbie was right on her heels, giving him a hard look, ignoring the fact that Nick was calling after her.

He yelled after her. "You would try the patience of Job,

woman! Will you at least stop a minute? I have something to tell you."

She stopped, still giving him her back, not bothering to turn around. "What is it now?"

"Come here, will you?"

"I've got work to do."

"So have I, and it's quite pressing, believe me."

"Then do it, I'm not stopping you."

"It's a private matter."

"Fine. I'm giving you plenty of privacy, all the privacy you'll need."

"I said it was private, not that I needed privacy. I need your help. Will you come here?"

She didn't budge.

"Tibbie, I know you're upset, but be reasonable. What would it hurt to walk over here?"

"I did that once, remember?"

"Yes, and if you'll remember, not a *damn* thing happened when you did."

"Only because we were interrupted." She started out the door.

"Tibbie!"

She stopped, sighing. "Whatever you have to say, you can say to me here."

"I'd rather not shout it so everyone in the house will hear it."

"Anything you have to say to me you can say to my family."

"Alright," he said. "Alright. I need to relieve myself, and if you don't help me out of this damn bed I'll do it right here!"

"Whatever you like," she said, and walked from the room.

"Tibbie! . . . Tibbie Buchanan, I'm warning you—"

Thwack! went the door as it slammed behind her.

"Bitch!" he yelled, throwing his tin cup, which hit the door and then the floor, rolling a few feet.

Tibbie smiled and walked down the hall, ignoring the

strange look she got from Mairi. "Aren't you going to help him?"

"No."

"But Tibbie . . . what if he's hurt?"

"He's not hurt. He's mad."

"What if he hurts himself?"

"Then I'll go see about him."

Tibbie had cooled down sufficiently to think more rationally. She knew Nick needed help to get out of bed and balance himself with his crutch. What if he really did need to relieve himself? If he did, there was no way he could make it even if he did manage to get out of bed by himself. He would need her to lean on. She remembered the sight of his blood spreading on the sheet when he pulled his stitches. With a sigh, she remembered how comical Nick had looked all propped up in his bed, blowing smoke in her face while she bathed him.

Her temper sufficiently cooled, she headed for Nick's room. She opened the door and stood in the doorway, watching him. He had managed to work himself out of the tightly tucked blanket and was leaning over the side of the bed, struggling to reach his crutch.

She fully intended to help him, but enjoyed seeing him like this; the strong, lithe body, the well-developed muscles that looked so smooth, though she knew they were hard to the touch. What a beautiful thing a man was, the wide muscular shoulders, the narrow waist, the trim hips with the hard, rounded buttocks. How different he was from her and how beautiful.

She watched him reaching for his crutch and her heart contracted painfully with remorse. He was a strong, proud man— such a contrast of powerful muscle and virile male in a helpless state. How humiliating and degrading it must be for him to seek the help of a woman each and every time he left his bed, and even now, the ordeal he was going through to reach that supportive piece of wood. Hoping she could salvage some of that bruised pride, she pushed the door quietly closed and started toward him, when he leaned just a little too far and fell from the bed.

His face was twisted with pain when she dropped to the floor beside him. "Nick—"

"Get away from me, damn you! I don't need you now," he said, clenching his jaws together to keep from screaming out in pain.

Tibbie sprang to her feet, rushing into her father's office and returning quickly with the tincture of opium. She joined him on the floor. "Here," she said, pouring some into a glass of water, "drink this. It will ease the pain, then I'll see to your leg."

"You've seen to enough, thank you. Now get out of here and leave me alone."

"Nick—"

"If you want to do something for me, send someone to find Porter Masterson and tell him to get over here as quickly as he can and bring a wagon."

"Why do you need him to bring a wagon?"

"So he can put me in it and take me home."

"You can't go home yet. You need someone to care for you—"

"Then I'll ask Cora Belle Hamilton."

"You've every right to be angry with me, Nicholas. Every right. This is all my fault. But you can't leave—"

"Oh, can't I? You just watch me."

She placed her hand on his arm. "I don't want you to leave."

"Why? Because you enjoy having some man pant after you so you can reject him at every turn? Because of what your father might say when he finds out? Well, don't worry your pretty little head about that. I won't tell him." He threw back his head with a grimace.

"We'll discuss all of that after you drink this," she said, bringing the glass to his lips. He drank it all, then rested his head against the bed, his eyes closed. Tibbie picked up the hem of her skirt and blotted the perspiration from his face, but before she could finish, Nick's arm lashed out and grabbed her wrist, squeezing painfully. "You must be terribly obtuse, sweetheart. I said I didn't want you to do anything for me. In plain English, I don't want your hands on me. Is that clear?"

"It's perfectly clear, you bellowing brute, but you're in no condition to know what in blue blazes you want. And I'll thank you to remember my father is ill and that makes *me* in charge here, not you, and until he returns, *I'll* say who needs what. Now, put your arm across my shoulder. I'm going to help you to your feet. But don't put any weight on that leg."

"Are you kidding?"

"No," she said, giving him a soft smile. "Oh, Nicholas, I'm so sorry. Really I am. I don't know why I behaved the way I did. I just felt so angry and hurt at the way Cora Belle came marching in here, fawning all over you. I'll invite her back every day if you like, only don't be angry with me."

He watched her in silence, feeling the anger drain out of him with each word she said. "Tibbie," he said, sounding very tired, "the last thing in the world I want to see right now is another woman."

Tibbie couldn't think of a single thing to say, because she knew in her heart of hearts, he was right. And she didn't blame him. She decided she would help him to bed and check his leg and then, after that she would see about finding a male to care for him.

And Tibbie did exactly that.

14

"Calm down, Nick, or you'll rupture something," Coll said.

"I've already ruptured something! My patience!" He glanced around the room. "Where in the hell is she?"

"Did you send for me?" Tibbie asked, opening the door to Nick's room.

"Yes," he said calmly, "I did." He pointed at the young boy standing just behind her and said, "Who in the hell is that?"

"Jeremy Pipkin," she said, watching from the corner of her eye as her father slipped from the room.

"How nice," he said. Looking at Jeremy, he said, "I'm Nicholas Mackinnon." Then looking back at Tibbie, he added, "And who in the hell, may I ask, is Jeremy Pipkin, and more importantly, what is he doing in here?"

"I hired him."

"For what?"

"To be your assistant."

"My assistant. I see. And what, pray tell, is he supposed to assist me with, since my present activities are, shall we say, somewhat limited—eating, sleeping, complaining, getting in and out of bed?"

"That," she said simply, "is what he's here to help with."

"Tibbie, you don't make sense." He paused. "I don't know why that surprises me."

"I was thinking—"

He threw up his arms. "God help us!"

She was finding it easier and easier to ignore those sarcastic stabs he periodically pointed at her. "After you fell the other day, I thought about the things you said."

"I was hurt. People sometimes say things they don't mean when they're hurt."

"Oh, I understand that, but the things you said did have . . . well, at least some of them did have merit."

"Like what?"

"I believe you said, 'The last thing in the world I want to see right now is another woman,' so naturally I thought it might be a good idea to find a man to do the things I had been doing for you." She noticed the way his eyes went to Jeremy, his brows shooting up as if questioning her words when she said the word *man*. "Jeremy is young," she said, "but he's strong and experienced."

"Strong and experienced."

"Yes. His father lost a leg last year in a wagon accident and Jeremy was a tremendous help to him."

"I'm sure he was, and I'm sure Jeremy is a fine, strong, young man, but I don't need him."

"But you said—"

"Tibbie, you drive me to the point of distraction; and when I'm driven to the point of distraction, I don't think rationally, therefore I don't always say rational things. When I said 'the last thing I want to see is another woman,' I was speaking of a very short time frame. An hour after I'd said those words they were forgotten." He folded his arms across his chest. "Now, you may tell Jeremy—"

She threw up her hand to stop him, then turned to Jeremy, who was looking very uncomfortable. "Run out to the kitchen and tell Granny to give you a slice of Mairi's applesauce cake. I'll be there in just a minute."

"I think I'll go with Jeremy," Coll said.

"As I was saying," Nick went on, "you may tell Jeremy that his services aren't needed. I get along very well with *you* play- ing nursemaid."

"But I don't!" she said in a higher pitch than normal. "One

hour around you and I'm in a nervous frenzy. It takes the rest of the day to calm down."

"I don't think it's as bad as all that," he said with a good-humored smile.

Irritated and put out with herself over the way he made her feel, she wasn't about to agree with him. "But it is!" she wailed. "Since you've come to convalesce here I can't sleep, I've lost weight, I'm cross and grumpy, snapping at everyone, and I cry all the time."

His look softened. "Tibbie, have you ever heard tales about the way a man has to have sexual release and when he desires a woman that need is even stronger?"

She hid her embarrassment well, but he caught the nervous wringing of her hands. "Of course I have, after all, I am my father's assistant. I am aware of the natural functions of the male body."

"Good, I'm glad you referred to it as natural. You have no idea how happy that makes me, because a lot of women find it repugnant and something to be scoffed at. But that isn't the point here. What I am trying to say is, a man will experience loss of appetite, irritability, and will go through a generally obnoxious period if those desires aren't satisfied. The same desires are every bit as normal for a woman as for a man, and the change in behavior when those needs aren't met are basically the same in males and females. Do you understand what I'm saying here?"

"Yes," she said, losing her control. "And I don't think it's very nice of you to point those kinds of things out to me. I know how to handle a lot of things—birthing babies, treating burns, bunions, and blisters, but you're a baffling vexation, Mackinnon, and I don't know what to do about that. I can't help what I feel anymore than you can, and you can believe me when I say that if I had a choice in the matter, I would choose to dislike you immensely!"

Her eyes were swimming in tears, and her temper was approaching dangerous levels, so the shocked expression on Nick's face didn't quite register with her. "And I can tell you something else too! I *hate* the way I feel around you and I can't wait until you leave!"

"Tibbie," he said like it hurt him to speak. "Sweetheart, come here."

"You must be out of your mind!" she shouted. "Go ahead, confuse me some more. I never know what to expect from you. One minute you're trying your best to seduce me, or yank me into your bed, the next minute you're angry and telling me you don't ever want to see another woman."

"Tibbie, love, will you please come over here . . . just for a minute?"

"Is that the only way I'm going to find out what kind of mood you're in? Well, I can tell you now, if you're planning to yank me into your bed, forget it. And if you're going to get mad and yell, you might as well do it from where you are. No wonder I'm so confused. I don't know if I should go forward or back up! I don't know what I want anymore."

"But I do," he said softly. "If you'd come over here, I might be able to give it to you."

"If you mean what I think you mean—"

"You need someone to understand you, someone who feels the same way you do, someone who cares and will listen, someone to put his arms around you and tell you everything will be okay."

And he was exactly right. It surprised her to hear him say it. It surprised her more to find out he had hit the nail on the head. For a moment she considered how embarrassing it would be to walk over to him. But then again, she would feel awfully miserable standing over here all alone if she didn't. Choosing embarrassment over misery, Tibbie walked the short distance that separated them and found herself wrapped in Nick's strong, comforting arms. How much better the world looked from inside that warm, nurturing circle. How much brighter the sun seemed to shine. How her past seemed to fade into nothing. How the future came more sharply into focus.

And then his mouth found hers and she forgot everything except the sweet madness that seized her, the fresh feeling of a new beginning here and now, with this wonderful, understanding man. There were no words, and through closed eyes, nothing to see; but oh, how her heart could feel—until she thought it might stop altogether or her brain would burst from the effort of analyzing something so impossible to understand.

But suddenly, Eric's face rose up before her, as if trying to steal the brightness of the moment. *Don't do this to me!* she pleaded. *You don't want me! Don't rob me of all happiness! I don't love you, Eric. I don't! I don't!*

But the fear was there, the memory returning so very strong. His had been her first love—bittersweet, then bitter, then turning to despair. But he had been her first love, and would always be special if for no other reason than that. More importantly, he was the father of her child.

Please, she thought. *Please help me. . . . Help me to get him out of my mind. You're out of my life, Eric. I want you out of my mind as well.*

As she gave herself over to Nick's drugging kiss, she fancied that Eric was not the only star in her universe, but one of many, a faintly glimmering object millions of miles away. But the thought loomed in the back of her mind that stars often weren't so distant to the naked eye as they seemed.

15

Nobody does much of anything on Sunday in the summer in Indianola.

The farmers don't plow. The mercantile isn't open. The sheriff gives his deputy the day off. The Glass Slipper Entertainment Parlour doesn't even open until late afternoon. And old Mrs. Whitely never takes her dog Baker—so called because he likes to loaf—for a walk on Sunday.

The past month had gone like a holiday, over too soon and crammed with delight. It was summer now, March winds and April showers having passed. All around her the world was new, the sky of purest blue; and looking out over the bay the water sparkled like dewdrops on a leaf of deepest green.

The worst of the yellow fever had passed, but Coll still showed the effects of the strain. He was tired and thinner, with deeper lines carved into his face. But he was happy to be through with the worst epidemic he could remember.

"I'm as happy as a dead pig in sunshine," he said.

Nick had been on crutches for some time now, having the run of the place, much like a stray puppy that is taken in and becomes the idol of the family. For truly, her family did dote on him. Even Granny—who normally didn't take to strangers right off—spoke of him in only the highest terms.

"He must be getting well," Granny said one afternoon. "He's got ants in his pants. Just look how fidgety he is. Raring to go and chomping at the bit."

Tibbie, who was sitting beside Granny in the porch swing,

looked across the yard to where Nick stood gazing down the road. "He received a package yesterday with some changes for the ship he's building. He told me this morning that the man he was building the ship for wanted to meet with him in San Antonio. And last week he said he should've gone to New Orleans weeks ago. He's been laid up too long, he's behind on his work, he's needed out of town. That's enough to make anyone act like he's got ants in his pants."

Tibbie didn't say anymore, for Beth, running across the yard to show something to Nick, distracted her attention. Beth was finished with her piano lessons for the summer and she was happy about that. Now she seemed content to follow Nick around, and what a sight they were, Nick hobbling here and there on his crutches, Beth and Precious tagging along behind. And Precious! He was growing like a weed, up to at least one hundred pounds, Tibbie was sure.

Down by the barn a spider's newly spun web glistened in the sun, and over in the pigpen a mama sow lay on her side in the cool, oozing mud and nursed eleven baby pigs. A family of wild ducks, which Tibbie identified to Nick as "gadwalls," had taken up residence in a brackish pond, and the tiny red wolf that lived in the yaupon thicket was spotted in the orchard the other day.

And now, June was looking like it was going to be a fine month, as far as the clinic was concerned, since most of the treatments prescribed were of a common nature, such as Rush's thunderbolts for constipation, or Glauber salts for the opposite affliction. Occasionally there was call to set a smashed finger, or for a snakebite remedy, or a blistering ointment or two. But all in all, it was turning out to be a quiet month.

The second week in June, Coll declared Nick hale and hearty enough to return home. Only that morning Tibbie had helped him pack his belongings, so he could ride into town with Coll in the wagon. Once they were finished, she picked up the small bag and started for the door, when Nick raised one of his crutches and blocked her way.

She turned to look at him and for a moment neither of them

spoke, being content to just look at each other. Nick studied the outline of Tibbie's face, the way her hair dipped to a widow's peak over her forehead. There were so many things he wanted to say to her, but none of them seemed important now. He watched her lower her head. Physically and emotionally weary, he didn't know what to say. The magic of the moment seemed to have passed them by. Her father was waiting outside in the wagon.

"I may not be able to see you for a couple of weeks."

"You don't owe me any explanations," she said.

"I'm not telling you this because I *owe* you. I'm telling you because I *care.* I want you to understand why I may not be back out here for a while. I know you. I know how you'll begin to imagine the worst. You'll begin to doubt me and my feelings for you the minute I walk out this door. I've got to go to Galveston as soon as possible. After that I need to find a week or two that I can go to New Orleans. We're way behind schedule because of my accident, since there's been no one to direct things."

"I thought Porter—"

"Porter is great for carrying out my decisions, but he can't make them."

"I understand. You take care, now. Don't go acting like a young fool on those newly mended legs of yours or you'll end up back here."

He saw the tears glistening in her eyes and he felt like hell. He knew she didn't understand a damn thing he'd been saying. To her he was just like that other bastard, walking out on her, and that made him feel like a traitor. He leaned over and planted a soft kiss on the top of her head. "I love you, Tibbie. And more than that, I care. I don't want to leave you for five minutes, let alone a couple of weeks. But I've given my word. People are depending on me. I wouldn't be much of a man if I fell through on either of those. I want you to understand. It's as important as breathing to me."

"I understand. Really."

He shook his head. "No, angel, I don't think you really do."

He started out the door.

"Nick . . ."

He turned and Tibbie ran to him, her arms going around his neck, gripping him like she would never let him go. He rubbed his chin across the top of her head. "I know," he said softly. "I feel that way too."

He kissed her gently on the mouth, then reached into his pocket and pulled out a small piece of brown paper tied with string. "A little something to help you remember."

She turned the paper over in her hand. "Where did you get it?"

"It came in the package with the other things." His face turned serious. "Don't open it until after I've gone."

She clutched the tiny bundle against her chest and followed him to the front door, where she stood until her father's wagon had rolled out of sight. Once he was gone, she walked outside. She didn't open her package until she had reached the orchard and sat down beneath that same tree she had sat beneath with Nick. It was wrapped in three layers of paper, the last one being a thin lavender tissue. When she unrolled it, a small angel carved in marble fell out. Tibbie clutched the angel in her hand and had herself a good cry.

Three days later, Tibbie had just finished braiding Beth's hair and was standing at the back door watching her run across the yard, with Precious squealing for all he was worth as he gave chase. Effie was making spoon bread while Granny sat in her rocker embroidering a pair of pillowcases.

"It's going to be a scorcher today," Granny said. "It's already hotter than a burning stump in here."

"There's no breeze today. That's why it seems so hot," Tibbie said.

Granny stood up, gathering her embroidery. "Think I'll move to the porch and fan myself."

"That's what half of Indianola is doing right now, I'll wager," said Effie.

And that was true, for Indianola summers are lazy days

when life seems to go into a state of hibernation, just carrying on enough functions to keep things going, but not enough to make any real progress. This Sunday was no different. The sun was shining so bright, it hurt your eyes just to look at it; there was nary a cloud in that pale blue sky overhead. Down below, most of the residents were sitting on the front porch looking static, or fanning. The women discussed the shameful way Ruby Jewel Singer dyed her hair *harlot* red, the men expressed their fears that it might go the whole summer before they saw a drop of rain.

Similar things were going on in the Buchanan house, where everyone was gathered in the kitchen, finishing up Sunday dinner.

"It's hotter than a hen laying eggs in a woolen basket," Granny Grace said as she went in search of her biggest fan.

"Oh, I don't know," Coll said, pushing himself away from the table and strolling to the back door. He stood there for a minute or two, his thumbs hooked in his suspenders. At last he said, "I was just thinking what a fine day it was. If I felt any better I'd swear it was a frame-up."

"I'm glad to hear that, Dr. Buchanan," Effie said, giving the leaves of her geranium a pinch. "It's time to talk of serious things."

"Why is that?" Coll said, as he made a beeline for the parlor.

Effie was right on his heels. "Because I've got a list of things for you to do. The well rope is frazzled, the lock on the front door is busted, there's a leak in the milk bucket, and three times last week the goats got into my garden through that wobbly gate!"

"Lord, woman! This is Sunday!" Coll said, slowly lowering himself into his favorite easy chair.

"And tomorrow is Monday and you'll have a clinic full of mashed fingers and runny noses."

"Make me a list, Effie." Coll put his feet on the footstool and leaned back.

"A list, my foot! You haven't done the things on the last list I gave you."

"I 'spect I'll get around to it one of these days."

"I 'spect you'll get around to it now," Effie said, picking Coll's feet up off the footstool and depositing them on the floor.

"I swan if you ain't the most pestiferous woman I ever did come across."

It sounded to Tibbie like there was fixing to be either a squabble or a fair amount of work going on, so she sent Beth a silent signal and the two of them slipped out of the house and made their way down to the orchard.

Beth ran down the path and through the gate, where she turned and waited for her mother, her skipping rope dangling from her arm. "How good it smells," Beth said, taking a deep breath. "It smells like summertime, doesn't it, Mama?"

"That's the honeysuckle running along the fence," Tibbie replied, coming through the gate. "That's what makes it smell so good, just like summertime."

They found a nice cool place beneath a twisted old plum tree and sat down. "I like it here. It's nice and cool," Beth said, pulling off her shoes and rolling down her stockings. A moment later she was wiggling her toes in the soft earth. "I see why Precious likes to root in the dirt," she said. "Do you 'spose it feels as good on his nose as it does on my feet?"

"I'm sure it must."

Beth wiggled her toes a few more times, then sprang to her feet with an announcement. "I'm going to jump my rope now. You watch me, Mama. Tell me how many times I jump before I miss."

Tibbie counted, but Beth was jumping in and out of trees so much it was impossible to see her all the time. Then she disappeared altogether. Fifteen minutes later she was back, breathless, her cheeks red, her blue sash dragging in the dirt behind her.

"Where did you go?"

"I went to get Precious."

Tibbie looked behind Beth. Sure enough, here came Precious, grunting with each step he took, his dirt-encrusted nose in the air, his beady little pig eyes shining and bright.

Beth, still breathless, dropped down beside Tibbie. Precious took a few swipes at the freshly plowed earth before grunting and dropping down beside them, putting his head in Beth's lap with a satisfied sigh.

There were times that Tibbie could swear that pig was almost human. *Why, just look at that ecstatic expression on his face!* Tibbie leaned back against the tree trunk, while Beth sat with her feet tucked under her, leaning against her mother, her chubby little fingers scratching Precious between the ears. "Mama?"

"Hmmm?"

"Do pigs go to heaven when they die?"

That question didn't surprise Tibbie in the least, for it was the type of question she got from Beth all the time. As she started to explain the answer, she was thinking that Beth would soon be asking more and more questions, some of them not so easy to answer. One question she knew Beth would ask one day was about her legitimacy. Beth would start school soon, and then it would only be a matter of time.

Tibbie had never really prepared Beth for that moment. She decided the best thing to do was just to wait until Beth asked, and then answer in the best way she knew how. Tibbie had never lied to Beth about her father, but she had never really told her much about him either. Beth knew she had a father, because from time to time she would hear someone in the family say she had her father's smile, or she had his eyes, or as Granny would say, "She's looking more like her papa every day."

And once or twice Beth had become curious and asked a question or two like, "Where is my papa, Mama?"

To which Tibbie would reply, "He's at sea."

"Will he come to visit us soon?"

"I don't think so. He lives too far away. To get here would take months and months and he's a very, very busy man."

Because Beth was only five, answers like this would satisfy her and she would suddenly change the subject to something she knew more about. Like Precious, for instance.

Speaking of Precious, he had recovered from being locked in the pigsty, but he was still a little standoffish around Tibbie.

This particular Sunday, however, Beth was interested in finding out all about school, for she would be six soon, and that meant she would be big enough to go.

"How big will I be on my birthday?"

"About the size you are now, Beth. It's only a month away."

"But Grandpa said I'd be big enough to go to school when I had my birthday!" she wailed. "I don't want to stay this size! I want to go to school!"

"And you shall, lambkin. You shall. Grandpa meant you would be *old* enough, because you can't go to school until you turn six."

Beth's eyes got larger and larger. *"Six?* Oh, boy," she said, clapping her hands together, "that means Little Pressy can't go!"

Little Pressy was the Sayers baby boy. His name was Preston, but Beth had nicknamed him Little Pressy, and before long everyone else was calling him that. The Sayers always sat near the Buchanans on Sunday morning. And just this morning, Mrs. Sayers had let Beth take Little Pressy outside all by herself.

"He can't go, can he, Mama?"

"No, of course not. Little Pressy is only two."

Beth laughed and clapped her hands again, turning to kiss her mother. Tibbie was brushing Beth's long blond hair, and smiled when Beth kissed her, but she did not look up. Beth turned back, looking across the orchard, following the path of rooted-up soil to see where Precious had gone off to.

"Mama," she said in a low, puzzled little voice that sounded like a whisper. "Who is that?"

Tibbie looked up to see a lone horseman coming up the

road. "I don't know. Just someone out to pay a Sunday visit, I suppose."

"Is he coming to see us?"

"I don't know. We'll have to wait until he rides up here. If he turns in our gate, he'll be coming to see us. But if he keeps going . . ."

"He will be going to visit the Dinwiddies."

Beth looked back toward the figure on horseback. "I hope he comes here," she said. "I just love company."

"You and your grandpa," Tibbie said. She looked up, seeing the horseman turn up the road that led to the Buchanan place. "Looks like he's . . . Oh my God!"

"Quick, Beth! Run and get Grandpa! Hurry! Run as fast as you can!" Beth took off like a streak of lightening, Precious's squeal coming a second later.

Tibbie never moved from her spot, but she did rise to her feet. "Eric," she said when the man drew rein a few feet away and sat looking down at her.

Eric . . . All the color drained from her face. *Eric* . . . One look and a thrill surged through her. *Eric* . . . *Oh, God! Eric* . . . *No*, she thought. *No!* But it was no use. Her palms were damp, her heart beat triple-time, her words stuck in her throat.

She looked up into the face that was etched like a beloved painting in her mind; those thickly lashed green eyes, the aristocratic nose, the curved, teasing mouth. But this was no painting, for those eyes that looked at her with bold, irrefutable desire were real.

She knew he must be able to read the uncertainty in the manner in which she looked at him, but she could not help looking. There was the face that had haunted her dreams for so long, and the desire to rush to him and feel his arms around her was hard to resist. She closed her eyes against the swirling dizziness that threatened her balance. In the darkness she could feel herself teetering on the edge of a dark abyss, a bottomless fissure in the earth that pulled and lured her to its edge, beckoning her to take one more step and fall forever into the pit of eternal darkness.

She opened her eyes, questioning her sanity, but the figure was real and Eric swam before her questioning eyes. "If you were in the neighborhood and decided to pay a call, don't bother!" she said. "You aren't welcome here."

She heard that old familiar chuckle, saw the light of delight dancing in his eyes. Was this the man she had loved for so long? Was this the strong, slender body that lay against her own and made love to her until the hot, sweet ache in her belly gave way to delight? A vision came to her: fingers moving rapidly over the buttons of a shirt; brown shoulders gleaming naked in the candlelight; the bed creaking under his weight as he sat down.

Eric.

Vibrant, alive, with a smile so bright it hurt your eyes just to look at it. He looked down at her with that same adorable smile, that same distinctive style of dressing that showed off his height and slim form. Eric, as golden and dazzling as a sunbeam. Eric, as forceful as the North wind.

Eric.

The prodigal lover had returned.

"Hello, Tibbie. You look more surprised to see me than I thought you would."

"After over six years, I can't imagine why I'd be surprised, can you?"

He flashed her a lazy smile. "Perhaps I should have written you to explain."

"To explain what, Eric? What could you possibly explain to me?"

"Do you mind if I join you? I don't want to sit here on my horse and talk to you while you stare at me like you've seen a ghost."

"Why not? That's what you are. A ghost. A memory. You aren't real anymore, Eric. That must make you a ghost."

"I'm no ghost, and I can prove that soon enough." He dismounted and stood by his horse, the reins held lightly in his hands.

"I don't want you to prove anything. I want you to leave."

Eric looked off toward the house. "Was that the child?" he asked. "The one you were expecting?"

"When you up and ran away?" Before he could respond, she added, "Her *name* is Bethany. We don't refer to her as *the child* around here."

He winced at her harsh words and Tibbie went on talking. But Eric was no longer listening. His eyes went over her, slowly, from top to bottom and back up again. He had not seen this woman in six years, but looking at her now, it could have been yesterday that she lay in his arms on the beach. He wanted to go to her and lay his head against her breasts and sob out all his anguish, begging her to forgive him, to take him back. He wanted to take her in his arms and hear her say everything would be as it had been then, but he dared not mention that to her. At least not yet. He fought for command of himself, realizing suddenly that she had stopped speaking and was staring straight at him.

"It isn't possible," he said, "but you are more beautiful than before." And it was true. She was more beautiful, for now her beauty wasn't just of the face. He had seen instantly that this woman had strength and poise and self-assurance. She was still beautiful. She was still young. But the difference was that now she was a woman in full bloom. "The years have been good to you, Tibbie." As he spoke she detected a hint of genuine wonder in his voice that was disturbing. Eric had never been the type for candid, heartfelt honesty, and certainly not one to give any indication of his true feelings.

His eyes were on her face as he said, "In so many ways you're the same as I remembered, yet there is something unmistakably different. You were always the kind of woman that would stand out in a crowd, but now it's more pronounced. You seem to have acquired a certain . . . shine . . . a gloss that will always brand you different from other women. It's obvious and quite mysterious, provocative almost—not a character trait exactly, but the faintest suggestion that beneath all that softness and submissive gentlewoman's exterior there lies a wild and uncurbed spirit. I have the strangest feeling that the timid young girl I once knew has grown into a woman capable of violence."

"Perhaps you're right. I could put a knife through your deceitful heart if I felt I had no other choice."

He dipped his head in mocking recognition, then came closer to join her. "So, I can see my coming back isn't going to go as smoothly as I had hoped."

"I've never been one to scatter pearls before swine."

"Ouch!" He smiled, reaching out to stroke her cheek. Immediately, she pulled back. "How do we proceed from here? What do we do about our past?"

"We have no past."

"Have you forgotten those few blissful months we spent together, the times you welcomed me to your—"

"You don't have to paint me a picture."

"Well, then, how do we proceed from here?"

"We don't. There's no reason for us to try."

"We have a daughter. Isn't that reason enough?"

She laughed cynically. "It wasn't reason enough six years ago. Why is it now?"

"I was a young fool then."

"You're still one if you think there's anything between us now."

"Tibbie, please. Can't you forget, or at least forgive?"

"Forget? Forget what? Forget the way your face froze into a mask the day I told you I was pregnant? Forget the way you did the manly thing and abandoned me? You must be mad!"

"Damn your hide! I didn't just abandon you. My father—"

"Yes," she said softly, "I remember you said your father had other plans for you. The daughter of a wealthy neighbor, wasn't she?"

He looked away. "Yes."

"And you married her—to please your father, of course."

"Yes, I married her, but that isn't how it was. I never loved her! I only married her because my father threatened me."

"And now you come here, after all this time, looking me up when you have a *wife*! Are you insane?"

"She died two years ago."

"Did you have any children?"

"No." He couldn't help remembering how many times he thought it so ironic that the woman he loved and didn't marry had borne him a child and the one he married but didn't love could not.

"A sad way to get out of a marriage, but I can't help feeling she's better off."

"Tibbie, please listen to me."

"Whatever for?"

"I'd like to see my daughter, to spend some time with her, to know her. I'd like to help—"

"You didn't want to help before. You threw the whole responsibility upon me."

He looked surprised.

"Don't tell me you don't remember! I do! 'My God! What are you going to do?' you said. Does it sound familiar?"

Her words stirred up an old memory and his face fell.

My God! What are you going to do?

I was wondering what we were going to do, Eric.

Your father's a doctor, can't he do something? You're too young to be a mother. You don't need a child right now. Don't look at me like that. You could have other children when you're older.

His mind snapped back. Tibbie was looking at him exactly as she had looked that day: angry, amazed, shocked. "I want to make it all up to you. That's why I came back."

"Whatever the reason for your return, Eric, it doesn't matter now."

"Yes, it does!"

"Does it? Did it matter enough for you to tell me good-bye? Or for you to leave me a note, some message? Did you bother to write me, even once, in six years? You left me. I thought it was because you didn't care for me, as I no longer care for you."

His head whipped around, and for a moment she thought him capable of striking her. But he battled with himself, gaining control, and in so doing, gave her the feeling that he was irritated with himself for letting her get his goat. One thing she recalled about Eric was that he couldn't stand to be bested, to feel someone had gotten the upper hand.

She knew he would take advantage of her momentary lapse into silence and changed the subject, steering the conversation back into waters he knew treacherously well. She wondered how many women he had charmed with that glib tongue of his since he left her. "You always took my breath away. You still do."

"Well, why don't you find where your breath's been taken, and join it? You aren't welcome here, Eric. Not anymore. There's nothing here that belongs to you, no reason for you to come back."

"I have a daughter."

She felt herself standing at the edge of a gaping fissure, the earth crumbling away beneath her feet. *No!* her mind screamed. *No! Get your wits about you. Don't let him back you down.* "You had a few moments of pleasure, Eric. *I* had a daughter."

"She's my daughter as well."

"I don't know how you figure that. *I* birthed her. *I* nursed her. *I* took care of her when she was sick. You didn't care when I told you I carried your child. Why do you care now? You never even wrote to find out if you had a son or a daughter. *That's* how interested you were."

"Tibbie, please . . . I didn't come back to fight with you."

"Why did you come back?"

"Because I still love you."

She felt dazed. Too many feelings, too many emotions held in such tight control for six years broke their bondage and rushed free, leaving her dizzy and slightly out of breath. Just the impact of seeing him again was devastating. So much she remembered about this man and the nights they had shared. But then she remembered how she felt after he left, how she needed him, yearned for him to the point of madness. She couldn't control the anger she felt. How dare he come back now. A flash of Nick's face hovered in the back of her mind and Tibbie fought to control the warring emotions of delight and panic. Eric. Here. Eric in the flesh, standing before her in impeccably tailored buff trousers, shiny tan knee boots, a pristine white shirt with the sleeves rolled up his sinewy arms and the neck open to show the tanned and hairless brown chest. How well she remembered the feel of that smooth, brown skin.

A memory of how he had looked back then, standing in the darkness on the beach, the moonlight highlighting a body that was naked and slim, the water behind him sparkling like dewdrops, the cool gulf breezes cooling his heated flesh. She remembered how he had come back to her and taken her hand, drawing her up to stand beside him, then leading her into the water where the two of them stood naked and let the sea wash over them. She couldn't forget how he had taken her into his arms. *I love you, Tibbie.* And then he had carried her back into the blanket and made love to her again.

I love you, Tibbie . . .

A short time later he was gone.

"Tibbie, I love you."

"Liar!"

"I came back to ask you to marry me."

Tibbie fainted dead away.

Eric was carrying her toward the house when he met Coll running toward them, his medical bag in one hand. He took one look at Eric and his face darkened. He looked at Tibbie. "What happened?"

"She fainted."

"That's understandable," Coll growled. "Let me have her."

"I want to carry her."

"Why? So you can drop her again?" Coll said angrily, taking Tibbie from him.

Some time later Tibbie woke up in her own room. Effie was standing beside the bed. Tibbie asked for Beth.

"She's drawing pictures for Granny. What happened, Tib? Why is Eric here?"

"Oh, God!" Tibbie said, her fisted hand coming up to cover her mouth. "I thought he came back for Beth." She started to cry. "I thought he came back to take her away!"

"How do you know he didn't?"

"He told me."

"Then why is he here?"

"He . . . He asked me to marry him."

"Hogwash! He's got some trick up his sleeve, sure as night follows day." She turned a concerned eye upon Tibbie, taking her hand and giving it a pat. "Don't you go believing anything that man says. He's so low you couldn't put a rug under him."

"Oh, Mama . . . I don't know what to do!"

"I don't know why you say that. Give him the boot. Send him on his way."

"But he looked different, not just older, but sad. I had the feeling he really did regret what happened, that he still loved me. . . ."

"If you think that, you've got a memory shorter than a frog's tail."

"What if he was telling the truth? What if he really does want to marry me?"

"Truth to a man like that is rare as a virgin, and don't you forget it."

"What if I said I still loved him?"

"Now, that would make a stuffed bird laugh!" Effie said. "You aren't in love with him anymore than I am. You're in love with a memory, one you've blocked all of the bad out of. You need to take off your romantic blinders, girl. You need to see that man for what he is. No good."

"Where is Papa?"

"He's in his office, talking to Eric."

"I'm right here," Coll said, entering the room and closing

the door. He came to stand beside Effie. He looked at Tibbie. "What did he tell you?"

"That he came back to ask me to marry him."

Effie looked at Coll. "Did he tell you that?"

"Yes."

Effie frowned. "You didn't believe him, did you?"

"Oh, I believed him, all right. I think he does want to marry Tibbie. I'm just not sure about the reason why."

"Tibbie thinks he's changed," Effie said.

"It's doubtful," Coll said. "Don't get hooked on hope, sugar."

But Tibbie feared she had done just that.

She was left alone to compose herself and to think things through, with her father giving her one last admonition. "Don't give into that mental magic that is bound to come. Thinking something will be different, doesn't make it so. You remember that."

"I will, Papa. Promise."

But it was hard. Eric was symbolic of the essence of her youth. His return was like an awakening, the return of her indefatigable spirit. Eric had returned. And he had sprinkled her with magical dust.

Eric came calling the next morning.

"I don't want to see him," she told Effie.

"I don't blame you none, but I think you should see him."

Tibbie's eyes widened. "Why?"

"Because you still haven't gotten completely over him and you never will if you send him away while you still have those feelings. He has things he wants to tell you. You need to hear him out and then decide. *If* you decide to send him packing then you won't be haunted with his memory."

Eric was waiting in the parlor, sitting in a chair by the window. He came to his feet the moment she entered. "Please sit down, Eric. I understand you have something to say to me, something you didn't say yesterday."

"Yes."

"We have a lot of patients to see today. I hope this doesn't take long."

"It won't take long."

She sat down, careful to sit on the sofa across from him instead of the chair next to his. "I'm listening."

"I've thought this over so many times, rehearsed it so much, I never thought this would be so difficult. I'm not sure where to start."

"The beginning would be a likely place."

"I—I wasn't completely honest with you before, when you told me about your pregnancy. I told you my father had arranged for me to marry, and he had. My father is a strong, determined man, but I was going to go back to break that engagement."

"Why couldn't you tell me that?"

"I was afraid you'd want to go with me, or want to get married right then. Tibbie, I know my father better than anyone. If I'd married you and taken you back with me, he would have made life miserable for both of us. I knew if I married you before breaking off the engagement, he'd disown me." He shook his head. "It's hard to admit it, but I was a coward. I couldn't face you with the truth."

The color had drained from her face and she whispered, "You weren't a coward, Eric. You were a bastard!"

His face was pleading. "Tibbie, I *loved* you. I was afraid to tell you, afraid I would lose you. I had every intention of coming back for you."

"Lose me or abandon me, what's the difference?"

"All I could think about at the time was being with you, having you. I kept telling myself I could work things out. Even when I left, I intended to go home and set things straight, to break off the engagement and stand up to my father, then come back for you."

"And so you ran off like a thief in the night?"

"I was afraid you would hate me when you found out. I knew you loved me, I gambled that it was strong enough to last until I could get back."

"And?"

"I told my father about you. He said the engagement couldn't be broken. Contracts had been signed. My . . . my wife's family was one of the wealthiest in Hawaii. My father is wealthy, but nothing to compare with her family. A great deal of money had already exchanged hands. My father not only said he'd disown me, he threatened to have me put in chains for breach of contract. There was nothing I could do. Marriage to you was out of the question."

"I see." She looked off a moment, contemplating. When she looked back, he could see the flame of a new anger, the fire in her amber eyes. "You've covered everything very well. Except for one thing. You haven't mentioned why you wanted me to see if my father could do away with Beth."

"I've regretted those words a million times. I was shocked and unable to think straight. It was so foolish on my part and really unlike me. My only defense is I put my love for you before the child." His voice quivered when he saw her look of disbelief and paused momentarily, gaining his composure. "My first thought was knowing I couldn't sail to Hawaii and back before you had the child. I was afraid that once I left you might marry someone else—anyone—to give the child a name. How could I stand the thought of coming back for you and finding you had married someone else?"

"What you suggested was murder. Your *own* child. How could you?"

"A question I've asked daily. A question with no answer."

"So you sailed to Hawaii and stayed, not bothering to write me."

"I did write. Many times."

"And you expect me to believe all your letters were lost at sea?"

"No, they never got that far. It wasn't until after my wife died that the letters I had written so carefully were returned to me by the man I had entrusted to mail them. He was a loyal friend, but he had a past, something my wife's father held over his head. He had no choice but to cooperate. But he refused to destroy the letters as he'd been told to do." Eric reached toward the table beside him, and she noticed for the first time a bundle wrapped in oilcloth and tied with string. He handed them to her. "They're all there, still unopened, just as they were when I gave them to Elias."

She took the letters into her trembling hands. "You said your wife died two years ago. Why didn't you write me then?"

"I wanted to tell you what happened, to talk to you, to see you in person. For all I knew you could have been married. I told myself that if you were, I would leave without seeing you."

"And it took you two years?"

"I barely had time to put my business in order after my wife died, when my mother became desperately ill. I couldn't leave then. She died six months ago."

"So now you're here."

"Yes, I'm here waiting to see what will happen between us." He saw her features harden. "Please don't say anything yet. I'm not asking you to make any decision. All I'm asking is for you to read those letters, to spend a little time with me, to let me get to know my daughter. Give me a little time to prove my feelings for you, time for your hurt and anger toward me to subside."

She stood and turned toward the fireplace, her back to him. "I don't know. It's been so long. I've met someone else."

"Are you in love with him?"

"If I'm not, I'm close."

She heard him stand and she turned toward him. He stood there like a shy boy uncertain of what to do next. "I would like to call again, perhaps meet Bethany, if that would be alright."

She nodded.

"Tell me what you're thinking, what you're feeling. Are you still horribly angry with me?"

She looked into his grave face and sighed. "No, I'm not angry. I was in the beginning, but I'm past that now. I was so hurt and heartbroken. I couldn't believe you could have done me that way."

"I told you I'd like the chance to make up for all that."

"I'm not sure you can, Eric." She walked to the door. "I'll show you out."

He followed her to the front door. "If I come again, will you see me?"

"I need time to think about that, but you may see Beth."

He nodded.

She watched him leave, wondering what she had agreed to. For some reason she couldn't shake the troubled feeling that she had scattered feathers in the wind.

16

That afternoon Eric came by again. When Tibbie took him outside to meet Beth, she was playing with Precious down by the barn. Eric was mortified to see she was playing with a pig. "But they're the nastiest things in the world," he said.

"No, they really aren't. Unbelievable as it may seem, pigs are really clean animals."

"Beth, don't you have anyone to play with besides this pig?" Eric asked.

"Oh, sure," Beth said. "At church I play with Little Pressy. And I see Melissa Abernathy at piano lessons. But I like to play with Nick. I like him the best." Turning to Tibbie, Beth said, "Is Nick coming over again?"

"Not anytime soon," Tibbie responded.

"He promised to bring me a surprise," she said.

"Well, I'm sure he will." Tibbie looked back toward the house. "It's almost time for supper. You come inside in time to get cleaned up, you hear?"

Beth nodded and let out a shriek, running after Precious. On the way back to the house they ran into Granny coming down the back steps. "You remember Eric, don't you, Granny?"

"I'd rather not," she said, giving him the once over. Turning to Tibbie she said, "Where's Nick?"

"Who is this Nick everyone keeps talking about?" Eric asked.

They walked through the house and out onto the front porch. Tibbie sat on the front steps, Eric settled himself in the porch swing, and she told him about Nick. She was tired of things being held back, secrets being kept. She had no idea how she would end up feeling about Eric, but she knew one thing—they had to be completely honest with each other from here on out, regardless of the outcome.

Eric listened, and when she finished he said, "I wish you had told me about him sooner."

"I've only seen you three times. How much sooner could it have been?"

"I mean volunteered it, without my asking."

"What difference does that make?"

"I don't know. Maybe you wouldn't have told me at all if I hadn't found out."

"Don't try to back me into corners, Eric."

"I'm not! I just wish you'd told me sooner, that's all. I don't like you keeping things from me, hiding things."

Tibbie shook her head and rested her head in her hands propped against her knees. When Eric saw the effect of his words he let out a sigh and moved to the step to sit next to her.

She didn't respond when his hand came out to ease the stiffness from her neck. He caressed her with his strong fingers, kneading away the tension with easy, firm strokes.

"I'm sorry. It just seems like I'm cut off at every turn. Sometimes I feel like Abraham waiting for Rachel."

She lifted her head and looked at him. "Why? Abraham was tricked into marriage with Leah. You married your wife of your own free will."

"I was forced."

"You had a choice."

"Is this always going to be between us?" He looked off. "Sometimes I don't think I'll ever have you." He laughed. "I'll probably still be chasing you when I'm as old as the hills and have a gray beard as long as the Colorado river."

"By that time I'll be so old you won't want to chase me."

His look turned serious. "I'll always want that," he said softly.

"Eric . . . I don't know what to say to you."

"Don't say anything. If I have even the slightest chance of

beating this Nick fellow out, I'm content to wait. If you've got plans to marry, please tell me."

She was touched by his gentle questions. "I . . . he hasn't asked."

"Thank God!" Eric said, then he jumped up and grabbed Granny, who was just coming out the door, whirling her around and around. He kissed her with a loud smack on the cheek, then swung over the porch railing, balancing on one arm; then he raced across the yard and hurdled the picket fence, swinging up onto the back of his horse. Spurring the animal into a fast run, he waved his hat and let out a loud yell that brought Effie to the front door.

"Whatever is going on out here? It sounds like we're being attacked by Indians."

"I wish it were something that simple," Tibbie said.

After he left, Tibbie sat on the front porch watching the cows grazing in bunches across the road, feeling a little stung by Eric's hasty retreat.

That night she lay in bed, awake for a long time thinking about Eric, musing over his sudden reappearance into her life. Never would she have believed she would ever see him again. Wasn't life full of one surprise after another? She thought about what he had told her, remembering the letters he had given her and how she had cried until she thought her heart would break over each one of them. There was no doubt in her mind after reading those letters that Eric loved her and loved her deeply. Even Effie, who had been so skeptical before, cried when she read them.

"Well," Effie had said, drying her eyes on the corner of her apron. "I don't suppose it was his fault that things went the way they did. I'm not saying what he did was right or that I agree with it. He took the coward's way out, but who's to say any one of us might have done the same thing if we were in his shoes. It don't sit right with a body to be unforgiving."

"Are you saying I'm unforgiving?"

"Don't put words in my mouth. I'm just spouting off, that's all."

As Tibbie lay in bed reflecting, she wondered how it would have been if things had gone differently. What if Eric had persuaded his father to let him marry her? What if his friend had mailed the letters Eric had given him? What if Eric had waited a few more months to come back for her? *Well,* she told herself, *this is all a waste of time. What's done is done and there's no calling back the wind once it's blown past. Eric has his destiny to fulfill and I have mine.* Only one question remained unanswered in her mind when she drifted off to sleep. Did her destiny lie with Eric or Nicholas?

The next morning Porter Masterson paid Tibbie a call.

"For me?" Tibbie said, when Porter handed her a long white box tied with a bright pink ribbon.

"Nick would kill me if I gave it to anyone else," he said with a laugh. "He sent it from Galveston by this morning's packet."

Tibbie hurried to her room after Porter left. She had the ribbon off by the time she reached the door. The lid was off by the time she closed the door, and by the time she reached her bed she had opened a beautiful white lace parasol and a note that said,

I counted nine freckles on your nose the last time I saw you. This will make sure there aren't ten by the time I return. Yours always, Nicholas.

That night her thoughts were all of Nicholas. Where was he now? Did he think about her often? She climbed out of bed and went to sit in the chair in front of her window. She leaned her head against the cool pane of glass, her sadness growing as she looked out over the yard, so silent and so still. The moon was high in the sky, huge and round and white, washing the earth below in the palest of tones, making even the harshest outlines soft and hospitable. *This same moon,* she thought, *is shining down upon Nicholas Mackinnon, wherever he is.*

The days flew by and she thought of Nicholas often, though she never saw him, and ironically, she saw Eric daily, but rarely thought of him. Perhaps if they had traded places it would have been the other way around. It seemed strange to her to think now of how easily she had come to love Nick, and how long it had taken her to realize it.

The following Tuesday, Eric took her boating in the bay. He talked at length about Hawaii, the island of Maui, its legends, its villages, its people. He told her about his family, his mother's death, his strong-willed father.

"I always loved him with all my heart, but I always felt he favored my brothers more. Maybe that's why I've always tried to please him, to do whatever he asked, hoping to win love from a man incapable of giving it to me."

"Oh, Eric," she said, leaning across from where she sat to touch his hand resting on the oar.

"It's okay," he said. "I'm getting used to it—having people I love not loving me in return. The only thing that surprises me is why I keep trying."

"Giving up is never the answer."

"Neither is being defeated all the time." He grinned crookedly and slapped the oar against the water so hard that she jumped, then shrieked as a spray of water came down upon her. Laughing and not bothering to remove her glove she skimmed her hand across the water, throwing considerably more on him than he had sprinkled on her.

"Hey!" he said laughing, his blond head gleaming. "You're gonna pay for that one."

She laughed and collapsed back against the bow of the boat, thinking that Eric and sunlight had to be close kin, for the sun verily worshipped him. With a sigh she dropped her hand over the side of the boat, trailing her fingers in the water. The sun was warm, the breeze over the water cool, and it was coming back to her now, the reasons why she had loved this golden man. She closed her eyes and remembered how it had felt to open her arms to him as he slid between her legs, laughing about the place they had chosen for their lovemaking and how the grit was grinding all the hair off his knees. And then he wouldn't talk or laugh anymore, as he spoke to her with his body. Afterward she would lie in his arms, listening to him talk, much as she was doing now.

"You look beautiful, Tibbie my love." And before she could open her eyes, Eric's mouth was upon hers, and the moment was brilliant and golden, like the sunlight dancing upon the waves of his hair.

But that night, when she lay in her bed, it was Nicholas who occupied her thoughts.

On Wednesday he took her to gather dewberries along the wooded areas that ran beside the creek. When her bucket was full, they spread a blanket beneath an oak tree, and he fed the berries to her. The juice ran down her chin and threatened to drip on her dress, until he tilted her head back and laid a careful network of kisses along the sweet trail.

But that night, when she lay in her bed, it was Nicholas who occupied her thoughts.

On Thursday Eric came into her kitchen with a bag of food he'd purchased in town. "I'm going to cook dinner for you and your family tonight," he said, and ran everyone from the room. When it was ready, they gathered around the table and sat down to the absolute worst meal anyone could ever remember eating and spent the next hour and a half laughing over mashed potatoes that were half-cooked and stuck to the spoon like glue. When Coll tried to dish some up and found them sticking to the spoon, he shook it harder. They came unstuck on the third shake, flying across the table and landing in Effie's soup. Her mother's blouse slopped with soup, Tibbie grabbed her napkin to help, knocking over her glass of red wine.

They had done a pretty good job of controlling everything up to that point, but when Granny looked down at the bloody piece of chicken in her plate and said, "Do I kill it or bury it?" the cause was lost. Everyone was laughing so hard by then, it didn't matter that the food was awful, or that Effie's blouse was soiled, or her best white tablecloth ruined. They didn't leave the table full, but they did come away satisfied.

But that night, when she lay in her bed, it was Nicholas who occupied her thoughts.

On Friday, Eric drove Tibbie to town to pick up supplies for Coll. She was sitting beside him in the wagon, listening to him laugh and watching the skin around his green eyes crinkle with delight. He whispered something in her ear and she laughed outright, and Eric reached across, picked up her small hand, and kissed her fingers.

It was not unexpected that Nick would return to Indianola. It just wasn't expected that he would have returned today, or that he would have chosen that particular moment to step out of the mercantile.

He was talking to Porter in an absorbed conversation, looking out onto the street as a matter of habit. Only then did his gaze settle on Tibbie. She never saw him or Porter, and a moment later the wagon rattled on down the street. Nick felt something shatter inside him. He could take almost anything Tibbie dished out, but playing him for a fool was not one of them. Without further explaination, Nick excused himself and headed for the livery.

But when Tibbie and Eric passed the shipyards, it was Nicholas who occupied Tibbie's thoughts.

It didn't take him long to show up at Tibbie's front door. An hour after Eric left, Effie came into the clinic to tell Tibbie, Nick wanted to see her.

Nick? Here? Now? Her stomach began to churn frantically, then the thought of seeing him again spread through her like a flower blooming. Her lips curved into a soft smile. *I'm going to see Nick. I'm going to see Nick.* But when she spoke, she couldn't think of a thing to say, except, "Now?"

Effie looked at her strangely. "I guess it's now. He's at the front door now. People don't usually show up at your door and ask to see someone later."

As she left the room, she was thinking how she had missed him more than she would have thought possible. She had proven to herself that she was in love with him, that she missed his quiet strength, his depth of understanding, his kindness, his lazy smile, even his anger.

Tibbie met Nick in the parlor, but they didn't stay long.

Grabbing her hand he led her outside. "What are you doing?" she asked.

"I want to talk to you," he said, his face a hard, expressionless mask. By this time, Tibbie, who was fairly skipping to keep up with him, was wondering how she ever imagined that she had missed this man, especially his anger.

Dragging her along behind him, Nicholas felt a tightening in his loins when he remembered the way she had run to him and thrown her arms around his neck the last time he had seen her. And then he remembered the way she looked today in the wagon beside that long-lost love of hers, laughing and getting her fingers kissed. He had a good idea that that wasn't all that bastard had kissed.

While Nick was occupied with his own thoughts, Tibbie was thinking that this was a Nicholas Mackinnon she had never seen before. He was still handsome as the devil, but now his jaw was clenched in a ruthless manner and there was a hint of cynicism in the deep blue of his eyes. This man looked angry enough to kill. "Can't we talk inside?" she asked.

"No."

"Why not?"

"Because I may lose myself and do something I've thought about doing for a long time."

"What is that?"

"Paddling your backside or shaking you until your teeth fall out."

Tibbie was astounded. "Whatever for?"

"I'll tell you in a minute," he said through gritted teeth.

By the time they reached the orchard, Nick's temper had cooled somewhat, but his determination to have it out with her here and now had not. When his anger began to subside, he knew there was no cause to blame Tibbie. But so damn much of his heart was held in her hands. That was an investment worth protecting.

When they went through the creaky iron gate, Nick released her arm and said, "I'm sorry I lost my temper."

"Thank you," she said, rubbing her wrist at the red spot he

had held tightly. "You certainly should be." She watched him swallow and take a deep breath. "You heard about Eric?"

"Yes, I heard. I also *saw*!"

"You saw what?"

"The two of you in town."

"And you're angry at me for going to town?" Her own temper was rising. "You mean to tell me you have come barging into my home, scaring me out of my wits, and dragging me like some cave woman to the orchard *because I went to town*?"

"Because you went to town with him and the two of you were sitting together like lovebirds."

"We were not! And just where would you expect me to sit? In the back of the wagon with the sack of barley?" Still disbelieving it, she said, "You're angry at me?" and threw up her hands.

"No," he said, his hand coming out to take her upthrown hands in his, lowering them and rubbing the soft knuckles. "I'm just angry that he's back in your life."

"He isn't."

"It sure as hell looks that way. The two of you have been joined at the hip since the day he arrived."

"You've certainly been busy snooping."

"You've certainly been busy giving me something to snoop about."

Her hands clamped on her waist, her elbows poking out. "What is that supposed to mean?"

"You've been with him constantly. You didn't send him packing. Everyone in town is talking about it. Fifty people asked me if I knew when you two had set the wedding. Just what are your intentions as far as he's concerned?"

Tibbie tried to understand Nick's anger, but his attitude toward her was making her just a little angry as well. He had no right coming over here like this, accusing her.

Before she could think further, he said, "Why is he back?"

"He asked me to marry him."

"Shit!"

The sting of tears came into her eyes. She had never seen

Nick like this. Nick, who was always so kind and considerate. Nick, who always understood. "Nick, please—"

"Please what? Please understand? Please be nice? Please let you stomp my heart in the dirt? Please go away? What in the hell do you want of me?" He grabbed her by the arms and shook her. "What is it you want? To keep me dangling on your every word until you decide which one of us you want?"

"That's not fair!"

"Fair? I'll tell you what isn't fair! His coming back! *That's* not fair!"

"Try to understand."

"Understand what? That you're confused? That you're having a hard time sending that bastard on his way? Boy, he must've gotten to you in the worst way, and it didn't take him long to do it."

She slapped him so hard his head jerked back. "Thank you for telling me just what you think of me. *That,* more than anything you've done, has helped me make up my mind."

"Tibbie—"

"Stay away from me. I don't ever want to lay eyes on you again." She whirled and ran. He caught her before she reached the gate. "Just what did you think I'd do when I found out you've agreed to see him again?"

"Leave me alone!"

He didn't let her finish. Jerking her against him, he said sarcastically, "Poor little Tibbie. Having so much trouble making up her mind. When he kisses you, do you compare it with mine? Or have you forgotten mine already?"

"I've never compared your kisses, or anything else for that matter."

"I don't believe you."

She threw up her hands. "I can't talk to you when you're like this. I don't even *want* to talk to you when you're like this. You're blaming me for things that aren't even true. I need your understanding, Nick, your comfort, not your accusations."

"What do you want me to do? Did you just think I'd come running just to comfort you when you've got another man on your mind? Do you want me to kiss the indecision from your mind?"

Before she could answer, he jerked her against him roughly, hooking his arm behind her waist. She went rigid against his punishing kiss. His hard mouth ground against her lips and teeth, kissing her in a way he never had, not being gentle or slow, not taking the time to make his bruising kiss anything but demanding and punishing. The humiliation of it angered her as much as his closeness felt so familiar. She knew the reason for this kiss, to degrade and hurt her as he had been hurt.

When he broke the kiss, Tibbie remained motionless in his arms. She closed her eyes and turned her head away, trying to calm herself, to gain control of her reeling mind. This man was so dear to her. He was hurt. Pain was something she understood well. She didn't want to add to his pain. She didn't want to say the wrong thing.

In the end she didn't have to. Seeing her closed eyes, her averted head, Nick had his answer. Eric was back in her life and he was out. "Damn you!" he said. "Damn you to hell!"

He shoved her away from him and she opened her eyes in time to see him go through the gate. "Nick!"

He stopped and turned. "You don't have to tell me anything. I'm not the fool you think I am, nor am I the fool you are. At least *I* recognize when I'm being rejected."

A moment later he was gone.

But she did recognize when she was being rejected, and the thing about it that hurt her most was that it was Nick who rejected her. That night she cried herself to sleep for the first time in six years.

The next morning, in spite of her headache and puffy eyes, she walked to town, hoping to find Nick. All night the hurt, wounded look in his eyes had haunted her. She didn't want things to be like this between them. As she walked, she considered the things she might tell him, the questions he might ask, the answers she would give. The thing that drove her on, conquering her pride, was knowing that Nicholas might be hurting. She could take anything but that.

All her worries were for nothing, for when she reached the shipping office Nick was not there. Porter was, however.

"Miss Buchanan," he said, smiling and holding the office door open for her. "Do come in."

"Thank you." Tibbie stepped inside and looked around.

"Please. Sit down." Porter pulled up a chair for her and she sat down, looking around as she did. As Porter sat behind his desk, she saw Porter's neat desk and another one that was cluttered, the chair behind it empty. "Nick's?" she asked.

Porter grinned. "Do I look like a sloppy man?"

She smiled back at him. "No you don't."

"Thank you. I suppose you're looking for Nick?"

"Yes."

"He isn't here. He was in earlier, in the foulest of moods, I might say, then he left with—" Porter began coughing, then said quickly, "I might add I was glad to see him go. I've never seen him in a nastier mood."

"Who did you say he left with?"

"I didn't."

"Please. It's important."

Porter sighed. "I'll probably have bamboo shoots driven under my fingernails and the hide peeled from my body for this." He looked at Tibbie's drawn and pale face. "Tansy stopped by and Nick took her to lunch."

He stood when she did and walked her to the door.

She stopped just outside and thanked Porter, offering him her hand. "I'd appreciate it very much if you wouldn't tell Nick I was here."

"I understand. Of course I won't."

Tibbie walked home slowly, so engrossed in thought she didn't hear the buggy coming up the road behind her until her father called her name. She rode the rest of the way home with him, but she didn't feel much like talking, though Coll was in one of his talkative moods and didn't seem to notice.

"You made your mind up yet?"

"Not exactly."

"You have to choose one of them, you can't have them both."

"Maybe I won't take either one of them."

Coll slapped the reins against the mare's broad back and she picked up the pace a little. "I'd hate to see you do that, Tibbie. You ought to be married."

"Why?"

"For a lot of reasons. You'd make a good wife. You were raised to be some man's wife. You're the kind of woman that needs a man to love her, children to raise. But the biggest reason I see is Beth. She's getting of the age that things people say will scar her. You can't protect her from that. She needs a home and a papa. I hate to see you deprive her of that."

Tibbie wanted nothing more than to go to bed and cry when she reached home, but Beth spied her getting out of the wagon and came running across the yard. "Mama, come and see Precious. He's so darling!"

Tibbie managed a smile and let Beth lead her around the house to where Beth's wagon was parked. But it was what was parked in the wagon that drew a real smile from Tibbie, for there Precious sat, wearing one of Beth's dresses, with a bonnet on his head. "You were right, Beth. He is darling."

Tibbie turned toward the house. "Come on in with me. I'll make us some chocolate." Beth took her hand. "Mama, is Eric going to be my father?"

Tibbie's heart pounded. "Eric *is* your father."

"But is he going to be my live-with-us father?"

"I don't know. Do you want him to be?"

Beth frowned. "Maybe." Then her face grew bright and her eyes huge. "But I like Nick ever so much better."

So do I, Tibbie thought. *So do I.* And her heart twisted painfully.

Eric came by that night after supper. Judging from the look on his face, Tibbie figured he'd gotten wind of Nick's visit.

Tibbie came outside to join him on the porch. A minute later Effie brought them a slice of gooseberry pie. Eric was his usual charming self with Effie and had her laughing when she went back inside. Tibbie couldn't eat her pie, dreading the moment Eric would mention Nick. Two arguments with two men in one day was too much.

But to her surprise he ate all of his pie, joking and talking with her, never making any mention of Nick.

Afterward they walked down the road a piece, talking. On the way back, Eric said, "You know I can't stay here in Indianola waiting forever to see what you're going to decide." He took her hand in his. "Tibbie, I love you. I want you to be my wife. I want to give our daughter a home, my name. Doesn't that mean anything to you?"

"Of course it does."

"I want you to tell me you'll come with me."

Tibbie wondered why things always went the way they did. If things had gone differently between herself and Nick today, she might be telling Eric to go on back to Hawaii without her. Perhaps she should do that anyway. But then she thought of Beth, thought of the things her father had said that morning and she knew Coll had been right.

"I need more time."

"Dammit! Is that the only excuse you know? Can't you at least be creative? Oh, damn, sweetheart! I'm so sorry." He took her in his arms, kissing her softly, whispering words of apology in her ear. "Forgive me, Tibbie. It's just that I need your answer."

"I know, Eric. I know. And I don't have one."

17

Late the next afternoon, Tibbie was sitting on the nail keg in the barn, thinking. Still unsettled over her latest confrontation with Nicholas Mackinnon, she had picked the barn because it seemed to be the only place she could go that no one would find her.

Trit-trot. Trit-trot.

Well, almost no one.

She looked up to see that porcine puzzle solver, Precious, hotfooting it toward her, his horny little trotters hitting the ground at a steady, even clip. She had gone to such lengths to see that she wasn't seen coming out here. *It's gotten pretty bad when a person has to hide in order to think.*

When he saw her, Precious stopped abruptly, his curly tail popping up as he gazed lovingly into her face.

"Go on," she said. "I want to be left alone."

The dreamy, rapt expression on his face disappeared—pigs being very sensitive creatures, and Precious being among the most astute when it came to sensing feelings. Tibbie studied him for a minute or two, then said, "All right, but you'd better be quiet. I'm not in a playful mood."

The pink piggy face seemed to light up and he squeaked triumphantly, trotting to her side and dropping to the dirt beside her with a satisfied grunt. His front feet were thrust out in front of him as he pressed his nose to the floor and poked the straw with his snout, raising a cloudlet of dust. Tibbie gave him a scratch or two between the ears, which put him into an immediate state of bliss, then she went back to her thinking.

It had been over a week since she'd talked to Nicholas. Oh, she'd seen him alright, with that sap Cora Belle Hamilton sitting beside him in the buggy, escorting Cora Belle and her cousin Ruthie to Sunday services, walking down the street with Honey Butler's arm through his, standing in front of the mercantile, laughing with one of the girls that worked at the Glass Slipper.

But he hadn't come to see her.

I'm a patient man, but I won't wait forever. . . .

Over and over those words returned to haunt her.

I won't wait forever. . . . I won't wait forever. . . . I won't wait forever. . . .

Faces began to swim before her. Cora Belle Hamilton, Honey Butler, Ruthie Faye Brewster, the girl at the Glass Slipper. And then she grew angry. Judging from the looks of things, he wasn't waiting.

With mounting irritation, she gathered her skirts about her and rose, stepping on Precious, whom she had forgotten all about.

Precious came to his feet and oinked piercingly ten times, running around in circles, squalling and oinking in earsplitting squeals before striking out at a dead run, digging up clods of dirt that flew back toward her, as if he were throwing them intentionally in her direction. His feelings were crushed. She would have to think of something to get back in his good graces.

As she meandered toward the house, she wondered what kind of end she had come to, worrying about what she could do to make amends to a pig.

No one saw anything of Precious for the rest of the day. Not even Beth could coax him out into the open. Knowing she would have to do something, Tibbie collected a pail of warm, steaming slops and headed toward the pigpens.

She found Precious standing by the wooden trough, staring forlornly at the watery mash he had been given earlier.

"Okay, you little grunter, I've brought you a peace offering. Potato peelings, crook-necked squash, toast, rice pudding, corn cobs, collard greens, all soaked in nice warm milk and wheat middlings." She poured the slops into the trough. "Am I forgiven? Are we friends now?"

Precious looked at the slops. He looked at her. He grunted a time or two, rooting his nose in the slops. Then he began to squeal, running in circles, kicking manure and mud into the air before rolling over and kicking his trotters in the air.

When he trotted back to the trough and began rooting and eating, making the most delighted noises, Tibbie said, "I take it my apology is accepted."

"Looks that way to me."

Tibbie turned to see Coll standing at the fence, his arms folded across the top rail.

"I stepped on him this morning. He's been sulking all day."

"I noticed it has been a little quiet around here. Not even Beth could placate him, huh?"

"No. His feelings were monstrously hurt, I'm afraid. I had other things on my mind when I stepped on him, and I didn't make a fuss to set things straight right then."

"So you had to bring him a bucket of his favorites."

"Yes."

"Apparently it did the trick. He looks enraptured right now."

"Oh, he is. It doesn't take much to make him happy."

"And what about you, Tib? What does it take to make you happy?"

"Why are you asking me a thing like that? I *am* happy. I thought you knew that."

"No woman is happy when she is trying to decide between two men."

"I'm not trying to decide. Or maybe I have. I don't want either one of them."

"Now *that's* a pail of slop."

"It's true!"

"What are you going to do, Tib? Seriously. Eric is wearing out his welcome. Either consent or send him on his way. And Nick—"

"I think he changed his mind."

Coll laughed. "If you think that, you don't know much about love or men." Coll started toward the house and Tibbie walked a little of the way with him, stopping by the fence. Coll walked on through the gate. "Don't stay out here in this night air too long," he said.

"I won't." A few minutes later she sat in Beth's swing, rocking herself back and forth in an absentminded way. The evening was warmer and more humid than usual, the kind of stifling heat that seems to draw the breath right from your body and sap the last reserves of strength. It was often in this listless, lackadaisical state of inertia that Tibbie did her best cogitation. She stopped rocking and leaned forward, her elbows braced on her knees, her chin resting in her cupped palms. Carried away by her thoughts, she heard no sound until Eric gave her a push, almost unseating her.

"I couldn't resist," he said.

"I came out here because I wanted to be alone."

"Do you find it necessary to growl at me?" he asked. "Have things between us regressed to that point? Can't you speak to me with softness anymore?" He stepped closer, running the curve of his finger across the hollow of her cheek. "In so many ways you're still the same sweet Tibbie I knew six years ago. Yet you've changed. . . ."

"I've grown up."

"Yes," he said pensively. "I suppose you have."

His gentleness softened her. "Oh, Eric," she cried. "Why do things have to change? Why can't we go back to the way it was before?"

"Are you saying you could never care for me? Not in the way you did then?"

When she didn't speak, only shook her head to show the emotion was too much for her, he stroked the top of her head, in the same manner her father might have done. "I realize there can be no going back for us. But I hate to think there is no way for us to move forward."

"Is that what you sincerely want?" she asked. "To move forward?"

"It's why I came back, isn't it?"

"I don't know, Eric. Is it?"

"Of course it is. But it's been difficult to convince you. I knew it would be hard, but I had no idea just how much opposition I faced."

"It's not just that I'm opposed to you—"

"I know that. I hurt you once . . . terribly, I know. It's been over six years. There's someone else—"

"It isn't just that."

"It's to be expected. You're a beautiful, desirable woman. I knew I couldn't just walk back into your life and pick up where we left off. At least I should be thankful you weren't married." His voice was no more than a whisper now. "But I had to try." He smiled, and the years between them seemed to melt before her eyes. Standing before her now was the love of her youth, the companion of her heart, her soulmate. She looked into his teasing blue eyes, absorbed the handsome lines of his beloved face, the way the wind ruffled the silky strands of his blond hair. He was the same arrogant, proud man that had swept into the life of a sixteen-year-old girl and turned her world upside-down. She wondered how many other women had been charmed by that handsome face, those flirty, laughing eyes and quick smile. It suddenly hit her that she didn't really care how many other women he had charmed. She didn't care because she didn't love him. She had loved him once a long time ago. But once a long time ago was not enough.

He leaned forward, his hands grasping the ropes on the swing and pulled her forward to meet his waiting kiss, touching her softly on the lips. "That's for the memory you gave me to cherish."

The first day of July, Cornelia Dickerson married Judge Wainwright's son, Dexter. The Dickersons and the Wainwrights were the wealthiest families in Indianola, so the wedding was something the whole town turned out for. And that included Tibbie Buchanan.

Tibbie stood in her room looking solemnly at the new dress she had sewn just for this occasion. But now she was having second thoughts. She had intended to sew something really different from anything she owned, but as the dress had progressed it was obvious it was heading for the same dull, plain end of all her clothes. The fabric was a rich golden amber that picked up the highlights of her hair and matched the flecks in her eyes, but the style and cut she had chosen did nothing for the beautiful fabric.

The dress wasn't ugly, exactly. It was just plain. Plain like a plate of grits was plain. Tibbie sighed. She felt like she had been eating cornmeal mush all her life. Once, just once, she wanted to feast upon something dripping with lavish excess.

But no matter how lavish she wanted it, there was no way around it. The dress was still plain. Plain like a glass of warm milk, or a warm, windless day. *How tired I am of clothes like this,* she thought. *Just once I'd like to wear something daring and . . . and red! Wicked, sinful, wonderful red. Crimson red. Blood red. Shameful. Scarlet. Something like the other girls my age wear.* But then she remembered that the other girls her age didn't have a mistake to live down. She eyed the dress.

"Well," she told herself, "there's no use crying over spilt milk. The dress is plain as dirt and it will have to stay that way."

"Oh, dear!" Effie said, coming into the room and eyeing the dress critically. "That will never do."

"I know, but it's too late now to do anything about it."

"Hmmmm," said Effie, walking around her. "Never go down in defeat! I think that must have been a Stewart motto or something." Effie eyed the dress some more. "It isn't beyond *all* hope."

Tibbie looked at herself in the mirror. "I'm not too sure," she said. The dress looked as common as a dirt-dauber's nest.

Effie circled her, lifting and bunching here, gathering and tucking there. "The color is exceptional on you."

"The dress is so average it makes me sick!" Tibbie said.

"The cut is plain, but not bad. It could be worse. I'll be right back," she said, and left the room.

A minute later she was back, carrying her sewing basket.

Tibbie stood in front of the mirror, still looking at herself. She had tried gathering and bunching like her mother had done, but no matter what she did, the dress looked commonplace. "I've been praying for a miracle," Tibbie said, "but perhaps I should just pray for a disaster, then I won't be disappointed."

"Oh, posh!" said Effie. "I don't know what's come over you. I'd take a miracle over a disaster any old day in the week." She pulled a long length of ivory lace from the basket and placed it on the bed. A moment later several yards of turquoise satin joined the lace. Then she studied the dress again. "Just a minute," she said. "I have an idea." Off she went a second time.

This time when she returned, Effie was carrying a tangled bundle of gold braid, and a nosegay of gold satin roses Tibbie recognized.

"Those came off your old tea-dress," Tibbie said.

"And the braid was off an old riding habit," Effie said. "Now, let's see what we can do here."

For an hour or more, Effie worked with her needle and thread, making a bow here, gathering a bit of lace there, looping braid, pulling up the skirt to gather into a bustle in the back.

"That looks good from the back," Tibbie said, "but what am I going to use to cover up my petticoats here in the front?"

"Hmmmm," said Effie. "Let me get that riding habit and see how that bronze fabric will look as an underskirt."

As it turned out, it looked beautiful. Everywhere she looked she was all rich bronze and gold with a bright turquoise sash that was worked into a bow and threaded with gold roses, gathering into a bustle in back. The plain bodice had been helped by three deep rows of lace ruffles that fell from the shoulders to a V point at the waist, piped in gold cord that gathered into several looped strands on her left shoulder.

"Needs more bosom," Granny said, coming into the room. "Men like a show of bosom."

"You think so?" Effie asked, eyeing the dress. "Maybe you're right. I felt like it needed something else on the bodice. I was thinking about another ruffle, or perhaps a bow . . . but maybe you're right." She studied the dress.

"Needs more bosom," Granny said again.

"I think you're right. The neck is too high."

Effie picked up the scissors and followed the V made by the lace. When she finished, Tibbie looked in the mirror and gasped. "Mother! This is cut almost to my waist!"

"Heh! Heh! Heh!" said Granny. "You'll knock the socks off Mr. Nickelson tonight."

"I may not even see Mr. Nickel—Mackinnon," Tibbie said. "I hear he's been showing Cora Belle Hamilton around lately."

"Don't you worry about that none," Effie said. "He's just biding his time."

"With every single woman in Indianola, from what I hear," said Tibbie.

"You were taught to pay no never mind to gossip."

"But I can't help hearing it."

Effie didn't say anything, so Tibbie changed the subject. "Don't you think we should add another row of lace so this isn't so low?" She pulled the bodice up some. Effie slapped her hands away.

In the end, they reached a compromise. They left the bodice low-cut, but Effie relented and covered the vast openness with a pretty piece of lace. "That way you see it, but you don't," Tibbie said.

To which Effie skeptically replied, "That's like saying you're making sense when you really aren't."

"Heh! Heh! Heh!" said Granny hobbling from the room. "Poor Mr. Nickelson. When he sees you in that dress he isn't going to know what hit him. He won't know *stand up* from *sit down* before the evening is over."

But once she was at the wedding, Tibbie wasn't so sure.

She was whispering to Mairi and Leticia Kildaire about how beautiful Cornelia Dickerson's wedding dress was, when she looked up and saw Nicholas Mackinnon across the room. "There ought to be a law against anyone looking that good," Leticia said, following the direction of Tibbie's gaze.

Tibbie was inclined to agree. Nicholas was, indeed, a handsome specimen of a man. In many ways he was simply devastating, especially dressed as he was now—the brass buttons of his jacket gleaming, yet seeming dull in comparison to the bright, flashing smile he turned upon Honey. Honey was sticking to him closer than the bark on a tree.

She wasn't interested, of course. Just simply making an observation. And she wasn't the only woman in church to do so. Quite a number of Indianola's feminine population, married and unmarried, cast lingering looks in his direction from time to time.

"Will you look at that," Mairi said, as they left the church and crossed the street to the Dickerson's house.

Tibbie did, looking in fascination as Honey did her best portrayal of an unconvincing stumble, which brought her flat up against Nick.

"That's the most disgusting thing I've ever seen her do," Leticia said, but Tibbie wasn't really paying too much attention. She was remembering how it felt to be that close to him.

"Tibbie Buchanan, don't you look . . . sweet," Honey said, coming over to say a word or two to the three women while Nick talked to a group of men.

"Thank you."

"Wasn't it a lovely wedding? Doesn't it make you want to . . . well, you know . . . tie the knot?" she whispered.

"No," the three said, in unison. "It doesn't."

Honey looked just a little put out. "Maybe that's because you don't have a man like Nicholas Mackinnon squiring you about," she said in inflated tones.

"Honey, I have a red dress that isn't as loud as you," Tibbie said.

Honey laughed. "Tibbie Buchanan, I know you never wear red anymore. Not since"—she gave Tibbie a triumphant look —"well, you know since when."

Tibbie, Mairi, and Leticia watched her walk away to rejoin Nick. For a while none of them said anything.

"Honey Butler is pretty disgusting," Mairi said. "But I'll have to admit, I wouldn't mind being where she is right now."

"Mairi Buchanan," Leticia said, giving Mairi a jab. "I can't believe you said that!"

"Why not?"

Leticia looked put out. "I thought you said you never noticed boys."

"I don't." Mairi's eyes drifted toward Mackinnon. "But then, he's not a boy."

"You might as well not look. It wouldn't do you any good. My mama heard from Cassie's mama that Mr. Mackinnon was a *very* frequent visitor to Honey's house."

"What does that mean?" Mairi asked, giving Tibbie a quick look.

"According to Cassie's mother it means there will be another wedding following Cornelia's before long."

Two hours of boring wedding party was more than anyone should be expected to endure, and even with the help of the spirit-laced punch Buddy Poindexter had given her, it was more than she was going to subject herself to. Feeling the floor tilting around her, she made her way to the back door, hoping the gentle gulf breezes would bring some relief.

The sun was almost gone now, and glancing back at the house she could see they were starting to light the lanterns outside, yet the last lingering glow from the sun left the faintest hint of light, which bathed her in a dull wash of gold, gilding her face and bringing the golden coils of braid to life.

The moment she stepped inside the house she saw Nick and Honey. And Nick, it was apparent, had seen her. Their eyes locked and she froze. He had been watching her all afternoon.

A few minutes ago he had noticed she wasn't inside, so he had been keeping an eye on the door. He saw her the moment she entered the house. Tonight there was a responsiveness about her, a yielding that was all feminine softness and seduction, that made his blood race. her skin looked as soft and pure as a baby's, while the graceful way she wielded her fan was all woman. He watched the way the golden loveliness of her bosom beneath its covering of lace rose and fell with each breath. He wanted to put his hands there. He wanted . . .

Tibbie jerked her eyes away from his, then ducked back through the door. Nick took a step forward, fully intending to follow her when he felt Honey's hand upon his sleeve. With a sigh, he turned back to Honey.

Tibbie was unusually quiet as they rode home, her thoughts on Nick. "What is wrong? Did it upset you to see Nick with Honey?" Mairi asked in a kind tone.

"I suppose it always hurts to see someone you love with another person, knowing they never think about you anymore."

"That," said Mairi, "is the most ridiculous thing I've ever heard. If I had a crying towel I'd give it to you."

"Well, it's true! People were even saying Nick and Honey are planning marriage."

"Horsefeathers! How can you expect me to believe that? I have two eyes, you know. I saw the way he watched you all evening. Honey might as well be a piece of marble for all Nick cares."

Tibbie flinched at the word marble, remembering the tiny marble angel Nick had given her. "Why would he watch me?"

"Because he's in love with you, you sap."

"Then why was he with Honey tonight?"

"For the love of God! The man is in love with you, but he's an honorable man. If he thinks you're in love with someone else, he isn't going to press the issue. If he thinks you want Eric, he's going to give you plenty of time and space to make up your mind. But he's no fool. He won't wait forever."

Tibbie felt her heart fill with misery and despair. Those words were painfully close to what Nick had said. He had also said she knew where to find him when she came to her senses. But the thought of going to him, facing him with her heart in her hands, waiting to see if he would accept it or grind it beneath his boot, terrified her.

Seeing the flood of emotion upon her sister's face, Mairi patted her arm. "You haven't given him much encouragement during the entire time he was telling you of his feelings. I think it's come to the point that if you want him, you're going to have to swallow some of that pride of yours and go to him. You think about that tonight when you're feeling miserable."

"I will," Tibbie whispered, seeing they had reached home.

"Good," Mairi said, "because if this goes on much longer, I'm going to go absolutely mad." The two of them climbed out of the carriage.

As Tibbie walked into the house and on into the parlor, she said, "This is the way people go crazy!" her voice carrying over the rhythmic clacking of Granny's knitting needles.

"What'd she say?" asked Granny, looking up from her knitting.

"She said, 'This is how people go crazy!'" Effie said in a loud voice.

"Oh," said Granny.

"You have a nice time tonight?" Effie asked Tibbie.

"Yes, I suppose," said Tibbie, dropping into the nearest chair.

"What'd she say?" asked Granny.

"She said, 'Yes,'" Effie shouted.

"Oh," said Granny.

"Are you still having trouble deciding which one you want?" asked Effie.

"I was," replied Tibbie.

"What'd she say?" asked Granny.

"She said she was," shouted Effie.

"Oh," said Granny.

"Like I said before, you can't have them both," Effie said.

"I only want one of them," Tibbie said.

"What'd she say?" asked Granny.

"She said, 'I only want one of them,' " Effie shouted.

"Oh," said Granny.

"Which one is that?" asked Effie.

"Nick," Tibbie replied.

"What'd she say?" asked Granny.

"She said, 'Where the devil can't go, he sends an old woman!' " Effie shouted, losing her patience.

"Oh," said Granny.

Giving Tibbie an exasperated look, Effie threw up her hands and said, "Tibbie Ann, when it comes to men, you were over-served."

And then she left the room.

Granny looked at Tibbie. "What'd she say?"

Tibbie passed her mother in the hall.

At half past three the following afternoon, Effie marched into Tibbie's room and said, "Why don't you go over to the cove and have a swim? You're much too pale. I think an afternoon in the sun would be good for you."

Thinking of the cove filled her with a terrible longing, and she tried to push back the unhappy feeling that she would never see Nicholas again. Fighting back tears, she went upstairs to change into her oldest dress, stripping off her petticoats. She took her straw bonnet from the hook by the back door and headed down the path that led out over the dunes toward the cove.

The cove was the loveliest of spots; a place where she and Mairi came to play as children. Later, when they were older and more daring, they had actually removed their dresses and gone swimming in their shifts. No one ever came to the cove. It was secluded. And private. And hers.

A return to one's childhood is a wonderful spirit lifter, even if it is for a few hours only. As she picked her way along the path, the warm air was as fragrant as the seagrasses it swept over. When she reached the cove, the surface of the water reflected the sunlight overhead, the smallest ripple of a wave washing upon the beach, for this cove was still inside the bay, and not on the ocean side. She went down the gradual slope of the last sand dune, walking toward the water that lapped gently against the shore. A few feet from the water's edge she stopped, dropping her bonnet to the sand, then sitting down beside it to remove her shoes.

Once they were off, she thrust her feet out before her, wiggling her toes and closing her eyes, her face tilted to the sun. Overhead, a seagull or two circled lazily, until deciding she wasn't here to toss them food, and flew on down the beach, eventually going out of sight.

She walked along the beach, holding her skirt between her legs, but when the skirt became waterlogged, she returned to her bonnet and shoes and removed the dress altogether. There was no one to see her except a few sandcrabs and a brown pelican that watched her from the top of a half-buried barrel. Once her dress was off, the sun felt wonderful, the breeze passing with ease through the soft, thin fabric of her shift.

She hit the water at a dead run, her speed slowed somewhat once in the water, but she did not stop until it was too deep to walk and she had to swim. She floated on her front. She floated on her back, squirting a stream of water from her mouth. It had been so long since she had felt this free. She wished she could float on her back forever, just keep on floating right out to sea, past the lighthouse, past Padre Island, past all the little boats bobbing in the distance, and to keep on floating away from all the things that plagued her.

She heard a fish flip and looked down, seeing a school of mullet pass beneath her. Flipping over to her stomach once again, she swam with slow, steady strokes until she could touch the sandy bottom. As she looked up, she saw the silhouette of a dark horse coming in her direction. The sun was behind him, so that when she looked at him, she was dazzled by sunlight, making it difficult to see his features. A sudden unannounced fear laid hold of her. How long had he been there? Without another thought, she turned and ran blindly through the water.

She heard the horse come into the water behind her, the hooves of the great beast hitting the water with a loud splash that seemed to follow her like an echo. He was so close now that she could feel the shower of water displaced by those hooves as it pelted her from behind. At first she was afraid he might drag her behind the dunes and rape her, but now another fear began to take root. The way he came after her, she was afraid the man sought to run her down.

She screamed as a strong pair of hands came out of nowhere to pull her, kicking and twisting, from the water. Thrust across a strong pair of thighs that straddled the horse's back, she struggled frantically until she felt a hard slap against the wet shift that clung to her fanny. "Tibbie, what in the hell is the matter with you?"

"Mackinnon!" she gasped.

He pulled up, taking her in his hands like a rag doll and bringing her up, none too gently, to sit in front of him. His hands were on each of her shoulders, his expression a mixed one, which she recognized as the same one that had always driven her to distraction because she could never fully read just what he was thinking.

"You could have told me it was you," she said, pulling at the wet fabric, hoping to separate it from her skin and therefore make it not quite so transparent.

"Save yourself the effort," he said. "I've already seen enough to keep me howling at the moon for days."

"Now, why would you do a silly thing like that?"

"Shut up, my naïve little mother," he said, his mouth coming down hard on hers, his hands going up to wrap around her head, holding her closer. Her mouth felt hot and hungry and she kissed him back with all the pent-up passion she felt. That seemed to encourage him, for he groaned and intensified a kiss that was too intense as it was. He was holding her so tightly against him, she could feel the wetness of her shift soaking into his shirt. Everywhere he touched her he was warm, living male, and she felt her body grow soft at the thought of it.

As he kissed her again and again, his hands began to wander

over her, touching her, warming her as the sun could never do, until she felt like she was swimming inside herself, and still he would not let her go. Everywhere it was warm, inside and out; and the feeling of him here, this close, his hands touching her in places they had no place being, left her aching, hot, and weak.

She felt the contraction of his thighs as he urged the horse from the water. "Are you going to rape me?"

"It wouldn't be rape," he said, and she was inclined to agree with him.

"But no," he went on, "I'm not."

"Good," she said with a heavy sigh.

"But I'm not ready to let you go just yet."

She pulled back, looking at him, just noticing that the horse had stopped again. "Why not? Why aren't you going to let me go?"

"Because I'm not going to let you face Eric and your father alone."

In answer to her puzzled expression, he nodded in the direction behind her and said, "They've obviously seen us and are headed this way."

"Oh, no," she said, trying to cross her arms in front of her chest.

"That's quite ineffective," he said, lowering her to the sand. "Try to cover everything major."

She picked up her dress, clutching it against her.

"You bastard!" Eric said, pulling up in front of them. "I ought to kill you. You couldn't let her make up her mind without trying one more time to get her into your bed. I have every right—"

"Eric," she said, "shut up!"

"Tibbie, be quiet," Nick said. "This doesn't concern you."

She looked at Eric. "I took my dress off to—"

"I can well imagine *what* you took your dress off for," he said harshly. "I only hope it was worth the effort."

"We didn't. . . . He never—"

"That's something I won't ever know, isn't it?"

"No," she snapped, "you won't know, and we both know just whose fault that is."

Coll rode up. "Tibbie, get your clothes on. We can settle this at the house."

"There's nothing to settle," Nicholas said.

"Where in the hell were you going with her, half naked and draped over your saddle?"

"Carrying her to dry land."

"The knight to the rescue," Eric snapped. "A likely story."

"I don't usually engage in the sort of thing you're accusing me of on horseback," Nick said. "There are beds for that."

"And I'm sure you've been in your share of them," said Eric.

"That's enough," Coll said. "Tibbie, you go on up to the house."

Tibbie could have shot her father and Eric with one shot and then taken the gun and beaten them both over the head with it. Just how long had she been yearning to be in Nick's arms, and then, when she was, half of Indianola had to show up? It just wasn't fair. She took one last look at Nick, her heart leaping as a pair of deep blue eyes looked straight into hers. She saw the regret carved into his handsome face, the longing in his eyes, and decided that she would go to Nick tomorrow and tell him all the things in her heart. And then she would tell Eric it was time for him to leave.

A short while later, when Coll and Eric came into the parlor, Tibbie looked at the two of them and said, "I don't want to hear one single word from either one of you." After that, she marched from the room.

⇥ · 18 · ⇤

That night Granny died in her sleep.

It was Tibbie who found her, coming into her room waving a note decorated with flowers and rainbows and bluebirds that Beth and Tibbie had made for her. Tibbie went to the window and drew back the curtains, turning and walking to Granny's bed with a scolding laugh and a comment about "those who sleep the day away."

When she reached Granny's bedside and saw her lying as slender and pale as a white narcissus, her great gray braid looking drab and time-worn across her chest, the words died on her lips.

That was when she screamed.

When Coll came, he said she hadn't suffered, but simply went to sleep. She was laid out in the parlor, devotedly attended to by those who loved her most, her hair brushed and rebraided, wound on top of her head, her face wearing the same peaceful expression Tibbie had seen whenever Granny knew some little secret that no one else knew about. Now she lay in her simple pine coffin, looking as regal and aristocratic as her blue-blooded Russian ancestors. Friends, neighbors, and members of the church came and went, ministering to the living in the name of the dead.

Tibbie had held up through it all. Not once did she openly show signs of grief—other than her pale, pinched face—never giving way to the tears she could feel inside. Seeing Tibbie like this, many friends commented about it to Effie.

"I know she's such a comfort to you at a time like this," Mrs. Timms remarked.

"There is always one who rises up stalwart and strong at a time like this to see the rest of the family through," was Rebecca Moody's comment.

And from Jeb Whittaker, "It's times like this that we need someone strong like Tibbie to lean on."

But as far as Tibbie was concerned, it was times like these that she wished she could cry and rid herself of the terrible grief that ached and kept on aching until she fell asleep that night.

Granny was buried two days later. And still Tibbie did not cry.

It wasn't until the following afternoon, when Tibbie stood beside Granny's grave with a bunch of fast-wilting flowers in her hand, staring at the freshly turned earth and seeing Granny's face as it had been the last time she had seen her, that she could cry. Their last conversation came back to her, as vivid and alive as the picture of her face.

Tibbie had been bringing the milk cows in from the pasture, when she met Granny and Beth coming toward her. Beth had immediately broken into a run. "Mama . . . Mama . . . Can I bring the cows in . . . please?"

Tibbie picked Beth up and whirled around and around with her, laughing and asking, "And why would a pretty little girl like you want to bring those *ugly* old cows in?"

"Because I love them. And they're not ugly! I think they're *beauuuutiful*!"

Tibbie looked back at the herd of Jerseys with their dainty black-tipped heads and gray-brown bodies, their horns curled like wreaths over their heads. As she looked, one cow in particular stopped and looked at her with huge, gleaming brown eyes, as if she knew she was being talked about. "Yes," she said, giving Beth's head a fluff. "They are beautiful, aren't they?"

Putting Beth down, Tibbie handed her the stick she had been using, then dropped back a bit to walk with Granny, the two of them watching Beth call out her soft admonishments to cows that had been around much longer than she.

Stealing a look at Granny, Tibbie saw her eyes glistening as she watched Beth. Touching her gently on the arm, Tibbie said, "What's wrong, Granny? Don't you feel well?"

"Hear what bell?"

Almost shouting, Tibbie repeated the question.

"Oh! Feel well! Of course! I'm fine. My old body is just wearing out."

About that time, Beth shouted at a delinquent cow, giving her a nudge with the stick and Granny smiled. "I wish I could see that one grow up. She reminds me so much of myself when I was a young girl."

"Don't talk like that." Tibbie forced a smile and a lightness to her voice that she didn't really feel. Shouting again, she said, "You'll probably be saying the same thing to her children."

"No, I won't. I've been dreaming of your grandpa a lot lately. It's the same dream, over and over. I see him—Lord! Looking so young! Like he did when I married him. And he's always standing in a grove of trees down by the summerhouse, where we used to meet when I'd sneak off from the house. It's like—like he was waiting for me, and I think probably he is. He's been gone so many years now, but I still love him as strongly as I ever did. I suppose that's why I never could remarry." Suddenly, her eyes seemed to come alive and her voice had a new quality, like floating. "Lord! The times we had, the love we shared. He was quite a man, your grandpa was."

"And you're quite the grandest lady I've ever known," Tibbie said, just a little glad they were out here in the pasture, where no one would hear her shouting like she was.

Granny winked at Tibbie and patted her hand. "Don't you let me go on like this—getting you all teary and sentimental. You're too young for such. Save that sort of thing for when you're old and don't have anything better to do. I've had a good, long life with more blessings than I can count. But I've been away from your grandpa too long, and I think it's time I went home."

Granny always kept a delicate Belgian handkerchief tucked beneath the cuff of her black bombazine dress, and today she had need of it, pulling it out slowly to dab at her eyes. She refolded the handkerchief, studying it carefully as she did. "My mother always carried a Belgian handkerchief like this. Of course, hers were much finer, the lace more expensive, but it's one of the things I remember about her. She told me once that as far back as she could remember, to her great-grandmother, the women always kept Belgian handkerchiefs." She sighed, and tucked the handkerchief back in place. "But they could afford to back then, back when Russia sparkled like a diamond in Europe's tiara."

Seeing they were nearing the house, Tibbie shouted again, but a mite lower this time. "You know, you look half your age."

"Of course I do! But inside, time is taking its toll. The obstinate beating of this old heart of mine is beginning to sound more and more like a funeral bell."

"Well, you'd better plan on holding it at bay a while longer. I refuse to let you go."

But Granny went on like she hadn't heard Tibbie speak. "My clock has just about run down, I'm afraid." Granny reached out to take her hand, pressing something into it. "I want you to have this."

Tibbie opened her fingers to see Granny's small silver watch lying in her palm. Her eyes went to the place on Granny's bodice where Tibbie had always seen the watch pinned. "No," she said, offering the watch to Granny.

But Granny pushed it back toward her. "It's a reminder that time doesn't stand still for us, no matter how much we dawdle along the way. I want you to remember that. Time passes, but it leaves its shadow. God sends us opportunity, but he won't wake us if we're asleep."

Tibbie stared down at Granny's grave and her chest constricted and her heart felt so swollen with grief, she wondered that it could beat at all. Death was so powerful. And now grief had somehow softened her heart. Silently the tears rolled down her cheeks to splash in great, fat droplets upon the bodice of her black bombazine dress.

Nicholas had been doing a lot of traveling of late, partly for business, and partly because of Tibbie. He didn't return to Indianola until the day after the funeral. As soon as he heard, he went to the Buchanans' to pay his respects, not only because she was Tibbie's grandmother, but because he had genuinely liked her. He visited for a time with the family and paid his respects, but Tibbie wasn't at home.

As he rode back to town, his mind kept wondering where Tibbie was. *With Eric, more than likely. Forget it, Mackinnon. Better yet, forget her.*

But Tibbie wasn't an easy woman to forget. Thoughts of her confused him, distracted him, ate at him constantly. Night after night he occupied his time with one woman after the other, paying no more attention to them than he did to the horse he was riding. His mood fluctuated between hope and despair. There had been such precious little encouragement coming from Tibbie that he was actually amazed he could dredge up any hope at all. But she belonged to someone else and if he had any sense at all he would forget her. Eric was a fortunate man, even if he didn't realize it.

That isn't my problem.

You're right, so stop thinking about her all the time.

I don't think about her all the time.

Oh, you don't, do you?

Not when I'm asleep.

You mean those short bouts of slumber between all that tossing and turning?

When I'm at work, I don't think of her then.

You mean the times when you're staring off into space? Or the times you're writing her initials on the sketches you've just completed?

It doesn't matter. It's Eric she wants.

Keep reminding yourself of that.

I do. It doesn't help.

Why not?

I guess we always want what we can't have.

And you want her?

I do.

Then go after her.

It isn't that simple.

Only cowards despair.

Wood was made to float, stones to sink. I can't fight destiny.

Destiny . . . Is that what you call the things that limit
you?

Some things you can't fight.

Not even with God's help?

I think He's got more important things to see to.

Yes, like tempering the wind to the shorn lamb.

She's going to be married, for Christ's sake! To someone else.

So? She isn't married yet.

She might as well be.

When God gives you milk, do you ask for a pail?

I'm not sure God has given me the milk.

Ahhh, ignorance . . . such a soft pillow.

What would you have me do?

If you want the fruit, you're going to have to climb the tree.

He had spent a grueling four days in San Antonio going
over the final details for completing the ship. He was dog tired.
That was probably why his mind kept returning to these spec-
ulative thoughts about Tibbie. Tibbie Buchanan was going on
with her life. He had to figure out a way that he could, too,
because he couldn't spend the rest of his life in love with another man's wife. He rode along, saddle weary and wishing he
had taken time to shave and clean up before riding out to the
Buchanan place.

He rode past the church, feeling degrees cooler as he passed
by the huge trees that shaded the graveyard. He looked out
over the grassy slopes, over the neatly placed stone markers,
over a mound or two of freshly turned soil, then farther over,

near the corner of the fence, the dark, rounded hump of another, enclosed by a black iron fence. He pulled up abruptly.

Something about that particular grave drew him. A moment later he understood why. Half hidden in the shadow of a tree, the mourning tones of her dress blending with the dark, glossy green of the foliage beyond, he hadn't noticed her at first. But then she moved and a filtering shaft of sunlight struck full upon a head as bright as a new penny. A blond head.

Tibbie.

He turned his horse through the open gate and up the winding road until he was close enough to see she was sitting with her back to him, the voluminous folds of her black dress billowy and swelling about her like her grief. He rode a little farther, stopping to tie the gelding to a sapling. He walked toward her, thinking she shouldn't be here all alone, and neither, for that matter, should he. As he drew closer, the pitiful, jerky sounds of her crying reached him. Then he saw the wilted buttercups held tightly in her pale hand, as if by holding on to them she could keep them from dying.

"Tibbie . . ."

At the sound of his voice she sprang to her feet, using the back of her hand to take a swipe or two at her face before she turned to face him, and his heart twisted.

Come here, sweetheart. Come here and cry on my shoulder. Let me hold you, lass, until the grief is gone. Take a step toward me, give me your hand . . . anything to show me it isn't too late, that you care. But seeing nothing in her face or in her manner that would indicate her willingness or love, he said simply, "Tibbie, you shouldn't be here like this. You're only making it harder. . . ."

Oh, Nick! Nick! Hold me please. Hold me and tell me I'm alive. Tell me you forgive me. Tell me it isn't too late for us. But as she looked at him, she saw nothing in his face or in his manner that would indicate either forgiveness or love, so she said simply, "I just came with some flowers." She looked down at the flowers in her hand. "Buttercups and wild carrot," she said. "Granny used to take me to pick these when I was a little girl." Then, with a faraway look and a sad, trembling smile, she said, "Funny, the things we remember. It's never the big important things, but the small, everyday ones—things we would think insignificant. Take these flowers, for instance. Of all the things I could remember, what comes to mind is that for the longest time I thought buttercups could be made into butter, but when I told Granny, she set me straight. She loved flowers. She taught me so much about them . . . and she taught Papa too."

"Somehow I can't see someone like Coll becoming too involved with flowers."

"Oh, but he was . . . at least in the things Granny taught him. They were practical things, of course."

"Of course. A drop of monkshood, ground wing of bat, eye of toad, two hairs off a bull's tail . . ."

She smiled at him and it was like the clouds had parted to let the sun shine through. "No, I'm not talking about superstition. Flowers have great medicinal value and Granny knew a lot about that. She taught Papa that violets made into tea will get rid of a headache; skunk cabbage relieves spasms and asthma; a drop of bloodroot on a lump of sugar is good for a cough; yarrow will clot blood."

She thumped the dense head of the wild carrot. "Some people call this 'Queen Anne's lace.' It's related to parsley. The Greeks would put parsley on graves to tell their loved ones they were still remembered. We don't have any parsley around here, so I thought . . ." She looked as though she were going to cry again, but she took a deep breath and composed herself. "Granny said parsley took a long time to germinate because it had to go to the devil nine times before it could sprout. She said they planted parsley on Good Friday when she was a little girl, just to spite the devil."

How rueful she looked, clad all in black and filled with sorrow, her face swollen and bearing the tracks of hastily wiped tears.

"That sounds like her," he said, aching to hold her.

"Oh, Nicholas, I miss her so."

He could never resist her when she called him Nicholas. "I know." He reached for her and Tibbie turned to him, her face burrowing into the hollow between his arm and chest. Once she started crying, she couldn't seem to stop.

"I feel like such a fool," she said in nasal tones, then as if realizing she was being held in his arms, she turned abruptly away. "I'm sorry, I've gotten your coat all wet."

"I don't mind. Why should you?" he said, intentionally keeping his tone light. He fished around in his pocket and pulled out his handkerchief, offering it to her.

She shook her head with a shrug, but she took the handkerchief, turning away to blow her nose. He stared at her back, noticing for the first time just how narrow her shoulders were, how small her waist. A tiny row of buttons ran from collar to hem, an hour's worth of discouragement to any man, but to him, a reminder of what lay beneath. He wanted to turn her around, to pull her against him and tell her it was alright to cry. He wanted to hold her while she did.

He stood, a thing apart, feeling helpless and without answers as she buried her face in her hands and cried harder, her frail shoulders shaking with the force of her sobs. Her pain reached out to him. Were those her tears he could feel banked in his eyes? What could he say? What could he do? Dear God! He felt so helpless. *Maybe I should just let her cry herself out.*

Nick couldn't stand to listen to any more crying. He placed his hands on her shoulders, feeling her flinch at his touch. "Hey," he said, "would it help to talk about it?"

She shook her head and he watched the tiny jet earrings swing to and fro. "No," she said, swiping once again at her nose. Through blocked nasal passages she added, "Grief isn't something you can share. I have to do it alone."

"But you don't have to *be* alone while you do it. Companionship helps."

But she didn't seem to be listening to anything he said. "It was too soon. I wasn't ready for her to go. I still had so much to learn from her. There were so many things I wanted her to live to see."

Yes, like your wedding.

"Death never seems to pick the right time. It's always too early or too late."

Just like love.

"But I miss her so much. I won't ever see her again."

Nor I you.

"It hurts so much."

Yes, it hurts like hell.

"I know," he said. "The loss . . . missing someone who was such a vital part of you. . . . That's the hardest part of it. But she won't ever be entirely dead. Her life hasn't been erased. You'll see her again. Memories don't die."

She turned her tear-stained face up to look at him when he said, "Blow on a dead fire, Tib, and watch a coal begin to glow."

The tears started to flow again, and the sight of her standing there all alone in her grief was more than he could stand. It didn't matter that he had held her for only a little while and now she had someone else. It didn't matter that once he touched her he might not be able to stop. "Tibbie, don't take on so." He reached for her and she came willingly into his arms, her wet face pressed against his throat until she was too exhausted to cry anymore.

Even after she had quieted he continued to hold her, his chin resting on top of her head while he searched his mind for the right thing to say, for words that would give her the solace he wanted so desperately to give. But he was drawing only blanks; and in the end he was forced to comfort in the only way he knew, by offering the strength of his arms.

They stood together, one clinging to the other for some time. Finally, Tibbie asked, "Why do we have to die?"

He drew his chin back and forth over her head, his hands spread wide upon her back. "I don't know, Tib. But at least it's equitable. There should be some comfort in that—in knowing we put an end to all life's unfairness when we go. Death puts its hand on paupers and kings alike."

"Granny Grace told me once that she felt like she had outgrown life, that it pinched her like a pair of too-tight shoes. Maybe this is what she wanted." She nodded her head. "She knew . . . the afternoon before she died she told me she had been seeing my grandfather. She gave me her watch. She told me God sent opportunity, but that he wouldn't wake me if I was asleep."

He could tell by her relaxed breathing that she was over the worst of it—at least for now. But she made no effort to pull away and he welcomed the chance to hold her one last time. A stiffness in her body accompanied by a change in breathing is what told him she was as aware as he that they had remained in each other's arms even after the thought of comforting had passed; noble thoughts moving to those more earthy.

He pulled back to look at her, seeing the coloring of awareness on her cheeks, knowing she had much the same thoughts as he. For a moment he stood on the threshold of indecision, wanting to yank her back against him, knowing he shouldn't.

She leaned forward, placing the flowers on Granny's grave, more to put a little more space between them than for any other reason. He looked at the rounded mound, his eyes going to the white marble marker. SOPHIA ANASTASIA

"Sophia Anastasia? Why did everyone call her Grace?"

"Papa would always tease her and say it was because she was so clumsy, but Granny said she simply wanted a name that sounded more American. Mama said Granny's papa always called her his graceful little swan."

She caught the way he was looking at her and she fought for some diversion. "Well, it looks like I've ruined your shirt. It's quite a mess."

"Yes, a real mess."

"As I'm sure I am. You were wise to leave your horse back there. I would've scared him, I'm afraid. I know I look a fright."

"Yes, quite a fright."

He watched her, picking out all the signs of her discomfort, the shaky warble to her voice, the quick little way she sucked in her breath, the manner in which she avoided his eyes.

Which was a good thing. If she had so much as glanced at him she would have found herself back in his arms.

He wanted to hold her against him and kiss her until she forgot all about death and family and responsibility and the burden of respectability she always carried around. But most of all, he wanted to kiss her until she forgot all about Eric. But he did none of these things.

She pulled away from him, looking self-conscious and out of place. "I suppose you'll be leaving Indianola soon," she said.

"Yes, it won't be too long now." He braced himself against a tree, his thumbs hooked in the belt at his waist.

"I think it would be wonderful to be free like that, to go anywhere you wanted to, just like that."

"It has its drawbacks."

When she lifted her eyes to meet his, they were so coldly distant and cynical, it took all the courage she could summon just to keep her eyes upon him. Couldn't he see her heart in her eyes? Didn't he know what the thought of leaving him was doing to her? She swallowed her pride one last time. "How exciting to build ships, to spend so much time near the sea. I would love to see the places you've seen, to be able to sail anywhere I wanted to." *Take me with you, Nicholas. Take me with you when you go.*

"Perhaps you will. Eric is from Hawaii, isn't he? And I hear he leads quite a grand life."

Her heart plunged lower than her shoes. She couldn't believe he didn't understand what she was trying to say to him. *Maybe he does understand. Maybe he just isn't interested.* It hadn't been so long ago that he had held her and kissed her, or told her that he loved her. Could his feelings have changed so suddenly? She wrapped her arms around herself in a hug and shivered, but not from any cold. "I don't suppose it will be any grander than a life of building ships."

"Much more grand, I would think. Do you find you have a sudden taste for shipbuilding?"

She looked away. "I have recently held a certain fancy for it."

"It's a good life, but at times a lonely one, for rarely can I stay in one spot."

"Must it always be a vagabond's life? Have you never given any thought to settling down in one place? Having a family? Children?"

"There are no castles in the clouds, Tibbie. I don't live a fairy tale." His voice was harder now, and curt. "My business isn't proven by past generations. It's fledgling yet, at best. My brother and I are racing against the clock, hoping to learn all we can before my Uncle Robert dies. I spend a great deal of time away, or at sea. There is little security in that."

She understood at last what he was saying. There would be none of the things she could expect with Eric, no husband from a wealthy, well-known family, no security that she would even have a husband except when he wasn't traveling or at sea. There would be no grand life of immense wealth, no mansion the whole community would covet. He was a proud man, but not apologetic for possessions which paled in comparison to Eric's.

The reminder of loss and death closed in around her. The air was sultry and hot, difficult to breathe. She felt as if she were already in her own coffin. A final place from which she would never escape.

"Well," she said with forced lightness, "I've stayed much longer than I should have. I'll be needed at home."

"Are you afoot?"

"Yes. I prefer to walk. I wanted to be alone."

His jaw clenched. "I see."

No, you don't, Mackinnon. You haven't understood a damn thing since you met her.

Later that evening, Tibbie sat in her rocking chair in front of her bedroom window. Outside, the warm red of the setting sun bathed everything in a fevered flush, giving emphasis to the long, slender necks of a gaggle of geese browsing around in the front yard and making the rainbow colors of the peacock's open tail more elaborate.

As she looked around the yard, memories came rushing back. She could almost see her grandfather harnessing the family goat to a wagon to take her and Mairi for a ride. And there, standing to one side of the wagon, was the old bloodhound she had named Burglar because he was always on the prowl. Up the road came her friend, Carrie Jo Newcomb, with a basket on her arm, and inside were four furry kittens she was giving away. But they were all gone: Grandpa died in his sleep at the end of that summer, and Coll shot Burglar after he was bitten by a rabid skunk. She remembered how she and Mairi were still playing with the goat when they heard that Carrie Jo had drowned while crossing Spider Creek with a basket of kittens on her arm. How she wished she could go back; to tell Grandpa she loved him and hug his neck for hitching the goat to the wagon; to change that morning that Burglar wanted to play and she was busy with her dolls and chased him away, not knowing he would go off by himself to find a skunk to chase; and would things have gone differently for Carrie Jo that day if she had given in and gone with her to give her kittens away?

How sad it was to realize the value of milk after the cow went dry.

It suddenly occurred to her just what she had said. Isn't that what she was going to do with Nick? Realize her mistake after it was too late? Her mind spun backward, to the week before Granny died and a talk she had with Mairi. *You haven't given him much encouragement during the entire time he was telling you of his feelings. If you want him you're going to have to swallow some of that pride of yours and go to him.*

"All right!" she said, standing up. "I'll go first thing in the morning."

19

At a quarter past seven the next morning, Tibbie Anne Buchanan sat at her desk composing a note to Nicholas Mackinnon, the wastebasket at her side overflowing with paper. A sweet whiff of the honeysuckle that climbed the tree outside her window floated into the room, but Tibbie hardly took notice. She was too busy wadding up another piece of paper and tossing it into the basket with the others. For a long moment she sat there looking at the blank piece of paper, as if by so doing, the words she wanted to say would magically appear.

Why can't I write this blasted note?

Simple, Tibbie. Keep it simple.

Of course! Since five this morning she had been making her best attempt at flowing, flowery eloquence, which was not, to say the least, Tibbie's greatest talent. With a fortifying sigh, she picked up the quill again, this time writing a brief, *simple* note to Nicholas, telling him that she would be waiting for him by the tree in the orchard tomorrow at three o'clock, and that if he chose not to come, she would understand that to mean that any affinity between the two of them was, for all time, severed.

The note tucked safely in her deepest pocket, Tibbie walked to the shipyard, rehearsing as she went, exactly what she would say to Nick when she saw him. She would hand him the note, telling him to please read it after she had left, then she would politely excuse herself and leave. Once she reached her house, she would begin the longest wait of her entire life.

Once she reached the shipyard, she made her way to Nick's

office. She found the door closed, so she knocked three times. When no one answered she turned, went down three steps, then paused. So what if no one was there? She could slip the note under the door where Nick was sure to find it upon returning. But when she reached the door and started to slip it underneath, she stopped. What if the note blew away when the door was opened, or slipped beneath the rug on the other side? She couldn't take any chances. Not with this note.

She tried the door and found it open, so she went inside. The office was just as she remembered it, Porter's neat desk on one side, Nick's cluttered one on the other. She went toward Nick's desk, passing the window and pausing to look down into the shipyard. She spotted Nick and Porter immediately. They were talking to a rather portly gentleman, who, just as she paused, handed Porter what looked to be a stack of papers. The men shook hands and Nick and Porter walked off, heading in the direction of their office.

Her courage gone, Tibbie liked the idea of leaving the note on Nick's desk ever so much better than a head-to-head confrontation. At least she would be spared the humiliation of watching him smash the paper between his strong fingers and fling it into the trash—*if* that was what he chose to do, of course.

She hurried to Nick's desk, placed the note on it and hurried away. For some reason, just seeing Nick and observing him had lifted her spirits. Nick cared about her. He did! Breathing a sigh of tremendous relief she hurried down the street, and when she reached the corner, she twirled around three or four times and said, "I'm in love. I'm in love. I'm in love."

"I'm glad to hear it," a deep, masculine voice from behind her said, and she turned around, her hands over her mouth to hold in her shriek of mortification. When she saw the voice belonged to Mr. Plummer's son, Archie, she was weak with relief. "Thank you," she said, giving him her best smile, then she whirled once more and hurried toward her house.

Porter and Nick arrived at their office, Nick holding the

door open for Porter, who carried the stack of papers. "Just put them on my desk," Nick said. "I'll go through them later."

Porter said something about Arthur Bradley having gained a lot of weight, then he placed the stack on Nick's desk and went to his own.

For Tibbie, the next day passed slower than the millennium. Why she had opted to have this long a wait for herself, she would never understand if she lived to be a hundred. Never, never, never again would she do something this stupid. *Why, nitwit, didn't you ask him to meet you yesterday?* Never had the day seemed so long.

Of course, part of it might have been because Tibbie was up at five and dressed by five-thirty—for a three o'clock appointment. But that was only the first time she dressed. By two o'clock, she had put on every dress in her wardrobe at least three times. Looking at herself in the mirror, she felt mounting disgust. *They're all so drab and plain, it wouldn't matter which one I wore. Why didn't I have the foresight to have at least one pretty dress?* She looked in her wardrobe again. Gray. Brown. Blue. Black. Russet. Dark gray. Dark brown. Dark blue. There was nothing worth wearing for an occasion as important as this in her wardrobe. But there was in Mairi's.

"Of course you can wear my green plaid dress," Mairi said. "Where are you going?"

"I—I took your advice, Mairi. I'm going to meet Nick at three o'clock."

"Oh, Tibbie, how splendid! Oh, this is so romantic." Mairi paused, looking at Tibbie. "My green plaid is not right for this occasion. Today, Tibbie, you *must* wear my graduation dress!"

"Oh, I couldn't!"

At precisely two-thirty, Tibbie stood before her oval mirror and looked at herself in Mairi's white graduation dress.

"How lovely you look. Once he sees you, he'll wish you had made this appointment for ten o'clock!"

Mairi watched her go. And then Mairi watched her come back.

"I forgot something," Tibbie said in a rush as she hurried up the stairs. A moment later she came rushing back down again. "My angel," she said, holding up the carved marble angel Nick had given her.

It was the longest walk of her life, but Tibbie enjoyed every minute of it. How delightful to walk down the same trails she had walked thousands of times before, but never with such enthusiasm, such rejoicing. The afternoon sun had burned away the morning dew that blanketed the fields, leaving everything dry and fragrant. The air was balmy and not too hot, and white fluffy clouds floated overhead, looking so close she felt as though she could reach up and pluck one right out of the sky.

She reached the last hill that led down to the orchard, feeling a twinge of disappointment when she didn't see Nick's horse tied to the fence. When she looked at Granny's watch pinned to her bodice, and that it was five minutes away from three, she knew Nick wasn't late. She was early. But she couldn't help feeling a wee bit disillusioned that Nick wasn't already there, for she had mused a time or two over the grand entrance she would make through that old rusty gate in Mairi's white graduation dress, her hair down and tied back with a bow for the first time since Beth was born.

Tibbie looked at her watch again. *Half past four.* He wasn't coming, and all the wishing and waiting in the world wouldn't make it so.

When she had almost reached the house, she met Mairi and Precious coming down the path. Beth, she could see, was in her swing. Her face a cold, emotionless mask, Tibbie felt her heart crack when she looked at Beth and thought about what might have been. Her mother's tenderness went out to Beth, knowing how she adored Nick, how disappointed she would be never to see him again. Turning to Mairi, Tibbie said, "Please take care of Beth for a while. I don't want her to see me like this."

"Oh, Tibbie, what happened?"

"Why, nothing. Absolutely nothing. He never came, you see."

"I don't believe it."

"Believe it."

"Nick wouldn't—"

"He already has."

"Let me go see him, I'm sure—"

"If you so much as breathe a word of this to *anyone*, I'll never speak to you for as long as I live."

"Oh, Tibbie, please don't do this. Let me come with you. I don't want you to be alone."

"I'm used to it."

She turned away, hurrying toward the house, hoping to be inside before Beth noticed her. Beth didn't, and Tibbie thought that was the only good fortune she had had in a long time.

All the way up the stairs she kept repeating over and over, "How could he have done this to me? How could he have coldly and deliberately let me wait, knowing what I must be feeling—Nick, the one who professed such a desire to put an end to my suffering, to ease my pain?" There were many things she would have believed about Nick, but liar was not among them—at least not before today.

Just before supper, Mairi stopped by her room. After a few tries, Mairi realized Tibbie wasn't going to talk about it, so she simply hugged her sister and said, "Beth is helping Mama with supper. I told them you weren't feeling well and that I'd bring your supper up to you."

"I don't want any."

"I know, but I have to bring it, otherwise Papa will be up here. When I told him you were ill, he started up here, but I stammered and stuttered and turned as red as I could—holding my breath and blowing—hoping he would guess. Of course, he didn't, but Mama did and whispered to him." Mairi went to Tibbie's bed and pulled back the covers, arranging her pillows and asking if there was *anything* she could do. Tibbie shook her head and went back to staring out the window. Her hand on the door, Mairi turned back toward Tibbie and said, "I've promised Beth we'd take Precious for a walk tomorrow, so don't you worry about anything."

All evening long Mairi came and went, but Tibbie sat huddled in her chair by the window, staring out at the very countryside that had looked so exceptional only hours ago. Around and around her thoughts seemed to swirl in a vicious, jeering circle of humiliation, misery, and blame.

She wondered just how long it would be before the story began to spring up around town, like poisonous fumes rising to the surface of a bad well. *Dear God! I can't go through all of that again.* How could she walk down the streets of Indianola, suffering the snubs and jibes, the leering comments from men, the spiteful looks from women. And Nick? She couldn't remain inside her house forever. She was bound to cross his path sooner or later. Of all the degrading things she would have to face, Nick would be the most difficult. No, not difficult. She simply could not face him, knowing each time she did that she would be reminded of how she had thrown herself at his feet, and how he had stepped right over her. So hurt, with her spirit crushed like glass beneath Nick's boot, all she could think about was getting away.

And the only ticket she had out of Indianola was Eric.

Without a minute to waste, she sprang from her chair with sudden renewed vigor. She picked Mairi's graduation dress up from the floor where she had dropped it, and removed Granny's watch, checking the time.

Half past eight. She looked at the tray Mairi had brought earlier, and going to it, she forced herself to eat a few bites and rearrange the rest so it would look like she had eaten well. No need to risk having Coll coming up to check on her. She guessed she would have to let Mairi in on what she was doing, because of Beth. Mairi would be needed to help her get Beth's things packed. A sudden flash in her mind brought Precious to the forefront. Beth would be distraught over the loss of her dear pet. Perhaps Eric could be persuaded to bring Precious along.

About that time, Mairi opened the door. "You're looking better."

"I feel like a pair of old worn-out shoes." Tibbie went to her wardrobe and pulled down her valise.

"What are you doing?"

"Packing."

"Whatever for? Where are you going? Has Nick . . ." The minute she said it, Mairi realized how ridiculous that was. Of course she hadn't heard from Nick, not unless he climbed the tree outside Tibbie's window. That had been done before—well, not that any man had climbed in, but as young girls Mairi and Tibbie had climbed out the window a time or two, just for the satisfaction of saying they had done it. And thinking upon it, Tibbie didn't look like she had received any positive reply from Nick. And judging from the horrid look Tibbie just gave her, she obviously thought Mairi's near blunder to be as poor as Mairi did herself.

"Tibbie, please tell me what you're about. What are you up to?"

"First, I'm going to see Eric." She slapped three nightgowns into her valise. "Second, I'm going to go to Hawaii with him." She rolled four dresses into tight little bundles and placed them over the nightgowns. "Third, I'm going to marry him the minute we get there." Next came five pair of bloomers. "Fourth, I'm going to do everything in my power to be a good, loving wife and make the best possible home for Beth and any other children that might follow." They were followed by more clothing hastily stuffed into her valise, including chemises, stockings, and shoes, and even a couple of books—one of them a Bible.

"You're taking Beth?"

Tibbie gave her a look which said that that comment was even dumber than the near-miss about Nick. "What else would I do with her? Drown her in the bay?"

"Are you going to tell Mama and Papa?"

"*You* are going to do that."

Mairi began backing toward the door. "Oh, no, I'm not. Tibbie Anne Buchanan, I will do almost anything in the world for you, and in fact I have, but that is where I draw the line.

Boil me in oil, burn me at the stake, poke my eyes out with a hot poker, feed me gooseliver until I choke, but don't you dare even suggest that I'm going to be the one to tell them."

"All right. I'll write them a letter and you can give it to them." Seeing Mairi's stubborn look, Tibbie amended that. "You can put it on the kitchen table for me, can't you? In the middle of the night, when no one is there?"

"Why don't you tell them?"

"You know what that would involve. They'd want me to wait awhile, or think it through, or get married here first, or leave Beth with them, or whatever other stumbling blocks they could toss in my path. The fewer people planning this, the better."

"Why did you tell me?"

"Because I need to tell someone. Because you're my sister. Because I need you to get Beth's things packed for me and get her out of the house, in case I can't."

Tibbie snapped her valise closed. "Now, you take that tray down and tell them I'm asleep."

"What are you going to do?"

"I'm going to write them a letter. And later, after everyone has gone to bed, I'll go see Eric."

Mairi rushed to embrace her sister. "Oh, Tibbie, this is awful! I may never see you again . . . or Beth!"

"But you'll have Precious!" Tibbie said. She smiled at Mairi, who burst into tears at her attempt at humor. "Don't cry. Of course you'll see us again. We're sisters, aren't we? We'll have you come visit us, and I'm sure we'll be back to Indianola on occasion. Thankfully, Eric can afford that."

"Yes, I suppose you're lucky in that regard. Still, I wish it were N—"

Tibbie's hard stare snapped Mairi's mouth shut so fast, she bit the tip of her tongue.

"Serves you right," Tibbie said.

After Mairi left, Tibbie paced the room, then wrote her parents a long letter explaining everything, then paced the room some more. At a quarter past twelve, she slipped from the house.

Once she located Eric's room, she knocked softly. He was still dressed when he opened the door. The surprise on his face was almost worth the effort she had been through.

"Tibbie! What are you doing here at this time of night?" Then suddenly noticing the valise at her side and realizing what was happening, he drew her into the room quickly and closed the door. He brushed her cheek with his fingers, pulling loose a strand of hair that had caught itself in the corner of her mouth.

"I've come to tell you I'll go to Hawaii with you if you still want me."

He opened his mouth to speak, but she cut him off. "You'd better hear me out before you decide. These are my conditions." He smiled at her businesslike manner. "One, I don't want anyone to know we're doing this until we've sailed. Two, I want us to be married as soon as we reach your home, or on board the ship, if that's legal. Three, I want Beth to come with us, and Precious too—"

"Wouldn't Precious be number four?" he asked, interrupting her.

"No," she said emphatically. "They're both small enough to count as one. And for number four I want your solemn word that at least once a year we can come back here or send for my family to come visit us."

His arms came around her. "Is that all, or is there a number five?"

"As a matter of fact, there is," she said, again emphatic. "Six, I want your promise that you will do your best never to make me regret doing this."

"Oh, Tibbie, you have my word on that." Before Tibbie knew what he was about, Eric took her in his arms and drew her against the length of his hard frame as his mouth descended with one purpose in mind.

"Eric, we don't have time for—"

He silenced her in the best way he knew, his mouth moving

sensuously over hers, his hand stroking her shoulder with reassurance, his other hand dropping to her waist to draw her against him more firmly.

And it really wasn't such a bad kiss. Considering who it wasn't.

It took some convincing, but she finally managed to get his mind on sailing and off kissing. "Why?" he asked.

"Because I *know* where sailing will end up. Kissing, I don't."

He laughed, calling her adorable, then settled down into a comfortable chair, drawing Tibbie into his lap and listening to what she had planned.

"In the morning?" He stood up, almost dropping her to the floor. "Sorry," he said. "Tibbie, my sweet, we can't possibly leave in the morning."

"I thought you had one of your father's ships here?"

"I do, but—"

"Then why can't we leave in the morning?"

"We need supplies, a course charted, the ship readied for sailing."

"Then we can sail to Galveston, or New Orleans, and do all of that." She gave him a serious look. "Listen to me, Eric. If you want me at all you're going to have to take me tomorrow."

He laughed and drew her against him. "Yes, *mon général*!"

But this time when he tried to kiss her, Tibbie twisted away and fled through the door. Pausing on the other side, she said, "I'll be at your ship at eleven o'clock tomorrow, Eric. Mairi will bring Beth a little bit earlier." She started off, wondering at the humorous look in Eric's eyes. Then she paused and looked back. "Oh, by the way, what is the name of your ship?"

He threw back his golden head and laughed, his white teeth flashing in the lamplight. "*Nordic Star*," he said softly. "Did you think I would come for you in anything else?"

The next morning everything was going as planned. At exactly eleven o'clock Tibbie walked the plank and stepped on board the *Nordic Star*, and into Eric's waiting arms.

"Beth is here?" she asked, knowing she was, for Tibbie had just seen Mairi and kissed her good-bye.

"In her cabin."

Her cabin, Oh, dear! She decided to tackle that one once they were underway.

"And Precious?"

"He wasn't as happy about coming aboard as Beth. We had to tie him up, I'm afraid."

"Oh, Eric, no!"

"We'll release him once we're underway."

Tibbie looked around. "How do I get to Beth's cabin? I need to be with her. She's probably frightened to death."

"I'm afraid not. Mate is showing her how to tie a knot, and the little sprite has a real knack for it."

"I want to see her."

Eric's arms tightened around her. "In a minute. But first, are you really serious about this?"

She pulled back to look him in the face. "This is a little too much for a joke, Eric, even for me! Of course I mean it."

Eric's smile rivaled the sun. "You mean that? You really mean it?"

"No, Eric. I spend all my time going around saying things I don't mean!"

Eric grabbed her and spun her around. "You won't be sorry, Tib."

"I'm already sorry," she said in a breathless way. "You're squeezing the breath out of me."

Eric put her down. "We can be married as soon as we get there." He put his hands on her shoulders, holding her at arms' length, his eyes studying hers. "What made you change your mind?"

She had already given much thought to the answer to that question, for she knew it would be among the first Eric would ask her. This man had hurt her terribly once, but she had no intention of doing the same to him by telling him the truth. What would it gain either of them? She made a decision to marry Eric, and she would do her best to honor him for as long as she was his wife. "A lot of things. Mostly, it just seemed the right thing to do. You are Beth's father."

"Do you love me?"

The floor seemed to open up before her, gaping wide and huge, like a bottomless pit ready to swallow her up. It wasn't important if she was only half truthful; it was the best thing for all those concerned. Only a selfish person would think only of themselves.

"I've always loved you." She saw the effect of her words and felt a stab of remorse.

But I have always loved him. He was my first love. He was the father of my child. The rest will come later.

If it came at all.

Yes, that morning everything went as planned. There was only one hitch.

Precious hated the sea more than anything. And he hated everything connected with it, including ships. The second thing he hated most in the world was being tied. The combination of the two proved volatile. Having been tied for over an hour now, Precious, who was usually an adoring pet, was anything but; and a pig when he is mad isn't to be messed with. Once he decided he had had enough of this business, he made short work of getting loose. The only problem was, when he was in the process of getting loose he was a noisy little thing, squealing and grunting and throwing an awfully big fuss. Beth, who loved Precious dearly and was as protective as a mother, was always tuned for his distress signal. And when she heard all the ruckus, she dropped the knot she was tying and climbed up on the bunk to peer out the porthole, just in time to see Precious streak across the deck and down the gangplank, squealing like the devil as he headed up the street.

"Precious!" Beth yelled. Without wasting a moment, she jumped from the bunk and rushed through the doorway. Mere minutes later she was off the ship and heading up the street, searching for her precious pig.

Meanwhile, Tibbie was doing her best to hold Eric at bay and was finding it hard to do so without making him angry.

He was no fool, and she knew that. The cabin she and Eric were in wasn't really close to the one Beth occupied, or to the place Precious had been tied. Consequently, she didn't hear the commotion or Beth's yell.

"Eric, will you please wait until we get away from here to badger me with all these questions? I'm jumpy as a cat and I admit it. It isn't every day that I run away from home."

About that time, someone knocked on the door and Eric opened it, stepping outside. "What is it?" he asked the first mate.

The first mate, having been the one who tied the pig, was also the one who noticed he was gone. And knowing Eric the way he did, he decided he'd better notify him of the pig's disappearance immediately. "The pig broke loose, sir."

"Damn! Is he still on board?"

"I don't know. I've got men searching."

Eric glanced back at his cabin door. "Keep it quiet . . . at least until we're safely away."

The second mate, who had been tying knots with Beth, didn't know Eric as well as the first mate, and when the little girl fled her room, he figured she was still on board—nothing to bother Eric about.

What this all amounted to was that Eric knew the pig was loose, but didn't know he was off the ship, nor did he know Beth had gone off behind him. Tibbie didn't know as much as Eric knew. And that is how the *Nordic Star* came to sail without Beth or her pig, Precious.

It could be said that both Beth and Precious were faring better at this point than Beth's mother, for Mairi, after leaving the dock and being in no hurry to get home, had wandered up the street, dropping first into one store and then the other. It was while coming out of one shop that she spied Precious heading up the sidewalk, *clickety, clickety, click*!

She had no more than called him to her and dropped down beside him to grab ahold of his leash when she saw Beth running up the street as well, her sash dragging in the dirt behind her. "Beth!" she called. "Over here!"

Without a moment to waste, Mairi took Beth by the hand and Precious by the leash and hurried them both back toward the dock, listening to Beth's tale as they went. They arrived in time to see the last of the *Nordic Star* as she sailed out of port.

"Is my mama still on that ship?"

Mairi hugged Beth to her side. "Yes, lambkin, I'm afraid she is." Mairi dropped to her knees, wiping Beth's eyes. "Now, don't you cry. Who does your mother love the most in the world?"

"Me."

"That's right. And as soon as she finds out you aren't on that ship, she will make Eric bring her right back."

Tibbie by this time was well into having a fit. "I want to see Beth, and I want to see her now!"

Eric, knowing the pig hadn't been located, didn't want her to see Beth until they found the pig, because he knew that once mother and daughter were united, they would want that blasted pig. "Tibbie, I've told you I'll take you to her as soon as possible." He was praying the pig would be located soon, so he could avoid having his first marital fight before the marriage.

He was a little late with that prayer, however, and he realized it as soon as an inkwell came sailing toward him. He ducked and the inkwell missed him. The ink, however, did not. To keep his cabin from being literally shredded by Tibbie's fury, he finally had to resort to tying her hands, and when she started kicking and calling him every name she could think of, he had to tie her feet as well. Splotched with ink, his cabin in ruins, he left Tibbie to finish her fit, hoping he could placate her later.

That was not the case, for later, as it turned out, was much worse. "What do you mean, my daughter left the ship?" Eric shouted to the first mate.

"I just found out, sir. Seems she was chasing after that pig o' hers, and they both left."

The first thing Eric did was pay a visit to the ship's doctor.

"I need a little tincture of opium or anything to help my bride-to-be rest. She's quite distressed."

"Give her two drops of this in a glass of water."

Eric did, having the devil of a time getting Tibbie to drink it. "Here, sweetheart, drink this. Your throat must be parched."

"What is it?" she croaked. "Poison?"

"It's only water. Drink it."

She did. Eric waited until he could see the effect of the drops in her heavy-lidded eyes and then he told her about Beth and Precious. "I did everything I could to find them. We'd been under sail for over two hours before I realized they weren't on board."

"Take me back," she said in a groggy voice. "I want to go back. This was a mistake."

Eric stiffened, grabbing her bound wrist and giving it a shake. "It wasn't a mistake, and don't you ever say that again."

"I want to go back!"

"You agreed to go to Hawaii, and by God, that's where you're going."

"Only if I had Beth."

"That's unfortunate. We'll get Beth later. I'll send someone for her."

"You bastarrrrd," she mumbled and then fell into a deep, deep sleep.

20

Nick and Porter stopped by the Glass Slipper for a drink after work. They were just coming out the door as Mairi walked by. "Hello, Mairi," Nick said, tipping his hat.

Mairi shot him a bone-chilling glare and said, "If I didn't have Beth with me, I'd tell you what I really think of you, you deceitful snake!"

"Brrrr!" Porter said, watching the beautiful dark-haired woman take off down the street, a little girl and a fat, white pig in tow.

Nick was puzzled by Mairi's outburst, but what puzzled him most was Beth. Beth, who always lit up like a lightning bug when she saw him, had only glanced at him once, and when she did, he saw the sad little face, the tear-trails, the benumbed expression. Even that pig of hers was acting sulky. *What in the hell is going on?* He didn't know, but he knew as well as he knew his own name that Tibbie had something to do with it. Nick shook his head.

"Where are you going?" Porter said.

"I made a mistake," Nick said. "I wasn't finished drinking. This was the night I planned to get drunk."

Porter stared at his friend, thinking there must be something going around that would be an epidemic before the week was out, if this was an example of how fast it spread. He wondered what was going on, as he watched Nick disappear behind the doors to the Glass Slipper.

Mairi, meanwhile, headed on home, thinking she would rather face a firing squad than her parents, with the story she had to tell them. By the time it was all out in the open and over, Effie had to be given a sleeping draught and put to bed, and Beth was afraid to sleep in her own room, and moved in with Mairi. And Coll? He went to his medicine cabinet and took out a bottle of French brandy he'd been saving for when one of his daughters got married, and moving to the back porch, he sat on the bottom step and consoled Precious, who had his head in Coll's lap, while he did his best to do something he hadn't done in thirty years—get drunk. About halfway through the bottle, he poured a little in a dish for Precious. It was the first time that day that Precious wiggled his tail.

The next morning Coll woke up and realized he had gotten his wish. He made it downstairs, hung a CLOSED sign on the door of the clinic and rejoined his wife in bed.

On the other side of town, Nick Mackinnon woke up with the worst hangover in history. Porter stopped by when Nick didn't show up for work, and seeing just how sick Nick really was, he decided to head on out to Dr. Buchanan's and see if he could get something to ease his friend's pain.

An hour later he returned. "Sorry, old friend," he said, "I went to Dr. Buchanan's, but something strange is going on out there."

Nick opened one eye and looked at Porter.

"Honestly, I'm telling you. Something fishy is going on. When I got there I found a 'Closed' sign on the door. When I knocked, that pretty little brunette that snubbed you in town yesterday opened the door. Before I could say a word she said, 'Can't you read?' and slammed the door in my face." Nick groaned. "Whoa! That's not all. When I left, I happened to notice this pig, the same one we saw in town, I think, and he was lying in the flowerbed, snoring. Honest to God, Nick, I would swear that pig had a hangover."

Nick threw a pillow at Porter and rolled over and closed his eyes.

* * *

Waking up the following morning was much better than the previous one, Nick decided the moment he opened his eyes. Never could he remember being so sick. He swore off liquor before he climbed out of bed. An hour later, when he sat down at his desk in the shipping yard, he swore off women. For it was then that he sorted through the stack of papers Porter had put on his desk days ago. And after sorting them out, he discovered a small envelope lying on his desk.

He opened the envelope and quickly scanned the note Tibbie had placed on his desk days before. He reread it, stopping at the part that said, *meet me by the tree in the orchard tomorrow at three o'clock.* Hastily, his eyes shot to the top of the note, where Tibbie had written in her lovely, flowing script, *Monday evening.* Monday evening. What was today? No, wait a minute, if she wrote the note on Monday evening, she wouldn't have placed it on his desk until Tuesday. He looked at his calendar. Tuesday was the day Arthur Bradley delivered those papers. It was coming back to him now: how he held the door for Porter, telling him to put the papers on his desk, never knowing that Tibbie's note lay there. Back to the calendar again. If she left the note on Tuesday, she meant for him to meet her on Wednesday. Wednesday? What did he do on Wednesday? He looked at the calendar again. It was blank. He remembered now; Wednesday he had spent most of the day down at the ship, and when he was in the office, he never touched the stack of papers, nor had he touched them on Thursday. That was the day . . . *Oh, God!* That was the day he ran into Mairi and Beth coming out of the Glass Slipper. No wonder Mairi said the things she said. His eyes flew back to the calendar. What was today? Saturday? What the hell happened to Friday?

You were drunk.

He groaned and buried his head in his hands. His poor little lass, how she must be suffering in her humiliation. That's probably why Dr. Buchanan closed his clinic the other day. Things were beginning to make sense.

Nick sprang from the desk and Porter looked up. "Something bite you?"

"Yes!" Nick shouted. "The love bug!"

Porter laid down his pen, and Nick, seeing he was looking at him strangely said, "I know you think I've lost my mind, and maybe I have. I don't have time to explain now." He was off like a shot.

Nick rode the chestnut right into Tibbie's front yard and bailed off onto the porch before the gelding had come to a full stop. In response to his pounding on the door, Mairi opened it, and seeing who was there, tried to slam it, but Nick wedged his boot inside before she could. Using all his force, he pushed his way inside.

"Get out!"

"Mairi, where is Tibbie?"

"Get out or I'll call my father, and believe me, he is angry enough at you right now to shoot you between the eyes and ask questions later."

Nick tossed his hat on the hall tree and went into the parlor and took a seat. "Then get him. At least maybe *he* will tell me what's going on, even if he does shoot me first."

Mairi whirled and headed for the door.

"I love her, Mairi. Will you tell her that for me?"

Mairi whipped around, tears pouring down her face. "I would if I could. But I don't have a sister I can talk to anymore, thanks to you!"

Nick leaped to his feet. "What are you talking about?"

"My sister! It's *your* fault she's gone!"

"Gone!" he repeated, feeling his body stiffen with dread. "Gone where?" he asked, knowing the answer even before she said it.

"Hawaii."

"Dear God in Heaven! Why?"

"You tell me. You're the one who pestered her day and night until she admitted she was in love with you, and when she did, you avoided her like she had the plague."

"What did I do?"

"It's what you didn't do, don't you think? You didn't meet her after she humbled herself and wrote you—"

"The note," he finished. Nick's mind at first refused to accept what his ears heard—even after he could feel his heart shatter into a million tiny fragments. All this time he had been working so patiently to teach her to trust him, and then when she did, he wasn't there. His voice unsteady, he told Mairi about the note, then he looked up, his face etched with grief, and saw her piano books open on the rosewood piano. "I . . . Mairi, excuse me for a while. I'll be back."

Nick had to get out of there, out of her house. He needed space and air to breathe. At first, when he left her house, he wandered aimlessly, not paying any attention to where he was going, until he found himself staring at the rusty old gate that led into the orchard. *Meet me by the tree in the orchard . . .*

He went through the gate, to the tree he had sat beneath with her that day so long ago. It had been winter then; the tree bare and brown and withered, like his heart was now. In the throes of despair, Nick rested his arms across his bent knees and dropped his head. He felt defeated. There was no other word for it. Tibbie was gone.

With a tired sigh, Nick came to his feet. There was no point in staying out here all night. He wouldn't find Tibbie here either. Suddenly Nick's head snapped up and he sucked in his breath. No, he wouldn't find Tibbie here in the orchard.

But he sure as hell knew where he would find her. He didn't care if that ship was ever finished. He was going to Hawaii and he was going to do his best to break all records getting there. At this point he didn't care if Tibbie had married that bastard or not. She was his, and by all that was holy, he was taking her away with him, if he had to gag and tie her to do it.

He spun around and started for the gate, kicking something with the toe of his boot. He glanced down, seeing the object roll ahead of his step, and just as his boot came down to grind it into the dust he saw what it was. He stepped aside and dropped down, picking it up. Coming to his feet, he rolled it over and over in his hand. It was the angel he had given her the day he'd left the clinic, the marble angel he'd ordered from New Orleans. She must have thrown it at the tree that day because the wings were both broken off. He dropped the angel into his pocket and walked through the gate. He stopped by the house and told Mairi he was going after her.

"Can you make it in time? They have three days on you already and Eric's ship is quite fast."

"So is mine," Nick said.

"When are you leaving?"

"At daybreak. Before I go, I have one question. Did Tibbie marry him before . . . before they left?"

Mairi smiled and touched Nick's sleeve. "No. She said they could be married in Hawaii."

"I hope Eric doesn't press her to do it sooner."

"I don't think he will. His family is quite wealthy. I'm sure he'll want to do the right thing and have a wedding no one will forget."

Nick grinned. "Oh, he'll have that," he said. "I'll see to it."

Later that night Nick was roused out of a deep sleep by someone pounding on his door.

"What in the hell is it?" Nick said, angrily yanking the door open. Seeing Mairi standing on his porch with her hood angled roughly over her hair, his mouth dropped open and he simply stared at her for a moment. "For God's sake! What are you doing out here at this time of night wearing your nightgown?"

Mairi looked down, seeing that her nightgown was quite visible between the open folds of her cloak. She drew the sides together as Nick said harshly, "Are you trying to get me shot?"

Nick stood back, buttoning his shirt up wrong and motioning for her to come in. Mairi stepped lively through the door, stumbling on the long folds of her cape and landing close enough to the green damask sofa that a slight shift made it look as though she had intended to sit there all along. "I know this will make you angry, and before you decide to cut out my heart and feed it to the vultures, I might as well tell you that I have made up my mind."

"To do what?" Nick asked.

"I want to come with you."

"If this is your idea of a j—"

"It's no joke. I'm quite serious."

"So am I, and the answer is *no*!" He walked to a desk scattered with papers and poured two fingers of Scotch into a glass and carried it to a small table beside her, placing it there and indicating she was to drink it.

"Oh, that's all right. I never touch the stuff."

"You never run around on a damp night in your nightgown either, I'll wager. *Drink it!*" His voice cracked like an acorn underfoot and Mairi hastily snatched the glass and tossed the contents down. About five minutes was lost in a coughing fit before Nick said, "If you want to go traipsing around town in the dead of night in your nightgown, I won't stop you, but you aren't going to set foot on my ship, and that is that."

"Please, Nick. Don't be so pigheaded. My sister is probably halfway to China by now and you act like it's nothing."

"You don't go to China on the way to Hawaii, and I know you're concerned about your sister, but you're *needed* here. At sea you would be, pardon me for saying so, a pain in the arse!"

"Don't go raising your voice at me! This wouldn't have happened if you had ever declared yourself."

"Declared myself?" he shouted. "What in heaven's name have I been doing for months?"

"You never asked Papa for her hand."

"It wasn't her goddamn hand that I wanted!"

Mairi looked frightened enough to bolt at his next word, so Nick calmed himself, lowering his voice. "Mairi, I'm going to take you home, *if* I don't get arrested or shot first, and then I'm going after your sister." A sudden idea flashed into Nick's mind. Grabbing Mairi's hand, he said, "Come on," and led her through the door.

"Are you going to let me go with you?"

"For a while."

A few minutes later Nick pulled Mairi up the steps of another house. "Who lives here?" she whispered, just as Nick pounded the door three or four times.

"You'll find out soon enough," he said, as Porter opened the door. He looked at Nick. He looked at his watch, then gave it a shake and put it to his ear. And then he looked at Mairi and let out a whistle.

"I brought this for you," Nick said, pushing Mairi against Porter and shoving both of them inside.

Porter, standing in better light now, gave Mairi closer scrutiny. "You brought her for me? What am I supposed to do with her?"

Nick raised one dark brow in faint suggestion.

"Now, you wait just a minute!" Mairi said, struggling to get through the door.

"Wait a minute, sweetheart, let's see what we have under all this cape." Mairi gave him a swift kick.

"You'll have to be gentle with her, Porter. She's soon to be my sister-in-law."

Mairi shrieked and lunged at him, but Porter laughed and drew her back and closed the door. Nick took the steps two at a time, listening to Mairi's shrieking and the intermittent sounds of shattering glass. He was wondering which one of them would thank him first when he returned.

Half an hour later Nick was standing on the dock, throwing the last of his bags on board.

≫ 21 ≪

Tibbie was no sailor.

She was sick before they sailed far enough for Indianola to be out of sight. It didn't help matters any when Eric, trying to be helpful, said she would soon get over it and be feeling well enough to eat a little squid soup.

That sent her scampering to her quarters for the chamber pot. Her quarters and the chamber pot. The two became synonymous after that.

Tibbie may have been brought up on the Texas gulf coast, but she had done little more than paddle around in the bay in a small rowboat with Mairi a few times when they were growing up. She had a landlubber's affection for going to sea. She didn't like it. She couldn't understand how two of her brothers could tolerate one voyage, let alone a life at sea. Five minutes was too long for her. Water to he had always been something you drank, bathed in, or looked at. Now she added a fourth description. It also made you sick.

While Tibbie was spending most of her time in her quarters humped over the chamber pot, Nicholas was four days behind her, having lost a little time putting in at New Orleans to move his belongings into his own ship, *Caledonia*. Once the *Caledonia* was underway, Nick spent most of his time standing at the helm, the warm gulf wind blowing in his face, and thinking of Tibbie. He would look out over the endless stretch of water before him, thinking that she was out there somewhere, three, maybe four days ahead of him. But the *Caledonia* was trim and fast. He speculated they would overtake the *Nordic Star* before she reached Rio de Janeiro.

Damn little fool! That's her way to solve everything: blind, stupid panic. Oh, I know what she is doing, thinking she can solve everything by repeating a few vows, that by uniting herself with him in holy wedlock, she can lock away her own feelings and desires. And then, as if she were standing right there in front of him, he said, "It won't work, my girl. It won't work because it's going to take more than a couple of oceans of water between us to get me out of your mind."

It was not a particularly pleasant voyage. Tibbie was no longer throwing a fit—even someone as young and hearty as she can throw a fit only so long—but she was adamant in her vow of not speaking to Eric. He had untied her several hours after the sleeping drops had worn off. By that time he had removed everything valuable from the cabin before leaving her to destroy what was left. She made pretty short work of that before wearing herself out completely and falling asleep once again. By the third day she realized the futility of such behavior. Eric wasn't going to turn around and that was that. So she turned her mind to other things, like escaping when they put into port.

That thought was shattered when Eric said, "And don't get any ideas about jumping ship. We're only making one stop and I'll have you locked in your cabin well before that."

There were only a couple of other times that Eric had said anything in her presence, having decided, she supposed, to give her plenty of room. Once was when he came into the cabin and caught her washing her hair with the pitcher of water left for her that morning. "That water is for drinking. Waste it on washing your hair and you'll drink salt water." The only other time was when she tried her hand at coiling rope, and though it was pulled through her hands for only a short distance, she received a nasty rope burn on each palm. Seeing her hands, Eric said, "I'll put the next man who tries to teach her anything on half rations."

So, to get her mind off her wretched bouts of seasickness, constant fear of drowning, Eric's refusal to take her home, and just plain boredom, Tibbie began keeping a journal. Her first entry was a rather awkward one dealing with the infinity of activities that went on aboard ship, as well as a brief index of seaman's jargon that could easily be digested by anyone at sea from the caterpillar stage upward.

The cabin was quite dark when she began her first entry, not even a glimmer of light coming through the stern windows. She lay in her cot swaying slowly and smoothly, huddled under the poor light from a small oil lamp, writing about life on board ship.

> Captain responsible for ship and navigation (but Eric helps out here some). Captain also takes observation at noon and then sets ship's course. He can marry; bury; and kill, if there's a mutiny.

Her second entry included a brief comment about stay tackles, an explanation of forward and aft, and what was meant by reefed topsails. Earlier in the day she had gone topside, where a westerly wind was laying the ship over as she thrashed along. "We're hoping to pick up the east trade winds soon, to help us on to the West Indies," she wrote as a direct quote from Trevor. Trevor, she wrote, was the cabin boy, and the only one Eric allowed to talk to her, besides himself, and since she wasn't speaking to Eric, that left only Trevor.

Further down she made mention of rigging, which she noted required constant attention. E.—she used E. because she refused to write his name—says they're just like a woman. When he explained that the sails had to be mended, protected from chafing, and replaced as necessary, she pretended not to be listening, but as he talked she was wondering if that applied to women as well.

By the third entry, she was at least coming to grips with the fact that she was at sea, which she decided was just as well, since there wasn't much she could do about it anyway.

The wind sings in the taut weather rigging, starboard side of the quarterdeck; must learn to balance to the roll and pitch of the ship.

Her last penned words were,

I am getting better at maintaining my balance between the massive gray waves that hit the ship one after the other. They strike the starboard bow first, heaving the bowsprit up, which is rather like a giant sea monster that has been pulled from his slumber and rises in anger from his bed at the bottom of the sea.

The following morning she found Eric had forbidden even Trevor to talk to her, so after sulking awhile, she decided she would go crazy if she didn't talk to someone. Later, she found Eric standing on the poop deck and she asked him when they would be putting into one of the islands she occasionally saw.

"We've supplies enough to make it around the Horn before we drop anchor. We'll be in the Pacific then and can make Valparaiso before we put in to land."

The next afternoon she stood beside Eric at the navigation table, looking at the chart that traced their route. "Where are we now?"

"Here, almost across the Equator, then we'll round Cape St. Roque and head for Cape Horn. It will be rough sailing until we're through Tierra del Fuego."

Tierra del Fuego. Nothing with a name like Land of Fire sounded too hospitable to her.

Her next journal entry read:

Friday, July 15, 1849
Today Eric conceded and said I could talk to the ship's crew. For the rest of the afternoon I watched the chief mate, Mr. Tripp, inspect the sails. He climbed up every mast and yardarm, checked each sail, spar, bolt, band, and rope. He kept notes of all needed repairs.

Saturday, July 16, 1849

We made a record run of 402 miles in the past twenty-four hours. The day aboard ship begins quite early. The cook and steward arise at one bell (4:30 A.M. for the novice). At two bells coffee is served to the watch. The crew eats at 7:30, noon, and 5:30. Their fare is mostly salt beef and pork—which the sailors call "salt-junk"—potatoes, beans, hard bread, and an occasional treat of plum duff, which is flour pudding with dried fruit and molasses. Sailors *hate* fish and fresh meat. Mr. Tripp said this was because they knew how to curse it better and "when sailors grumble, all is well."

Sunday, July 17, 1849

Last night the slop chest was opened for the crew as it is every Saturday night, so they could buy clothing, tobacco and such to be charged against their wages. The rest of the evening was spent reading, mending clothes, and smoking.

Monday, July 18, 1849

We're in typical equator weather now. The wind is gone, and now it's nothing but calms and cat's paws and plenty of hot, damp heat. Everything is sticky and wet and nothing will dry. Everything is in slow motion, with the sails slapping against the masts like the crack of a pistol. With each deep surge the timbers creak. Although quite hot, the nights are quite the most beautiful seen anywhere, with spectacular sunsets (perhaps enthralling would have been a better word here). Once night has taken hold, the sky is littered with stars and the sea is aglow with phosphorus trails. The Southern Cross is low to the south, but Eric says it will be above us soon.

Tuesday, July 19, 1849

Today we are at latitude 1 degree 28'S, longitude 29 degrees 32'. We had a sudden squall that whipped the mirrored surface of the sea into a froth of angry whitecaps. The crew quickly braced yards to catch the wind in a whirl of activity, but then, as fast as it came, it was gone. Mr. Tripp calls this a "miniature tempest." Late in the afternoon we crossed the equator. It was my best day at sea yet, for I was feeling much better and the ceremony of welcoming Neptune and being shaved by him—done only when crossing the equator —was great fun. A sailor dressed as Neptune, wearing a robe of canvas with a wig and beard made of rope. The razor was a barrel hoop and the shaving soap was grease applied with a paintbrush. I wished Bethany had been here to see it. It was the first day my thoughts lingered on her for any length of time without crying. I miss her dreadfully and worry about her missing me so much. My only consolation is in knowing that Beth is loved and well cared for by my family, and that she is smart enough to understand I am not away from her by choice. I have been drawing pictures of the ship each day to give to her when we are together again, which I hope will be soon.

Fifteen days later she wrote in her journal:

August 3, 1849
Mr. Tripp says we will be rounding the cape at the worst time of year, because it is winter in the southern hemisphere. Already the breezes are nippy and Mr. Tripp says there will be fights breaking out among the crew. Eric showed me my first cape pigeon with their speckled wings. It looked like they couldn't decide if they wanted wings to go with their black heads or white bodies, so they opted for both. Cook gave me some scraps and I threw them to the pigeons. They are noisy, hungry birds that will eat anything, because I tossed them a piece of rope and one swallowed it right off.

August 8, 1849
The crew has been busy dressing the ship in its heaviest sails, preparing for the pamperos—dangerous gales that will soon come thundering out of the mouth of a river 130 miles

wide. The weather today is squally. Mr. Tripp says it could
turn bad overnight.

August 9, 1849
Mr. Tripp knows a lot about sailing, because the weather
today has turned bitterly cold, with stiff gales and howling
hail and snow. Fighting the heavy head seas, the crew must
man the pumps constantly. Eric sent me below and I have
remained in my quarters wondering how the cape can be
worse than the roaring forties. Eric came down later to tell
me that there had been another fight on deck, but that it was
quelled. Mr. Harkins, the second mate, received a knife
wound in the arm. I was able to assist the ship's doctor and
we dressed the wound after cleaning it with disinfectant.
Eric was in an amorous mood after that, but I pleaded ex-
haustion and went back to my cabin. Eric has been patient
so far, but I know he isn't a patient man and this enforced
patience won't last. My thoughts are constantly with Nicholas now, and I wonder at my own sanity in doing something
so stupid as agreeing to marry Eric. How foolish I was to
make such an important decision when I was hurt and angry. Now that I've had time to think, I know something
went wrong, that Nick is the kind of man who would have
come, even if only to tell me good-bye. I wonder if I will
ever learn what really happened? I feel sometimes like my
proud reason has turned upon me like a pet serpent and bit
me.

August 13, 1849
The days are shorter now—the sun rises at 8:30 and sets at
3:30. The Strait of Magellan lies to our west. It separates
South America from Tierra del Fuego, of which Cape Horn
is the most southern island. Everyone is prepared for the
worst. The gales are colder and heavier now, making it necessary to lash the deck with life lines to protect the crew that
often works waist-deep in water. They have five minutes at
the end of each watch to dry their clothes in the *bogey room,*

which is the sail locker that has been cleaned out and furnished with a stove. The fo'c'sle remains cold. To heat it and have the crew going from heat to cold constantly would have them all sick. It was dark when we passed Staten Land and I was disappointed not to see land, but Eric said it was nothing but rugged land where nothing but sea birds will live. Tomorrow we head into the Cape Horn rollers, huge waves a thousand feet from crest to crest. I am afraid I won't sleep tonight.

August 14, 1849
We spent the better part of the day clawing for westing. We passed two larger ships standing to Southwest. The weather was too severe to identify them. Mr. Tripp said he had heard of ships fighting for westing for ninety days before finally giving up. I find it most amazing that the cape pigeons and albatrosses soar about us constantly, apparently not mindful of the weather. I read one of Captain Peterby's books, which said that the horn was named for Schouten, who discovered it in 1616. Mr. Tripp tried to cheer me today by telling me about a squall he was in once that was so bad, a sailor who opened his mouth to speak was turned wrong-side out. The ship was rolling badly, the lamps swinging wildly on gimbals. The highlight of my day came at supper, when the ship gave a great lurch and Eric was baptized by fish chowder. After supper, Mr. Tripp told tales of sea and superstition, but it did little to counter my own doldrums.

August 17, 1849
This morning we passed yet another cape hazard, Diego Ramirez Rocks—gray, jagged rocks jutting out of the windwhipped water. By afternoon the gale was subsiding. Mr. Tripp's jokes are at last funny. I cannot help but feel immense relief and bow my head in prayer that the dreaded cape is behind us. Tierra del Fuego is to our east now, and that is a comfort to know. I looked in the log book today and shuddered at the names I saw there: Last Hope Inlet,

Useless Bay, Deceit Rock, Desolation Island, Famine Reach —all points that lie behind us now. It was a good omen that I looked out my porthole and saw the Southern Cross high overhead. Tonight I will sleep to the sound of a stiff breeze playing in double-reefed topsails.

August 31, 1849
Completely around the horn now. In the roaring forties again. Eric said the glass was falling. Mr. Tripp predicted gales ahead. Eric said we would be in Valparaiso in less than two weeks. I cannot imagine walking on dry, solid land again. But what is worse, I cannot imagine returning to ship once I have. I am finding it harder and harder to live with the mistake I made. Today was the first time I asked Eric to let me return home.

September 7, 1849
Mr. Tripp was right. We had gales. One solid week of them —not as cold or fierce as those coming around the horn, but frightening and uncomfortable nonetheless. I mentioned returning home twice more and Eric threatened to lash me to the mast if I mentioned it again. At least the seas are calm now. Tonight will be the first peaceful sleep in many, many weeks.

September 8, 1849
After breakfast I found Eric leaning over the navigational charts and begged him to put me on a ship bound for New Orleans once we reached Valparaiso. He didn't appear too angry when he denied my request, but later, when I had dressed to go ashore, I found my door locked. Apparently, Eric hadn't forgotten his earlier promise. I saw Valparaiso from my porthole. When Eric returned, I didn't have many options as far as reciprocity was concerned, but my Scots blood was heated and so I locked my door from the inside.

"You'll come out when you get hungry," Eric said.

A drinking cup thrown against the door was the only reply.

The fourth day of my fast, Mr. Tripp and three sailors broke down the door to my cabin. I was so weak I had taken to my bed earlier in the day. Eric was there, ready to give me a tongue lashing, but Mr. Tripp carried me to the kitchen and gave cook his orders. Lifting the lid from a huge pot, he peered inside. "What's this?"

"Turtle soup."

"Then spoon-feed her turtle soup until she grows flippers."

On October first the *Nordic Star* sailed into port at Lahaina.

⇥ 22 ⇤

"You push me one more time and I'll flatten you where you stand!"

Two ornately carved mahogany doors opened to reveal a pale and fragile Hans Neilson lying in a magnificent four-poster bed on the other side of the bedroom door as it opened to admit his son, Eric, back after a year's absence.

Where had his travels taken him this time? China? Africa? Egypt? Greenland? And more importantly, what had brought him back? Word of his declining health, more than likely. His eyes traveled over his son, seeing that he looked as fit and healthy as the day he had stormed through those same two doors claiming, "I've waited too long as it is. *This* time I'm going to marry the woman I want."

Hans wondered if that was the woman that Eric had wanted all this time, but she didn't look to be too happy to be here. What had Eric done now? He was always too impetuous for his own good.

He sighed, remembering Eric as a beautiful, fragile child, who had always been too well groomed and too perfect to run half-naked on the beach like a savage, as his two brothers had done. He had always been the perfect child. Perfect and grown-up. Hans had always worried that beneath all that golden godliness was a man who always wanted his own way, and usually got it.

But he was still his son, though he bore more physical resemblance to his mother and his brothers, and dear to him.

As Eric stood just inside the door, taking in the situation in the room, Hans was studying the young woman in a wrinkled traveling dress standing slightly behind him. He assumed she had been the author of the hostile words he had just heard outside his door—but she looked too fragile to flatten anyone. But he knew looks could be deceiving. Hans's ire was raised at his son's behavior, at forcing the young woman to come and see a sick old man on his deathbed, for he assumed that to be the reason behind her obvious displeasure. But at the sudden warmth of Eric's dazzling smile as he crossed the room to his father's bedside and came down on one knee beside him, Hans forgot about the young woman and her displeasure.

"You've just arrived?"

Eric laughed. "This very moment. As you can see, I haven't allowed myself the privilege of a bath or clean clothes. Is your condition . . . ?"

"Declining rapidly. I'm glad you're home."

"I came as soon as I could."

"You've seen your brothers?"

"Only Lars. Hans is in Honolulu, I understand."

It was then that Eric stood, making the girl behind him visible.

She was an American, he decided, as his eyes fell on the small-framed woman. He pegged her as American with as much certainty as knowing hers was the voice he had heard threatening Eric only moments before. No woman from a more civilized part of the world would have dared, but those American women. . . . They were a strange lot. Full of fire and brimstone, and this one looked like she had more than her share of both. Knock Eric flat, indeed! He hoped he lived long enough to see it.

Hans looked from the girl back to his son.

"This is Tibbie, Father. Tibbie Buchanan."

"You're American."

"No, I'm a Texan."

"Ahhh," Hans said, his eyes suddenly growing bright. "That explains it."

"Explains what?" Eric asked.

"Nothing. Just her loveliness. I've heard American women were quite lovely, but those from Texas were by far the most beautiful." Even at his outlandish compliment the girl's expression did not soften.

"Come forward, my dear. Let me see you better in the light."

As she stepped forward, Eric lifted the cloak from her head and shoulders, releasing a sudden dance of honey-gold curls. She spoke not a word, but her eyes, hot and furious, flashed up at Eric in defiance.

Flatten him now! Hans found himself thinking.

Hans was no connoisseur of women, having been raised by missionary parents who disdained such activities. But he did have an eye for beauty. And this girl was a beauty. Especially standing beside Eric, as the two of them looked so angelic— bathed in liquid gold in Michelangelesque splendor. So perfectly matched they were in beauty they could have well been God's perfect creation, Adam and Eve.

In spite of the girl's wrinkled appearance, there was a classic regality about her, almost to the point of severity. In her eyes, he saw she had experienced more pain in her life than her years warranted, and he wondered at her story.

"I'm Hans Neilson, Eric's father. I'm sorry we can't be introduced under more formal circumstances."

"Don't worry," Eric said. "As she said, she's from Texas. It's their habit to dispense with formality whenever possible."

The girl's show of spirit wasn't dampened in the least by Eric's verbal jab. If anything, the amber eyes were glaring at him with even more animosity than before. It was then that Hans noticed the faint purpling beneath her eyes, the tired arch of her brow. The poor child must be exhausted.

"Then let's dispense with the formality of your having to present yourself immediately upon your arrival. The young woman looks weary to the bone, Eric. Take her out and call Liliha to show her to her room."

* * *

Upstairs, Tibbie was pacing the room. Her bath water was growing cold. She had already ripped to shreds the lovely new dress that had been laid out for her. She had been pushed about as far as she was going to be pushed. It was time Eric realized this.

The door opened and Eric peered in, ducking behind the door as a chamber pot came sailing toward him, hitting the door with a shattering crash. Half the porcelain in the room followed, leaving such a pile of shattered shards it was difficult to wedge the door open. Once he managed to get inside, Tibbie was halfway out the window. Eric caught her before she leaped to the tree a foot away. She landed a couple of good kicks to his midsection before he succeeded in wrestling her back into the room. Once she was inside, she desperately tried to kick him some more, but he deflected her attempts expertly.

"I demand you release me at once!" she gasped, struggling for each breath as she twisted and turned in his hands, despairing at the set resolve she saw on his face.

"Stop fighting and I will."

"That's not the kind of release I'm talking about. I want to go home."

"I'm afraid that's not possible. You and I have an agreement. I intend to see that you keep your word."

"I won't marry you, so you might as well get that idea out of your head. I was stupid ever to agree to it in the first place."

"That's immaterial. The point is, you agreed and I intend to carry through as planned."

"You can't force me."

"I don't intend to. I feel we can reach some kind of civilized agreement in all of this."

"The only agreement I want from you is your agreement to send me home."

"Tibbie," he said, breathing hard, "be reasonable."

"Why? So you can tie me up again?"

"That was your fault. Since we docked three hours ago

you've tried to run away three times. I tried to overlook your jumping overboard after knocking your escort—"

"Guard," Tibbie interjected.

Eric continued. "After knocking him into the water. And I warned you after I put you in the carriage and you climbed right out the other side that I would be forced to tie you up if you tried anything else."

"So it's my fault."

"I certainly didn't force you to take off when we were were tangled up in traffic and I got out to see what the problem was. I had to chase you for a bloody block before I caught you."

Tibbie had endured all of this in the best frame of mind possible. She had seen the man she had loved, the father of her child, evolve from jilter to jailer. And now, after months at sea, he was refusing to honor her request to return home, insisting that she promised to marry him, and he had the insolence to say he expected her to do just that. There is something unexplainable yet predictable about a woman who has been pushed to the limit and backed against the wall. Every shred of strength she could muster went into the rapid movement of her arm; every despicable act, each hateful word, every minute she had suffered by his abandonment was clenched in the fist that landed a staggering blow to his left cheek. Little did it matter that the impact of bone meeting bone rippled up her arm as if the earth itself trembled—at least she had the satisfaction of seeing that his nose was broken.

She realized it even before he did, for it was several minutes before he fully recognized that he had been hit. By the time it registered and he pulled out his handkerchief, he was bleeding a river and in no mood to talk. Without a word he left her, slamming the door and leaving it to rattle on its hinges from the impact.

For three days Eric stayed away and Tibbie busied herself with several attempts to leave.

Her first attempt had been simply to climb out her window. Only when she turned to leap to the tree she had seen the other day, did she realize it wasn't there. Apparently, Eric had it chopped down.

Her second attempt was to steal out of her room in the dead of night, since Eric had been fool enough to leave her door unlocked. She understood why a locked door had not concerned him. The beast had a string attached to her door and tied to a bellpull. When she opened the door, the bell in Eric's room clanged. He intercepted her before she reached the staircase.

The third time, she feigned deathly illness, requesting a doctor, whom she was sure she could enlist to help her. After a quick examination the doctor informed her he would apply leeches and finish up with an enema. Her near-deathliness was forgotten when he pulled the apparatus from his bag, which proved to be a ghastly instrument about a foot long.

Her final attempt had been to hide herself in the hamper for soiled linen that she found parked in the hallway. For over an hour she nearly suffocated at the bottom of a heap of smelly laundry, feeling some small elation when the hamper was rolled to what she hoped was the room where the laundry was done. When the hamper was parked and the sound of voices had faded, Tibbie slowly fought her way to the top and lifted the lid, only to discover she was not parked, as she had hoped, in the room where they did the laundry.

She was parked all right, and in a room too. In the room that belonged to Eric's brother, Lars.

"Hello," Lars said to the tousled confusion of golden curls arranged over an overly large pair of startled amber eyes. "I've never had anyone go to such lengths to pay me a visit."

"I must confess," Tibbie said, climbing from the hamper, "that wasn't my original intent."

Lars was sitting behind a gold-inlaid desk, a quill in his hand. He put the quill down and indicated a chair on the other side. As Tibbie seated herself, he said, "I can only guess that you must be the woman my brother has brought back to marry, and from where I sit, you don't look like you are too soft on the idea."

Tibbie shook her head violently. "I'm not."

"There's someone else."

"Yes. Only I didn't realize it until it was too late."

"It's never too late." He laughed at the look on her face and Tibbie saw his striking resemblance to Eric.

"I'm afraid it is. You see, I've about exhausted all my resources." She looked sickly at the laundry hamper. "It was my last hope."

Lars laughed readily. He looked at the enchanting creature parked woefully on the chair next to his bed and wished with all his heart he had met her before Eric. But it was small consolation to think of sitting back with ease and watching his brother bumble this one, and there was no doubt in Lars's mind that he would. This woman appeared to be too resourceful. He knew, if given enough time, she would think of something. And Eric had always had his way. It would do him good to be taught a lesson.

The lesson was watching him with large round eyes. "You can call the dogs on me if you like. And imprisonment and starvation won't make me give in. I've been hounded and treated ill before. I come from strong Scots stock and we've faced worse hardships."

"You take it surprisingly well. A king could go to his death no better."

"My great-grandmother was a Russian princess."

"My goodness," he said, doing a poor job of repressing a smile. "With a background such as yours, I'm surprised you didn't drive a stake through my heart the moment you discovered you were in my room."

"We Scots aren't inclined toward murdering the innocent."

"But he is my brother. His guilt is mine."

"Did you put him up to this?"

"Of course not."

"Then you're innocent."

"Eric said you bore him a son."

"If I had it to do over again, I'd pick Beth, but a different father."

Lars threw back his head and laughed. "Tell me about your daughter."

For an hour, Tibbie talked on about Bethany, telling Lars all about her infatuation with Eric, his abandonment, and Beth's birth. She left nothing out, even telling him about Nicholas. When she finished, Lars looked thoughtful.

At last he spoke. "Sounds to me like Eric needs a taste of his own medicine in the worst way."

"It can't be worse enough to suit me."

"You think he needs to be taught a lesson?"

"I'm not his judge and jury. I just want him to leave me alone and let me go home."

"Why don't you agree to the marriage—"

She sprang to her feet. "Absolutely not!"

He motioned for her to calm herself and sit down. "Let me finish. Then you may leap from your chair like a frightened sheep if you please."

She sat down on the edge of her seat in readiness, just in case.

"I never meant to suggest that you go through with the marriage, just agree to it. Then Eric will stop pestering you about it. That should free that clever little mind of yours enough to come up with something."

"And if I don't think of something?"

Lars studied Tibbie thoroughly. Even in the subdued light her eyes were a bright amber. She had a strong mouth and jaw, and her speech, her every action revealed a typical Scots rock-hard determination, with a Texan's swaggering assurance. She was a paradox, and interested him. In every aspect she was as feminine and dainty as they came, and soft-spoken as well, yet he had seen her muster a brassy boldness that would put a seasoned sailor to shame.

"You can still refuse to marry him at the last minute. Brides have been known to cry off a day or two before the wedding."

Tibbie considered this for a moment, then smiled. "Eric will be furious."

"Yes, but he will be in any case. In time, he'll see the way of it."

"After I'm throttled, or before?"

Lars laughed. "I must say I almost regret my offer to help. I find I will sorely miss you."

Hearing voices in the hall, she said, "I'd best be on my way, before someone reports me missing." Lars nodded, and she stood. "I'll come see you again soon." She turned toward the door.

When she reached it, Lars called to her. She turned, her hand on the doorknob. "Don't be too hard on him," he said.

"Within reason," she drawled, hearing his soft chuckle as she closed the door behind her.

She kept her word. She was back to see him, and soon. Two days later in fact. Only this time she didn't come in a laundry hamper. This time she requested a visit.

"I've decided what I'm going to do," she said, staring at her hands folded in her lap.

Lars looked at her thoughtfully. "I don't suppose you'd trust me enough to tell me, since I'm Eric's brother."

"I'll think on it," she said, "as soon as I've worked out all the details. This plan is still in the nursling stage, you understand."

Lars gave her the same smile she had seen so often on Eric. "I understand." He folded his hands across his chest. "How are things with Eric?"

"It's been just like you said. Since I've agreed to the wedding, he's leaving me alone. I hardly see him at all."

"I understand he's planning quite a wedding . . . by far the biggest this island has ever known."

"Good," Tibbie said. "The bigger, the better."

➤ · 23 · ◄

Three days before the wedding, Tibbie was praying for good weather and a big turnout. This may have sounded strange, coming from a woman who did not want to get married in the first place, but according to the plan she had worked out, the bigger the wedding, the more assured she was of success.

Eric was still making himself scarce. Last night there was a big luau for them and it was the first time she had talked to him in almost four days. He was so attentive and sweet that she would find herself forgetting, at times, his ill treatment of her. He was getting what he wanted, wasn't he? No wonder he was attentive and sweet. There was no doubt in her mind that if she suddenly changed her tune and announced her refusal she'd be dealt with in the same way as before.

The wedding morning arrived with the sun, which lingered all day in a sky that was a rich, liquid blue. Tibbie stood on a balcony with its lacy iron frames looped with corkscrew branches that dripped scarlet hibiscus and white orchids that lay in masses of exploding color. From here, she could see dormant volcanic peaks rising up in the distance over tropical forests that rushed down to the sea on one side of the island. The other side was windswept and washed in sunlight, which warmed a narrow strip of gray sands that fringed an aqua bay. Primitive beauty lay all about her, for Eric's home lay in the sloping hills that formed a verdant valley dotted with farmland that dipped toward the beach. Sea moisture kissed her skin, and the soft, gentle beat of the foaming surf rang like silver-toned bells in her ear. All in all, it was a good day for a wedding. At last, God seemed to be hearing her prayers. She ardently hoped He had been listening when she had gone over the details for the rest of it, because she was in this thing all alone if He decided to back out.

Fifteen minutes before the ceremony was to begin, Tibbie gave the orchids in the curling ribbons of her hair a poke or two, then looked at herself in the mirror. Nick's smiling face stared back at her. With a gasp, she whirled around, seeing the smile in his deep blue eyes.

"Nicholas!"

"In the flesh."

"What . . . ? Where . . . ? How . . . ?"

His grin grew wider and he stepped closer, taking her in his arms. "Is this a test to see if I can finish the questions? *What am I doing here? Where did I come from? How did I get here?* Does it matter? I'm here now. That's what's important."

"This is serious." He stood there, looking more handsome than she had ever seen him, the early afternoon sun glinting off his hair, his face darker now from the sun. And here she was, feeling terribly awkward, gawking at one man with lovesick eyes while she was beflowered and bedecked in her wedding dress, about to marry another . . . almost.

It was an act of instinct that propelled her into his arms, and Nick closed his eyes, thinking that of all the things he had expected her to do, he had not anticipated this. Her arms locked around him, her hair encircled him like a golden net. His hands cupped her face, his thumb brushing her moist mouth just before he drove his fingers deep into the coiled curls to draw her face up to his. His mouth hovering above hers, he said, "Tibbie, sweet lass, I have so much to tell you, but there isn't time. I didn't find your note until after you had left. I came after you as soon as I found out what happened. Now that you've admitted you love me, do you think I'd let you marry someone else?"

She broke away from him as if she suddenly realized she had

thrown herself at him and had suddenly gone shy. "How did
you find me? How did you know where I had gone?"

"Mairi told me." He stepped closer, his hand coming out of
his pocket to stroke the side of her face with his knuckles. She
took another step backward. Once he had her backed up
against the wall, he lowered his hands, blocking any movement
with his body, and she found little comfort in the fact that his
hands were rammed in his back pockets. This man would look
formidable with no hands at all.

"You have to leave," she said vaguely, finding it hard to
keep her mind on anything but looking desirable enough that
he would be overcome with emotion and kiss her, for initiating
contact with him was still awkward for her. "Can't you see
I'm getting ready for my wedding?"

She must have looked desirable this time, because suddenly
she was in his arms, her mouth covered with his, her body
burning with desire that dissolved everything real about her,
leaving her helpless and drifting. She sighed, melting against
him, thinking it was good to be kissed by a man who knew
what he was doing. Suddenly he broke the kiss, the delayed
understanding of what she had just said breaking through.

"What did you just say?"

"I said you have to leave. I'm getting ready and I don't have
much time left."

"Tibbie, I want to talk to you."

"Nick, I don't have time. I have to walk down the aisle in
less than five minutes. Find me afterwards. You can talk to me
then."

He looked astounded. "Now, *that* would be a dandy time for
me to propose."

"Well, it certainly took you long enough. Why now?"

"I told you I loved you. I thought that was enough at the
time. I wanted you to have time to adjust to my loving you
before I started pushing you about marriage. And strange as it
may seem, I've never fancied myself proposing to a woman
who hadn't said she loved me in return. Besides, you never
gave me many opportunities to say much of anything. I figured

if it irked you as much as it did for me to tell you I loved you, what would happen if I proposed?"

"Thank you for the explanation. Now, get out of here before someone sees you."

"You aren't going anywhere, except out of here with me."

"We wouldn't get five feet and you know it. Half this island is employed by Eric's father."

"You don't have a lot of faith in me, do you?"

"Nick, you don't understand."

"I sure as hell don't."

"Just calm down and trust me. I'll explain everything later."

"You take one step out of here and you'll be sorry."

"Nicholas Mackinnon, don't you dare threaten me!"

"Stop talking and listen to what I have to say."

"I need to finish dressing."

He grabbed her by the arm and pulled her behind the dressing screen. "You look fine." He picked up her veil and plopped it on her head.

"That isn't the way it goes. You've got it on wrong."

"Then it's a perfect match for this wedding, because we both know *it's* wrong." She tried to leave but his arms came around her and he hauled her in, pulling her flat against him. His hands were everywhere. Suddenly she realized his hand was beneath her skirts and touching her with bold strokes, high on her thigh.

Her admonition was neither faint nor timid. "Stop that! Are you crazy?"

"About you."

"I can't go walking down the aisle panting. Stop that!"

"Do I make you pant, Tib?"

She slapped his hands away. "You always did have more hands than any man I've ever known."

He raised one scandalized brow. "How many men have you known?"

"Don't think you can change the subject."

He looked at her standing there like a cameo all in white. Fresh flowers, still dew dappled, nestled in her hair. The mirror behind her gave him a full view of a nipped-in waist and volumes of a creamy silk taffeta skirt gathered into a bustle and long train, embellished with hundreds of small satin rosettes.

While Nick was looking her over, she was debating whether she should tell him, suddenly deciding the least he knew the better. He would just have to trust her. She saw the look in his eyes and felt a twinge of guilt. But she dismissed that, telling herself she had a million reasons to be furious with him, namely that he hadn't shown up that day in the orchard and saved her from going through all of this. How on earth had she ended up as she had, halfway around the globe, on a tropical island, pretending marriage to one man while being hounded by another proposing marriage?

He made a grab for her and she said, "You are a cad to tease me this way." She struggled against his rock-hard grip, praying she could talk some sense into that thick head of his. He just wasn't going about any of this in the right way.

"Look, you don't just barge in on a woman on her wedding day—"

"You aren't going to marry him. You're going to marry me."

"I told you it's the wrong time to ask me."

"Why? Personally, I think it's a great time. Here you are, all dressed for the occasion."

"You're crazy as a bullbat."

"Never was a man in love sane. It's a proven impossibility. Now, quit squawking and tell me you love me."

"I love you! Now will you—"

He cut her off with a kiss. When he finally stopped kissing her and eased his hold, he was breathing as hard as she. His eyes were pleading, earnest. "I've loved you and watched you waver with your indecision, giving you time to see where your heart lay, never understanding that you were too damn stubborn even to be honest with yourself."

The sound of music drifting up the grand stairway from below reached her ears. "They'll be coming for me now. I have to go." She placed a hand on his arm. "Nick, if you love me, trust me. I don't have time to explain more than that."

The naked urgency in his features shook her to the core. From Nicholas, proud and secure, the last thing she would have ever expected to see was a look of hopeless vulnerability. It gave her such power. It made her feel so low. She looked at him, feeling her heart crack, deciding to tell him what she was about. For a moment they stood staring at each other, determined blue eyes meeting determined gold, Scots both of them, locked in a stalemate if she had ever seen one. The tension around them vibrated like a strummed wire. She saw his features harden. With a swiftly indrawn breath she watched him turn on his heel as he said, "Very well, have it your way."

A moment later he was gone.

She turned to stare at herself in the mirror. Her mouth felt hot and dry. A sickness swept over her, yet she could not swallow to ease the nausea. The tears that burned so badly began to seep beneath her tightly closed lids and streak down her face. Would he trust her and wait, or was he leaving without her?

The thought that she might never again see him was almost more than she could bear. Everything within her urged her to give in to her pain and suffering, to collapse in a grieving heap, billowed and consoled by the cool rustle of silk gathered about her. But the fiery defiance in her Scots blood, the generations of imperial Russian ancestors bred to withstand untold hardships combined to keep her on her feet.

She would never know how she managed to make it downstairs and into the ballroom that had been decorated for the wedding, or how she was able to walk down the aisle between the rows of more than five hundred wedding guests with such frozen poise. But she had come this far and she wouldn't back out now. She glanced at Eric standing stiff and arrogant, a look of proud victory on his face. He thought he had beaten her, but that was his mistake—assuming by her backing down that he had won. She remembered Granny telling her once that even a billy goat will take a step or two back before he butts. She had taken her step back. With a radiant smile, she took her place beside Eric.

Looking at Eric, the minister said, "Eric, wilt thou have this woman to be thy wedded wife, to live together after God's ordinance in the holy estate of matrimony? Wilt thou love her, comfort her, honor and keep her, in sickness and in health; and forsaking all others, keep thee only unto her, so long as ye both shall live?"

"Yes, I will."

Turning to Tibbie, the minister repeated the vow, "Tibbie, wilt thou have this man to be thy wedded husband, to live together after God's ordinance in the holy estate of matrimony? Wilt thou love him, comfort him, honor and keep him, in sickness and in health; and forsaking all others, keep thee only unto him, so long as ye both shall live?"

"No."

The minister gaped and his face turned a mottled purple, his jowls flapped as he strangled to repeat a stunned, "No?"

For a split second Eric was unable fully to absorb what he had just heard. But when it hit him, it hit him hard. He whirled around, his face a portrait of twisted rage. For a moment she thought he might strike her, but then his eyes shifted to look out over the throng of people, as silence echoed like an empty tomb. Composure slid over his face as easily as heated oil. He looked at her one last time. "Why?" he asked. "Do you hate me that much? Am I some vampire, that you must drive a stake through my heart?"

"I'm sorry, Eric. It was the only way to stop you. You would have never let me go." Like an explosion from five hundred guests, a horrified gasp went up in unison.

"It was quite effective, for I hope to God I never lay eyes on you again." He spun away from her, waving off some of his men, who had started her way. "She's free to go," he said. "Get her out of my sight." But even as he left the room, the weight of humiliation heavy upon his shoulders, he saw Tibbie's face shining before him as it had been the day she told him about the baby—the day he turned his back on her and walked away.

The room was soon smothered with the sound of frenzied chatter, vibrating at a fevered pitch. The minister raised his hand, but before he could say anything, the thundering sound of approaching horses overtook every sound in the room. Everything lay in suspended silence.

The ballroom, which was a wing of the house, was built with doors on three sides—doors which were now flung open to admit the cool sea breezes. But Tibbie hardly felt them, nor was she aware that the room had grown strangely quiet. She was still standing in the same spot, her hands clenching her bouquet. Her eyes were wide open and filled with wonderment. She turned to stare in the direction of the sound of hoofbeats, through the open doors that led out to a grassy hill that sloped down to the sea. As the riders approached—a dozen or so—the assembled guests stared incredulously at the horsemen that rode into the ballroom. If she hadn't been frightened herself, she would have laughed at the sight of it, a whole room of people staring like a bunch of prairie-dogs at a stampede.

One of the masked riders, more brazen than the others, rode in front and Tibbie saw him coming right toward her, clearly dominating the others that followed behind. Before she could scream, or even jump out of the way, a strong arm came out of a voluminous cape, and leaning low over his horse and never breaking his speed, the rider swept her off her feet and threw her across his saddle.

Through the doors on the other side of the ballroom they rode, quickening their pace around the house and down the grassy slope, the deep bite of hooves turning up clumps of volcanic turf. She was unable to see where they were going, for each time she tried to raise her head, the rider shoved it back down. Only when the horse's flashing hooves hit the pounding surf and splashed into the water, did she realize the fool was riding straight into the sea. Had Eric hired them to abduct and drown her?

Overcome by panic, she began to fight and kick, almost

making her way to an upright position, when out of nowhere a fist connected with her jaw.

When she came to, she was inside a ship's cabin. Nicholas Mackinnon's face was the first thing she saw when, at last, visual acuity connected with mental faculties. She watched him standing across the room, wearing leather britches and a doublet that lay over a white cambric shirt, looking as tanned and hearty as she remembered.

In the distance a church bell tolled. "An angel is getting his wings," she said.

At that reminder, Nick reached into his pocket and pulled out the carved marble angel he had given her. "Speaking of angels, I think you lost yours."

He came to stand beside her, holding the angel in his extended hand, and she took it, remembering the day she had fled the orchard when Nick didn't show, and how she had thrown it against the trunk of the tree with all her might.

"The wings are gone, I'm afraid."

"That's all right," she said, her arms coming up to lock around his neck. Then burying her face in the hollow beneath his throat she said, "Oh, Nicholas! Don't you see? I have my own wings now."

He was still furious with her for the stunt she had pulled. "You're lucky you survived to get them. What in the deuce were you thinking about, marching down the aisle and telling Eric *no* in front of five hundred people?"

"That was my plan."

"It was plain crazy, that's what it was."

"No, it wasn't. Nick, listen. It was the only way, don't you see? If you had simply abducted me before the wedding, they would have sent a dozen ships after us. Eric's family is very wealthy and very powerful."

"And because of that, you decided to humiliate him in front of half the islands. He'll be sending headhunters after you now, you little idiot."

"I know Eric, how his mind works. It's finished between us. I'm afraid he wouldn't spit on me, now, if I was on fire."

Nick laughed. "I can't say that I blame him."

With a groan she dropped back to the bed. "What I don't understand is why you rescued me in the end? When there was no need."

He threw back his head and laughed. "Sweet Tib, will you go through life muddleheaded?"

"If it's my fate," she said sourly and he laughed again.

His expression turned grave, but his eyes were still warm and full of love and life and laughter. "I came, sweet Tibbie, because I figured you had some scheme cooked up that was likely to get you killed or thrown in jail."

"I don't know why you'd want to go to so much trouble to save me from anything. I'm headstrong, opinionated, temperamental, and too outspoken for my own good. My family sticks to me like glue, I talk too much, and I have the infuriating habit of leaping before I look, and when they handed out patience I must have been standing behind the door. And to top it all off, Mairi said I snore."

He laughed, taking her in his arms. "Sweet Tibbie, don't you know I'd rather have you with all your faults than lose you?"

"You couldn't say that if you really knew me."

"But I do know you. I know the haunting hunger of the memory of fair, honey-colored curls and amber eyes, and a mouth that can spit brimstone and kiss me in a way that heats my blood to boiling. You are as sturdy and strong as the ships I build, with lines as sleek and tapered, and your sails are full and filled with wind. You will hold true to the course, for you are as fierce and loyal as they come. Do you think I haven't remembered such on the many long and lonely nights since I saw you last?"

She looked at him with newfound understanding, knowing at last what he was thinking. She had loved him, but in the traditional, proper way. She had wanted him to come to her on bended knee, to promise her a house with a white picket fence and a rose garden. But she had loved a dream, not the man. Deep within her she wanted both Mackinnon and everything else tied up in a white satin bow. She had wanted him to be like every other husband, promising to spend his life in the insipid dullness of humoring his wife. What he had admired in her was her resolve and her spunk. He would never be satisfied with a woman as tepid as bathwater. She could be hot as Hades, or cold as fire, but he would love her because she was true and honest to her feelings. And in his strength and honesty and integrity, she suddenly found hers. For there was only one man she could ever be happy with, only one promise she wanted,—that he would love her and be there for her, patient and understanding as he had always been, waiting for her to understand the way of it.

As if he had suddenly been transformed, he was all that she had ever loved. He was the sparkle of sunlight dancing across water on a red-rimmed summer day. He was the song in a mockingbird's throat, the blue in the bluebonnets that overran the orchard. He was the indescribable joy of holding one's newborn for the first time, the fierce pride and beauty in her grandmother's face when the wind blew strong in remembrance. He was the comfort of warm, living arms after the cold sting of death, the pulsing throb of Scotland and Russia that ran fierce and proud and passionate in her blood. He had offered her nothing. He had given her everything, a living breathing awareness of all that was lovely and beautiful, the whole of life: peace, pain, passion, and happiness, free for the taking, asking nothing in return.

"You've turned suddenly quiet. Has the battle been fought and won?"

"There will always be battles," she said, "and I doubt I will win them all."

He said nothing, but remained quietly looking at her in the same manner as before.

"There should be some way out of this mess I've made of things, running off in the middle of the night with one man, being abducted on the day of my wedding by another, returning home with someone other than the one I ran off with. How will I ever live this down?"

And then she knew none of it really mattered. People would whisper and gossip and talk, they would make suppositions and color each story to make it more believable, adding fiction to fact to give credence to the tales of their own invention. But they would never know.

They would have no way of knowing how she looked at him with sudden understanding, and asked him saucily if he was up to having a wife as hardheaded as she, or how he looked standing there with the sunlight that poured through the window bursting around him like star-points, as he threw back his beautiful head and laughed. They would never imagine the way he crossed the tiny cabin in three swift strides and took her in his arms, lifting her from the bed and swinging her around the room until she was dizzy from the force of it.

For how could they, in their provincial, narrow minds understand how he took her hand and pulled her with him, down the narrow corridors and up the tiny steps to the bow of the ship, then stood with his arms around her as they stared out over the green water, toward the future, the wind in their face?

Perhaps in time, visitors will go to Lahaina and stand on the windswept hills and look beyond the sleepy village to the sea. They will know nothing of the once-magnificent home that stood there, or of the young woman, Tibbie, and the man who stole her away. And as they look down upon the silvered stretch of water they might think they hear the tinkling sound of laughter riding to them on the crest of a wave, or see the shape of a horse rising out of the ocean's spray. And on days when the sun is right, they might fancy they see the sleek form of a clipper ship, with her black bowsprits gleaming and her canvas filled with wind.

And if they happen by when the *Moae* winds are blowing in from the sea, they might hear the natives sing:

Where are you, O Moae wind
You're taking my love with you.

* * *

They will be sitting in the shade of a *kukui* grove, talking about a time long ago, possibly before the demigod Maui slowed the sun, a time when the sun, La, beat down upon Maui, Molokai, Lanai, and Kahoblawe. And they will tell how a horse as dark as a moonless night rose out of the mist of Haleakala Crater and sped over rivers of black lava, his feet shod with brimstone and breathing fire, *Ka-poho-i-kahi-ola,* the spirit of explosions, upon his back. They will tell how he ran faster than a *hōlua* sled, pursued by *Ke-o-ahi-kama-kaua,* the spirit of lava, his hooves ringing louder than *Kane-Hekili,* the god of thunder, as he raced across volcanic domes and wind-cut terraces, down to the coast where the whaling village of Lahaina lay. They will tell how he thundered up a mountainside, and stole a bride from her groom, and throwing her across his horse, raced across wave-cut beaches to disappear into the sea.

EPILOGUE

Together, Tibbie and Nicholas stood in a grove of trees that ran along the Tehuacana Creek, east of Waco, Texas. The old grave markers were there, but the names had worn away with time.

Behind them, sitting in the buggy, two young women shaded themselves with frilled parasols, and near them, three impatient young men sat mounted on blooded horses.

"Pa," one of the young men called out. "How long are we going to be here?"

"That depends," Nicholas said. "I wanted your mother to see the place. If she likes it well enough, we might live here one day."

"Here?" one of the young women, a girl of sixteen, croaked. "You mean leave Nantucket and live in Texas? In this place?" She looked around her. "Why, there's nothing around here for miles and miles except grass."

"But it's good, rich grass, Molly-mine."

"What do the gravestones say, Papa?" It was the other girl talking. She was older than her sister and fair, with gleaming blond hair.

"The words are all worn away now, Beth. I think they only had my mother's name and that of my brother, Andrew."

"Can we ride on ahead into Waco, Pa?"

Nick looked around at his oldest son, John. He was seventeen and busting at the seams to live a little—not that Nick could blame him. Of all his children, it was John that inherited his looks and coloring from Tibbie's Russian blood. He was as tall and straight and dark as an Indian and as aristocratic and proud as they came, and better looking than two sunsets come together.

Matthew, fourteen, gave John a poke in the ribs. "You just want to go show yourself around Baylor and listen to the girls swoon."

"You're just mad because they wouldn't swoon if you went," said Stewart, who was barely twelve.

"Papa, let's go. I'm broiling hot," Molly said, fanning herself vigorously.

Nick took Tibbie's arm and she switched her parasol to the other side. "Are you hot, my love?"

"A little," she said. "But I'm glad we came."

"So am I," Nicholas said. "It's been a long time."

He helped Tibbie into the buggy and went around to the other side and climbed in, picking up the reins. Giving the mare a slap on the back, he made a sharp turn in the buggy and rode down a grassy slope toward the gate. "I remember when this used to be a well-metaled road," he said.

"Lord deliver us," John said. "Papa's getting philosophical again."

"He's reminiscing," Molly said, sitting in the back of the buggy, looking as pert as a cricket.

"A person can take only so much reminiscence," John said.

"Grandpa says the best way to be happy is to be healthy and have a bad memory," Matthew said.

"He should know," Tibbie said with a laugh as the buggy crested the hill and Nick pulled up, looking back over the grassy stretch of land toward the grove of trees. He couldn't see the grave markers now, but he knew they were there.

Tibbie placed her hand on his arm. "Don't look so sad, Nicholas. The past will always have stories to tell, but the young and restless present will never listen."

"If you had it all to do over again, my love, would you still marry me?"

"Yes, but sooner."

He looked back toward the pecan grove one last time, bidding his past farewell at last. He slapped the mare, and the buggy rolled down the hill and out of sight, leaving behind nothing but stillness and the sound of the wind sifting through the tall grass.

They used to tell how the Comanches were the fiercest Indians in the Southwest.

Experience the Passion and the Ecstasy

Heather Graham

☐ 20235-3 Sweet Savage Eden $3.95

☐ 11740-2 Devil's Mistress $3.95

Megan McKinney

☐ 16412-5 No Choice But
Surrender $3.95

☐ 20301-5 My Wicked
Enchantress $3.95

☐ 20521-2 When Angels Fall $3.95